T0036157

Sugar Birds

Praise for *Sugar Birds*

"Bostrom's prose is propulsive and detailed. Aggie is a wonderfully magnetic character: a scrappy, stubborn preteen whose father has taught her to survive off the land. The supporting characters are equally strong, including the teenager's bird biologist grandmother and Aggie's autistic brother, Burnaby. The story is a true page-turner all the way to the end. An engrossing tale of survival and redemption in the Pacific Northwest."

KIRKUS REVIEWS

"Bostrom takes her readers gently by the hand and plunges them into an immersive tale straight from page one. *Sugar Birds* is a powerful coming-of-age story of betrayal and loss, rebellion and anger, friendship, forgiveness and redemption, all woven into a testament to the wondrous natural world . . . packed into one heart-pounding read. Highly recommended!"

CHANTICLEER REVIEWS

"Suspenseful. Lyrical. Redemptive. Bostrom's voice reminds me of Delia Owens' *Where the Crawdads Sing* and Annie Dillard's *Pilgrim at Tinker Creek.* I loved this coming-of-age tale."

TARYN R. HUTCHISON, award-winning writer and author of *One Degree of Freedom*

"Exquisite setting, unique characters, and a gripping plot blend with complex family storylines to make *Sugar Birds* a page-turner that stays embedded in your soul for a welcomed long while."

SARA EASTERLY, award-winning author of *Searching for Mom*

"A riveting, redemptive story! I couldn't put it down. Bostrom drew me into souls of beautifully drawn characters and planted me in farmlands and forests where those characters fail, suffer, grow and love. I cannot recommend this book highly enough."

SY GARTE, PhD; award-winning author of *The Works of His Hands: A Scientist's Journey from Atheism to Faith*

"Since her first books over two decades ago, I've longed to see how Cheryl Bostrom's gift of scientific, elegant thought and language would shape her fiction. Stirring, intelligent, and lyrical, *Sugar Birds* was so worth the wait."

MONA STUART, author of *Raising Children at Promise*

"Cheryl Bostrom's hard-to-put-down *Sugar Birds* reminds me of the classic, *My Side of the Mountain*—one of those rare books that appeal to every age; full of depth, pages that turn quickly, and most of all, ebullient truth."

KATHERINE JAMES, award-winning novelist; author of the memoir *A Prayer for Orion*

"A new heroine is born! Ten-year-old Aggie's voice is innocent, fresh, and compelling. Bostrom's deft language, deep reverence for the natural world, and keen understanding of the human condition merge in this enduring novel of forgiveness and hope."

ASHLEY E. SWEENEY, award-winning author of *Answer Creek*

"This novel illustrates truth I know in my bones—that there is a great mending for all of my life-gashes and deep aches. *Sugar Birds* is the best book I have read in ages, and is a book for all ages."

DONNA VANDER GRIEND, former chaplain; author of *Out of the Mouths of Grandbabes*

"*Sugar Birds* is a tour de force, with protagonist Agate as uniquely powerful as *The Hunger Games's* Katniss. This story will take readers where they've never been before. I plumbed my own depths as I followed Aggie and Celia through physical and emotional hinterlands of spirituality, pain, guilt, and redemption. . . . An incredibly good book."

DR. LYNNE CURRY, columnist for *Anchorage Daily News* and author of *Beating the Workplace Bully*

"What an adventure! Cheryl Bostrom skillfully intertwines compelling storylines of two girls lost in wilderness of their own making—who find rescue and freedom through gifts of trust, healing of deep hurts, and forgiveness. It's a book of hope restored."

EMILY POLIS GIBSON, M.D. and poet, photographer, and essayist at Barnstorming.blog

"Captivating . . . Compelling . . . An intuitive understanding of people as a part of wild nature has been almost entirely lost in modern society. This book brings a glimpse of the importance of the outdoors to children's development and indeed, to their very souls . . . Highly recommended!"

KAREN STEENSMA, biology professor and farmer

Sugar Birds

A NOVEL

CHERYL GREY BOSTROM

Tyndale House Publishers
Carol Stream, Illinois

Visit Tyndale online at tyndale.com.

Visit Cheryl Grey Bostrom online at cherylbostrom.com.

Tyndale and Tyndale's quill logo are registered trademarks of Tyndale House Ministries.

Sugar Birds

Copyright © 2023 by Cheryl Grey Bostrom. All rights reserved.

Previously published in 2021 by She Writes Press under ISBN 978-1-64742-068-0. First printing by Tyndale House Publishers in 2023.

Cover photograph of foggy trees copyright © Tim Gartside/Trevillion Images. All rights reserved.

Interior photograph of forest by Jay Mantri on Unsplash.com.

Author photograph copyright © Laura Buys. All rights reserved.

Map copyright © Emma VandeVoort Nydam. All rights reserved.

Cover design by Julie Metz/metzdesign.com

Published in association with the literary agency of Books & Such Literary Management, 52 Mission Circle, Suite 122, PMB 170, Santa Rosa, CA 95409.

Sugar Birds is a work of fiction. Where real people, events, establishments, organizations, or locales appear, they are used fictitiously. All other elements of the novel are drawn from the author's imagination.

For information about special discounts for bulk purchases, please contact Tyndale House Publishers at csresponse@tyndale.com, or call 1-855-277-9400.

Library of Congress Cataloging-in-Publication Data

A catalog record for this book is available from the Library of Congress.

ISBN 978-1-4964-8163-4

Printed in the United States of America

29	28	27	26	25	24	23
7	6	5	4	3	2	1

To my Gwynie,
with more love
than all feathers since
birds first flew

Oh, I took a little boat,

such a pretty little boat,

just as the day was dawning.

And I took a little oar,

and I pulled away from shore,

so very, very, early in the morning.

—TRADITIONAL LULLABY, CIRCA 1890

"Consider the birds . . ."

—MATTHEW 6:26

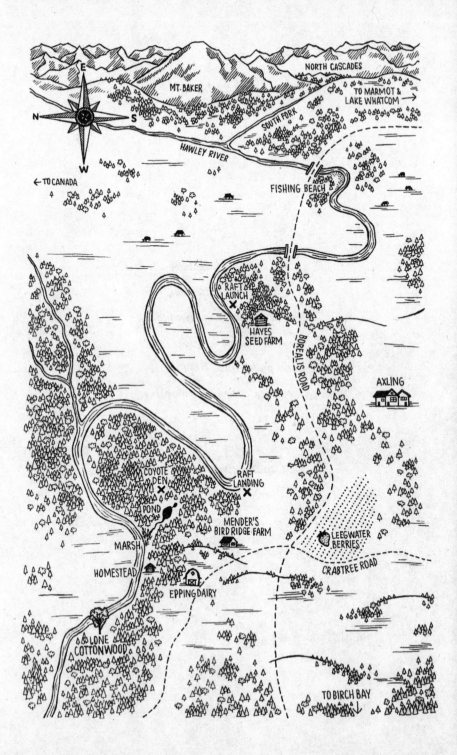

1

AGGIE

MAMA

"You stay on the ground, Agate!"

Aggie scowled as her mother shouted across thirty rows of foot-high corn. Teeth clamped, the girl slammed her gloves into a bucket, then lengthened her stride until she reached the four-wheeler beside the barn. The words lay sharp against her spine. Mama must have seen her eye the crow's nest near the alders they cut that morning. *Of course she did.*

Without looking back, the girl cranked the engine and revved the throttle. The tires skidded sideways, spewing gravel behind her before they caught and fishtailed into the pasture in a streak of crushed grass. The machine bucked uphill across uneven ground—too fast, she knew—but the engine's whine would drown out anything else Mama might yell.

When she crested the rise, she dropped the throttle into an idle and ran her eyes along the ridges of the North Cascades, their slopes blue beneath the snowline. Then she shifted sideways in her seat to look back toward her family's log house, the cupola-topped cedar barn, and the garden. Shrunken in the distance, her parents bent over baby onions in the June afternoon sunshine, weeding. Beyond them, sprinklers irrigated the tree seedlings Aggie had been hoeing since lunch. She clenched her arms and felt the ache in them, thankful that Dad called her off the job to retrieve the chainsaw he'd left in the woods.

She drove down the back side of the hill, nosed the vehicle alongside a pile of firewood rounds, and clicked off the ignition. As if dismounting a horse, she swung her leg behind her and jumped to the ground, then trotted toward the Douglas fir that held the nest. Mama expected her to find Dad's saw and return right away. Nothing else. No climbing.

But her mother would never know. Aggie could make it up and down the tree in under five minutes and be home with the saw before either parent missed her.

Her eyes crawled up the old fir to a dark cluster of twigs, where a sharp-beaked silhouette brooded her eggs. The male crow watched Aggie from an adjacent tree and bobbed to his mate, who waddled from the nest and hopped to a nearby branch. Aggie tilted her head at them and pressed her finger to her lips. "Nothing to worry about," she whispered. "I just want to see 'em." The fir was an easy one; the nest only the height of a telephone pole. She had scaled trees like this, what, a hundred times? Five hundred?

With no sign of Mama, she entered the tree, her feet and hands deliberate as she climbed, her movements brisk. Boughs heavy with needles offered a quick ladder. The silent crows watched, squatting, wings poised, their necks stretched low.

Halfway up, the foliage grew sparser, and her heart raced at her high visibility. If Mama had followed, she would spot her for sure.

2

Aggie picked up her pace, planting her foot on a limb the diameter of her wrist and, without testing its strength, pulled her full fifty-five pounds onto it.

The limb snapped. A flailing arm snagged a branch and she dangled, scrambling for toeholds. Both birds squawked and took to the sky, spreading the alarm. Startled sparrows launched from the grass below as the crows circled and dove. Aggie found her footing and braced against the onslaught. When a beak speared her shoulder, she pawed the air behind her, intercepted a crow across its breast and flung it sideways. Both birds arced skyward, protesting as she hoisted herself to the bowl of the nest and peered inside.

There, arranged in a circle like the petals of a flower, the olive-green eggs' narrow tips touched at the center. "Five," she said to the raucous, hovering birds—and stuck her thumb in the air.

A thrill surged through her. In two weeks she'd begin to visit daily. Though the crows were sure to jab her a few more times, they'd get used to her, like they all did. When she watched their first egg hatch, she'd memorize it and draw the cracked shell and emerging beak. She'd record every hatchling in her book, just like Dad taught her.

Now, though, she had to move fast, and the fir's twiggy branches slowed her descent. A young birch, skinny and limbless as a fire pole, intersected a bough below her. *Yes.* The birch would give her a straight shot to the ground. She sidestepped along a horizontal limb until it narrowed dangerously, then leaned into the thin tree, caught the trunk and swung her weedy body over. With a bear cub's grip, she shinnied lower—until a shriek ricocheted through the woods.

"Aggie!"

The crows vanished into the trees. Still clamped around the trunk, Aggie arched backwards as her mother appeared. Even upside down, she saw fright scrape across Mama's face, and it lodged like a stone in Aggie's chest. She jumped the last few feet out of the tree and stood on one leg like a heron, her eyes locked on her mother's knees.

Mama gripped Aggie's chin. "How many times have I told you not to climb so high? After yesterday, I thought you understood. *Tsch*. Ten years old. Still can't trust you." She jerked Aggie's jaw higher, her eyes blazing. "No more. Starting tomorrow, you will either stay within visible range of me or you will help Aunt Nora at the dairy while your dad and I are working. Someone has to keep an eye on you."

Aggie eased away from Mama and studied the ground. Her aunt rarely left her airless house and never opened her curtains. She would have to do their dishes. Clean those dingy rooms. And who knew when Uncle Loomis would sneak up on her and yell if she messed up. She wondered how her brother could stand to milk for him.

The alternative was no better. Tethered to Mama, she'd feel like a mouse with an owl overhead. And her parents would fight about her.

"But Mama. I wasn't—"

"You are going to break your neck. Or worse."

Aggie's face burned hot with something more than Mama's fear. She felt like spitting. Spitting at her mother who was trying to steal her joy over eggs, her joy at running up a tree into the sky. She crossed her arms and turned sideways to Mama, who again reached for her, more gently this time.

Aggie dodged her. From now on, she would climb only when she and Dad worked on the far edge of their eighty acres. Or when her mother kneaded bread dough or bought groceries or shipped seeds. Aggie would chart nests deeper in the woods than ever before, or along the Hawley River—where Mama wouldn't look. And if Mama came after her? She would be a squirrel and skitter through the trees like one. Way higher than before.

Her father approached over the hill, and Aggie ducked behind a fat, leaning alder. She did not want him to witness her anger, this awful feeling that made her mouth pinch and her head hurt above her ears.

Mama watched her hide, then turned toward her dad. "Harris!"

"I saw her."

"How many times will you see her and do nothing? Wasn't yesterday enough? From now on, that girl stays out of trees."

Yesterday. Big whoop. Aggie had found a nest of red-shafted flickers, only twenty-five feet up. Dad didn't worry at all.

"I always look after her, Bree."

"How can you look after her when she's on a branch as high as our house?"

Aggie pictured their two-story log home, with its steep gables. She had never considered the size of her trees in comparison.

"Like you did better keeping her at the barn with you? How'd that work for you?"

Exactly, Dad. Mama really overreacted that time. Hadn't she pulled herself into the cupola with a strong rope, over the cushy straw in the haymow? *Baby stuff. So safe.*

And she'd found six barn swallow eggs in that flawless mud cup.

Her mother's cheeks flushed. "You are her father. You can't let her win."

"This isn't about winning. You're strangling the girl. If you keep treating her like she's five, she'll never grow up."

"She won't be doing any growing if she lands on her head."

Aggie strained to listen as he lowered his voice. ". . . hardly growing now. Doctor charts don't lie." He stroked his stubbled chin. "Look, Bree. What if we send her back to school in the fall? She hasn't been around anyone her age in a year. Maybe this time she'll—"

Mama threw her hands in the air, then spun away from him and strode fast toward the house.

. . . *make some friends.* Aggie finished her father's sentence, mouthing the words and stretching out *f-r-i-e-n-d-s.* She didn't like the boys at school. James Marking had called her a freak when she picked up those baby possums crawling on their road-killed mama in front of the gym. So what if she put them in her sweatshirt pouch and took them to class. So what if she pretended to be a marsupial until she got them home. They'd have died otherwise.

She didn't like the girls, either—especially big Trina Boonsma, who had flunked fourth grade twice and scared Aggie on the playground. Trina stalked her at church, too. Good thing Aggie was quick, or, she suspected, Trina would have kept pinching her privates in that hallway behind the sanctuary. Aggie had shown Mama the bruises Trina left on her chest, but she never expected her mother to block Trina and Mrs. Boonsma right there in the foyer after the service.

"Tell that cow of yours to keep her hands to herself!" Mama had waved the church bulletin in Mrs. Boonsma's face.

Twenty heads snapped toward her. Mrs. Boonsma pulled Trina close.

Dad reached Mama through the crowd, caught her arm, and extracted the tube from her hand. "Terribly sorry." He tipped his head at Mrs. Boonsma, then Trina. "Bree hasn't been herself lately."

"No way I—" Her mother wrenched, but Dad's grip held.

"Not the time or place, love. Let's go." He spun Mama—almost like he did when they danced in the barn to the radio—and hurried her outside. By the time Aggie and her brother got to the car, Mama was shouting, smacking the dashboard with Dad's worn leather Bible. "We're done with church." *Whack.* "Done, done, done." *Whack.* "Can't keep my children safe *anywhere*." Her father had flinched with every swat.

No school and no more town church meant no more Trina. Aggie was relieved. Mama's erratic behavior was worry enough. Besides, kitchen church was way better. And short, usually; she and her brother recited the week's memory work from the catechism, Dad read Scripture. Aggie would sing from their *Psalter Hymnal* while Dad jazzed it up with a Celtic riff or two on his fiddle. Sometimes she even danced on the linoleum, where her feet clacked out the rhythm.

Besides, who needed school for friends? Aggie found real friends in the woods. Birds. Raccoons. Trees. And homeschool took less time.

In a way, Mama had recovered. At least now she no longer rolled her wild eyes, shouting at people she hardly knew. She worked in the garden again. Mailed out packages wrapped in kraft paper, with *Hayes Heirloom Seeds* stamped in the corner.

Her mother did, however, yell when Aggie climbed.

If only she had waited to visit the crows.

Her father, his hands hanging, watched Mama stomp up the hill, swiping hip-high orchard grass out of her way. He nodded to Aggie's hiding place. "Let's head home, my girl." He strapped the chainsaw into the basket behind the ATV's seat. "You practicing everything I taught you out there?"

"Yes, Dad. I think about it all the time." At least the parts that interested her. Like tracking animals. And bird calls. And, usually, checking tree branches for soundness.

"Good. Good. One way or another, we'll figure out how you can grow those wings of yours without testing God—or your mom. No need to dare either of them to keep you alive."

"She doesn't get it."

He leaned against the machine's fender and crossed his arms. "Actually, I think she does." He looked past Aggie at Mama's retreating form. "She just doesn't want anything to happen to you."

"Dad. She even worries when I eat grapes."

"Being a mother has distracted her." Her father plucked a leaf from her hair. "Those jars of agates in the kitchen? Ever ask her about them?"

"You're changing the subject."

"Ask her about that cliff in Oregon. And those waves. If she had fallen . . ." He whistled a descending note, like in a cartoon before someone crashed. "See if she'll tell you that story."

"I don't know how that'll help."

"Your mom hunted those stones like you hunt nests. Insisted we name you after them."

So her mother could scale cliffs to find rocks, but she wouldn't let Aggie climb trees? Her face grew hot again.

Dad mounted the four-wheeler and patted the seat behind him, and Aggie clambered on. "Eggs like daisy petals in that nest, Dad. Five of 'em." She clamped her arms around his sides and laid her cheek against his shirt. He steered up the hill after her angry mother.

RUBBLE

AS THE FOUR-WHEELER APPROACHED the house, Aggie spotted her brother standing by the open door of his truck. *Ah. Burnaby to the rescue.* Mama's searchlight would swivel to him when they went inside. She hopped off the slowing vehicle and ran ahead to meet him. Her dad pulled up behind her.

Burnaby, his eyes dodgy, patted the Ford's cab. "F-100," he said. "Delivered 1968. Seventeen years ago. Like me."

Her brother brushed a speck off the shiny paint and twisted the lock button on the door. How often had he said that in the two months since he bought the truck? Each time he repeated himself, Aggie caught the excitement his face never showed, and she felt kindness toward him. Now he drove to his job at Uncle Loomis's dairy. No more bicycle. She smiled and visualized a stork delivering a miniature red pickup and baby Burnaby together in its bundle. *If only he liked jokes.*

"Night milking, huh?" Dad pulled a pack of Beemans gum from his pocket and set it on the dashboard. "Chew it when that rowdy second string comes in the parlor. Settle your stomach." He reached for her brother's shoulder, but let his hand fall, unwilling, Aggie knew, to elicit Burnaby's typical flinch at any human touch besides Mama's. Longing flitted through Dad's eyes.

Burnaby nodded. "Double shift. Uncle Loomis is cutting silage. I'll stay there tonight." He retrieved his domed lunchbox from the passenger seat and raised it, as if toasting them, before he followed Aggie and Dad into the house.

The three entered the kitchen as her mother flung a saucepan into the sink. Burnaby stood in the doorway like a supplicant, his lunchbox balanced on his uplifted hands. Aggie shrank toward the wall. Her dad stepped behind Mama, slid his arms around her waist, and pulled her into his chest.

Aggie's hands clenched at the compressed line of her mother's lips. Only when Dad whispered, his mouth right beside Mama's ear, did her mother relax and lean her head back onto his shoulder. Aggie heard her sigh and say, "I know, I know."

Wearily, Mama gestured to Burnaby. He set the lunchbox on the counter and opened it, then flipped the latch rhythmically while Mama brought food from the fridge. She laid one hand atop his until his fingers stilled, then stood two individually bagged peanut butter sandwiches—crusts removed—upright in the left end of the box.

"Eat. And. Read. From. Left. To. Right," Burnaby said, tapping the red metal lunchbox in time with each syllable. Aggie mouthed the familiar line with him and poked the wall behind her in sync with his clipped words. Mama pushed a baggie of carrots, cut in precise, half-inch rounds, against the sandwiches.

Burnaby held three fingers like a bookend against the food until her mother washed and dried an apple, then set it stem-up in the box, to the right of the carrots. With a clean napkin, he dabbed a water drop from the base of the stem as Mama folded three more napkins, held them vertically against the carrots, and chose a small block of wood from five of graduated sizes lined up against the counter back-splash. She nestled it into the box, glanced at vigilant Burnaby, and replaced it with a larger block, one that more tightly filled the void between the napkins and the right end of the box. They all knew that if the food wasn't just so, her brother would be late for work because he would stand beside Mama with his cheek twitching until she made everything fit.

Almost done. Aggie watched through half-lidded eyes as Mama poured milk in a Thermos. Burnaby spooned in a level half-teaspoon of Ovaltine, chose a dinner knife from the utensil drawer, and stirred—not nine times, but ten—before he rinsed the knife, tapped it on the edge of the sink, and closed the Thermos. *Good enough to . . . ? Yes!* Burnaby clamped the Thermos into the lid and clicked the box closed. Aggie picked it up and followed him onto the porch.

"Mama's mad again, Burn."

"I suspected so." He stooped to pick a marigold from a clay pot by the stair and handed it to her, his eyes on the flower. "Think yel-low." She passed him the lunchbox, and he touched two fingers to his forehead, saluting his goodbye. Aggie wound the flower's stem around her finger like a ring.

At the truck, he settled his food behind the seat and whistled for Pi. The brown dog leaped in ahead of him and stood on the passen-ger side, her prick ears tilted forward as her thick tail thumped the window. Burnaby traced the dog's muscled shoulder with his index finger, slung the door closed and shifted into gear.

Aggie watched the truck lurch down the potholed lane, then peeked sideways at the house. She'd be on her own in there. Without Burnaby and Pi to distract Mama at dinner, she would have to find another way to evade the climbing issue. But what? She swayed from foot to foot, antsy. Already the red-tails by the river were flap-hopping and stretching their wings. If Mama kept her home, the baby hawks would fledge before she said goodbye.

She wandered out to the treed side of the house, where branches from the previous night's windstorm littered the ground. A web of twigs crunched underfoot. *Tinder.* "Keep it dry and your flames will grab every time," Dad told her whenever they built a fire.

She scuffed the debris with her foot as an idea took hold, then patted the knife in her jeans. *Fuzz sticks.* Best kindling ever. She would make some for the fireplace. Mama would like them for sure. Opening her pocketknife, she plopped into the grass and began to whittle. She nudged the blade into a finger-thick twig as if she would skin it, but left thin curls of bark attached. A dozen feathery sticks later, she folded her knife and eyed the pile, pleased.

Come winter, she would light them in the woodstove for Mama. A fuzz stick's flame reminded her of a Christmas tree with its lights blazing. She liked that. She wished she didn't have to wait.

But why wait? She'd light one right now. Give it a test run. She hurried to the laundry room for matches, returned to her pile, and crumpled a handful of toothpick-thin tinder onto the ground. She built a teepee over the top of it with larger twigs and shoved a fuzz stick inside. Then she sat, straddling the little structure to block the rising breeze, while she lit a curly peel. She shielded the fire with her hands until it bit the tinder and caught. The flame's gentle wobble calmed her.

Mama's afraid I'll fall. Sure, she slipped on a branch now and then, but she never fell. Even so, Mama said she couldn't climb anymore, ever. She lingered on the word *ever* and sighed. She hated feeling this hot anger at her mother. She didn't know what to do with it and was glad that, for now, it was going away.

The flicker spread inside the teepee, and the tinder crackled in response. She rationed the fuel to keep the fire small: a stem, a leaf, and another few twigs. As an afterthought, she cleared a little firebreak around the flame—a barren circle, like her dad had taught her: "Make it wide enough that the blaze can't jump." The powdery dirt puffed as she exposed it.

Kneeling, she stared into the flame until a garter snake caught her eye as it slithered from a hole near her fire circle and hurried toward the flowerbed.

"Too hot for ya?" She jumped to her feet and stepped lightly on the snake, holding it in place, then pinched its tail and lifted. The creature twisted as it dangled, and she nearly dropped it when Mama called her for dinner, her voice shrill. Aggie turned away from the house, lowered the snake headfirst into the pocket of her windbreaker and zipped it inside. She fingered its contours through the fabric before she flicked the campfire's burning twigs apart with a piece of tree bark and kicked dirt over the flames.

Mama shouted again. Aggie gathered the pile of fuzz sticks and carried them inside as a peace offering.

"Won't work this time, Agate. Enough's enough." Mama jerked her head toward the woodbin and sat stiffly beside Aggie's dad. Spaghetti steamed in the center of the table. "Hurry up. Food's getting cold."

Aggie shuffled toward the fireplace and lowered the sticks onto the kindling pile. She scooted into her seat across the dining room table from Mama and hunched sideways, fidgeting with the zipper on her jacket.

"Agate Esther."

"Hm?"

"Look at me when I'm talking to you."

Aggie felt like an egg, splitting open. One of these days, Mama would look in her eyes and see only the shell. Yep, while Mama laid down the law, or while arugula seeds distracted her, or while she drained herself giving Burnaby her last ounce of patience, Aggie would crawl out of her shell and fly away.

She looked at her dad, who winked and nodded, then dropped

her eyes again. The snake needed air. She tugged the windbreaker's zipper open half an inch. The animal poked its head through the opening and Aggie quickly covered it with her cupped hand. When the snake's tongue tickled her palm, she bit her cheeks against a smile.

The phone rang. Mama signaled "wait" with her upheld finger as she rose to answer. Her voice from the kitchen sounded friendly, musical.

"Dad. Save me. Not Aunt Nora's."

"No drama, Aggie."

"Dad. That place is a mess. And Uncle Loomis scares me."

"He doesn't bite. A few days won't kill you. Your mom's settling next season's contracts this week and still has to work out details for the seed catalog. Dave Hoff asked me to don my arborist cap and consult with him on that pine beetle outbreak."

"Around here?"

"No. East of the mountains. I leave for Winthrop tomorrow."

"Take me with you? Mama will have me on a leash when you leave."

"Honestly, Aggie, I—"

The phone clattered onto the receiver, and her mother reappeared.

"Nora's picking you up first thing in the morning. No shenanigans, hear me? If you don't behave yourself with her, I can make things much, much worse for you."

"Bree." Dad's voice was low.

Mama smacked the table with the flat of her hand. "No, Harris!"

"Let me go with Dad, Mama. Please."

"*Phft.* And turn you loose in eastern Washington? You're following in Zach Spinner's path. Only a matter of time."

"The Spinner kid? C'mon Bree. Calm down. Listen to yourself."

Aggie's jaw went slack. Last Fourth of July, Zach Spinner had tossed a handful of wire clothes hangers into an electrical substation, then watched the show as the circuits arced, exploded, and torched a nearby shed. A fireman died, and the town went black for days. Only seventeen, but they tried him as an adult. "He got his fireworks," Uncle Loomis said. Aunt Nora said Zach would be middle-aged before he got out of the slammer.

"I hear myself just fine, thank you. Aggie doesn't listen to a word I say. If she keeps it up, she'll be in juvie before she's twelve."

"I'm not hungry." Aggie shoved her plate away as a small, reptilian head and its slinky, shoestring body emerged from her pocket, slipped to the floor, and trailed across her mother's bare foot.

Mama's knee bumped the underside of the table hard as she recoiled from the snake. Her mouth formed an O, and she swung sideways and clenched her knee to her chest. The creature slid into the living room and disappeared under the sofa. Mama watched it hide, then turned slowly to Aggie, her eyes hooded, her breathing fast and shallow. "Get to your room. Now."

Aggie streaked upstairs and crouched beside her bedroom door, listening. The rise and fall of her parents' voices—punctuated by her mother's stomps and slams—droned on. She couldn't make out the words. Oh well. She'd heard them all before. The wooden door felt cool against her cheek.

She wanted her soft mother back—the mom she loved and could talk to. Not the frantic-eyed lady who talked too fast and banged around in the kitchen in the middle of the night. Not the mama who had mostly stayed in bed last spring. And definitely not the mean mother downstairs, who yelled at her and took pills that made her barf.

Dad had promised that Mama would get better, that her moods would level out with the medicine. He had held Aggie by her shoulders and crouched to eye level. "I know this is hard, Agate, and that you're sadder than you've ever been. But there's a better song out there. Find it and draw what you hear. Ask the Father to show you. When your mom's ready, you can share it with her."

Aggie pulled her sketchbook from under the bed and opened the cover to her first picture, drawn the previous spring while her pallid, depressed mother lay upstairs. She ran her fingers tenderly over the finch's rosy crown and breast, remembering.

———✍

"Start with him," Dad had said, singling out a house finch cracking sunflower seeds at their feeder. He had found Aggie slouched at the kitchen table, worry bowing her spine like a daisy stem, her fingers wilting sprigs. He pushed her untouched sketchbook and pencils toward her. "See where he flies."

She did. Not too willingly, at first. But after the finch made three trips to the same cedar, Aggie followed. When a dowdy, striped female flitted past her, she found the bird's launch point: a nest of the tiniest rootlets, tinder, and horsehair, probably from that sorrel mare upriver. A smooth cup of fescues and dusky contour feathers—from some duck, she guessed—curved around three perfect, perfect, perfect eggs, all pale blue with black specks.

She memorized them before she hurried inside to draw, first the father bird, then the nest and those eggs. A few days later, she turned over a fresh page and drew the mother feeding wobbly hatchlings, still blind and splotched with down.

There were more, throughout that spring and summer. Shy Swainson's thrushes deep in the woods. Practical robins in that maple tree. Juncos, hummingbirds, chickadees. Beaks punching through shells. And the hawks . . . Whenever a clutch fledged, the joy of their launch opened more sky to her, and another piece of her sadness shriveled and blew away.

———✍

She slammed her sketchbook closed. If only her anger would blow away, too. Down in the kitchen, Mama ranted on. If she came upstairs and yelled, this time Aggie would climb out the window right in front of her. She would take her drawings and jump into the tree beside the house and leave Mama lecturing into her curtains. She would do that. *Yes.* Right in front of her.

Sneaking out would be easier, though. She thought of her red-tails and, if she counted twilight, of June's nearly eighteen daylight hours. If she left by 4:30 a.m., she could see the little hawks and be back to the house long before her parents rose at 6:00. *Yes.* She stroked the sketchbook's cover. *Tomorrow.*

She wriggled out of her jeans and tank top, pulled on navy pajama leggings and a long-sleeved, gray T-shirt, then closed the drapes to block the lingering summer sun. She set her alarm clock for 4:15, tucked it behind her pillow, and crawled into bed. Her parents' voices thrummed below.

Stay on the ground? She burrowed under her blankets, fuming. *Never.* How would she keep track of her birds if she didn't climb? How would she record their hatches? Draw their nests and babies?

If she quit climbing, how would she shrink the sadness?

———⟑

Sometime in the night, she startled awake as Mama snatched her blankets and hurled them from the bed. "Aggie! Hurry!" her mother shouted, raspy, as she hauled Aggie from her mattress onto the carpet. "Fire!"

Aggie rose to her elbows, coughing. Her movements were jerky, her brain ragged with sleep and fumes. Mama dropped to the floor beside her and tugged her shirt. "This way."

Smoke bellied over them as Aggie crawled after her mother, her hammering heart a blood drum in her ears. When they reached the stairs, Mama gripped her hand, and they groped their way to the back entry. Mama fumbled with the lock, threw the door open, and yanked Aggie past the porch and across the yard to the ancient maple at the lawn's edge.

She pushed Aggie's shoulders against the tree. "Stay here," she barked, wheezing from the smoke. "Your dad . . . his fiddle."

"No, Mama!" Aggie snared her mother's nightgown, clawed it toward her. Mama wrenched, ripped the fabric from Aggie's hands, and darted back to the burning house.

Aggie flattened herself against the trunk and slid into a crouch. And then, horror: flames gulped air through the open door and jumped into her mother's hair as she disappeared inside. "Noooo!" Aggie fought her seizing muscles, leapt the porch steps in stiff strides. A whip of fire stopped her at the doorway. Unbearable heat bullied her backwards.

"Harris!" Mama wailed from somewhere inside. Voices melted in the roar.

Aggie flew off the porch through a swarm of sparks and raced the log home's perimeter, skirting wide past windows that, opened for night air, now spewed licking tendrils of flame. A timber popped and sprayed pulsing embers across the lawn. Numb from adrenaline and terror, she plowed across them in bare feet.

At the front door, she hesitated at the handle's thumb plate, glowing red with heat. Covered her ears at the maniacal crackle of flames inside. Then she jammed her hand into a boot on the landing, struck the latch, and shoved.

Locked.

Panting with fear, she pounded the boot's heel on the door and bleated, "Mama! Dad!"

She flung the boot onto the lawn and again sprinted around the house, searching for access, but all the windows bloomed in the darkness, pushing, pushing fronds of flame out toward the sentinel firs at the yard's edge. Could she climb in through the crawl space, through the trapdoor in the pantry? There had to be a way.

But no. The house screamed as the logs whistled and exploded in the heat. Flames punched outward from every window and doorway.

She sped the circumference of the house again and again, but no route inside remained to her.

Beaten back to the trees, she doubled over, struggling for air and coughing up the acrid taste of ash. She pressed the heels of her hands into her eyes, sealing them against the smoke's sting, and rubbed until she could again squint at the flames, at the charred ground, at a seared circle in the grass at her feet.

Her campfire circle.

Her campfire.

A scorched trail led from the circle to some blazing lumber stacked by the house. With temples pounding, she stared at the smoldering path. This nightmare. Her fault. Her head hung over the blackened earth, her mouth agape.

The realization dizzied her, gutted her with dread. She tripped, righted herself, and tore back to the big maple where her mother had left her. She scrambled up the two-by-fours nailed to the old trunk, a ladder to her leaf-veiled treehouse, where guilt collapsed her over the little cabin's half wall. Riveted to the unfolding devastation, she flailed against blame until shock lifted her outside of herself, detached her from the body she no longer wanted to claim as her own. Until denial, in a brief respite, made her an observer, not the cause. *Yes. An observer.* Of that girl in the treehouse. That girl crying. That girl who lit a fire.

Sirens wailed along the road. Smoke billowed around her, and she held her sleeve over her nose and mouth as fire trucks and an ambulance rolled in a procession down the driveway, their lights strobing the yard and barn. Men in heavy brown suits shouted, hefted fat hoses, and sprayed.

Water dented the blaze, then vaporized. The fire roared back, engulfing the logs and penetrating them until curved trunks glowed and exploded. Firefighters receded into the inferno. Aggie watched dumbly as a section of roof collapsed and her bedroom opened to the spark-filled sky. Fire stormed through the hole.

A firefighter crossed the porch carrying a limp body. Behind him, two more emerged with another lifeless form slung between them. When a man shouted, Aggie's hands flew to her open mouth. Had he said, "Gone"? She wasn't sure, but she thought so. *Gone?* Did that mean they were *dead?*

She fell forward on the treehouse planks, her breath shallow, the whump of falling timbers thundering around her. Sirens screamed. Orange light shimmered through cracks between boards; shadows contorted on the ceiling.

Then even more smoke, as firefighters fought the blaze. Someone called her name over and over, but trauma immobilized her, rendered her thoughts erratic and muddled. She wouldn't answer. Couldn't.

By the time dim morning light crept over her, the dying fire chewed quietly. Aggie pulled herself up the half wall and absorbed the scene. Embers snapped in black rubble where her home once stood. Only one man sprayed hot spots; others coiled hoses and stowed ladders.

And then they got into the trucks and drove them away down the road.

Her mind tripped and stalled with exhaustion and shock. Oh, her mama. Her dad. *Gone. Gone.*

To the hospital? A blip of hope rallied her, then died. She had seen those bodies, heard the firefighters yell. Her chest clenched, wringing her insides hard, like a dishcloth. Dad. Mama. She killed them with those sticks. With her fire. She beat her legs with clenched fists, bit her cheeks, tasted blood.

Her eyes flitted randomly. *Think, Aggie.* She couldn't stay here. If they caught her, they'd take her to jail. Well, to juvie. And according to scary Mike Mackey, who knew firsthand, that was as bad as jail any old day.

She had slouched low in her school bus seat in front of Mike while he told Joe Paulson how an officer patted him down and searched his pockets and then took all his clothes and felt him all over for hidden stuff. How they put chains around his belly and irons on his legs when they took him to court. Chains! How the toilet was out in the open and he had to poop right in front of everybody. When he lowered his voice and told Joe what the dirty boys there did to him, Aggie had started to shake.

The memory galvanized her, nearly propelled her down the treehouse ladder. She would find her uncle's farm. Find Burnaby.

Then a terrifying image of Uncle Loomis, his face skewed with rage, floated enormous and close.

She flattened herself against the treehouse wall and shut her eyes, reliving the fright from two months earlier, on the Saturday Burnaby first drove his new truck to the farm. After she promised to rake compost for Aunt Nora, Mama had agreed to let Aggie go with him.

Aggie had waved at her aunt through the kitchen window and skipped to the calf shed to let the newborns suck her fingers with their foamy mouths. From a mound by the door, she scooped a bucketful of fuzzy cotton seeds and poured little piles of them near yearling heifers grazing outside. A few were nosing the treats when Uncle Loomis climbed through the fence and lunged at her. He gripped her shoulder, leaving dirty fingerprints on her shirt, then bent low and thumped her chest.

"Wasting rations! Lost your brains?"

She dropped her head.

"Listen up, girl," he hissed, his spittle spraying her face. She focused on his tangled eyebrows, dodging his speckled eyes. "I don't need no more rats around here, stealing my feed."

Aggie had avoided her uncle ever since. And now? If Uncle Loomis threw a fit over a few cotton seeds, what would he do to her *now*, after she burned down her house?

And killed my parents. She plucked at her pajamas and cringed. She was too bad for anyone to help. Too awful. Uncle Loomis. Burnaby. Everyone would hate her.

Such a tiny, practice fire. She put dirt on it, didn't she? But not enough. And she flicked those embers all over the place. Mama was right. She was too hasty. Careless. *Ohhh.* The groan roiled inside her. Grief punched her guts.

A car engine alerted her to a sheriff's rig crawling up the dusty lane. In the early sunlight, smoke hung over the wreckage like gold fog, blurring the uniformed men into specters who circled and poked at the smoldering ruins. One of them said her name.

Still trembling, Aggie dropped down the far side of the tree, where they wouldn't see her, and fled.

3

CELIA

DETOUR

WITH THE ROAD MAP ACROSS MY KNEES, I traced our progress north toward Seattle along I-5 and checked my watch.

"We're on track for the cabin by eight tonight, Daddy." I flipped down the visor mirror and twisted the stud in my infected earlobe, my teeth set against its sting. "Remember how I went off on you during spring break?" My father drew a slow breath and nodded. "And how pissed I was when you kept me from going to Meredith's party?"

He shifted in his seat. "That I do."

"I'm sorry, Dad. Mother did a number on both of us, and I haven't made things any easier. But the second we left Houston, my pity party was done." On the map, I circled SeaTac, where we'd just landed, with a wide swipe of my marker and wrote June 15, 1985 in block letters across the top. "Fresh start. Right now."

He cleared his throat like he was going to say something, but I kept talking. "I'm through with her. I'm done missing her."

He glanced at me, his expression skeptical. And sad. I couldn't remember his last belly laugh. Forcing a smile, I patted his shoulder. "See Dad? I'm fine. We're fine. A few days at Lake Chelan and we'll be straight-up awesome."

He slowed to let a two-toned Chevy pickup merge in front of us, then ran the back of his hand across his forehead. *Strange.* A sixty-five-degree day in Seattle, but he was sweating more than he did in Texas.

"You okay?" He nodded as I drummed on the dashboard. "Our exit is coming up." I read traffic in the side mirror. "Right lane, right lane—or that semi will block you out."

"The way you watch the road, I'd have given you your license in a heartbeat, Celia. What was that examiner thinking?"

"I ran a red light in downtown Houston, Daddy. That's what he was thinking." I cranked up the radio. He turned it back down. "Now. I-90 East. Right there." I sat up straight as the turnoff approached, and cocked my head at him. "Use your blinker."

"I know how to get there."

He checked his mirror. His hands, perfectly placed in the prescribed ten and two position, tightened on the steering wheel. But did he move into the exit lane? No. No, he didn't. Instead, he eased into a lane farther left and accelerated.

And he drove right past the exit. My head swiveled, watching that turnoff go by.

"You missed it. What are you *doing*? Lake Chelan is that way." I snapped my thumb to the right—back toward the ribbon of freeway heading east out of Seattle and over the Cascade Mountains.

"Change of plans. We're not going to the lake."

"What?"

"I only found out Friday. Didn't get a chance to tell you."

My voice left me. Seconds ticked by.

It returned loud.

"You didn't get a chance. It's Sunday. You couldn't tell me Friday night after work? Or when we were packing? Or at the airport?"

He tapped the steering wheel. I glared at him. "I was afraid, Celia."

"Of *what?*"

"That you wouldn't come."

"Come where? Where are we going? Why did you have me pack for a month if we aren't going to our cabin?"

"To my mom's. I thought you'd enjoy seeing your grandmother."

"You're dodging. We'd go there anyway—after the cabin, like always."

"Nothing's 'like always' anymore. I've been offered a remote assignment. If I don't take it, I'll be out of a job. All the layoffs—"

"What about our plans?" I sounded screechy.

"Campos Oil doesn't send their exploration geologists to Lake Chelan. I'll be working with their deepwater exploration team off the coast of Brazil. That offshore data acquisition I told you about. Three-D seismology."

I gaped at him, absorbing. "We get to go to Brazil? I didn't pack the right—"

"Not this time. I'll be on an offshore rig, so no dependents. Too dangerous. Sorry, sweetheart."

"You're *leaving* me?" Why not throw me to the wolves and be done with it. I scooted against the door and crossed my arms tight against my sternum. From the corner of my eye I saw him glance sidelong at me, but I did not look his way. No sir. He cleared his throat.

"Those turbidite reservoirs are turning out better crude than any of us anticipated. Once the oil industry recovers, we want to be ready."

"You said 'yes' to an assignment in South America and I can't go with you. You didn't even tell me about the offer. Do I have any say in this?"

"Celia, I hoped—"

I fanned my hand to silence him and leaned across the console, inches from his ear. "What am I supposed to do while you're gone? For what, three, four weeks?"

Air escaped through his teeth like radiator steam, and he drove on without saying a word. He sped up, checked the speedometer and backed off the gas pedal. I knew it was killing him that the car lacked cruise control. The man never got tickets. Never got pulled over. A ridiculous rules guy. Oh, yeah. Always doing the right thing.

Except for me.

"You didn't answer me, Daddy. Give me a timetable—and a home. Where are you going to store me while you're away? At Gram's for a month?"

"You may need to stay there a little longer than a month."

"*What?* How long? Details, Dad." I pounded my pen on the map, leaving spotty red marks all over western Washington.

"Well, a few months from my start date. Six months max. If it goes past August, Mrs. Derby will send you whatever you need when she checks the house. Maybe you can even begin the school year here in Washington. The counselor at Axling High School said she'd duplicate your first semester schedule. And the cross-country coach liked your times."

"You *called* them?" I wadded the map. Pressure was building behind my eyes.

"Well, yeah, I—"

I pitched the crumpled map at his head. He ducked and swerved toward a sedan in the next lane. The driver laid on the horn and braked hard.

Daddy jerked the wheel. "Hey! What the—You trying to get us killed?"

"I don't care."

He straightened his arms, pressing into the steering wheel. Lifted his shoulders and held them there. Inhaled, long and slow.

"You love it at Grandma Mender's."

"But I don't want to live with her!" I shouted. "Why can't I stay with Meredith?"

"I think you know."

Unbelievable. My best friend ever, and he called her a bad influence. "Loose as ashes in the wind," he said, like he was talking about cleaning a fireplace or something.

He reached across the console for my hand, but I yanked it away.

"So. Following in Mother's footsteps?"

"Don't be absurd. It's a job, Celia. We have to eat." He changed the radio station to some boring newscast and flipped his sunglasses off his forehead onto his nose. Then he turned up the volume.

Stupid tears. I stretched the hood of my sweatshirt down over my eyes and rubbed them through the fabric. Mascara smeared onto the fuzzy aqua lining. Great. Just great. A raccoon mask to complete my ensemble. I hugged my knees to my chest, stiff as a mannequin in my brand-new, travel-to-Seattle tracksuit. My nose clogged.

"When do you start?"

"In a week. I fly back to Houston first thing tomorrow."

"Daddy, no!" He winced when I yelled. "You're *exactly* like Mom. You care more about your stupid deepwater seismology than me."

"Sweetheart. That's not—"

I pushed up my hood and turned to him.

"Don't 'sweetheart' me. Go ahead. Dump me with your mother and see what happens. I may not be there when you get back."

"C'mon. After all we've been through together?"

I felt like a yo-yo. Before Mother left, I dove for any scraps of tenderness from the woman. A smile? A compliment on my grades? A little concern when I hurt my knee? I took what I could get. Then she would hoard her kindness and I'd starve. I had watched her leave and banked on Daddy. Now he was leaving me, too. I had trusted him with every bone in my body.

I was an idiot.

I pulled my arms inside my sweatshirt so the sleeves hung empty and curled my hands, fetal position.

If he was going to ditch me, I would show him I didn't need him, either. I didn't need anyone. I would get home and start my junior year in Texas, not some hole-in-the-wall in Washington State. No way I'd miss out on this cross-country season. Or miss our math team events; the four of us were totally killing it.

And since the day Meredith moved into our district after semester break and extracted me from the chemistry lab, my looks were working for me, too. Hair. Makeup. Clothes. Meredith credited her makeover as the reason that stud calf-roper Luke Ralston talked to me when she and I hung out by the chutes at the high school rodeo finals, and why he walked me to the bonfire afterwards.

Dancing flames didn't cause those astonished stares when I walked through that crowd in Meredith's hand-tooled cowboy boots with Luke hanging on me. I swear Meredith sensed that I was about to ditch him and run to the ladies' room to scrub my face and calm my hair down a little. She trotted up beside us, looped her arm in mine and whispered that I was a Harris County version of Sandy in *Grease*. Making my entrance, she said, and *oh, was it ever grand.*

Luke stopped by before Daddy and I flew north, saying that after I got home from this trip, he'd like to hang out, if I was up for it. Made me a little nervous, but I told him I just might be willing. Yessir.

I felt my prospects dissolving. If I didn't get back to Houston *way* before Christmas break—Daddy's six-month forecast— Luke would be long gone. And that Jeep waiting in our garage? Oh yeah. I wanted my license.

I fingered the paint swatch in my pocket. Moss green. For the cabin. Daddy and I had waded through the Benjamin Moore sample rack to find it. Well, we wouldn't be doing any painting now. Or lying in the sun. Or water-skiing.

What *would* I do for *months* at Gram's? Hoo boy. I supposed I'd occupy myself with that insane rain problem Mr. Maurer had given our math team. Run those endless country roads. And read. I'd brought a few requisite AP English books and a dog-eared paperback Meredith had stuffed in my bag at the last minute. "Brace yourself, girlie," she said. "You won't find *that* in your sweet little school library."

My library? Hers now, too, though socks fit a rooster better than Meredith fit into any library—or into my structured world of academics and sports—which suited me fine. Meredith Prescott was a curriculum unto herself, and from the minute our school counselor asked me to give her a campus tour, I was a happy enrollee.

Mer wouldn't like my detour one bit. She'd made *plans* for us this summer. Parties with friends she wanted me to meet from Lamar High, from which she'd been *unfairly* expelled. "Big plans," she said. "You will be SUR-PRISED, library girl." I had been counting the days.

Not to be. Instead, by the time we passed Everett, an hour north of the airport, I was suffocating, and we weren't even halfway to Gram's. "I need a rest stop, Dad." Once he stopped the car, I would run. With only five bucks in my wallet, who knew where I'd go, but at least *I'd* be deciding.

"Coming right up," he said. But he missed several exits leading to strip malls and shopping centers, places where a girl could disappear fast. A half hour later, he pulled in at a country store outside Conway and pointed at the door. "Left at the doughnuts. First door past the Mountain Dew."

"Very funny." I glared at him and beelined to the restroom at the back of the store, where I locked myself in a nasty stall to consider my options. They were few at the moment. After what happened to Meredith with that creep who picked her up on the gulf road, Daddy knew I would never hitchhike.

I could, however, take a bus.

At the end of the hallway leading to the restrooms, I found a pay phone. I paged through the directory, sneaked a glance over my shoulder for Daddy, dropped my dime in the slot and whispered to the dog-bus lady. For seventy-five dollars, she said, Greyhound would get me from Washington back to Houston. By the time Daddy learned I had scrammed, he'd be climbing an oil rig off the coast of Brazil. Unless he wanted to call in reinforcements, he'd have no choice but to let me stay with Meredith until he got home.

One problem: I still needed seventy bucks. Daddy was a cosigner on my savings account, so that was out. Meredith was usually flat broke, so she'd be no help. If I asked Gram or Daddy for money outright, they'd smell a plot. I didn't need money at Gram's. Even if I did, they would expect me to work for it.

Okay, then. I would earn it somewhere. And once I accumulated the funds, I'd find that bus and split.

On the way out of the restroom, I leaned in close to the mirror. My normally clear skin was blotchy from crying and streaked with black mascara. *Too gross.* I made a mental note to buy waterproof next time and held a paper towel under the spigot. I poised it under one eye, then changed my mind. This was perfect. War paint. And the mascara matched my hair. I tossed the towel in the trash, finger-combed my ponytail, and rewound my scrunchie.

When I stepped outside, Daddy was pacing in front of the store. "You get lost in there?"

"What do you care?"

He reached for my car door, but I aimed my best stink eye at him and yanked it open myself.

I rolled the window down, shut my eyes, and stuck my head outside so the wind blasted my face and I wouldn't have to talk to him while he drove. If those bugs hadn't kept hitting me, I'd have stayed there the rest of the way to Gram's. I itched to get out of that car, away from Daddy.

An hour later, almost to the Canadian border, we left the freeway and turned toward the mountains. At a stop sign on Borealis Road, I couldn't stand it anymore. Couldn't stand *him*. I jumped out of the car and slammed the door. Daddy rolled down the window.

"C'mon, Celia. It's only two more miles. Get in."

"Leave my stuff at Gram's and you can be on your merry way." I jogged along the quiet road as the car crawled next to me.

His head tipped sideways so he could see me through the window. "I'm sorry."

"You're dumping me twenty-four hundred miles from home. We'll see how long your little Celia stays at her grandmother's."

"Celia, don't."

I sprinted away from him, up the hill, where grass rolled from either side of Crabtree Road like a lumpy green blanket, pasture for all those little dairies that dotted the valley. Along with plenty of berry farms, they propped up the one stoplight town of Axling, seven miles southeast. I'd loved this land for as long as I could remember, but now the rusty barbed wire quilting the fields may as well have been razor wire topping chain link, with me gripping the mesh.

Angry as I was, the beauty still found me. I slowed to a jog and took in the swath of rugged peaks, the North Cascades, hemming the valley's far edge before they marched on into Canada. Their white caps already showed shadowy streaks from early snowmelt. Enormous trees lined the fields and hills between me and those mountains and beckoned me like mothers who care—*nothing* like mine.

Daddy followed alongside for a hundred yards, but when I snubbed him, he closed the window and drove past me. At Grandma Mender's open gate, I turned down the long, treed lane where I practiced hundred-meter sprints whenever I visited. Our rented Chevy sat at a weird angle in front of Gram's sprawling farmhouse. She stood on the porch, no doubt watching for me, her elbows cupped in her hands, her gray braid draped over one thin shoulder. Daddy's stocky frame filled the doorway behind her.

I ignored them both as I approached. I crossed the lawn, hopped the rail fence and whistled for Gram's setters, out digging for voles by the woodshed. Zip and Clover ran to me, their tails whipping, their russet fur sleek in the sunshine. I rubbed their ears and tried to hold myself together as I walked past the house, out of Gram and Daddy's view. To calm my brain, I counted my strides, ninety of them, which landed me at the field's distant boundary. At ninety-one, I folded into the warm grass. The dogs licked my face then sprawled beside me, bellies up in the late afternoon sun.

How long would Daddy stay in there? An hour? Two? With that early flight to catch, he wouldn't spend the night. Would he come find me? Part of me wanted him to. Wanted him to come sit by me and wrap his arms around me. Tell me again that he was sorry and that he loved me and would return for me as fast as he could. And I'd hug him back, tell him I'd be fine. That I was disappointed, but that I understood. And that I loved being with Gram—and I loved him.

But the other part of me, the sizzling mad part, wanted him to hurt. Sizzle was winning at the moment, hands down.

He walked to the fence half an hour later and ran his eyes over the meadow where I lay hidden in the thick, waist-high grass. He had no idea where to look. "Celia?" He'd never locate me. I massaged the dogs' ears to keep them quiet. Clutched their collars. "Celia?" I held my breath. "Ceel-ya?" His voice echoed off the trees by the river this time. He paced the fence at the lawn's edge, held fingers to his mouth and whistled. Shaded his eyes, inspecting the field. Cocked his head and listened. Eventually, he dug his hands in his pockets, coughed roughly, and returned to the house.

I waited, but he stayed inside. What did he expect? That I would crawl to the door? No way I'd give him that satisfaction. I would hide until he left. I'd outlast him. I would sleep in the barn if necessary.

It seemed like a worthwhile plan until I heard his car start. Then ice rolled up my arms and legs. I *did* outlast him. My daddy was *leaving me.*

I buried my face in Zip's scruff. By the time my sobs squeezed out every salty drop, Clover was trotting to the house—and the vengeful side of me had won. No doubt in my mind; I'd be gone before Daddy returned. There were other ways to hitch a ride.

4

AGGIE

FLIGHT

AGGIE DIDN'T DARE use the road as an escape route. Those people pawing through the rubble would see her there, catch her, and take her to jail. Instead, she tore down the hill trail toward their pond, gritting her teeth against the pain in her burned feet. Her hands shook as she untied the yellow dinghy her dad had inflated the week before, on her tenth birthday.

She dragged the raft over the nearby river's grassy dike before she buckled, sobbing. Then she remembered the deputies, sprang like a startled cat, and aimed the boat into the water, where sunlit fog and smoke gilded the air above the surface. She entered the craft nimbly and, with a bare foot shoving hard into the bank, pushed off. The Hawley River, still high with snowmelt, urged the boat downstream. Water wrinkled against its sides and tugged it along.

The boat veered into the main current, and she shivered at the exposure, open to water and sky and trapped in her yellow boat. As her panic rose, she stood to jump overboard, but when the dinghy wobbled, she fell onto her bottom and stared dully into the swirling drink. *Salmon,* she thought. If only she were a salmon, she would smell the water and know where to go. Sniff out a place to hide. Somewhere safe.

Was there anywhere safe? She huddled in the morning chill as the little boat's oars dangled from the oarlocks. At last she curled up on the rubber deck, and when the day warmed her, slept.

Midmorning, heat and thirst woke her to an unfamiliar landscape. From her drift down the middle of the river, she saw a wide pasture peppered with dairy cows, all ambling toward a long, squat barn at the field's far border. A man with a pair of cattle dogs eased them forward. Surreal. Calm. Detached from her, as if they were in a snapshot, or on TV.

But Aggie's mind jigged. She ducked beneath the gunwale and hunched into the boat's inflated side. That man with the cows. Was *he* coming for her, too? She peeked. He was still herding animals—and walking below dike level. So he couldn't see her, right?

Wrong. Everyone could see her. *Everyone!* She flattened her trembling body onto the craft's floor and waited.

Minutes passed. Where was he now? No one called or appeared at the top of the dike, so she lifted her head, her eyes darting. The man and his cows were behind her, mere slivers entering the barn. Still, she imagined him spotting her, pursuing her, sounding an alarm. He would. She knew it.

The boat swung, forcing her attention to the water. The current swirled her toward a partially submerged tree, where protruding branches pointed jagged, knife-like tips at her raft. Her fingertips tingled with another infusion of fear. "Dad!" She screamed over the water and the vacant fields beyond the dike, emptying her lungs until her tongue felt huge and dry in her open mouth.

Facts flitted by: Brian Hatch. High schooler. Swim team. Drowned by a water-logged tree in the river. Then her dad's voice, banging in her ears. "His thrashing entangled him more. That's why you can't panic, Aggie. Think instead. Choose."

She glared at the woody tentacles, jerked an oar loose, and pushed against a limb with the blade. Her dinghy swerved, then floated toward a sprawling pancake of roots inches beneath the water's surface. On her knees now, she hoisted the oar, rammed its tip into the twisty mass, and heaved her weight against it.

As if deciding, the boat paused before it responded to Aggie's pressure and shifted direction—toward the open current. *Free.* Sweaty, with her hands locked tight around the oar, she watched the threat shrink behind her.

Row. She had to row, but the swirling water disoriented her. On the pond she rowed often, but the oar now seemed foreign and she fumbled with it.

Think, Aggie. She willed her fingers to drop the oarlock into place and grasped the oars' handles. She dipped both blades under the surface and pulled.

Ahead of her, its talons leading, a black and white blur splashed and sank into the river—until even its outstretched wingtips submerged. Then the skinny raptor erupted from the water, a trout glinting silver in its claws. Aggie took a deep breath and tracked the bird as it regripped the fish midair, then flapped to a messy nest in a cottonwood beside the dike. *Osprey.* Recognition momentarily calmed her before her thoughts again rushed away, this time in a swirl of flames and diving birds.

She rolled her shoulders, trying to relax, then forced herself to study the shoreline. Downstream from where the osprey landed, dense trees, their needles and leaves knit together above thick undergrowth, lined the bank. "Impervious and cold," her uncle Loomis called these heavy Washington forests. Aggie didn't think so. The forest was the friendliest of places, if you knew your way around. The kindest place. She extended her arms toward the waiting branches. She would land there and go to them.

But first, water. Releasing the oars to trail from their locks, she stretched over the dinghy's pillowy bow, balanced on her belly and sniffed the silty river's hybrid scent of rot and growth. When she slurped a mouthful, its taste wormed in her throat.

Beavers swim here, Dad, I know, I know. At least this water came from the middle of the river. Fast flow was safer, wasn't it? And what was the name of that sickness where beavers swam? She lay dazed over the side of the boat, wishing she had paid attention, refusing to drink more.

If only she could touch those trees.

Determined now, she sat up and steered for shore, pulling hard at the oars. When the boat scuffed gravel, she straddled the gunwale and stepped into ankle-deep water, then thrust the raft under a scrubby, overhanging willow. The dinghy bobbed—leaf-shrouded but ready for her, should she need it again. She tugged the line around a branch and crawled like a salamander onto the dike, where she flopped onto her belly in the tall grass. Algae clung to her chin.

She lay there breathing, breathing, trying to calm. *Slow*, she told herself, but she panted and gasped. Dad's whispers came to her, soothing her panic: *Full lungs. Slow.* The sun moved higher as she refused the night's horrors and searched for different thoughts. Better ones. *Kitten. Egg. Nest.* Anything to crowd out the fire.

After a long time, she took one deep, unhurried breath. And another. The pulse in her neck quieted.

New glimpses of Mama came to her. Mama peaceful, reading under the aspens in the hammock on a warm day before she got sick.

Aggie closed her eyes and concentrated. The memory stuck, briefly. She pictured herself creeping beneath her mom and brushing the ends of her mother's coppery hair as it trailed through the hammock's loose weave. Sun glinted heat off the curls.

———∿

"My hair doesn't shine like yours, Mama."

Her mother had laid the book across her lap and rolled onto her side, evaluating Aggie through the webbing. "Your hair has soft light, baby. Like mist. Or moonbeams." Mama's gaze caressed her. "And those agate eyes of yours? Warm light. So lovely."

Aggie wanted to believe her. She believed the misty part, but the light and beauty? She didn't buy it. That night washing dishes she pulled a metal spatula out of the suds and analyzed her own elfin reflection in its surface, confirming what the bathroom mirror told her. Ashy blonde and pale as paper, she could not have looked more different from her radiant mother. She was dull, invisible.

She had recalled her dad laughing when she melted into a wild cherry tree. "You can hide right in front of me, Aggie. When you climb those trees, I can't tell you from the branches and leaves."

———∿

Branches and leaves? A startled mallard rose squawking from the river and intruded on the memories. If resembling foliage kept her hidden, then she liked her appearance just fine. Her gray top and navy bottoms would blend in, too—and mud already mottled her pink, bare feet. She parted the grass for a clearer view of the woods. She would crawl there, she decided. Disappear into the undergrowth, climb and get her bearings. The trees would hold her while she figured out what to do next.

HAWK

THE FIELD GRASS had cooled and the mountains turned pink when Clover led Gram to me, two hours after Daddy drove away. My grandmother knelt down beside me, but I kept staring at the cumulus clouds overhead, velvet pillows gone all gold and violet. Zip, dozing in the crook of my arm, rose to greet her, and both dogs bounded off.

"Hungry, honey? For dinner? Talk?" She ran a wrinkled hand along my shin.

"No thank you, ma'am." I withdrew my leg. Things had changed between Gram and me. She had colluded with my daddy.

"Fair enough. I could use your help, though." She sounded tentative. "Jake Brim just called. He's bringing over a Cooper's hawk he found snared in his garden's deer fence. Tore a talon."

That shifted my gears. Regardless of my grandmother's betrayal, we had work to do.

During my last visit, Gram left a magazine on my nightstand, opened to a glossy photo of her with a recovering barred owl and the feature headline, "Acclaimed Biologist Considers the Birds." The piece began with the story about her grandfather nicknaming her Mender after she revived a snowy owl, then recounted how Marta Burke, a researcher by trade, retired at sixty to rehabilitate birds, and had done so for the past six years. Midway through the article, Gram described a kestrel we had worked on and called me her "kindred spirit" and "a passionate, tireless assistant."

A bit of a stretch, since I only visited three or four times a year, but I liked reading it. Felt like a little feng shui for my clashing insides. Passionate? Tireless? When it came to birds, *yes*. I was a lot like my gram.

But skilled? Intuitive? Hardly a lick like her. I wondered what my double-great-grandad would have called me. *Nothing* to do with mending. My solo attempts at healing failed miserably. I tended that finch for an hour after it hit the window. It died anyway. A duck with a fishhook through its beak escaped me and flew away, trailing twenty yards of nylon line. And my parents' marriage? I tried. Oh, I tried. I doubted *I* could save anything.

———✲———

Gram had pondered the clouds for five minutes before I answered from my nest in the grass. "Is he bleeding like that barn owl did last year? The one the Webster kid shot with that pellet gun?"

"Enough to put him at risk, from Jake's description." When I stood without taking her extended hands, she clasped them in front of her. "Will you kennel the dogs? I'll get your gloves."

Minutes later, a rangy, wire-haired farmer in a sweat-stained cap lowered a wobbling box into Gram's hands. Bird feet scraped the cardboard inside.

"He didn't like me untangling him, that's for sure."

"C'mon in." She hugged the box to her chest. "We'll take a peek at him."

"I'd rather leave him with you, if you don't mind. I'm not dressed for a visit." Cow manure spattered his coveralls and rubber barn boots. "I still have to feed calves."

"Thanks for bringing him by, Jake. I'll keep you posted."

"Sorry to interrupt." He flashed me a wide smile.

"Not at all. This is the granddaughter I told you about. Celia? Jake."

I knew it. My grandmother was telling every random person with an injured bird that my dad had dumped me here.

"A pleasure." He touched his hat, turned and waved without looking back.

Gram hummed while I pulled on my long-cuffed leather gloves and checked over the supplies laid out on the laundry room counter: a leather raptor hood, styptic and talcum powders, superglue, gauze, scissors, a tiny paintbrush, paper plates, tongue depressors, and tinctures in little brown bottles with squishy eye-dropper tops.

"You ever see a Coop, Celia?"

"I don't think so."

"Looks like that sharp-shinned boy we worked on, but with a bigger head, thicker legs. More of a barrel body." She snipped the duct tape sealing the bird's box. "Nape is lighter, too." Her hands stabilized the box's erupting lid flaps as the hawk struggled beneath them. "Remember what to do?"

I nodded, irritated. I had helped her for years. She stepped away as I lifted the flaps and quickly secured the wild bird's legs and wings— like I always did.

But as I lifted him, my hold shifted, and he wrenched a wing free. I still held his legs, but he flapped hard and pitched forward. His foot dripped red.

Gram flinched. Just the slightest twitch, but it felt like a slap, and the muscles in my neck constricted.

She reached around me and immobilized him in one smooth motion. "We've got him, honey."

I scowled, slid my hands behind hers and reclaimed him.

She pointed at his tail. "Rounder than the sharpie's."

I raised the hawk to see. He rotated his head from side to side, his open beak threatening. *If I were you, I'd want to bite someone, too.* His talons jutted in front of him like sickles, and his stub oozed.

Gram was studying me. "He's a handful. Thinks if he can get away from us, his pain will stop."

Her words hit close to my core; I bristled. "How do *you* know?"

She shrugged, then ran the leather hood under his beak and slid it over his head. With his eyes covered, the bird quieted. "Now let's see what he did to himself."

I wrinkled my nose. "Too much blood."

"He left his toenail behind when he fought that netting. If Jake hadn't found him, he may have bled out or died of shock by morning." She held the toe and bent close to study it. "Fortunately, the tear is low on his digit. The claw should grow back with no irregularities. We'll patch him up to help him along."

She applied lidocaine to numb the injury, then dusted gauze with styptic powder and pressed it on the bird's wound until the bleeding stopped. "Now we'll dry it so the coating will stick." She swabbed the site with clean gauze and blew on it. Even blinded by the hood, the bird wrestled against my grip, bit my glove. "He's a fierce one. Hold him steady now."

Well, that rankled me. *Like I wouldn't?*

"Once the finish hardens, it'll protect those nerve endings, and they won't be so sensitive. Then he can use those spectacular feet of his to hunt again." She whistled to the bird and dabbed his foot with the gauze. "He knows we're helping him. Such a brave boy."

Gram mixed talcum powder with the glue and painted it over the toe. "After it dries, we'll add another coat. That'll be enough for tonight. A volunteer will take him to the raptor center tomorrow. I expect they'll thicken the claw a bit more when he gets there."

She palpated the bird's crop at the base of his neck. "Hm. Empty. He must have been zeroing in on a meal when that fence waylaid him. Time to set this boy up in his hotel room and give him some dinner."

Between applications of the custom-made nail, she lifted a travel crate onto the washing machine, hooked a water dish to the door, and set two raw chicken legs inside. I eased the bird, his toe sealed and dry, onto the crate's floor. Gram removed his hood and shut the gate.

"Thank you, dear."

"For what?" My tone dared her to answer.

She opened her mouth to speak, closed it, and quickly stowed supplies in their respective drawers and cupboards. She glanced at her watch. "Oh, my. Ten thirty already. Time for this old bird to roost." I averted my eyes as she touched my cheek and padded to the door.

Alone with the resting hawk, I wiped the counter, then dropped my head to his eye level, assessing him through the door's grille. "You. So exquisite." I wanted to stroke his steel-gray feathers, arrayed like a cape against the tawny mottling on his breast and underside. He glared at me with cranberry eyes and sidled toward the food. "You want some room. I get that." I stepped back against the wall and stood motionless until the bird gripped a chicken leg with his good foot and tore into the meat. Relieved, I watched his crop swell and turned out the light.

6

AGGIE

HUNGER

WIND. FROM THE SOUTH. Aggie figured. Gusts spanked the river's surface before they leaned the grass blades toward the woods, like little pointers inviting her into the trees. Smaller puffs petted her as she crawled away from her boat.

The breeze made branches flick at her in welcome. "Wet-foot trees," her dad called them: spruce and birch, western red cedar. Big-leaf maple, alder, cottonwood. They all liked the damp peat that flanked the river.

Aggie knew these trees. Well, she knew their relatives, which put her on familiar terms with these cousins. She touched one after another in somber greeting as she wove her way deeper into their midst. At a spruce tree, she shook her head, refusing its prickly needles and rough jigsaw bark, then nodded at the Douglas and hemlock firs—old friends growing farther up the hill, where the soil was drier.

I swear, Aggie. You study trees like a dog sniffs for game.

Dad. Aggie figured that she studied trees like her dad studied her. Sometimes, without raising his eyes, he would say, "Maybe not that way," as if he could hear her thinking about where to climb next. She'd sense him beneath her and draw from his strength. Her nostrils flared, smelling the memory. She must have dreamed the fire. Surely her dad was tracking her now, like he always did.

A towering Doug fir caught her eye. This one hadn't surrendered its lower limbs to the dim forest understory; this one, she could climb. The wind whipped her hair as she gripped the first handhold and effortlessly pulled her spindly frame skyward until she settled onto a chair-like trio of boughs she calculated to be over sixty feet up.

From her new lookout, she watched a tractor drag an irrigation line across a far pasture. Only two days before, she and her father hauled pipe to a field of young trees. "Too dry." He had thrown a handful of dusty soil into the air. "We've never watered this early."

"Too dry, too dry," she hummed unevenly. Why hadn't she listened? Left those matches alone? She wiped her wet eyes with her sleeve, scanned the hill and then startled with a jolt that nearly pitched her sideways off the limb.

Farther up the slope, the same tiny woman who helped Burnaby with his projects and who visited Mama was setting a sprinkler in her garden. *Mender!* The old lady brushed her hands over her jeans and retrieved a sweater from a fencepost. She draped it over one tanned, skinny arm and strode toward the house, her long, gray braid bumping her back with every step.

Aggie took in the familiar white farmhouse, the gambrel barn, the garden, the horse arena and, beyond it all, the road. Since this was Mender's place, somewhere up that road was her uncle's dairy. Where her brother was working when she lit the fire. When she killed their parents.

Her lungs tightened, and her burned feet stung as the haunting scene replayed. Her stomach growled. But it was thirst that interrupted the overpowering flashbacks and drove her to the ground. She plowed through the tangled brush, then followed a game trail until she caught a whiff of water. The scent led her to a small artesian pool, where she sank to her ankles in soothing mud. In its center, clear water bubbled from a deep hole, then spilled into a larger, duckweed-covered pond a baseball toss away.

Dad would drink here.

A nurse log bridged the pool's upper half. She crawled past baby trees growing on its mossy trunk, extended dished hands, and sucked the water down, wild with thirst that intensified with every swallow. She plunged to her elbows and lifted her hands again and again, the taste of snow from some faraway glacier rousing and reviving her until, satiated, she splashed her swollen eyes. Rinsed her ears. Snuffled water from a curved hand and blew—rinsing, rinsing, as if she could sluice away the sounds and smells of the fire. Extinguish those images.

When she got to her knees, her hair dripping, a reflection on the water's surface drew her attention. *Elderberries.* She and Mama picked them every summer after they turned purple. Boiled them into jam. These berries were still red, but she recognized the foliage. She clambered over to the bush and shoved a handful in her mouth, puckering at their sourness. Obviously, they weren't ripe in early June, but they were elderberries, and they would do. A roar in her stomach insisted. Her hands shook from hunger as she picked.

She ate her fill and returned to the lookout tree, ascending to her breezy perch just as a white car drove the lane to the house. The old lady Mender came outside and propped her elbows on the car's open window, talking to someone in the driver's seat. Then a dark-haired man climbed out. Mender wrapped her arms around him and held him for a long time, swaying as if rocking a baby. *Her baby?* He shook his head, pointed toward the road, and the two walked into the house.

Within minutes, a girl in turquoise workout clothes jogged onto the lane. She reminded Aggie of one of those girls on the basketball team at Burnaby's school. Tall. Lean. Two lanky, reddish dogs with floppy ears ran to her, then led her into the field. They all dropped into the swaying grass, out of sight.

Aggie watched the location, but the trio had vanished. Fallen asleep? The man came outside and called a couple of times. What was he yelling? The girl's name? The third time he whistled and shouted louder, his voice overriding the wind.

Cilia? Those tiny little hairs? What kind of name was that?

The man's shoulders slumped, and he returned to the house. Was he the girl's father? Even if the name embarrassed her, why didn't she answer her own dad?

Aggie stayed in the tree, reading the scene. She had nowhere else to go, anyway. A red-tail circled overhead and she imagined herself a rabbit nibbling grass beneath it. Then she envisioned the hawk diving and hauling her off with its puncturing talons. It would shred her with its beak. Would the pain feel something like this horrible sadness? She rested her forehead on her arms, the berries heavy in her belly.

A long time later, she heard an engine; the dark-haired man's car rolled slowly down the lane. Was the girl still in the grass? Aggie wasn't sure and didn't care. An aching lethargy overwhelmed her. Wedged between two branches, she closed her eyes.

———Λ———

Before moonrise, Aggie bolted awake, muzzy. Coyotes yapped across the darkened landscape. Had they roused her? The answer came as sour bile rose in her throat. Her belly churned. She leaned with the spasm, and vomit exploded from her mouth. She scarcely had time to shake her head and spit before the contractions resumed in a fury of successive swells. The cramps wobbled her. She reached for a branch, missed, and grabbed a lower snag.

A new fear, foreign and invasive, gripped her. In all her climbing, she had never felt off balance, but she did now. Never had she been afraid in a tree, but then she had never climbed in the dark before. What if she couldn't get down? The tree's bones were shadows; she couldn't see much else. Reeling, she felt around with her toes until she found a branch, but when she stepped onto it, her foot skidded off into the air.

Her body followed.

Branches tore at her as she plunged past them—ten, fifteen feet. She flailed, caught herself, then slipped and fell again. When her arm hooked over a limb, she lurched to a stop and hung there, skinned and shocked.

I fell. I fell! She gained a foothold on another branch and peered into the gloom beneath her, but couldn't see the ground.

A fresh wave of nausea wracked her body. She trembled and retched again and again, certain her eyes would burst and her belly turn inside out. Between heaves, she tested each branch with her blistered feet and lowered herself slowly, until she landed on the blanket of needles around the tree's base.

She staggered, then slumped in a ball, holding her stomach and shivering with cramps. When she shut her eyes, her mother and father called her from every direction. Frantic, she crawled in a delirious half-sleep, searching for them. Whenever her hands closed around one of their ankles, the ghosts evaporated, and her eyes popped open. Her heart thundered. Grief and nausea pinned her to the ground. She didn't care if the dogs found her. For hours, she didn't care.

As night wore on, the wind calmed, and damp air from the river moved low through the trees. Chilled, Aggie lay motionless, stirring only when soft fur rubbed against her injured foot. The animal walked the length of her sore, abraded body, leaning into her and purring before it poked its noisy nose into her ear. She lifted her hand and a small cat arched under it. She ran her fingers along its back, and the creature kneaded her as Aggie clutched it to her chest. Her nausea was subsiding, and the vibrating purr soothed her until she relaxed and slept.

When hunger woke her in predawn gray, the cat was gone. Disoriented, she listened to the forest birds' first chirps and whistles until her alertness returned and she remembered where she was, and why. Savage cravings for something, anything to eat grew as she rose, spit, peed in the bushes and climbed her lookout tree. She gazed at the fenced garden, then sighed and tightened her empty stomach.

A milk truck whined up the hill to the house. A man in overalls and a dark cap stepped from the truck's cab and shuffled in a familiar gait to the house. Aggie brightened. The same milkman she knew from home. He set his wire basket of clanking bottles on the side door's step.

She wanted to run to him like she always did, calling out little jokes. "Hey, Mr. Binks. Don't try to butter me up," or "If you fall down our stairs, you'll get creamed." But she stayed put. What would he think when he drove down their lane and saw the rubble, when he heard that she burned her parents? He would hate her. Her breath caught in small hiccoughs.

Oh, she wished she could go to Mender and ask her for some of that milk. Tell her about the fire, and how it was all an accident. But how could she? Mender was friends with Mama and Burnaby, not her. Along with Mr. Binks, Mender would hate her, too.

Still, the bottles were right there for the taking. A sure thing. She would be stealing if she took one, and she didn't want to do any more horrible things, but what difference did it make? She was already a murderer. She assessed her dirt-streaked pajamas. *Dirty inside and out. Infected with badness.*

A bat wheeled past her, hunting its insect breakfast in the remnants of twilight. What if she swooped to the house like that? She could be a bat, her legs like wings, darting toward her own meal.

She tracked the retreating milk truck until it receded down the road, then began her descent. Halfway down the tree, her eyes shifted to a small flock of goldfinches that ribboned toward the house. As the sun squeezed over the mountain, chickadees winged along the finches' trajectory. A flash of orange found her peripheral vision— *grosbeak.* The bird sailed from a branch below her, straight to the feathered gathering near the patio, and her eyes widened. Mender owned a bird feeder. That meant sunflower seeds. Millet. Maybe even peanuts. She imagined herself a finch flying straight toward that food.

She laddered the rest of the way down the tree and circled the empty arena, then crept through the tall grass and under the fence to the base of a cedar tree. Drooping branches and a thick trunk hid her. As she viewed the yard through a gap in the greenery, a familiar rub tickled her calves.

She petted the cat's back and they watched the feeder together. The animal's chin quivered at the birds crowded around the teeming tray, which hung at the bottom of a seed hopper hooked on a pole a few feet from a window. Aggie took in the closed window blinds and, emboldened by her hunger, imagined chewing the seeds, pretending they were oatmeal.

At the count of three, she scooted across the lawn, then crawled under a rhododendron bush. Cautiously, she flattened herself against the house and inched toward the feeder. Her stealth didn't trick the birds; they scattered when she approached. She scanned the windows, hoping the cat's appearance on the lawn behind her would convince any early risers that nothing was amiss, that the birds spooked because of a plain old calico.

Under the feeder now, Aggie held out her shirt and tipped the hanging container sideways until seed poured into the pouched fabric. She gathered the cloth around the bulge and made her way along the side of the house, crouching beneath the windows until she arrived at the side door where the wire milk basket waited.

A door closed inside the house as she reached, salivating, for a bottle. Her hand stopped midair. Were they coming for milk? She swallowed hard.

And yanked a quart free. The glass clanked against the basket's sides and scraped on the stair as she secured her grip. Did they hear her? Without waiting to find out, Aggie hugged the food to her chest and charged across the open field for the woods.

7

CELIA

HOOKS

AFTER THE REPAIRED HAWK settled in his crate, I crawled into bed, exhausted. Next thing I knew, a chemistry beaker broke in my dream and my eyes flicked open. Something clinked under my bedroom window. I thought I heard a scuffle of footsteps, but wasn't sure, so I edged off the bed and lifted a slat on the blind.

In the fragile light I could see young sunflowers and peas in the garden and, below my window, Gram's side porch. The milk basket, its bottles holding their creamy contents, sat askew on the step. I craned my neck, looking for a spill, but the bricks beneath the basket were dry. Still groggy, I released the blind and slipped back between the sheets.

———∿———

The courier had picked up the hawk before I wandered into the kitchen two hours later. Gram came through the patio door. "So odd. I filled that feeder yesterday. How could those chirps empty it that fast?" She set an empty Mason jar on the counter. "How'd you sleep, dear one?"

Kind words, but she seemed rattled. Probably irritated from whatever Daddy told her about me. I poured a glass of orange juice. "Dead to the world until I heard the milkman at the crack of dawn. He slammed that basket so hard I thought a bottle broke. Must have been heading to a fire."

"Something else on his mind, I suppose. He left us three quarts instead of four." She set a bowl of oatmeal in front of me without a utensil, realized the omission and, distracted, pulled the spoon from the sugar bowl for me. "Heading to a fire." Gram whispered the words to herself, then faced me. "Do you remember the Hayes family? Harris and Bree—and their kids? Burnaby? Aggie?"

"Harris . . . Isn't he the guy who sawed that heart-rot maple? Last time I was here? Came in for coffee?"

"That's the one. The arborist . . . He and Bree raise native trees . . . and heirloom seeds." Her eyes brimmed. "They bought the Staubs' farm back when Harris left the Alaska Forest Service. Wanted to be near family when Aggie was born." She fanned the air. "Not important now. Their place burned to the ground night before last. I just heard." The words choked her. "Long-time friends."

"That stinks. They okay?" *Time to get a newspaper, Gram. Or a TV. Or to turn on the ra-di-o.* How often did I *beg* her to get a television?

"Not all of them. Don't have many facts, but it was bad . . ." She inhaled sharply.

I shouldn't have asked. I last saw her cry when my granddad died, and I didn't like it then, either.

She held her hand over her mouth and nodded until her voice steadied. "Their neighbor was driving home from swing shift . . . saw flames. She called the fire department, but too late. Burnaby was milking at his uncle's farm, so he's safe, but they airlifted Harris and

Bree to Harborview. Both burned, but Bree's worse. Lung damage . . . She may not make it. A timber smashed Harris's leg." She lifted her coffee, brought it to her lips, then poured it down the sink. "And they can't find Aggie."

"Can't find her?"

"They combed the rubble. No trace. Her uncle called an hour ago, beside himself. A fisherman found her boat spinning over a whirlpool in the river, at the open bend straight east of here." She gestured toward a sunlit window. "Swamped."

"Is he sure the boat's hers?"

"Positive. Her name's on it."

"You think she was in it?"

Her tears spilled. "Oh, I don't . . ." She collected herself, drew a deep breath. "It *is* her dinghy, and she *is* missing, but . . . Search and Rescue's meeting here after breakfast."

"So you think she's in the river?"

"I don't know. If not, she's alone somewhere out there. Terrified. Maybe injured." She stretched her fingers wide toward the woods. "She's only nine. No, ten. Turned ten last week." She clasped her hands and scanned the trees.

At that moment, Aggie was one more problem added to my heap. Why was Gram dragging me into this? Still, I felt sorry for the girl, so sure, I'd help search for her. We'd have time before I caught my bus.

———⚓———

A familiar, round woman almost as short as Gram rang the bell promptly at 8:00. I swung the door wide, and she flew into my grandmother's arms, her shoulders heaving.

"Oh, Nora." Gram stroked her head until the woman pulled away. "Celia, you remember Nora Epping?" The woman sniffed, pulled an elastic off her copper-colored bun and rewound it tighter. She drew her sleeve under her nostrils, leaving a slug-like trail along the

SUGAR BIRDS

cloth, before she lifted her hand at me in a half-hearted wave. Gram
wrapped an arm around her waist. "Nora and Loomis. Next place
north of us. Aggie is their niece."

Nora's eyes watered. "When we heard about her boat, the
tracker—that sheriff with the German Shepherd—" She pointed at
a serious, ruddy man with a majestic black dog on the front driveway. "Well, he drove straight to Bree's." She hesitated and dropped
her chin. "The dog sniffed a trail down to the river, but the sheriff wasn't sure it was hers. Then he found the skid. She must've
dragged the boat. Dog tracked that path." She wiped her nose on
her hand this time. Her voice squeaked. "She's alive, Mender. I can
feel it."

Unless she drowned. The boat was empty, after all. Aggie may
have pushed a rubber raft into the river, but could she handle the
river's surge? I imagined her fleeing that fire and her burned parents.
Dragging that boat. Floating off. Falling overboard.

Or maybe she escaped. If she wanted to get away that badly, part
of me hoped she succeeded. Just like I would.

A brick-shaped man with a shock of bedraggled yellow hair
knocked on the window and signaled Nora outside. Gram and I followed. "Hello, Loomis," Gram said. His beefy paw swallowed her
hand, and he shook it vigorously.

"Burnaby!" The man's voice boomed, and he released Gram. A
walking beanpole with hair even lighter than Loomis's appeared from
behind the horse trailer. He was about my age and at *least* six foot
six—as skinny as Loomis was broad. Loomis jutted a stumpy thumb
toward the guy. "My nephew." A sturdy, fudge-colored dog stood
between the two, her eyes on Burnaby.

I smiled at the beanpole, but he didn't respond. Gram withdrew
a red licorice vine from her pocket and held it out. Burnaby nodded, slipped the candy up his sleeve, then gazed past us with eyes the
color of my moss green paint chip. He seemed faraway, gentle. And

58

intense, if his fidgeting hands meant anything. Quiet on the surface, but churning down deep—like the river that may have swallowed his sister.

The dog sniffed my hand warily, then dropped her ears and tail in submission when I scratched her chin. "She have a name?"

"Pi." The dog nosed Burnaby's hand. "Australian Kelpie. Part Dingo. She musters livestock." He touched his thigh, and the animal quickly heeled, her head at his knee.

We stepped aside to make way for two others wearing the team's signature orange hats: a balding man with a smoker's cough and a grim, bow-legged woman, who each hoisted ends of a long bar wrapped in chains. Hefty hooks dangled along its length. "What's that for?" I whispered to Gram.

"To drag the river bottom. It's a long shot, but if Aggie drowned anywhere near here, they may snag her body. Search and Rescue is sending a boat to meet us." Gram could have been carrying the hooks herself. Her shoulders sagged with the weight of what we were doing, searching for a lost child, the daughter of friends.

My throat constricted.

A paunchy cowboy in a chambray shirt and neon orange vest held the reins of a stout buckskin, whose ears swiveled to sounds of the gathering crowd. The man adjusted his straw Stetson authoritatively, tightened the saddle's cinch, and mounted. Leather squeaked under his weight.

"Listen up." The rider checked his watch as he waited for the searchers' attention. "Sheriff Tom will assign your teams down by the boat. Walkers will fan out at this end of the woods." He bumped the horse with his heels and followed Tom and the shepherd through the grass and down the hill to the river. The rest of us fell in line. Pi flanked Burnaby like a soldier.

Then a river skiff pulled to shore, and I forgot about the child. I couldn't help myself. The bald man handed the chain-wrapped bar to the boat's driver, who happened to be *the* best-looking guy ever. *Ridiculously* good-looking. I just may have gawked.

Celia. You're searching for a little girl. They are dragging the river for her BODY. Knock it off.

Didn't matter what I told myself. I was riveted. Dark-haired and olive-skinned, like me, he was, what, six foot one? Two?

A trace of beard shadowed his jaw. He was older—twenty? Twenty-one? I visually outlined muscles through his shirt. Athletic, soccer-player lean. *Mmm.*

Too delicious, Meredith would say. He looked up and smiled at me. *Oh, don't blind me.* Meredith would say that, too. I laughed aloud as he attached the bar to the boat's transom.

"Ready, Cabot?" the older man shouted.

"You bet."

Cabot. So that's his name.

He shoved the boat into the current with an oar and dropped the chains and hooks into the muddy wash. I watched, transfixed, as they crossed to the center of the river. The engine surged against the heavy water.

The sheriff reeled me in. "You. Team with Burnaby. He's done this before. We're doing what's called a hasty search. That doesn't mean careless. Pay attention. It's our best chance of finding her fast if she's alive. We'll cover the parcel of woods between the river and those farms in pairs. The chopper will run a pattern over us, but will concentrate on the open fields. Keep your partner in sight. Observe everything: broken twigs, footprints, feces, bits of paper or clothing . . . everything."

Even broken *twigs*? This sounded tedious.

Paired now, Mender and Nora, Loomis and the orange hat lady, and then Burnaby, Pi and I waited until the man on the horse turned us loose.

"Burnaby," I said. He faced away from me, so I touched his shoulder. "Sorry about your family."

When I made contact, he threw his arm back as if I'd stung him. I quickly scanned the other searchers, but they hadn't noticed. So *embarrassing*. If I wasn't his type, he could have told me a bit more discreetly.

"Whoa, Burnaby. I'm not hitting on you. Just extending a little sympathy."

He acted like he didn't hear me. My face heated. I weighed the possibility of trading places with Gram, letting her hunt with this cranky guy.

But before I made the swap, Tom and the tracking dog receded into the brush. The cowboy nudged the horse's sides with his heels, and the rest of us set off behind them, pushing through undergrowth.

———⚶

We'd been searching for fifteen minutes before Burnaby said a word. "I was milking, or I would have been there." He swiped a low-hanging branch aside and Pi sniffed the ground beneath it. "I would have gotten them out."

My defensiveness melted. What was I thinking? Burnaby was upset, but not with me. That fire wrecked his family. Of course he'd be off.

"Aggie climbs. If she's not in the river, she'll be in a tree." Burnaby squinted into the leaves overhead. "If we find her tracks, we should look up."

"Where do you think she is? River or tree?" I walked toward him.

"I don't know. Aggie rows competently, but a diked river can't spread out. Mountain snowmelt speeds the currents. Currents can flip boats. Drive objects to the bottom." A muscle in his face jumped.

Like bodies. "Well, let's hope she's in the trees." Then, stupid me, I patted him on the back.

He spun as if I'd shot him this time. "Don't touch me." His voice landed on me flat and calm.

Awkward. I felt like a leper. And irritated. I raised my arms, hands uplifted in surrender. What was the guy's deal?

"You got it." I almost added *jerk,* but restrained myself for the sake of the search.

Burnaby walked past me as if nothing happened, so I resumed my position a little behind him and several feet to his left. We soon fell into a rhythm. He took two long-legged steps. I took three to keep up. He brushed a branch out of the way to check beneath it, then his head rotated as his eyes swept a wide circle over ground, shrubs, rocks, downed logs, and trees. Down. Side. Up. Side. Down. The guy's gangly legs resembled ones on those cobweb spiders that lived in our garage back home. He moved like a machine. Mechanical.

I kept an eye on him, and before long, my ire subsided. Something about the boy. He was no jerk. Just . . . different. Sensitive. So sensitive I didn't dare surprise him by touching him.

Meredith would call that a waste, not touching. I wouldn't know. Boys usually steered clear of me. Like Josh Hebert did. I remembered exactly.

"You're one scary chick," he had said, after word got out that I'd conquered that National Merit practice test. "A freshman. Geez."

"Good," Daddy said, when I told him. "Keep intimidating them, sweetheart."

Meredith had scoffed. "You wait, book girl," she said. "Your train's coming. Strap in for a *ride.*"

———A———

Burnaby ignored me while we searched, but I did my best to follow his lead through the woods, hunting for anything in those trees that stood out, and concentrating so hard I didn't even think about talking. I was also listening—for girl noises and for hoots or whistles from the rest of the searchers signaling that they located a track or a clue.

But after a helicopter whumped over the surrounding fields, the forest seemed almost shy in its quietness.

At 2:00, I checked my watch, weary. If the team planned to stay out here until we found Aggie, I needed a little stamina boost. Was it against Search and Rescue regulations to talk? The guy seemed like a rules dude, so I asked.

"Uh. Burnaby. You in school?"

Step. Sweep. "Yes."

"So . . . what grade?"

Down. Side. Up. "Grade twelve on September twelve."

"Funny, twelve and twelve. What are the odds of that?"

We moved six feet through the brush before he answered. "In this case, the probability of the matching numbers is almost one out of thirty. One out of thirty—or zero point zero bar three."

Was he kidding me? Who talked like that besides *me*—and my school math team, when we were out of math-haters' earshot?

"Yep. Threes forever. Do you think—?"

"What's this?" Burnaby said. Bright red berries lay in slimy glops around the base of an old fir tree. He poked one clump with a stick and answered his own question. "Vomit, I suspect."

Pi sniffed the piles. Burnaby bent over, mulling, before he tagged a branch with a neon green strip of surveyor's tape and blew his whistle.

Tom's orange hat bobbed as he and his dog wove through the woods toward us. "Whatcha got?" he asked.

Burnaby pointed at the berries. "Can you identify?"

Tom handed Burnaby the dog's leash and snapped a picture before he filled a specimen bag with samples. "Don't know. Probably nothing. Animals puke all the time. We'll send it to the lab and see what they say."

The shepherd sniffed the remaining berries and wagged his tail like a windshield wiper in a downpour. Burnaby braced himself against the dog's pull. When Tom retrieved the leash, the animal locked his nose to the ground and urgently tracked an area in a twenty-foot diameter around the mess, lingering in a depression at the base of an adjacent tree. "Something bedded down here." Tom lengthened the dog's leash. "Where'd it go, buddy?"

The dog dragged him over the rise toward the house. The pair returned minutes later to a nearby maple, coursed two short loops away from the tree, and stopped at the chewed berries under the fir. The dog barked shrilly into the tree, jumped up on the trunk, then spun in a circle. Tom frowned. "He's stymied. Trail begins at that maple and ends here."

"She climbed." Tom and I traced Burnaby's gaze into the fir tree and we all scrutinized the branches overhead.

"You see anything?" Tom dripped condescension. "I sure don't. I know she climbs, but honestly, Burnaby. She's not a criminal. Why would she hide from you?" He shook his head. "Ridiculous. There's no kid up there." He reeled in the leash. "If she'd gone up, she'd have come down again, and there's no trail off this location. Nobody else has found anything either. We'd be more accurate with a grid search, but with no evidence besides that boat, I'm redirecting our personnel into the next forest quadrant downriver when our second team joins us at three." Static erupted from his walkie-talkie; he pushed a button to silence it. "We're bringing in another boat, too. We appreciate your help, miss, but our team will hunt for her from here on out."

"We're *quitting*? You're sending me *home*?" I shouted in Tom's face. Even though I needed some lunch, his dismissal enraged me. Burnaby pulled a leaf off a shrub and tore it into a circle shape. His lips pursed.

Tom spat brown liquid into the shrubbery, then faced me, annoyed. "No, we're not quitting. We're covering a sizeable area fast, and Burnaby's coming with us. We'll have more teams here by evening, so if we don't find her downstream in the next few hours, we'll return before dark. You, Mender, and the Eppings can revisit this quadrant again. We'll be glad if you do."

Oh, I was livid. How could they move on? They found her raft right under our noses. And what about those *berries*?

Burnaby, his neck craned, stepped away from us, studying the trees. My detachment dissolved. I could feel his grief. Or was it mine? Such familiar pain. His family, my family: ruined.

Maybe we could understand each other. And we could look for his sister. I could stick around long enough to do that.

At least until I earned seventy bucks. Strawberries were ripening at the farm down the road—within jogging distance. They'd need pickers.

8

—

AGGIE

SEARCH

AGGIE DIDN'T TURN AROUND until she propped the stolen milk bottle at the foot of a mossy big-leaf maple, where she bent over, her breath ragged. She couldn't see the house. Couldn't tell if anyone came after her. She stood watch, ready to run.

Minutes passed, and nobody showed. Still gripping the shirt pouch with her right hand, she plucked a few platter-sized leaves from a low-hanging branch with her left and set them on the ground. She dug a shallow indentation in the forest duff, layered the leaves inside it, and emptied her cache of seed into the makeshift bowl.

Only then did she tear off the bottle's waxed paper lid and gulp. When she paused for breath, the quart was half empty. She set the bottle down, scooped a palmful of seeds and crammed them in her mouth. Chewing fast, she pulverized the sunflower shells, swallowed, and then—more intentionally this time—picked out her next mouthful.

Her tears returned. Here she was focusing on her first decent meal in two days, but when she separated the sunflower seeds out of the mixture to shell them, she remembered Mama sorting seeds at the long table in the barn. How her mother's lips moved as she counted coriander balls and thorny little chard beads. How her freckled hands grouped tiny carrot crescents and lettuce seeds shaped like so many punctuation marks. How, when Mama slid the seeds into little envelopes, Aggie licked them closed. The image comforted her. Her kind Mama was here. With her.

She shelled a few sunflower seeds, mixed them with a handful of millet and naked peanuts, and chewed for a long time before she washed the slurry down with another gulp of milk. Her stomach was full now, and her eyelids drooped. But the sun marched higher, and she heard voices and car doors slamming near the house. A horse whinnied. What if those people went for a walk and found her sleeping under a tree with the stolen milk bottle? She felt dirty again, but when she rubbed her hands on her legs, her guilt smeared and grew bigger.

Rousing, she poured the rest of her seed into the bottle with the milk, pushed the waxy lid back into place, and scattered duff over her makeshift kitchen to erase it. No walkers or riders or dogs would stumble over *her*. With the bottle clamped in her armpit, she climbed the maple, then hid the precious food at a branch cluster. She would come back for it before the milk soured.

At a long, lateral bough, she crossed to her lookout tree. Halfway up, her hand landed on something slimy, and she recoiled. *Ew. Berry barf.* She wiped her palm on the trunk, chose her grips with greater care, and tuned in to noises near the house as she ascended. Even in the rising wind, sounds clattered like dishes in a sink. When she took her elevated seat, her body went stiff at the scene below.

Colors cascaded down the hill: red, green, yellow, and neon orange windbreakers, caps, T-shirts. Search and Rescue people. One

wore a cowboy hat and rode a horse. Another, in an orange shirt with
SHERIFF across the chest, walked a black German Shepherd. Two of
several wearing orange caps, a middle-aged woman and a big-bellied
older man, carried a long bar wrapped in chains.

Her dad led search parties like this. *Wait.* She recognized some of
the volunteers: Uncle Loomis, gesturing wildly to the older man; the
black-haired girl named after ear hairs; Aunt Nora, rubbing her nose,
her shoulders bowed; Mender. Lagging was Burnaby, *oh Burnaby*, who
seemed to be studying trees upstream. Pi trotted close to his heels.

She nearly cried out at the sight of her brother. Burnaby, here for
her. She could run right over to him, could bend over Pi, and the dog
would lick her ear. Burn would drive her home in his truck to Mama
and Dad. She couldn't take her eyes off the pair.

But something was wrong with Burnaby. He tilted with every
step, as if he didn't have knees, as if his legs were stilts. His arms didn't
swing. And Pi was on high alert, her head down in that bodyguard
way of hers, her muscled legs tensed and dodgy. What were they—?

Oh, oh, oh. How could she forget? There'd be no ride from her
brother. No Mama at home. No Dad. Burnaby was upset. So upset.
He and the others were helping the sheriff. Her chest felt sweaty.
They're after me. Even Burnaby. Especially Burnaby. And, as she suspected, Mender.

An engine revved down by the river. Another searcher in an
orange cap pulled a skiff to shore. The two with the bar called to the
man in the boat and unwound the chains, exposing large hooks that
hung from them. "They'll snag her if she's there," Uncle Loomis bel-
lowed across the field.

Snag who? Snag me? With those hooks? She trembled. *How did they
know where . . . ?*

Then she saw it: her yellow dinghy. Someone had pulled it ashore
so close she could almost hit it with a fir cone, if she threw her hard-
est. The black dog sniffed it. The boat was hers, all right. She had

written her name on it with a Magic Marker as soon as her dad pumped it up on her birthday. She couldn't make out the letters, but there was no mistaking that green ink. *Stupid of me to write my name. Stupid of me to shove the boat under the willow without tying it better.* Did the wind pull it loose? *Stupid of me to think I could hide a bright yellow raft, anyway.*

The searchers gathered around the boat and listened while the sheriff talked and pointed. When he finished, the men in the boat lowered the hooks and bar into the water and motored down the river. The rest of the team headed her way.

She inspected her clothes. Her navy leggings could pass for a shadow. Her gray shirt was more conspicuous, but at least it wasn't pink. And in two interminable days, her long-sleeved tee had picked up a layer of grime. If Mama saw her, she would insist that Aggie strip to her undies in the laundry room before she came inside.

She needed to be dirtier still. She pinched earwigs out of a crevice in the bark and smeared the insects across her chest and down her arms, adding smudgy streaks to further disrupt the solid field of fabric. She smiled wanly. *Much better.* If she kept her knees pulled up, her legs would block even more of her shirt. Or should she take it off? She peeked down her neckline at her pale chest. *Nope. Too pasty.*

When the searchers entered the woods, she forgot her camouflage efforts. Four teams combed the forest floor. She quickly dismissed any threat from old Mender and Aunt Nora, and from impatient Uncle Loomis and the orange cap lady, who fell backwards when Uncle Loomis released a branch that whacked her. She doubted the cilia-girl and Burnaby would be much help either. Sure, her brother was a skilled tracker, and he knew she climbed, but he hated heights. Whenever she scampered above his head, he averted his eyes so he wouldn't get dizzy. He didn't know her climbing habits or how high she traveled.

And Pi? She wouldn't give Aggie away. The dog wasn't trained to track. Besides, she had been smelling—and ignoring—Aggie forever. Unless someone or something threatened Burnaby, or unless she sat right in front of the dog, Pi cared only about her brother.

The searchers' other animals worried her, though. Dad called horses "prey beasts." He said searchers liked them because they watched for threats from above as well as at ground level. If a horse could detect a cougar overhead, it could easily sense her. When that horse drew near, if Aggie so much as itched her nose, the animal would alert its rider to look up. A horse had a keen sniffer, too. She wished she had rubbed a smelly plant on her body to mask her odor.

Her nape tightened as she watched the sheriff. He poured water over the dog's nose—a scent-sharpening tactic, according to Dad. Then the pair plunged ahead of the others, moving fast along the river on a route she hadn't traveled. *Why?* Wouldn't the dog have snagged her trail where she crawled to the woods? Why leave it? *Oh, yeah.* They were heading downwind. The dog would track her from the opposite direction on a trail uncontaminated by the other searchers, closing a lariat around her.

She picked at the dried mud on her feet, visualizing her tracks beside the spring. But so what? They'd dead end, wouldn't they? Her footprints wouldn't show on rough bark, and even when the dog caught her scent, it couldn't follow her as she moved between trees in the canopy.

Or could it?

Her best hope to evade them all, she decided, was to climb even higher. Become an owl, sitting so daytime still she blended in with the tree trunk bark and lichens. Nobody would expect her to go as high as she did, to hide right above their heads. All summer, if she must. But then what?

The horse approached, and Aggie saw its ears flick. It sensed her! Apprehension broke her resolve to stay still. She rose and side-stepped around the tree, positioning herself behind the trunk—and dislodging some debris; a clump of tree litter fluttered toward the forest floor. She shrank. Hadn't she had known better than to move? Mama's voice rang in her head: *Impatient! Careless!*

The horse halted and snorted, not fifty feet from her tree. The rider turned in the saddle and panned his surroundings. When the animal blew and stamped, the man dismounted and draped the reins over the saddle horn. He watched the horse's ears first point forward, then swivel. "What is it, boy?" He read the ground before he aimed his eyes higher.

Methodically, he traced each tree around him, far into the branches. Though she was pretty sure her tree stood outside the radius he was studying, she kept the trunk between them. She willed herself to tree bark immobility and breathed in sips as the man's eyes crawled the woods.

At last the easy sound of a horse tearing grass replaced the silence. "Unh-uh. No eating. We're working, remember?" Aggie peeked to see the man tug the reins and the horse's head lift. "Must have been a false alarm, if you're thinking about lunch." He swung into the saddle and rode on.

She filled her lungs as the pair moved away, and climbed higher than ever, glimpsing only flashes of color while the teams hunted below. Their search pattern was erratic; they missed wide swaths of ground. Maybe they would even miss her footprints by the pool. The tension in her body eased. Momentarily.

———A

She heard the helicopter before she saw it advancing like a giant blue dragonfly. The craft crawled low along the riverside fields toward her, then lifted to skim the canopy. Aggie cowered as the deafening pulse of the rotors thumped against her. The pilot, his head cocked toward her tree, talked into a microphone on his helmet, his eyes hidden behind sunglasses.

She was too high! Too visible from overhead. The searchers were squeezing her from above and below. Spinning blades swept the tree-tops, and the wind slammed her body with a concussive force that nearly hurled her from her perch. Aggie clung to the trunk and cried out from pain in her eardrums.

The chopper made three passes. With each one, she weakened with terror and hurt and the force of the wind. If it returned a fourth time, she doubted she could hold on. The downwash would blow her right out of the tree.

And then, as quickly as it arrived, the machine flew downriver and left Aggie and her thundering heart alone. *He didn't see me.* Her head lolled, and she squeezed her eyes closed, gathering her wits, blocking out the searchers below.

She had scarcely stopped panting when louder voices injected her with additional dismay. The girl and Burnaby had changed course and were angling her way. Could they spot her through that sea of branches? The conversation's cadence reached her, but not the words. Burnaby blew his whistle and showed the girl something on the ground. Aggie blanched. *The berries!*

She had vomited her address at the foot of her tree.

9

CELIA

BURNABY

AFTER THE *OFFICIAL* SEARCH TEAM moved downriver, I stood at Gram's front door and watched the Eppings' Buick turn toward the dairy. We all needed to regroup. And eat. Gram set a salmon sandwich on the kitchen table and pointed me to a chair, calming me with a promise that we would keep hunting for Aggie.

"That Burnaby's a piece of work," I said.

She shot me a cautionary glance. "I'm very fond of that boy."

"Obviously." I thought of her handing him the licorice. "You've known him awhile."

She ran her eyes across the ceiling and spoke slowly, assembling the chronology. "Yes . . . since Aggie was a few months old. He was . . . uh . . . second grade. I stopped by for fall seeds and found Bree pulling her hair out."

"That doesn't surprise me."

"Aggie was screaming. Burnaby was hiding in a kitchen cupboard because Bree stepped on some of his macaroni shells while she was walking the baby. He had lined up hundreds of them, alternating them with LEGO pieces arranged in some kind of binary code, near as Bree could tell."

I snorted. "I can picture it."

"I imagine you can, after today." She dunked her tea bag and watched it spin on the string. "When I offered to hold Aggie, Bree practically tossed the baby to me. Your dad had colic. I ever tell you that?"

"Nope." As if I cared.

"Anyway, Bree and I ended up at her table like old friends. I held Aggie. Burnaby stayed in the cupboard."

"So you didn't actually *meet* him."

She smiled. "I guess not. But I learned what Bree was dealing with."

"Why was it his fault? If my mother ruined a major project, I'd hide too."

"I didn't mean that, Celia." Gram sighed. "Nobody blamed him. Bree had bigger issues with the boy. Burnaby was already seven and still not talking. He never made eye contact with her. Backed away from her from the time he walked."

"He didn't look at me, either," I said.

Gram pushed her plate aside and folded her hands on the table. "I've seen him every few weeks for years now, either here or at their place and I—"

"Wha—?" I coughed water onto the table. Burnaby spent more time with my grandmother than I did. "Go on. What did macaroni boy do next?" I dabbed the spill.

She eyed me gently. "Well, a month after my first visit, I stopped by again. When Burnaby came in off the school bus, Bree asked him about his day. Neither of us expected him to answer. But this day? My word. His voice sounded like BB gun pellets hitting cardboard."

"So he talked."

"Oh, yes. He answered her question. In *detail*. He recalled everything, Celia. I mean *everything*. Like how he squeezed one point five centimeters of toothpaste onto his toothbrush at 7:12 a.m. Opened his spelling book to the middle of page forty-six at 9:14. How at that moment his teacher blew her nose.

"Bree and I stared at each other over the boy's head, dumbfounded. Next, he told her about story time and recited *at least* a full page of the chapter book his teacher was reading, verbatim. He kept talking until Bree offered him some peanut butter toast."

"So his brain filmed the entire day."

"In living color." She scraped a fleck of dried oatmeal from the table with her thumbnail.

"He talked about probability today," I said. *Beautiful math.* I picked up our plates and carried them to the sink. Gram didn't seem to hear me. She turned a spoon in her hands.

"One night at bedtime—he was about nine—Bree was sitting on Burnaby's bed praying with him." Gram laid her palms down on the table and splayed her fingers. "Burnaby fixated on her hands. *Then* . . ." Gram held a finger to the back of her wrist, her eyes wide. "Then he touched this little knob with his forefinger. First time in his life the boy touched his mother without her asking. He traced the bones in her hands, tapping the knuckles. He touched the other knob." She demonstrated, pointing to the bony protrusion near her opposite wrist. "Styloid process of the ulna.

"The next day, on a hunch, she brought him a book of skeletal diagrams. Humans. Birds. Various animals. Burnaby devoured it. After that, Bree studied bones herself, so she'd know enough to engage him. When she found an old toaster oven at a yard sale, she taught him how to sterilize the owl pellets they found in the woods. Then she called me.

"Burnaby arrived here with a pair of tweezers and a shoebox full of owl castings. I showed him how to extract the bones from those pellets. Over the next couple of years, we cataloged them, clear down to the caudal vertebrae of mice and the pygostyles of passerines. The birds fascinated him most, especially the osteology of perching birds."

She pointed at the chair beside her. "He sat right here and glued vole skeletons together. Bored holes in bird bones and wired them so they appeared to be flying."

"Point taken, Gram. The boy's a genius. I get it."

She ignored me.

"Next he modified the incubator. He took an egg from our coop, cracked it into a Saran Wrap hammock hanging in a Mason jar, and put it inside. He sat in front of that incubator window as if it were a TV, while that chick's bones grew without the shell. Eyes, beak, feathers. The complete bird. Can you imagine?" Mender inclined her head. Her eyes were dusty.

I finished wiping the counter and sat back down. She had my complete attention.

"I called his mother to come see the wonder. She brought Aggie along. That child—she was about four by then—lifted a peeping Rhode Island Red chick out of the incubator. It imprinted on her."

"Was it *normal*?"

"Normal as any chick hatched naturally. Nothing short of amazing."

"What did Burnaby do?"

"He lost interest. He'd watched the bones form, and that was sufficient. The boy's brain runs on a narrow-gauge track: one rail scientist, the other rail, artist. He rolls right past whatever would connect him socially or emotionally."

"That explains how he was acting in the woods."

"What do you mean?"

"He could have been searching for Easter eggs."

"I would expect that." She set our water glasses on the counter, walked to her study, and returned pinching something. "Math, physics, art, beauty. He sees it all in his bones." She handed me a small one.

"A toy tractor seat."

"It's an owl's ilium. Actually, the complete hipbone. I've been meaning to give it to him, but you can, if you'd like."

"If I think of it." *If I'm still here.* I'd be riding a Greyhound before I did any bone-swapping. I slid the hip into my pocket and carried mustard to the fridge.

So the boy kept to himself. *Brutal.* No wonder he freaked when I touched him. Well. I'd at least talk to him. Not long-term or anything. Nothing that would interrupt my escape plans. I felt sorry for the guy. Besides, I needed a distraction until I earned the money for my ticket. Burnaby was interesting enough, unless—

"Gram. That guy on the skiff. Know him?"

She pulled her head from a cupboard. Assessed me warily. "He's too old for you, Celia."

"I didn't say—"

The shrill of an incoming call cut me off. Gram answered quietly, stretching the curly phone cord to the pantry as she shelved leftover pretzels. "Oh, hello Wyatt. Good to hear from you. Yes. Yes, she's right here."

Daddy. I stiffened.

Gram pulled the handset away from her ear. "Celia?" She held the phone out to me and arched her eyebrows. "Isn't it time you talked with your dad?" I turned my back to her and covered my ears before I tripped toward the door. If I stayed in the room, I would have to engage my father or argue with my grandmother. I was not willing to do either.

"No offense to you, Gram, but please tell him to shove it." I pushed past her extended arm and that handset with my dad's voice inside it. He could talk to his mother, not me. I wanted nothing to do with him. I bumped open the screen door and headed for the barn.

10

AGGIE

SECRET

THOUGH THE SEARCHERS had dispersed hours before, Aggie stayed high in the tree, suspicious, her rear end gone numb, her elbows and knees creaky as old hinges. Now she had to *move*. Find somewhere to sleep. Eat.

But near the tree where she'd cached her food, she caught sight of two striped tails disappearing into the brush. Her bottle lay behind a log fifteen feet away, and spilled seeds clumped like milky little islands along the game trail. A line of ants hauled off dregs.

Woeful, hungry, she lifted her empty bottle like she would a baby and cradled it all the way to the pool. She was rinsing it when she realized something important, there in the mud: those searchers never found her footprints near the water because four-legged visitors *trampled* them.

Outlines of small paws, their thumbs extended and splayed, trailed through the muck: opossums. They'd be no help to her. Neither would those thieving raccoons, whose long-toed prints appeared by the dozens where the rivulet exited the pool. On the pond's periphery, she found the oblong tracks of coyotes, plain as day, same as those left by the whelps Dad had chased from the garden.

— ⋀ —

"They're weanlings, Agate. Den will be abandoned. Want to find it?" She got her jacket. Within half an hour, they found the entrance, a burrow dug into the slope, hidden under a salmonberry bush.

"Someone else is hunting here, too." Dad pointed at a fresh earth hill beside the den's opening.

"C'mon, Dad. Not moles."

"Definitely not." He pulled a tape from his pocket and measured the width of a paw print recorded in the molehill's soft soil. "Five inches. M-shaped heel pad. No visible claws." He pointed at each feature. "Guess."

Aggie ticked through the prints she had learned when they tracked in the snow. Dad had quizzed her until she could identify them in her sleep: possum and raccoon, but also squirrel, bobcat, muskrat, skunk, rabbit. She counted them on her fingers and added porcupine, beaver, mink. She even saw a bear track once, in late spring—and she knew the difference between deer and elk. But this one?

"Beats me."

"Mature cougar. Male, given the size."

— ⋀ —

Aggie wiggled her nose like a rabbit, remembering. Could she find an abandoned den without her dad's help? If she did, she'd stay warm at night—and safe, even from a cougar.

Sure enough, coyote tracks led away from the pool, but within a few feet of the water, the ground hardened, and the detritus topping it proved too difficult to read. Oh well. Today she would be a coyote. She crouched low, sniffing as she crawled. When the air gave no hints, she veered uphill along a faint path through the understory. She inched along, probing under every bush and stump and log for piled dirt that would suggest a creature had dug beneath it.

She was about to quit when she saw the hole. Under a decaying cedar log, something had hollowed out an oval doorway the size of a lopsided soccer ball. She found a long stick and jabbed the dim interior as she crouched, ready to spring away and run if an animal came after her.

The cavity seemed empty, so she put her head near the door and inhaled. A faint odor like their neighbor's lab after he swam in the pond wafted her way. Doggy, but not awful, and yes, like the scent of the den she and her dad found. Had the coyotes left fleas inside? She scratched her leg and hoped the cedar oil from the old log would keep them away. With a shorter, fatter stick, she expanded the opening, digging into the earth where the log touching it had rotted.

She squeezed inside. Not very tall or wide, but deep enough for a full-grown coyote and a litter of pups. The den held her small body comfortably. And if she found some padding, she wouldn't have to sleep on dirt.

To break her scent trail, she waded in the shallows along the river's sloped dike, straight to where female cottonwood trees puffed out silken down. Pods lay gaping on the ground, spilling out fluff that accumulated like snow near bases of the massive trees and rocks, or wherever any obstacle interrupted their flight. Single seeds, each wrapped in a cloudy wisp, floated through the air by the millions. Aggie batted at them before she swiped her hand through a drift and compressed it into her shirt pouch.

While daylight lasted, she gathered the fleece and hauled it to her den, stopping only to gulp orange salmonberries—she recognized them *for sure*—that grew in thickets along the river. By dusk, a cottony mattress lined the floor and partway up the sides of her little cavern—a soft insulation against the cool soil and rotting cedar. Stars blinked through foliage overhead when she surrendered to exhaustion and grief, folding herself against the fluff until her body warmed the tiny space and her teeth stopped chattering.

That night the calico found her again and curled into her belly. Aggie welcomed her, even as she worried. Was human scent stronger than the coyotes'? Why else would the cat risk entering an enemy's den? She vowed to find a pine tree, crush its needles, and rub the fragrance over her entire body to cover her smell.

What other animals could detect her?

She found out. Late that night, heavy footfalls thumped across her log, and a flashlight beam crossed her cave's mouth. A dog snuffled the opening. "Whatcha got, Mesa?" A man's voice. More voices in the distance.

At the dog's appearance, the little cat growled and sprang to life. Hissing, she batted the intruder's nose and, when the dog yelped, streaked from the hole. The dog's feet skidded in the leafy duff as he gave chase.

"Give it *up*, puppy. A real shot to prove your nose and—"

"Find somethin'?" Another man.

"Just a cat." He whistled, and she heard a dog's rhythmic panting. Metal collar tags jangled as the dog scratched. A leash clicked, the tags clinked again, and the flashlights moved past her through the woods. Unnerved and hungry, she lay listening, sleepless.

Still awake at moonset, her hunger grew so insistent that she rose and crept through the blackness to the garden, where she yanked carrots, gathered pea vines. Not enough to fill her up, but she stumbled back to her cave and chewed her feeble plunder in the dark.

Her dead parents pushed all else from her thoughts. The horror descended on her, shriveled her. The cedar walls of her den muffled her wailing until, spent, she drifted in and out of disjointed, tormenting dreams. She writhed against a dark bird of sorrow that pecked at her with a sharp beak before it turned into the terrifying mouth of a wolverine, its teeth filling her with rough-coated terror. Her fingernails clawed at her throat as a strangling, ropy snake of guilt tightened around her neck with each image of the burning house and her parents' bodies. An angry rat with eyes like hers chewed on her dead mama's ear.

By morning she was gasping and gulping, submerged and drowning in loss. She relived the deadly hours—from building her campfire until her mother ran back into the burning house—in a fragmented loop of memory that she revised again and again. In one scenario, she poured water on the campfire, and no fire rekindled. In another, she awoke to the acrid smell of smoke, roused her parents, and they escaped unharmed. In a third, she clung to her mother's legs and kept her away from the fire, and Dad joined them both at the treehouse. At the end of each imagining, an inner voice sneered at her like a possum, hissing. *No, Aggie. You burned them. You did it. You!* Then the wrenching mental battle would begin again.

She felt utterly alone.

———❦———

But Dad had said she was *never* alone. He said it for the hundredth time that day on Blanchard Mountain, when they played Homing Pigeon. As usual, he tied a cover over Aggie's eyes and led her into the woods, away from the trail. Then he took the blindfold off and told her to locate the truck.

She figured Dad was following her like always, but this time when she turned around, he was gone. She retraced their path, scoured the ground for tracks, but came up empty. Only when she had screamed at the top of her lungs did he run to her, there all along. "Like the Father is," he said, enveloping her in his arms. "Even if you can't see him."

———— ⚛

By early afternoon, the storm inside her abated, and she crawled from the den. Her belly throbbed. How would an angleworm taste? Or a beetle? A yellow slug oozed in the shade by her foot. Could she eat that? *Never.* She nudged the slimy creature with her toe until its antennae retracted.

Dad taught her to follow streams if she got lost. Would a stream lead her to food, too? Worth a try. From the pond's outflow, she tracked a rivulet past the woods, through a swale and into a marsh where blackbirds gurgled as they clung to cattails.

Cattails? She hopped as she recognized them and waded into the swamp toward the plants. Her dad peeled them like leeks and ate the tender stalks raw.

"Try 'em, Aggie. Full of nutrients. We can cook the roots, too. More starch than potatoes." Dad's words prodded her as she pictured the two of them gathering bowlfuls of toothy young corms and baby rootlets for Mama, who chopped and stirred them into pots of vegetable soup.

Aggie stripped a round stem from its sheath and snapped off a pliable section several inches long. It smelled fresh, mild, like the ones Dad pulled, so she nibbled, took a bigger bite, and ate it all. *Like cucumber.* She ate three more before she rinsed a root in the creek and dissected it, tearing corms and rootlets from the rhizomes and peeling them with her teeth and fingernails. Then she chewed forever, until the root parts released their nourishment and she swallowed her starch-thickened saliva.

The leftover fibers felt like wood in her mouth, so she spat them into the creek before she repeated the process. *So much chewing.* She'd have to think of the roots like her sticks of Doublemint gum, only

with food in them. She plunged into the soggy peat and started pulling, found a fat stick and dug deeper. Her hands roughened and
stung, but now she knew she could survive.

Her first thoughts the next morning were of the cattails. She
wriggled outside and retrieved her digging stick and a hand-sized
piece of shale. Eager, she waded midstream to the marsh. The reeds
continued far down the little draw, an endless food supply.

At the end of an hour, her shirt bulged with roots and the tasty
stems. She stashed half of them in her den before she sat in the sunny
grass several feet from the trees and ate more. For the first time since
the fire three nights before, the land looked pretty again. Maybe she
could pretend to be happy, like Dad had wanted. Maybe, if she did
everything Dad wanted, God would erase the fire. Chase off the sadness. Change this misery into a dream. Only a dreadful dream.

If Burnaby were here, he'd suggest a routine to help her do the
right things. She made a list:

1. Get water.
2. Pull cattails.
3. Climb trees.
4. Explore.
5. Spy.
6. Visit nests.
7. Sleep.

Time for number three. Pretending to be a squirrel, she leapt onto
a low branch of a maple laden with samaras. "Hello, old tree." She
hugged the trunk like she would a grandmother. "Whirlybirds? Don't
mind if I do."

The dark ache didn't leave, but pretending helped. She plucked a
cluster of the winged seeds, tossed a few in the air and watched them
helicopter to the ground. When she split a fuzzy seed casing, a tiny,

immature bead lay inside. Too small. A squirrel like her wouldn't eat any of these yet. Not for a few more weeks.

She scampered higher, intersected a limb, and crossed first into an alder, then another maple. At a sturdy fir beyond her reach, she returned to the forest floor then climbed it, passing from its long lateral branches through more trees, denying the fire and pretending her dad was below her as she skirted sleeping owls and a porcupine and bedded deer.

And nests. So many nests. Their eggs were food for her sad heart, but never for her stomach.

———⚡———

Midafternoon, she climbed toward a commotion in a hemlock tree, where three raccoon kits noticed her and scrabbled her way. She sat owl quiet while they patted her arms and lifted her hair in their fingers.

A chitter from below interrupted them. The kits forgot Aggie and somersaulted down the tree to their mother, who pierced the girl with her black bead eyes and hurried the babies across the forest floor. Aggie tumbled down the trunk after them. She would avoid that fierce mama. But those kits? They could be her friends if she hung out near them.

She raced to keep up. When the animals dissolved into a thicket, Aggie clawed through tall ferns and found herself in a ring of familiar, dilapidated buildings. Years before, she and Burnaby took an overgrown trail from the dairy and found this small, collapsed barn, punched through with alders. Blackberry vines mounded where the house had stood. A river rock chimney rose toward a blue patch of sky overhead—a pioneer's chimney, Burnaby said. Nearby, immature plums, apples, and pears dangled from gnarled, neglected fruit trees. *Food for later.*

A root cellar's mossy roof blended into the hillside behind the orchard. She remembered this tiny house. Could she sleep *here*?

She was lifting the door's wooden latch when a branch's loud crack stopped her.

Brush rustled as something large pushed through it, coming down the hill. Aggie dropped the latch, ducked behind the plum tree, and climbed, entering its leafy cover just as a tall figure stepped into the clearing. He walked toward the root cellar, right under her tree, so close she could smell him. *Cows. He's been with cows.* Burnaby smelled like that after he milked.

He seemed older than Burnaby, though, and didn't resemble Burn at all. Black, shaggy curls grew over his collar and forehead. His arms, poking out from short-sleeved coveralls like the ones Uncle Loomis wore, were hairy and tanned. He looked *beautiful,* even with his face scrunched in concentration. He reminded her of a raven, all dark and strong and shiny.

As if expecting someone, he surveyed the rim of trees and slowly ran his eyes over the decaying buildings and the ground around them. Lingering. Ingesting the farmstead like a dinner. Aggie fretted that he would look up and see her, but he instead pulled a clear plastic bag from his pocket and pushed the air from it. Aggie glimpsed little red circles about the size of quarters inside. Though she wasn't sure, they appeared to be rolls of caps for a toy pistol, like the ones in the cap gun she fired to shoo crows off the corn. After each little pop, the paper would roll away from the gun's hammer, charred and smelling of burned kitchen matches. She liked the scent.

Her mouth drooped. Her caps, like everything else in the house, had burned in the fire. Besides, the toy gun was Burnaby's, and the caps were his, too. Dad thought they might keep her brother from lighting fires whenever he got upset. The plan worked, sometimes. Though now and then Burn still lit paper, he often pulled a roll of caps from his pocket or the glove box of his truck, walked to a private spot, and pounded a few of the little gunpowder dots with a hammer or stone. Mama said the tiny explosions calmed him like fire did.

The man tied a knot in the bag, stooped under the jamb of the cellar's small doorway, and emerged a minute later, his hands empty. His actions puzzled her. Why would he hide a bag of caps way out here? Something was fishy.

He shut the door and slipped into a fringe of greenery at the edge of the clearing. Aggie counted to forty before she left the tree, then tracked him. For her own safety, she had to know more about him. She wanted no more close calls. If he had shown up a mere minute later, he'd have intercepted her inside the cellar. And what if he came here again?

Her skin prickled as her mind returned to the bag. Why did he bring it *here*? And from where? Where else in these woods did he go? She climbed to a crossing branch from another tree and set out.

Numbers three and four? Check. Climbing and exploring complete. Next up: number five. Time to spy.

11

CELIA

BONES

I WANTED TO DISTANCE MYSELF from that phone, far enough away that Gram wouldn't try to call me back, make me talk to my father. I would not tolerate any strategic affection from him, and I certainly would not agree to stay put and wait until he returned. He lied to me. I did not owe him my allegiance.

Gram's barn sat on a knoll about fifty yards west of the house—typically an easy dash, but I was wheezing after the first few steps. Reminded me of the night after my mother left, when Meredith dug in her purse and handed me her asthma inhaler. "Allergies," she said, but I knew better. A spell like this didn't happen often, but when it did, anxiety gripped my throat in a slow squeeze, trying to tell me something. What this time? To talk to Daddy? Make up with him? Or to run even faster in the other direction?

After how he tricked and abandoned me, I opted for the latter. I had a right to be pissed off. *Royally* pissed off. Besides, anger made me feel powerful. I liked the way it moved me, and I did *not* want to pop its tires. I'd have relished it even more if I could have filled my lungs.

When I reached the barn, I stretched my arms overhead, fighting for breath and waiting. Experience told me that these wrestling matches with my airway eventually ended, so I waited without surrendering for that unseen hand to release my throat. I imagined myself buying that bus ticket as I addressed a crowned sparrow, hunting bugs in the grass. "I'm outta here, little guy." The bird tilted its head at me, pecked something, and flew off. "Yeah. Like that."

When my respiration calmed, I lowered my arms and watched the house. Gram came out the side door, waved a trowel at me without smiling, and continued to the flowerbeds. Remorse bit me. I owed her an apology. Trouble was, I found apologies to be exhausting—and they made me feel naked. My ire didn't seem so sturdy after telling someone I was sorry.

I turned toward the big old barn. As a child, I often ran out here as soon as Mother, Daddy, and I arrived from Texas. I would be eager to find my grandfather holed up inside, engineering his latest invention. His shop filled an attached shed about ten feet wide that spanned the full length of the barn. Seven small, square windows over the long workbench faced the mountains and the house.

Granddaddy would park me on a stool beside him, where he taught me bits of plane geometry, algebra, and physics before I knew what to call them. From illustrations he later framed and hung over the workbench, we built prototypes of gadgets and tools, which he displayed in our own private museum at the far end of the shop. On each of my trips north, we worked on designs for future projects and put finishing touches on old ones, which he spent his free time dreaming up and building.

My favorite was a life-sized pony we called Picker, built on a padded frame, covered with tricolored cowhide, and wearing a real leather saddle and bridle. Granddad finished her when I was ten—Aggie's age. Designed to replace the orchard ladder, the pony lifted me to apples and cherries on hydraulic legs that I raised and lowered by tugging on opposing reins. When I dismounted and pulled the reins out front as if I were leading her, wheels lowered, and I rolled her to another tree. When I looped the reins over the saddle horn, the wheels retracted and Picker's legs regained their stability. I held apples in front of her blocky, hide-covered muzzle and imagined her crunching them, her rough tongue licking my palm. Lying under her wooden belly in the orchard, I pretended she could talk.

Was Picker still inside? I had to see. Be alone with my thoughts at the site of some of my sweetest memories. Gram had locked the workshop after Granddaddy died. I hadn't asked to enter the building since.

A heavy padlock still hung from the latch. Disappointed, I ambled around back, where I stopped short. The huge sliding door gaped. A red pickup truck idled outside with a board ramp sloping off its tailgate.

Who was in Gram's barn? Yet *another* person sideswiping my plans? I slipped up next to the opening and listened as someone dragged something heavy across the concrete. A door deeper inside the barn opened, squeaked shut.

Anxiety still toyed with my throat, so I waited for, oh, two minutes. Three. Hearing nothing more, I peeked inside. A large insulated cooler sat askew near the interior workshop door. Then, from inside the shop, an unearthly, muffled wail seeped into the barn's cavernous expanse. I tried to make sense of the sound and concluded that someone, or something, was crying.

I sidestepped the cooler and knocked. "You okay in there?"

The wailing subsided, so I stooped and pressed my ear against the wood. From that compromised position, when the door opened, I stumbled into the room and nearly tripped over Burnaby, who had reached up to let me in. He sat cross-legged beside the door with a little glass bowl in his lap. His moist eyes recorded me with a blink before he again hung his head over the bowl's clear rim.

"Stay there, Burnaby. I'll turn off your truck." I dashed outside and shut down the engine, then returned and sat across from him. Our knees nearly touched. Funny how a few hours of hunting in the woods with him gave me permission to sit there like his counselor. Well, *I* gave myself permission.

He wasn't sobbing anymore, but his tears still dripped into his little bowl, which almost held enough liquid to sauté vegetables. I had never seen such an emotional wash. After we sat there awhile, I couldn't contain myself.

"Why the bowl, Burnaby?"

"I've wasted too many."

I waited for him to say more. He didn't.

"Too many. Too many what?" I racked my brain. Guessed. "Tears? What do—?"

"According to Mama, tears carry our feelings."

"Really."

I was trying, I truly was. I didn't intend to mock him, but the guy was catching tears in a *bowl*, for heaven's sake. I saw no counseling credentials in my future. Or poker playing.

"She says the best artists put feelings into their work." He hiccoughed in that twitchy way children do after a tantrum.

"What's *that* got to do with the bowl?"

I may have rolled my eyes. Or simply shifted them to the ceiling. Either way, they landed on a mobile of bird skeletons overhead, wired into positions of flight and gyrating from the sloped ceiling. I jumped to my feet to get closer. "What is *this*?" I blew on the nearest skeleton and the entire mobile, composed of dozens of birds, tipped and spun in perfect, floating balance. It was breathtaking.

Burnaby rose slowly and set the bowl on the workbench. His

gaze sharpened, alert and protective. Both hands swiped his eyes. "A murmuration of starlings. Or it will be, when I finish."

A murmuration. I saw one once, flying over a bayou along the Gulf Coast. A mesmerizing cloud of birds swam through the sky like an amoeba. And now, right here, Burnaby was creating one from skeletons.

"Gram didn't give you all these birds. Where'd you get them? And how in the *world* do you strip them all?"

"*Sturnus vulgaris*. Starlings. Uncle Loomis calls them sky rats. They eat his cow grain. So he shoots them." He stepped outside and opened the top of the cooler he had dragged into the barn. Damp topsoil, laced with clumps of uprooted grass, filled it to the brim.

"I bury them in here. During cold weather, I store the tub indoors to keep the temperature elevated for microbial activity. Bacteria and beetles facilitate decomposition. Then I screen out the bones. Bleach them in hydrogen peroxide solution. Assemble them." He scraped away some dirt, exposing loose feathers.

If my eyes bulged, Burnaby didn't notice. "Where did you keep them before?"

"Mama wanted them out of my bedroom. So I placed the cooler in our barn. Put a heated seedling mat over the soil all winter. Now that I am staying at the dairy, Mender suggested I bring them here."

Of course. A guy must have his garden of dead birds handy. "Makes sense. Now. About those tears."

"Never mind the tears." He closed the cooler and sat on it.

"Burnaby. Seriously. Talk to me."

He frowned and tipped his head. "I *was* talking."

"I mean about this." I tapped his chest over his heart and he jumped away, rubbing his shirt as if to obliterate my fingerprint.

"No touching."

I sighed and cast my eyes around the rest of the workshop, finding no evidence that my granddaddy ever spent time there. Nothing remained of his work. Instead, an orderly riot of skeletons in various stages of completion covered every available surface.

"When did Gram move Granddaddy's things out of here?"

Burnaby's eyes outlined a ceiling beam. "August 17, 1984, 367 days after Dr. Burke's funeral. That day, my dad told Mender that he would be removing my projects from the seed barn. To make way for more supply bins. Mender offered me the shop. On the condition that I help her remove Dr. Burke's belongings. I complied. Relocated them to her garage."

"I see." I fed the dogs in that garage. They slept there in chain-link kennels next to Gram's car. Far as I could tell, they didn't share that space with Granddaddy's stuff. Did Gram stow it all somewhere? Pitch it?

I chalked her up as yet another family member who made decisions that *affected me* without my consent. Or at least without my input. Or at the very least, made family decisions without *telling me*. The heat in my burners was rising.

And Burnaby came here constantly. Why had she kept *him* a secret?

12

—

AGGIE

SHOTGUN

THE BEAUTIFUL MAN outside the root cellar crunched through the woods, crashing brush until he stepped onto a neglected trail up the hill. *The trail to the dairy.* Aggie watched from a maple until he dropped into a draw and hiked the next rise, where the trees were farther apart. She lowered herself to a bear crawl and crept after him to the edge of the forest.

Ahead of her, the man crossed a weedy pasture and passed behind the smaller of two barns—a low, weathered building where Aggie helped Aunt Nora bottle-feed calves. Beyond it, cows ate their sweet-smelling hay in a larger barn where, according to Uncle Loomis, they *loafed* on fresh sawdust bedding. Her brother's truck was parked near the big barn's newer section, a slope-roofed addition that housed the gigantic milk tank, an office, and the parlor where Burnaby milked all those cows. Across the barnyard, chattering swallows rocketed through the interior of the three-sided machine shed. Her aunt Nora and uncle Loomis's farmhouse, most of its blinds closed, as usual, sat nearest the road.

For years before he got his truck, Burnaby had ridden his bike here. He checked the odometer on his handlebars after every trip. "Exactly zero point six miles of gravel and seven point three miles of pavement. One way." She could hear him saying it for the thousandth time. Then he would push the reset button and measure again the next day. She imagined him measuring the distance from the milking barn to her cave, and her insides warmed. Compared to his bike ride? *Not far at all.*

She dodged toward a fencerow lined with densely leafed poplars, from which she could spy without being seen, keenly aware that her real invisibility came from the fact that people didn't *expect* to see her. As long as she stayed still, they wouldn't. She copied killdeers and rabbits, who hid right under predators' noses. Even so, sneaking around the dairy would be risky. She would have to be careful.

She climbed a few feet higher and craned her neck to locate Burnaby. During the search he'd been walking funny. Funny *wrong.* She had to see him again. Had to know if he was okay. She would wait here until he showed.

But then two blasts echoed past the calf shed.

Aggie dove to the ground, sprinted along the fence line. She dipped under an electric wire and hid in tall grass behind the well's pump house just as Uncle Loomis walked around the barn onto the gravel between the buildings, his shotgun broken open over his arm. Heat bent the air, wrinkling him into undulating waves.

Burnaby appeared next, uninjured. Her heart banged against her ribs from the scare—and at the sight of her brother, who lagged behind Uncle Loomis and toted a metal bucket between himself and Pi. The dog walked to a dead starling and nudged it with her nose. Burn laid his hand on Pi's head and knelt by the bird.

Aggie calmed as she watched him. She studied his face, saw the inscrutable features that hid his dismay over the killings. He cradled the carcass in his palm and lifted its feathers to locate exactly where the pellet had struck and which bones had broken. He ran his fingers over the small body, examining its beak and skull. Between thumbs and index fingers, he gripped the leading edges of its wings and held the bird in front of him, like Mama would hold a shirt up by its shoulder seams before hanging it on the clothesline. He rolled his fingers slightly, and the wings spread as if in flight.

Aggie knew he was deciding whether or not to repair the bird. If shotgun pellets had damaged the bones too badly, he wouldn't want it.

This bird interested Burnaby, though. Maybe a pellet had entered the starling under its wing. Maybe the lead ticked a rib, then quietly interrupted lungs or heart and sent the bird plunging to earth without shattering a single bone. He could resurrect this one.

He laid the starling in the bucket and retrieved two more of the limp birds. He pushed back their iridescent feathers, mottled purple and brown and blue-black in the sunshine. This time he touched an unnatural jog in one bird's fractured wing and palpated the other's broken back before he carried both birds to the dumpster.

Aggie stifled a sob. Though Burnaby would never let her hug him, she wished she could at least go to him, ask him questions, and listen to lengthy explanations she rarely understood. She longed to call out to him, but dismissed such an action outright. *He knows I lit the fire.* He wouldn't acknowledge her now, even if she stood right in front of him.

At least she knew where he was. Secretly, she would come to the farm and watch him. Be near him. Each day when she spied, she would spy on Burnaby.

The besieged flock of starlings circled back and landed in a chestnut tree shading the lawn between the pump house and the gravel.

Burnaby returned to his bucket and knelt there as Loomis angled two shells into the barrels, snapped the gun closed, and steadied the stock's butt against his shoulder. Aggie watched intently until he swung the barrel in her direction. Astonished, she flattened herself in the camouflaging grass, smashed her eyes closed, and waited.

The blast's percussion vibrated into her, translating into the fear of a hunted animal. It grew into a tremor of renewed anger at her uncle—at Uncle Loomis, who bruised her collarbone when she stole cottonseeds. Who yelled at her. And now *this*.

"Take inventory, Aggie." Her dad said that to calm her, to get her to think. She blinked and inspected her body. No blood. No pain. *He missed me.* Relief drenched her as leaves fluttered, landing in her hair.

"How'd I do, Burnaby? Get any?" Uncle Loomis gawked at the dispersing flock, the gun still at his shoulder.

Burnaby perused the tree and the short turf beneath it before he picked up his bucket and stepped into the big barn's shade, out of the heat. Pi lay ten feet away—on duty, Dad called it—watching Burnaby and panting.

"None this time."

Aggie quivered as she evaluated the torn branches. Her uncle didn't aim at specific birds. He didn't even try to lay eyes on them. He fired in the direction he last saw the flock and hoped that the pellets inside the shell would scatter enough to hit a few. If she had been hiding in that tree, he'd have shot her.

"Hey, Loomis." The man she'd been following emerged from the calf shed and approached the pair.

Her uncle lowered the gun. "Ah, Cabot. Where'd you go?" Aggie shifted onto her side, still cloaked by the grass. Where had she heard that name?

"Checked heifers down in the lower pasture. Two of 'em are bagging up. I'll get them into maternity tomorrow." He began coiling a hose. "Any news on Aggie? You look by the river this morning?"

Hold on. The man in the boat. One of the searchers. *Cabot—with the hooks.* Yes, the same man. Was that why he was traipsing through the woods and prowling that old farm? Was he hunting her? But why that stuff in the root cellar?

Uncle Loomis adjusted his cap and cleared his throat. "Yeah. Nothing yet." He nodded at Cabot, then turned and walked toward the house. Burnaby knelt by the bucket again and flipped the handle, which clanged against the rim.

Cabot watched her uncle's retreat, then scuffed gravel at Burnaby with the side of his boot. Rocks pinged off the bucket. Pi flattened her ears and crept toward them.

"I've been scouring those woods for your sister as much as you have," Cabot said. "So don't get any bigshot ideas. I'm not going anywhere." He aimed an imaginary handgun at Pi and fired, blew on the end of the imaginary muzzle, and strode into the cow barn.

Burnaby's shoulders rose and fell before he pulled a wooden match from his pocket and struck it on the galvanized bucket. He held the flame to a napkin he took from another pocket and dangled the burning paper between his middle finger and thumb until the fire licked him and he let go. The paper fluttered to the ground, blackened, and cooled. He crushed the char into the gravel with his heel.

A movement in the barn's doorway caught Aggie's eye. Cabot was watching Burn, staring after him as her brother walked to his truck. An expression she couldn't decipher bent his mouth.

She stayed prone in the grass until Cabot slipped back inside the building, then crawled up the pellet-torn chestnut tree. From there she continued to spy as Burn's truck started up and turned toward Mender's. Cabot steered the tractor along the barn's interior alley, pulling the mixer wagon that augered silage onto the slab. Stanchions clanked as cows swept their tongues in circles, swiping for feed.

Half an hour later, Cabot shoved his rubber boots and stained coveralls into the trunk of his car and strolled to the milkhouse. She heard water thrum against the metal sink. *Done for the day. Washing up.* He paused in the doorway, ran his dripping fingers through his hair and walked across the barnyard onto the farmhouse porch. Delicious smells wafted from the barbecue.

Dinnertime. Hired help didn't go in her aunt and uncle's house, much less eat with them. What was the man up to?

13

CELIA

PAINT

BURNABY DRAPED A CLOTH over his bowl of tears, slid it deeper onto the workbench, and shadowed me as I meandered through his skeletons. Until I could buy that bus ticket, I would escape right here in the barn with Burnaby's magnificent reconstructions.

Amidst bones in all stages of reassembly, skeletal voles and mice scampered along level surfaces. On one shelf, a rabbit and squirrel faced each other, hunched and startled. A fragile, bleached salamander climbed behind them. On another, rebuilt songbirds smaller than starlings hopped, fed, and flapped, their miniature bones wired and glued.

"Where did you get these littler ones?" I touched a tiny skull.

"In pellets from the woods. Under owl roosts." He adjusted the foot of a miniature skeleton. "An owl eats small creatures intact. Bones, feathers, fur won't digest. So his body forms a pellet, coats it with mucus, and he regurgitates it."

He lifted a bony vole, curled for sleep. "Mama says I should ask if a person wants me to keep explaining. Do you?"

"No thanks. I believe I understand." I was clear on that scenario. Night predators choked down prey, coated the hard and fuzzy parts with slime, and burped them up. Then Burnaby dismantled the package and reassembled the victims.

Another bird mender. Like Gram, in a way. I stepped in slow motion deeper into the room. "And these, Burnaby. Where'd you find them?" All down the workbench surface, larger skeletons preened their bleached wings and pecked bony prey.

"Birds Mender couldn't save. On roads. At the airport. Found one under an electrical transformer, scorched."

"All these wouldn't fit in your cooler. How do you clean them?"

"Ants."

"Huh?"

"Western thatching ants. *Formica obscuripes.* Above fifty degrees Fahrenheit, they can strip a bird in days."

"Oh, *man.* Show me?"

He lifted a shoulder. "I suppose. They are currently consuming a barred owl. Should be ready in a week."

"I'm in. You'll let me know?" I wouldn't be on the bus yet.

Burnaby nodded once, then trailed after me as I moved along the bench. "I prefer mornings to repair them." He pointed at the row of windows above the work surface. "Before noon, sunlight illuminates bone details. But that light changes by the hour, so I wait to paint until the sun passes the barn's peak."

"Paint?" None of the skeletons had paint on them. "You varnishing the bones or something?"

He ambled to the back of the shop, pulled a stiff paper from a portfolio, and laid it next to a raptor skeleton diving toward a bony pigeon. "Peregrine," he said. There on the page, a watercolor falcon dove from a cloud, its wings tucked and blurred with speed.

Burnaby's liquid eyes lit as they swept the painting. "A peregrine uses gravity's acceleration of 9.8 meters per second squared to increase her own flight velocity." He slanted his arm along the diving bird's trajectory, with his elbow pointed at the ceiling. "She considers gravity and adjusts her angle when she aims at her moving prey."

Lost in his description, his tension eased, and his sentences smoothed and lengthened. He stroked the skeleton's spine before he continued, his hands fluid.

"When she pulls out of a dive, the g-force stress concentrates on her wings, which connect to her body right here at the sternum." He pointed to invisible tissues on the skeleton. "Muscles more powerful—and proportionally larger—than any others she has. Exactly what she needs."

"Wow." I touched the breastbone where those muscles would attach. His painting captured the *feel* of the height, the plunge, the bird's hunger. Reminded me of that hang-glider cliff near Chelan when a hot updraft dared me to leap.

"I'm on to you, Burnaby. You *could* talk about those tears if you wanted to."

"I don't want to." His cheek started twitching.

"But you . . . Never mind." I didn't mean to make him nervous. Maybe he really didn't know what he created here.

Or maybe I was the one who didn't get it. Didn't get him. Suddenly I wanted to. I gave him a thumbs-up and returned to the portfolio.

"May I?" I lifted the cover a few inches.

He opened it the rest of the way, and I entered an astonishing collection of stories told in ochre and vermillion, raw sienna, and Prussian blue. Swallows dived at an indifferent bald eagle. A great horned owl brooded her eggs protectively. A satisfied osprey tore at a fish beneath its talons. Every bird carried a passion that coursed straight through Burnaby's paintbrush, each a resuscitation of one of his skeletons.

He pointed at a skeletal falcon's hipbone. Was he breathing faster because of the bird? Because of me? *My* pulse raced.

"The shape of the ilium mimics current mathematical theory about the universe's gravitational fields."

"Yeah?" My brain was firing on all cylinders.

"This part of the bone." He touched an arch on the hipbone. "See the hyperbolic paraboloid?"

Seconds passed before the beautiful, curving imagery meshed for me. I eyed the boy with wonder. Burnaby wasn't trying to impress me. He wanted me to *understand*. And he was speaking the language I loved most, the language my granddaddy taught me: mathematics, tossed into the mix of physics and birds. And watercolor.

"I sure do. Hold it right there. Back in a sec." I raced to my room to retrieve Gram's little owl pelvis. I returned minutes later, panting, to find Burnaby holding a small, stiff brush and digging through a box of paints. I unclasped a chain from around my neck, removed the silver C Daddy gave me for my birthday, and slid the tiny hip onto it. I held the ends of the chain in front of him, showing him the bone.

"Hipbone." He petted the ilium with one finger, then twisted the links until the bone swiveled.

I smiled at him. "For you." I passed the chain around his neck and clasped it. He looked scared as a cat at a dog pound, but he stood still.

"Perhaps a barn owl." Those mossy eyes shone.

"If you say so."

Awkward, for both of us, so I returned to his paintings and pulled one from the stack—a rendering of a Canadian goose pacing a highway's shoulder. Open-billed, it stretched its neck as if calling. Its mate lay dead on the pavement.

"Oh, Burnaby." Something in the honking bird's posture. Grief?

"This one needs more feelings." He touched the goose's throat.

"No way." That picture ripped my heart. Geese mated for life, and now these two . . . I thought of Burnaby's parents. And my own.

He retrieved his bowl of tears, dunked his fingertips in the liquid and brushed them over the mourning goose's breast. Then he dipped a stiff brush into the bowl and blended tears with a dab of red paint he squeezed from a small tube. With the brush upright, he flicked the bristles, sending a shock of speckles over the area of the painting he had dampened.

I gasped. He was ruining the image with those little red dots, which smeared on the wet paper and marred the pacing goose's creamy breast.

"*What* are you doing?"

"Alizarin Crimson. Fugitive paint."

"Which means . . . ?"

"Focal points. The color lands like fresh blood. Tears carry the emotion."

I locked my eyes on the goose's foot until his words registered. Literal Burnaby believed his tears turned that red into actual anguish. Sorrow. Goose pain. *Whatever.*

"Whoa. Why fugitive?"

"An unstable lightfast rating of four. The color will fade with age and UV exposure. Changeable as pain."

So. Given time and light, the spattered goose would heal.

Either he wished, or he knew.

14

AGGIE

PROWLER

AT SUNSET ON AGGIE'S FIFTH DAY in the woods, a dragon wind arrived. Gusts from the rogue southeaster bowed trees heavy with new leaves and licked them with its hot breath, until flocks of green shriveled, broke from their branches, and flew. Leaves slammed and flattened against Aggie as she adhered to her schedule and scaled the last tree of the day, a young cottonwood along the river. Defiant, she aimed her face into the escalating current. Wind or no wind, she would climb. Since morning she had felt like fighting everything. Especially the wind.

Dad liked wind. On a blustery hike to Dock Butte, he said it reminded him of the Father's breath. "Invisible. On the move." He had stopped her on the trail and tapped her chest. "Inhale. There. Breathe him in, Aggie. He's oxygen. So close and good."

Aggie scowled, remembering. *Oxygen fed the fire, didn't it?* Now she had no parents. God's *good* breath? Good *how?* "Not FAIR!" she wailed toward Mender's house. Gusts muted her yells.

The gale kicked up even stronger after sundown. Aggie crawled into her den to escape the pummeling, to wait out the storm. Her log damped the noise and, wearied by the howling air and anger, she slept.

Until a low rumble purred outside.

More wind? No. The squall had blown itself out hours before. This sounded like an idling engine. The vibration grew louder until something blocked the dim light at her burrow's entry.

Goosebumps erupted on Aggie's arms, legs, torso; her mouth went dry as the interloper marked its arrival near the mouth of her cave. Not with a skunky scent. More like a litter box. She thought of the little calico and knew this was no litter box cat. This was rough, musky. *Musky pee.* She gagged at the smell.

Frantic, she leveraged herself away from the entrance, but slipped. Her hands skidded forward on the silky mattress and bumped a dry cushion and some bristles. *Nose. Whiskers.* She yelped and shrank to the rear of her cave. The head withdrew, and a giant paw replaced it, swatting the space in front of her until it snagged her shirt.

Her hysterical shrieks thinned the cramped hollow's air as she pummeled the invader's foot. When the claws let go, a furry muzzle appeared, its mouth wide and yowling foul air at her.

Cougar!

As if bailing a sinking boat, Aggie scooped dirt and downy fiber and flung it into the mountain lion's immense face. It retracted, growling, so she edged toward a piece of shale between her and the doorway: her cutting stone, mere inches away, but within range of those terrible paws, those monstrous teeth.

Her hand shot to the entry, and she snatched the rock. A paw flew past, narrowly missing her. Panting, she clutched the shale to her chest. The lion lay on its side, slapping at the air in front of her as if playing with a ball of yarn.

Slowly, she raised the rock like a hatchet and waited. When the lion again reached for her, she plunged the stone's sharp edge across the animal's toes. The cat screamed and recoiled. The retreating foot tore the stone from her hand and flipped it toward the door. When she scrambled to grab it, the paw, claws extended, struck at her, ripped her shirt.

And snared her. One razor-sharp hook dug deep, slicing the underside of her forearm between elbow and wrist. Aggie squealed in pain and clamped her injured arm to her body as the claws resheathed and the puma's foot receded like a seaside wave.

The smell of her blood mingled with the animal's odor as the cougar paced outside. *Ten, eleven, twelve.* She counted every pass of a leg until the motor-like purr again filled the cave and the mountain lion's head blocked the hole a third time.

This time, she screamed from the caverns of her lungs. The pressure from the sound she hurled at the puma spread into her head and eyes, threatened to rupture and spill her guts beside the dark clots beneath her. Undeterred, the cougar, its ears flat, lowered its muzzle, bared its teeth, and hissed.

Finally, emptied to her marrow, Aggie stopped screaming to breathe.

The lion seemed surprised by the quiet. It inclined its head as if listening, closed its jaws, and rumbled a breathy purr before it slipped into the night woods.

Uncontrollable shaking began in her torso, spread to her limbs. Her dripping arm stuck to her shirt, and cottonwood batting clung to her in tacky wads. Cowed by the lurking cougar, she lay immobile and pressed the wound harder against her grimy clothes to stanch the bleeding.

How much longer could she sleep underground? Live in this forest? She had called wilderness friendly? *Hah!* How did she ever think that?

Her arm ached as she argued with herself, remembering that she needed the trees and thickets, the ravines and marshes and caves. Needed every inch of the untamed forest to hide her from Cabot and the other orange caps, whose plans for her were far worse than a cougar scratch, any old day. Since that night when the dog passed her cave, searchers had returned four times, missing her only because their noisy advance forewarned her, told her to climb. Only because the forest concealed her.

Well, she couldn't climb now. Pain speared her arm. Next time those dogs would smell her blood.

15

CELIA

HOE

GRAM WAS NOT HAPPY WITH ME. I had left her with a dangling phone and a nasty message for my dad. Regardless, I waited two days to make amends. I would have stalled even longer, but unless I earned some cash, I'd never get home. And in my restricted position—miles out of town with no car—the strawberry farm down the road was my only potential employer. I needed Gram's signature as my guardian. My *temporary* guardian.

Besides, when she didn't give me reasons to buck her, she was pretty cool. I wanted to smooth things over with her before I terrified my father by running off, so on the third morning after he called, I put on my gardening gloves. "Want to pull a few weeds, Gram?" We hadn't unearthed a single dandelion root together since I blew her off. With all of us searching for Aggie, the closest I'd been to the garden was two mornings earlier, when I opened my bedroom blinds, saw

the gate swinging, and ran outside in my jammies to close it before
the dogs could chase a rabbit into Gram's lettuce.

"Do you?" She smiled at me. Searched my eyes.

"Yes, ma'am." I waited while she retrieved her hat and hoe and
followed her to the fence. Inside the gate, she lurched to a stop.

"What happened out here?" Strewn vines led to a ruined row
of pea plants. Baby carrots lay crushed, their lacy foliage shredded.
"Were you that angry, Celia? Why not talk it through?"

Her accusation landed on me like an uppercut. She thought I
ripped up her garden to get even. I shook my head in little snaps
and crossed my hands over my chest. "Gram. No *way* . . . I would
never . . ." I didn't want to act defensive, but I had already heaped my
plate with misdeeds. I did not need this one for gravy.

Her glare pierced me. She didn't blink, so I turned my gaze to
some adolescent beet greens.

"I saw you running back from the garden in your pajamas."

"The gate was open. I ran out to close it. I am *not* responsible for
this, Gram. Really."

She weighed my words, then turned to appraise the torn rows.
Her countenance softened. "You were so angry. I assumed—"

"I closed the gate to keep the dogs out. I didn't come in here." She
flicked my ear lightly and locked her eyes on mine.

"But if you didn't do it, who did?"

So she was still blaming me. *Great way to talk it through, Gram.*
I broke eye contact and sent my sightline to the ground, where it
landed on a strange print. A pad with five faint dots above it marked
the soil where peas were missing. A foot away, another set of inden-
tations. An animal could have made them, I supposed, but they
resembled tiptoes. Human. Child-sized. The only wild child who
could have danced in the garden was Aggie. Was she hiding right
here on Mender's farm?

I walked the rows looking for more, but the rest of the thickly mulched garden showed only a few weeds poking through. I was searching through the strawberries when Gram whacked her hoe into the mutilated pea patch.

"Gram! You'll *wreck* them!"

Too late. The footprints had vanished into the soil.

"Wreck what? They aren't growing back, Celia. I'll replant."

I glared at the hoe blade, fuming. Not only was Gram falsely accusing me, but she had destroyed evidence everyone was hunting. She would never believe I had seen those tracks, and I was too irate to try to convince her.

Had I seen them?

"I need a walk." Bent over the carrots, Gram waved me off.

I spent an hour in the woods but saw no more of the peculiar little marks. Did the child drop out of the sky? I found the tree where Burnaby and I located those chewed berries. The lab report had been inconclusive, but who besides Aggie could have barfed them up? I shaded my eyes and examined the hulking fir for any sign of activity in its branches. *Nada.*

If I hadn't seen those prints, I'd have blamed some crazy raccoons for fiddling with the garden gate's latch and having a heyday in Gram's tidy rows. But those were no raccoon tracks. With each passing minute, I grew more certain that the prints belonged to a child. A girl who had evaded all of us so far.

Lingering in the warm field, I let my thoughts roll over the trees. Why was she hiding? What was she thinking?

If I were in her skin, I'd be coming to terms with my parents falling in that fire. My home burning. My belongings enriching the soil as charcoal. My next closest female relative, Aunt Nora, would get snot all over me if I got near her, and I would go deaf from Uncle Loomis telling me what to do at 10,000 decibels. Besides, I'd smell like cow pies if I lived with them.

Okay. Rewind. I paused and tried to visualize the ten-year-old girl. What *really* was going on with her? For one, she had to be starving. And heartbroken. And scared. So scared. If my suspicions were right, she had witnessed her home's incineration. Didn't know if her parents were dead or alive. Now she couldn't go to her dad when she was curious or worried or just wanted to talk to him. Like I could with Daddy. Before.

The child was probably missing her mom, too. Why didn't she at least want her aunt? Was something keeping her from going to Loomis and Nora? Would she choose these woods over them? Burnaby said she liked trees. Or did she come here to find *him*?

The sun-dappled forest crowded around me, fragrant with summer. *If I were you, Aggie, I'd run here, too.*

I took my time walking back to the house.

———✲

"Gram?" The kitchen was empty, so I checked the rooms on the main floor. Climbed the stairs to the landing and scouted the hallway. All the doors stood open. "Gram, you here?"

She wasn't.

But from the window at the top of the stairs, I saw her below me, in the side yard. She was kneeling near her roses, facing the sky with her eyes closed, lips moving, hands in her lap. Her Bible lay open in the grass. Again.

I swear my grandmother spent more time praying than anyone I knew. Daddy, *raised* by her and Granddaddy, tried to be perfect, not devout. Mother was outright hostile to people with trust in anything other than themselves, and, frankly, I believed in things I could prove. So Gram was something of a curiosity to me.

I knocked on the window. Not the most courteous thing to do, interrupting her and her God, but I needed to clean off the mud between us. I hoped my sour stomach would benefit.

She smiled up at me and waved me outside. My insides warmed, and I hurried to her. My sweet gram. Despite her conspiracy with my daddy *and* her secret purge of Granddaddy's shop *and* her alliance with Burnaby *for years,* I didn't want to be unkind. My parents were the problem, not her. She patted the grass beside her and I plunked down.

"Gram. When Daddy called? I lost it."

She swiped her arms and thighs like she was brushing off lint. "That's behind us, honey. Clean slate?"

A ladybug landed on my foot. "Not that simple."

"I understand your anger, Celia. But what do you want to do with it? Let it run wild? Wouldn't it be better to deal with what's beneath it?"

She reached for my hand, but I pulled it away.

16

AGGIE

POULTICE

HER THROBBING ARM WOKE HER. Aggie jerked with the remembered fright, and her shoulder bumped the hollow log's ceiling, sending pain the length of her wound. Beneath her, blood staining the cottonwood fluff showed as black gum in the predawn dimness.

This was bad. She fingered the slice and shut her eyes, wincing. She had to tend it, but how?

As if answering, Mama surfaced behind Aggie's closed lids.

——————

"Don't tease that cat, Aggie. He'll nick your hands." Her mother had stood on a ladder in the orchard, picking August apples. Aggie's tomcat slept under a nearby pear tree—or tried to. Aggie lay on her stomach in the warm grass beside him, flicking his whiskers, dodging his claws until, finally, the cat drew the line. A bloody red line, straight across her palm. Aggie squealed and splayed her fingers as he sped off.

"Those dirty claws. So much bacteria." Mama scouted the ground from her perch on the ladder. "There, Aggie." She pointed at the fence. "Yarrow. Plantain. Let's get a poultice on that scratch so it doesn't get infected."

Aggie knew yarrow and didn't like it. She once brought her mother a bouquet of the lacy flowers and they stank up her hands and the kitchen. And plantain? A nuisance. Stems topped with pointy, wreathed heads poked out of their lawn. She had pulled a million of them in the garden.

She spotted one nearby. "Weeds?" She pursed her lips and wiped her bleeding hand on her shorts.

"Leaves only, please."

Aggie picked a handful of feathery leaves off a yarrow plant and brought them to her. Mama stripped out the rib, shoved the greens in her mouth and chewed.

"Oh, my. So bitter." She blinked and puckered, but kept chewing. Green juice leaked from the corners of her lips. "Now you. Plantain." Aggie shook her head vigorously and backed away. "C'mon, girl." Mama's words garbled through the pulp. "You love asparagus. Plantain tastes like that."

Aggie nipped a tiny edge from a plantain leaf and waited. When the flavor reached her, she raised her eyebrows, nodded at her mother, and then poked several small leaves into her mouth.

Mama stepped off the ladder. "Chew them into a paste. Like this." She spat the mash into her hand and held it out in front of her daughter. With her teeth, Aggie scraped the plantain from her tongue and plopped it on top of the yarrow.

"Now let me see that cut." Mama massaged the two plant pastes together and smeared them on the scratch. "Close your hand and hold it there." A breathy, mnemonic *puh* had escaped Mama's tight lips. "Plantain for pain and itching. *Yuh.* Yarrow for *yikes*—deeper wounds. Both fight infection."

———⚘———

That day Aggie thought her mom silly for giving all that attention to a measly little cat scratch, but now she was grateful. She climbed out of her cave, sat on her log, and scrutinized the six-inch wound in the day's first light. It was deep. Ugly raw. And so sore. Could plants heal it? She sure hoped so. If this cut got infected, she might have to surrender.

Surrender? No, no, no. Nobody would get their hands on her and put her in juvie. She would patch herself up.

First, she'd give herself a good washing, something she hadn't done since before the fire. And not just her arm. Every inch of her was gritty, especially her feet—and her privates were stinky. She headed for the spring, but when a twig scraped the cut, pain buckled her. Guarding the wound, she sidled the rest of the way to the water.

She lowered her arm into the pool, but the frigid water stung so fiercely that she gasped and yanked her arm skyward. She forced herself to think of the Polar Bear Swim at Birch Bay on New Year's Day. Twenty-five degrees that day, and her standing there in her bathing suit. She and Dad had run into the sea, pumping their arms and laughing. Had dunked to their chins.

But my arm wasn't slashed then. She gawked at the oozing flesh and turned her head away. The cut's depth worried her. Mama would say it needed stitches. A full-body bath would have to wait.

She plunged her arm into the water a second time and nearly fainted, but held it there until the icy water dulled the pain. Her fingers traced the wound underwater. Skin flapped over it in places, and even in the numbing cold, it hurt too much to rinse deeper.

Good enough. With nothing clean to dry herself, she drooped her arm at an awkward ninety-degree angle, away from her body, like a sparrow airing its wings after rain. The gash hurt worse at that tilt, though.

"Keep it above your heart." Mama again. She had elevated Aggie's hand on a pillow the night after she caught it in the car door.

Above my heart. Aggie tipped her forearm up and laid her palm on her scalp, so the injury was above her shoulder. Yes, above her heart felt better. And sunshine would dry it off. She lay back in the sloping field where the woods met the grass and extended her arm uphill, over her head. Warmth soothed the wound and she closed her eyes. *Ah.* If she kept her body stationary, the pain eased.

Instead, a new sensation took its place: tickles. Mama said that cuts itched when they were healing. *Tickles. Itches. Same thing.* She lay still as a stick with her arm outstretched, with the wound facing upwards as she relaxed into the low buzz of summer insects. Not a mosquito whine. Mosquitos stayed in the shade. This sounded like bees. Honeybees, with little pollen bags on their legs. She pictured the bees in their seed garden, climbing into bright nasturtium blooms, gathering flower dust.

Or these were plain old flies, humming away like the ones at her uncle's farm. A calming, summer sound. Almost a serenade. Her mind wandered until the tickling in the wound intensified and called her back.

Reluctant to reawaken the pain, she stalled, like Gulliver from her old storybook, tied to the ground with Lilliputian ropes and not yet ready to pull free. She would let the sunshine shrink her cut and heal it. Did she really need a poultice?

With her eyes closed, she was home again, hose in hand, watering the young trees. She splashed each one to wet the needles and leaves and surface soil, and then moved on, hurrying, until Mama called to her. "You cutting corners, Agate? No deep soak?"

Cutting corners. Yep, if Aggie bandaged the wound without a poultice, she'd be skipping steps again. Then how would she heal—and escape the cougar if it returned?

When it returned. Now the animal knew where she lived. Good thing those lions mostly hunted at night and didn't like to dig. If she hadn't been inside her cave . . . well, she wouldn't dwell on that. When she got better, she would find a rock to block her den's door when she went to bed.

She raised both arms into the air and a compact cloud of flies lifted with them. *Shoo. Pesky things.* She swatted at them, and the tickling quit, thankfully. She didn't need that annoyance on top of everything else. The gash marked her skin like a huge red leech. She felt sick if she inspected it too closely.

After collecting a fistful of plantain leaves, she hunted the river-bank until she found the tiny white flowers and floppy fronds of yarrow. "Good to see you, smelly things." She sat cross-legged amidst the patch of blooms, steeled herself against the throb in her arm, and gathered fuzzy leaves. With hamster efficiency, she stuffed both plantain and yarrow into her cheeks and began to chew.

When the plants released their juices, she retched and nearly coughed out the whole gloppy mouthful. She needed food, not this. Her stomach was crying again. But instead of spitting out the mess, Aggie stopped chewing until her gagging subsided and the saliva pouring into her mouth diluted the yarrow's bitterness. She emptied the mash into her hand and, looking sidelong at the cut, dabbed the green goo from her wrist to her elbow.

Now what? She couldn't sit there all day. She needed a bandage. And a mouth rinse. Unless she kept moving, she would have neither. She considered the river, thought of muskrats and beavers pooping in the water, and spat. She lifted her shirt, pressed her poulticed arm against her bare stomach, and retrieved the bottle she had stashed near the pool.

———🜔

Back at her den, she swished her mouth and blew half of the spring water from her bottle into the shrubs. She drank the rest, ate a few leftover cattails, and crawled inside the cave, trying to ignore the bloody bedding. A bandage could wait. Stiff and cold, with her arm immobilized against her belly, she clenched her teeth to stabilize her trembling jaw.

Mama said plantain helped with pain, too. Mama knew. Later in the afternoon she would feel better. Besides, the wind was rising again. Ominous, steel-colored heaps of clouds piled up outside, darkening by the minute. She would lie here until the storm passed and let the plants work. Only until then. If she stayed here too long, she would run out of cattails. If she didn't eat, she would grow too weak to climb.

She might even die.

The churning clouds exploded, shaking the ground beneath her. *Thunder.* Would death be like that thunder? Would it shake the ground like that? She held her breath and waited. The door to her cave brightened with a flash, which pulsed in her teeth and her ragged arm. Another boom followed, louder than the first.

And rain. Rain, on a billion leaves and needles. Rain that washed all of her hunkered birds and porcupines, raccoons and possums, streamed down the face of her cave, and soaked into the thirsty ground.

She stretched her good arm through the cave's opening, palm up.

17

CELIA

ANTS

AFTER I ESCAPED GRAM'S LECTURE in her rose garden, I found Burnaby in the barn. "Bone-hunter, you ready? Let's find that owl you fed to the ants."

We both needed the break. People were going crazy looking for Aggie. I hoped I might see signs of her while we collected, but to protect Burnaby's sensitive self, I didn't tell him I had seen footprints in the garden. For *two seconds*. And had no proof. No need for a painful red herring.

Burnaby stood at the workbench with a bucket of dead starlings at his feet, while he folded toilet paper and laid it in a shoebox. Gram's garden basket sat beside the box, with tongs, two pairs of tweezers, a trowel, and a pancake spatula laid like medic's tools on the hand towel inside.

"Can I carry something?"

He handed me the box and strode out the door toward the river, scanning the trees again for Aggie as both basket and starling bucket dangled from his elbows. Pi trotted beside him, and I trailed the two, still steaming about Mender's accusation that I had wrecked her peas and carrots. Still baffled by those footprints.

I was so busy frowning into the ground that I almost plowed right into Burnaby at the first anthill, rising three feet tall in a sunny spot between two spruces. He bent deep over the pile of twigs and fir needles, his face inches from the squirming insects as he introduced them.

"Thatching ants."

Paths led into the mound from all directions, thick with black and red bugs carrying grass and beetles, dead flies, tinder, and conifer needles. A few ants crawled across his boot and up the leg of his jeans, but he ignored them.

"Don't those bite?"

"They do."

I stepped backwards, but he let them climb right over his denim as he scraped bare and stomped flat a three-square-foot dirt patch bordering an ant trail. He pulled a bird from the bucket and laid it on its back in the center of the cleared space, talking as he worked.

"The first time, I arranged the bird directly on the mound. Later I found the skull and spine, but the ants had dispersed most of the skeleton." With the spatula he scraped away a piece of the matted anthill. "I dug inside for missing bones, but the insects swarmed." He pointed at the tiny creatures, rolling like sea waves into the damaged section.

"Like that."

He waved the spatula toward the scrape. "Thereafter, I left the birds farther from the hill."

"Don't you have a jar of spare parts?" I suppressed a smile. *Unlikely.* Given his penchant for accuracy, he would hate to jury-rig a skeleton.

"Yes, I do. Substitutions—in a box, not a jar. I prefer originals, however."

Hoo boy.

At a second, taller anthill, Burnaby brushed debris off a nearby stone, flat and large as a Thanksgiving turkey platter, then cleared the surrounding ground. "My first bone plate. From the shallows upriver. Still need a few more."

He again laid a bird on its back, this time in the center of the stone. We knelt and watched. Two ants crawled to the starling and traced its feathers with their antennae. As others diverted off their trail in the direction of the supine bird, the original explorers scurried back to the nest. Within minutes, platoons of ants marched toward the carcass. With the temperature in the high seventies, insects soon covered the bird in a collective writhe.

Burn rose abruptly. "Five more."

"You rationing?"

"One for each hill. Animals eat these birds too, so we'll distribute. Cut our losses."

At the last mound, we found the owl. A few ants lingered around its skeleton, picking their teeth, I figured, after chewing all the bones clean. The lower half of the beak lay a foot away from the rest of the body, moved by a zealous ant squadron. Feathers and the smallest wing bones, those delicate hands of the bird, lay strewn in a trail across bare dirt.

Burnaby opened the shoebox, so I picked up what looked like a femur. I was just trying to be helpful, but he appeared to have an internal conniption over my effort, given the size of his eyes and how his mouth sputtered. My hackles rose. Settled.

"Easy, Burn." I set the bone in the box, then wiggled my cigar stub digits at him. "I get it. No touching." I actually did get it. Bones were his deal, and he was good at them. He'd been kind enough to bring me along. He didn't need a bull crashing his china.

When I folded my hands, he relaxed, and with tweezers and fingertips he recovered the bones with the delicacy of a surgeon. Then he laid both box and tools into the garden basket, sat cross-legged in the shade, and morphed into a maître d'.

"Would you like a snack?" He spread a bandanna on the ground and produced a package of M&M's, which he tore open with bone-gathering precision and poured onto the handkerchief.

"Why, sure." I reached for the pile, but he raised his hand to stop me. From a baggie in his pocket, he withdrew a damp cloth and cleaned his fingers, then passed the rag to me.

"Alcohol. Bacteria deterrent." He waited until I wiped down my bone-touching paws before he sorted the candies by color, then arranged them on the cloth according to the chromatic spectrum, leaving gaps for the missing colors. Quite a few gaps, given that he was working with green, yellow, orange, and those random brown and tan outliers. When the piles lay in neat order, he extended his hand. "You first."

I took a yellow one. Burnaby swallowed and blinked. I suspected that choosing one out of sequence had a visceral effect on the guy. He stayed with the green. Ate them all.

"I'm not good at this yet." He took a candy from the next pile.

"There's a skill set to M&M's?" Couldn't help myself.

"At conversation. Mama says I give speeches when I should be conversing. Misplaced monologues are selfish, she says. Talking should be reciprocal. Unselfish. Like tossing an apple back and forth so each hearer can catch it. She says I should listen without having a speech ready. Consider. Respond. Listen again."

My mockery smacked me this time. He was so *sincere*. "At least you realize it, Burnaby. Most guys don't get that. Girls either." Did I? I understood the law of quadratic reciprocity, but he was talking about people. About *relationships*. He seemed concerned about *me*.

"See?" he said. "You did it right there. Heard me and responded."

He lifted his hands like a referee calling a touchdown. I wouldn't have guessed he liked football.

"And you did the same right back," I said.

"I did?"

"Yessir. We are having a proper conversation."

A brightness washed over his face. He scooped up the remaining candies. I knew he was making a sacrifice, stirring them all together.

"Here," he said, and poured the mixture into my palm. Beneath all his weirdness, the guy was almost cool. Maybe sturdier than I thought.

"About Aggie . . . I saw something."

Burnaby plucked a dandelion leaf and began tearing it.

"Might be nothing," I continued. "But I swear I saw footprints in Gram's garden."

His eyelids fluttered. "Did Mender see them?"

"No, and it was too late to tell her. She wouldn't have believed me. Thinks I lie to her."

"Mender knows tracks. She didn't notice?"

"Apparently not. Chopped right into them."

Burnaby panned the foliage overhead. "Those would be the first prints anyone has seen. You certain they were human?"

"No, I'm not *certain*. I only saw them for a second." He nodded slowly. Folded the bandanna.

I felt fidgety. "You see your parents yet?"

"Yes."

I waited. "Well? How are they?"

His eyes dulled, and he shoved the kerchief into his pocket. "Critical. Especially Mama. Necrotic expansion. Immunosuppression."

"And that means?"

His shoulders hunched. The explainer was still holding the apple.

———※———

Thunderheads were piling up like mashed spuds when I got back to the house. No sign of Gram. I changed my clothes, assessed the sky, and figured I could get in a quick five miles before it rained. I jogged fast down the lane and turned downhill at the road, into the wind.

About a mile and a half out, thunder rumbled in the distance. I thought of Aggie. Where would she go in a storm? Was she out in the open like I was, a target for the nearest lightning bolt? I hadn't seen a flash, so I quickened my pace and kept running, determined to make it to the stop sign before I turned—my two-mile mark, according to Gram's odometer.

The sign was in my crosshairs when a fork split the sky, and my feet buzzed. I sprinted toward the intersection, gauging the interval between flash and boom as I pumped my arms. "One Mississippi, two—" Thunder detonated overhead. Not even a mile away. I was speeding into the storm's teeth.

Lightning sliced a soggy cloud as I reversed course and raced back uphill. One second I was running fast along dry pavement, and the next I was sopped and splashing at a jog, with bolts and thunder exploding around me. Open fields lay on either side of the road, and my body vibrated with the charged air. Panicky, I sprinted again, this time for a tired old house ahead of me on the left, a few hundred yards away. I hoped someone would let me inside.

A car swam toward me with its headlights on high beam, its windshield wipers flailing against the deluge. The blue Camaro slowed as it approached, and I veered onto the grassy shoulder. The driver stopped and flung the passenger door wide.

"Get in!" he shouted. "Don't touch the door!"

I squinted at the man inside, wondering whether I should race for that creepy house or jump in a car with someone I didn't know.

But I recognized him. Cabot! That hot guy from the search. No mistaking him. I dove onto the front seat and he stepped on the gas.

The door swung partway closed with the momentum. "Okay. You can shut it now. Didn't want you electrocuted."

"Thanks." I pulled my dripping ponytail over my shoulder. "Sorry about your car." Water puddled around my shoes.

"It'll dry." He grinned. "What are you doing out in this storm?"

I nearly told him I was running, but my saturated appearance compromised my eligibility to sass the man right out of the chute. He was far too good-looking. And he had just saved my life. Maybe.

"I miscalculated. What about you?"

"Heading home. I work up at Epping's farm."

"The dairy? I'm at the next place south of there. Bird Ridge Farm. Marta Burke's my grandmother."

"Mender. I've heard of her. Saw her for the first time last Monday, when we were looking for Aggie. Saw you, too." He winked at me and smiled again. *Winked.* "I'm Cabot Dulcie, by the way. And you are?"

"Celia. Celia Burke. Here from Houston, while my d-dad's on a job." The man had me stuttering.

"Houston, huh? You're a long way from Texas, Dorothy. Want me to show you around Oz? An old lady like Mender can't be much of a tour guide."

He clearly did not know my grandmother, but protecting her reputation was not foremost on my mind. "Yeah. I'd like a tour. I'd like that a lot."

"Ever see Lake Whatcom?"

"Heard about it."

Maybe the guy water-skied, too. I stood by the window after he dropped me off. My heart bounced like a kangaroo.

18

AGGIE

ITCH

THE POULTICE DRIED TOO FAST. Though Aggie guarded it, without a bandage, the mash fell off in chunks by morning. The flesh along the edges had swollen like a sponge, sending jags of red lightning into the surrounding tissue. *Uh-oh. Infected.* She dabbed pus away with her pinky finger. *You are hot, hot, hot. Cold bath coming right up.* She stood to go, but swayed, so she braced herself, hands on knees, until the dizziness waned enough for her to plod to the pool.

The spring water stung; she ground her teeth and waited. Gradually the chill countered the pain that pulsed with her heart-beat's rhythm. A few of the green flecks from the poultice and some white, rice-shaped particles floated free in the water, but the skin flap had adhered to the ragged tissue. Though she rubbed until she cried out, she could only access half the cut. The water clouded with the wound's discharge.

By the time she finished, the prospect of gathering herbs for another poultice exhausted her. Couldn't she bandage the cut without all that goo? Would it really help? The mash hadn't worked yesterday. Maybe it made the infection *worse*.

Her fever, which was rising by the hour, decided for her. Her body ached as she struggled to refill her bottle at the pool. After she peed in the rain-drenched bushes, she lay on the cool, damp duff near her log for the rest of the day. That night she burrowed into her cave, where black possum dreams haunted her until they gave way to a detached euphoria, like she felt when her dad played his fiddle under the stars.

———A

Her body burned for three days. Fever riddled her sporadic sleep with hallucinations, so that she hovered in a partial wakefulness that left her sapped and confused. Though her cattails lay in a heap by her head, she ate little, and rose only when she crawled outside to pee again and to stumble to the spring, where she forced herself to fill her bottle and drink.

After moonset on the fourth night, the itchiness plaguing her since the preceding day melded into fitful dreams of chicken pox and woke her. Sweat plastered her hair and clothes to her skin, and her arm itched so ferociously all she wanted to do was scratch.

She resisted. In the darkness she was blind. And so dirty. If she scratched with her filthy fingernails, she'd load the wound with even more bacteria, or tear away a good scab without realizing it. She forced her hands under her thighs and refused to touch her arm.

But apart from the itching, she felt better. Her fever had broken, and though weakened from lack of food, her mind was clear. Before dawn, she crawled outside and waited for enough visibility to see the wound. She wanted to claw it with the cougar's savagery. Wanted to gouge out the itch. As light seeped over her, she saw why.

Maggots.

Little white larvae protruded from under the skin flap, and more wriggled and burrowed around raw islands of granulating flesh. She wasn't itching because she was healing, but from these horrible creatures crawling inside her wound.

On wobbly legs, she jumped and shrieked, snapping her arm like a bullwhip. When only a few larvae fell to the ground, she rushed, stumbling, toward the spring. She flailed her arm against the clear surface, ignoring the pain until she saw grubs writhing in the water. With the flat of her hand, she rubbed the gash until more of the worms came free and floated off.

The itching subsided. Weak with shock and hunger, she crumpled onto the forest floor and inspected her injury in the growing light. A few white wigglers still squirmed inside the cut. From fly eggs, she remembered. Grimacing, she extracted the creatures one-by-one and flicked them to the ground.

Maggots eat dead things.

Maybe death had been closer than she thought.

She plucked the last grub and let her shoulders sag, her body and mind depleted. A great weariness came over her. Hiding took so much work. How long could she keep this up?

She forced herself to study the wound. The angry swelling along the sides of the cut had shrunk and paled. Red streaks shooting out from the gash had retreated, and a clear serum now wept from the wound, instead of that smelly green pus. She clenched her fist and opened it. No throbbing.

Wait a minute. Did those nasty squirmers heal her? Though the idea revolted her, she would face facts. The maggots had eaten away her infection. Without them . . . she shuddered, as the ground she counted on shifted, and her thinking took a turn.

Dad had made all of life in the forest one gigantic game. Even when they played Homing Pigeon out in the foothills, he spun her in both directions before she could take the scarf off her eyes. *A game.*

But this was no game.

That something horrible could happen *to her* if she refused Dad's advice never occurred to her back then. That bad things could get her if she followed it? Unthinkable. But now? She made a list of things that had tried to kill her:

1. Cougar.
2. River.
3. Trees.
4. Plants.
5. Fire.

She surveyed the forest as if she had never seen it before. Rough, prickly spruce trees glowered at her. Branches proved untrustworthy. Hadn't she stepped onto fat limbs only to have them snap off underfoot, weak and brittle? *Liars!*

Before the fire, death was something that happened to Brian Hatch in those underwater tree roots. Not to her parents. And definitely not to her. Most of the time she had felt ridiculously safe, never imagined that anything would kill *her*.

Now her bug-bitten arms and legs stung with proof that even the smallest insects were out to get her. Only a stray maggot near her foot suggested otherwise.

19

CELIA

KISS

THE MORNING AFTER THE THUNDERSTORM. I sat in an Adirondack chair on Gram's patio with my heels propped on a watering can and a legal pad of equations for Mr. Maurer's rain problem balanced on my lap. Under the heady influence of calculating the vertical component of rain falling in feet per second, the fragrance of Gram's roses, and a long shower, I was entirely focused. My steady preoccupation with Aggie sat in my mental back seat. I wore no makeup, a baggy white T-shirt, and faded cutoffs shorter than my tan line. My hair was drying in the sunshine.

So when Cabot appeared at my elbow, I think he read my distraction as a rebuff. He stepped backwards.

"Uh, remember me? Your grandmother said you'd be out here."

"Hey," I stammered. I leaned away from him to lay my worksheets on the ground—and to hide the blush I felt climbing my neck. "What's up?"

He set a matching chair at an angle and stretched sinewy arms down the armrests. Leaning back, he beamed at me, gap-toothed, tan; the corners of his eyes sent two sunbursts of lines down the sides of his cheeks. His heat bounced at me, pinning me in place.

"Day off. Want to climb a mountain?" He inclined his head toward the peak dominating the eastern skyline.

"Mt. Baker? Don't I need some serious equipment? And training?"

"Not for Artist Point. Road opened yesterday, a good month early. Still snowy in places, but hiking boots will do." He pitched forward, assessing my bare feet. "You got some?"

"Of *course*. A girl can't come to Washington without *boots*."

I thought of the back country around Chelan—where I usually wore them. Hadn't even pulled them out of my suitcase yet.

He settled back in the chair, grinning. "A nice little four-miler."

I shaded my eyes and took in the mountain, stalling. The man didn't waste any time. I needed to compose myself. *And* ask my grandmother.

"Maybe. If you can answer a riddle."

He angled toward me. I smelled soap and something else. Something musky. Noticed a shaving nick on his chin.

"Ooo. The girl's playing games. I like that." His eyes danced. "Fire away."

I handed him my yellow pad and pointed at the numbers. "It's raining. I'm on foot and I have to get home. I also want to stay as dry as possible. Should I walk or should I run?"

He gave it back without looking at it. "You wouldn't have to walk. I'd take you home."

"I'm serious."

He laughed. "You'd run."

"How do you know?"

"What do you mean?"

"If I really, really needed to stay dry. If my life depended on it, and I was travelling on foot, are you sure I should run instead of walk?"

"Well, yeah. You'd get there faster."

"What about other variables besides my speed?" I turned my calculations toward him. "Would droplet size matter?"

Cabot's head tipped back, then upright, as if it were hinged. "Woman. You need a new hobby." He took my wrist and pulled me to my feet, sending a surge of that heat into my arm. "Let's go."

So he didn't like math.

He waited in his car while I went indoors to change and inform Gram of our plans. She glowered at me for a good five seconds. "You're telling me?" Her mouth pursed, and she turned toward the door. "I'll chat with that boy first."

I followed her outside, mortified. She bent close to Cabot's window, and he rolled it halfway down. Flashed me a grin.

"Hey, Mrs. B."

"You be careful on that road, young man." She rested her hands on the glass.

Cabot laughed. "You worried about *me*? Sunday driver here." I couldn't see her face.

"I mean it. Have her home by four. Without a scratch."

He laughed again. Shifted in his seat. "I ain't got claws, Mrs. Burke."

"Don't grow any." She patted him on the shoulder and stepped back to the sidewalk. Crossed her arms. Smiled at me. "Let me know what you think of the air up there, sweetie."

"Whatever."

Cabot got out and held the car door open, and I climbed in. I spied on Gram in the side mirror as we drove off. In a wide stance with her fists on her hips, she shrank to a dot in the mirror's frame.

And just like that, I was *alone* with Cabot Dulcie. *Oh, Meredith.* I imagined her slow smile and slower inhale, her nostrils flaring at his complex scent. *Animalic,* she'd call it, before she shuddered with delight. Some kind of cologne. An air freshener shaped like a little green tree dangled from the mirror. *Yeah. And that.* He took a roll of Mentos from a pocket in his cargo shorts and held it toward me before he slipped one into his mouth, chewing and talking. Peppermint.

The car whined as Cabot punched the accelerator after every stop sign, testing the upper limits of each gear as we crossed the wide valley, flushing roadside birds as we sped by. His hand didn't leave the shifter until we stopped in the foothills for sandwiches-to-go at a cramped little restaurant packed with broad-backed loggers leaning over their coffee and pie.

Then he aimed his car up the mountain. My senses reeled with trees and views whizzing past and the great-looking guy driving me through high-altitude curves in a low, blue Camaro, while Van Halen wailed out the open windows. *Eruption. Jump. On Fire.* Perfect accompaniment for a trip up an active volcano on a day that felt like one.

Cabot's voice hummed and surged over the car's engine. ". . . I did the bike leg of the Ski to Sea Race on this road last year . . . team took second . . . faster this time . . ."

Who cared? If he'd said he sold parakeets at the farmer's market, I still would have hung on his cadence. He talked with an energy that leapt into the next moment, the next sentence, and I drank in every carbonated word.

Near a small lake, he pulled over. "Warm-up hike," he said. He popped another mint onto his tongue and sprang from the car, his jaw working fast. "Mt. Shuksan." He ticked his head toward a snowy, dentate peak that actually resembled a molar, its mirror image reflected in the lake's shiny mouth. "Picture Lake. They named it right, yeah?"

"You think?" I said. *Unbelievable.* "Belongs in a magazine."

"You ain't seen nuthin'." He looked like I felt. Edgy. Exhilarated. He shook his arms like a swimmer on a starting block and shifted side to side.

"Race ya," I said. Without looking back, I dodged an elderly couple bent over a shrub and sprinted along the shore of the lake. Within seconds I heard him behind me, his breathing strong and even, his strides longer, gaining. We finished the loop in a dead heat. Not bad for hiking boots. Cabot slapped his cap on his thigh and reseated it over his forehead. He high-fived me and laughed. The sound rolled into me.

By the time we wound past the shuttered ski lodge, I couldn't stop smiling. I thought of Meredith telling me about a guy she'd gone out with, and how she'd felt chin deep in a Jacuzzi with a view, leaning into the jets. *Something like this*, I guessed.

At the trailhead, he put our sandwiches in a pack, then led the way up a narrow path arrayed with alpine firs and boulders and, where the snow had melted, patches of greening meadow. A spicy scent rose from the warming conifers. We shaded our eyes against the snowfields' glare and surveyed the nearby tree line. Above it, craggy peaks surrounded us like kings, conferring.

"Kulshan Cabin's that way." Cabot pointed into the distant trees. "I stayed there in seventy-nine, before I summited Baker."

A mountain climber, this guy. I liked that. Liked him.

Along a hogback trail with wide views of the Cascades on both sides, he swung the pack to the ground and sat on a log silvered with age. I breathed in the valley, my hands on my hips. "Queen of the World," I whispered into the sky.

He patted the gnarled wood beside him. "You got that right."

He heard me. I shrank and sat, lifting the pack between us. He dug for a sandwich and handed it to me, brushing my fingers with his, injecting my arm with a jolt of warmth; I recoiled reflexively.

He didn't react. His eyes traveled quietly from the food in my hands to my face and rested there before he set the pack on the ground. Then he swiveled the bill of his cap like a baseball catcher's and moved into the gap between us, pressing his thigh and shoulder against mine. I caught my breath and lowered my head, but he lifted my chin between two fingers and held it there until I raised my eyes to his.

Then he tilted, closed his eyes and kissed me. Just like that, his mouth slid over mine. No time for me to worry or wonder what to do or practice in a mirror. A small, warm sip. Minty.

Stunned, I didn't pull away, so he took a longer drink of me, then kissed the tip of my nose and beamed. I think I smiled back, at least a little. I felt shy, even as I felt like a candle on that big old cake of a mountain, lit for the first time. My lips seemed connected to my every nerve, buzzing from my fingertips through my torso and down into the soles of my feet. Could he tell? My face burned. I bit into my sandwich, still tasting the sweetness of him.

I took another bite, then stood and rewrapped my food. "Lost my appetite."

He was studying me, grinning. "For food, maybe." I tugged the strings of my hoodie. I couldn't look at him. "You're smackin' gorgeous, you know that?"

I shook my head and smiled weakly, tensing my shaky legs. "C'mon Cabot. Let's go. You're embarrassing me."

He really laughed then. "Your wish, my command, Queen of the World."

How did he mean that? I couldn't read him.

He slid the pack over his shoulders and lead the way across a hillside and up a steep incline. My eyes dogged his calf muscles as they worked the grade, my mind replaying each kiss. At the base of a jagged boulder the size of a small cabin, he turned to me, holding his index finger against those lips. Islands of snow dotted the talus slope spilling down either side of the massive rock.

"Why?"

"Shhh." He gripped a notched projection and ascended the creviced rock face hand over hand. I climbed behind him, shadowing his toeholds, curious.

At the top he crouched and pointed. In a wooded draw below us, woven into a windswept alpine fir, a rough stick nest lined with moss and matted white tufts teemed with baby birds.

"Ravens." He was whispering, rapt. Two large black birds were riding thermals across the valley, headed our way.

"Here they come, Cabot." *Corvus corax.* I wanted out of there. Tales of ravens protecting their young were the stuff of legends. We did not want to be hanging over their nest when they arrived. "Let's go." I backed down the boulder and took a shortcut through loose scree to the trail below.

Cabot didn't follow. He lay prone on the rock, his feet jutting past the edge, patiently watching those parents with their chicks. I was sorry I had spooked. I could have been lying up there, too—right beside a guy who *liked birds*, maybe as much as I did. Nobody I rubbed shoulders with at school gave a lick about them.

"Think they were sleeping on fur?" We were back on the trail, heading toward the car.

"Yeah. From mountain goats." He shaded his eyes and swept the slopes. Pointed at a cluster of white dots on an outcrop across the valley.

I zeroed in on the distant animals. "How'd you know about that nest?"

"Came across it on a hike four years ago. I've watched this pair every year since. Biggest clutch was seven. The male's blind in one eye. If I'm ever reincarnated, I'd like to show up as an egg, right there."

Reincarnated? Spiritual, too, this guy. Cool, I guess, though Gram would say his ladder was up a dead tree.

"Yeah? Why's that?"

"Ravens dominate. Strong. Smart. Crafty. Live long, never quit. Know what they want and will take on anything, even eagles, to get it."

Ravens had nothing on this guy. I didn't know about the crafty part, but from what I'd seen so far, he'd just described himself. "Cool that you watch them. I'm partial to raptors, myself." Oh, the stories I could tell him, but he changed the subject to his work schedule.

No big deal. From the sounds of what he had in store for us, we would have lots of time to talk. On the way home, however, when he *told* me we were going to Boulevard Park the following Tuesday, my caution light flickered.

Then I relaxed. So what if he failed to *ask*. The man was a planner. By the time he parked in front of Gram's house, he was laying out the rest of our week together. I scanned the windows when he pulled me close, hoping she wasn't watching. But when he kissed me, I forgot about her. His lips dissolved something in me. I was still woozy from our connection when he leaned across my lap and opened the door for me from the inside.

Good thing Gram was getting groceries. She'd have sent him packing in a heartbeat if she'd seen us. Half an hour later, I met her at the porch and carried bags to the kitchen.

"You got some sun today." She brushed a wisp of hair from my forehead and studied my face. "Hike far?"

I avoided her eyes. "Picture Lake. Artist Point. Pretty up there. Saw a raven's nest."

"You must have enjoyed that." She was trying to read me. "Handsome boy, Cabot."

"He's okay."

"And he's twenty, Celia. I remember when he was born."

"So? You know his family?"

"Not well, but I do. He tell you about them?"

"Not yet. We talked about other stuff."

"Mm-hm." She hesitated and turned her head. Praying, I guessed. She prayed in the middle of sentences sometimes. Buying time, I figured, until she shut me down. "You make any other plans with him?"

"Yeah. He wants to see me again. I'd like that, Gram. We had fun today."

"I'm sure you would, honey, but—"

"Twenty's not that old. His birthday was only a couple of weeks ago."

"You've never dated, Celia. A man changes a lot between sixteen and twenty. Besides, it's not just his age. He's been through a lot, and—"

"Thatta way, Gram. Judge him without even knowing him. You can't keep me in a cage forever."

She sighed. "Your father said—"

"And *why* would he have *any* say in this? He's *gone,* Gram. Lied and left me."

"He'll be back, sweetie. And in the meantime, I'm looking out for you. I didn't say you can't spend time with the boy. Only that you'll have some limits. Follow them, and we'll do fine. Agreed?"

"What kind of limits?"

"I'm serious, Celia. Toe the line and you can see him. Cross it and you won't."

"Whatever." I didn't know what I was agreeing to, but at least I'd get to hang out with him again.

———⅄

That night after Gram went to bed, I crept into the kitchen and dialed Meredith's number. Her dad answered, groggy. I looked at my watch. 1:00 a.m. in Houston. I stretched the cord and hid under the counter between the barstools.

"Mr. Prescott? Celia. Sorry to wake you. May I speak with Meredith? It's important."

"Humph." The phone banged when he dropped it. Footsteps trailed off.

I was about to hang up when she answered. "Hullo? Ceils? You okay?"

"Sorry so late, Mer. Waited for Gram to fall asleep."

"Not a problem, hon'. Just got home." I heard her teeth clink glass, heard her swallow. "Your gram? She at the lake with you?"

"We never made it to the lake." I filled her in on Daddy's untimely deposit of me on my grandmother's doorstep before he absconded.

"Your four-foot leash dad? Who'd a guessed? You must be *pissed*. Shoulda stayed here. I saw Luke Ralston."

"Yeah?"

"He's been askin' 'bout you."

I puffed my cheeks and exhaled. "I think I can be home in three weeks." I told her about the strawberry farm. The dog bus. "Will you pick me up? I can stay with you, right?" My request lacked conviction. Leaving would be different after today.

The line crackled. "Mer?"

I heard her breathing. "Uh. No question, baby girl. I'm here for you. Lots happenin' this summer you don't want to miss. The twins' parents went to Europe for six weeks and left their crazy uncle in charge, so it's carte blanche over there. Pretty sweet."

I saved Cabot for last. Embellished the story.

"He *kissed* you? You *let* him?" She choked on whatever she was drinking. "Whooeee! My little Celia's comin' outta the library. How old is he, anyway?"

"Twenty. Works at the dairy north of Gram's."

"Oh *yeah*. You are makin' up for lost time. That's my *girl*."

The toilet flushed upstairs. "Gotta go, Mer. Gram's up."

"Okay. Keep me posted." She giggled. "Be ready. I expect he'll surprise you. Or you may surprise yourself."

20
—
AGGIE

HOUNDS

SIX DAYS AFTER HER INJURY. Aggie loitered around her den, famished. The gash kept her from plowing mud for cattails, and she'd eaten the last of her stored food the night before. She wished the afternoon breeze moving the treetops would blow her way, where she slouched against her log. Even the forest shade seemed steamy, the birds lethargic. She emptied her water bottle over her head and contemplated a trip to the spring, but stayed put.

Until she heard them, barking and baying in the distance upriver. *Hounds.*

The fuzz on her neck and arms stood like gophers. These weren't dogs like those that had come through with locals in the days preceding her injury, but real hounds. *Probably bloodhounds.*

Bloodhounds, Dad said, had noses like no other—except for German Shepherds, and then only the outstanding ones. Hounds could sniff out anything, he said, and their handlers were usually experts, too. Hound teams found who they were looking for.

She assessed the area around her log. *Loaded with scent.*

Climb, Aggie. Now.

Trembling, she crawled into her den and scraped away the cottonwood fluff that lined the old log's walls, heaping it onto the blood-soaked down that covered her dirt floor. Then she wadded up every bit of the mess, crammed it under her shirt and tucked the hem into her pajama bottoms to contain it all. If she left no physical evidence or fresh trail, she might throw them off, slow them down.

Fortunately, she tried to leave *no* footprints *ever*, and she always pooped on maple leaves and tossed them in the river. She traveled along branches or in waterways whenever she could, interrupting her foot trails, and since her injury, she hadn't wandered far. The heavy rain would have smeared aging scent on her wider-ranging routes toward the homestead and the dairy, and she hoped the heat would have lifted her smell off the ground. Could they still follow her?

She threw her digging stone and stick far into a blackberry thicket, cinched her waistband's drawstring around the lip on her bottle, and climbed. Her only hope to evade the hounds completely would be to dead-end them. Leave them yammering into trees she had already departed. She thought about the routes she had tested through the leafy canopy and examined her weakened body, her damaged arm. Could she still make the passes between trees? Climb as high as she did when she was stronger?

Reduced to prey, an animal hunted, she listened to the tenor of the dogs' voices, waiting for their excited barks and yelps to change to a sustained bawl once they caught her trail. Her every sense heightened; her body wound taut. And from somewhere, she garnered reserves she didn't understand.

She climbed a wide maple and moved through the trees, stowing her bottle above ground, distancing herself from the oncoming dogs, and following the hot, treetop breeze that carried her essence away from them. She returned to the forest floor multiple times, whenever trees were too far apart, or whenever weariness or her compromised arm limited her, trusting mere patches of ground scent to confuse the animals and redirect them to places she had already abandoned.

Far downriver from the homestead, she spotted a cottonwood on the riverbank, offset from the rest of the forest. Risky, climbing a tree she'd also have to descend, but she needed a height open to the breeze for her plan to work.

A fresh shot of energy infused her veins when distant, dreaded bawling reverberated through the trees. The vocal shift meant one thing: the dogs had caught her scent. Racing to the cottonwood, she climbed, gripping branch stubs and bark, tearing her fingers and toes in her rush to get high enough to release the bloody fluff.

Her hands shook as she let it go in bits, dropping some, tossing some, but always into the wind, which seemed glad to lift the tufts and carry them farther still. Downy wisps landed on the riverbank, in the water's currents, in fields surrounding her and between the trees that lined them, planting her smell everywhere—but without scent trails attached—in an area she hadn't traveled and didn't intend to. Quickly, she rubbed the last clinging shreds from inside her shirt, scrambled down the solitary tree and hurried into the denser woods, where she again climbed and cowered from the advancing hounds.

Their baying ramped up, shifting to a frenetic, urgent chorus. Noises played tricks in the woods, she understood that, but they sounded close now. Aggie pictured them, noses to the ground, smelling her every step, every pee. Where she slept, sat, washed. What clues had she left behind? A sweaty sheen covered her forehead and cheeks, dampened her chest and underarms. The dogs were yelping, leaping, she imagined, on each tree she had climbed.

She cringed, listening with every cell in her body.

Until the howling shifted direction and faded to sporadic yelps. Her hesitant smile grew. The detours had bought her time.

———◢◣

An hour later she left the silent woods. With bottle in hand, she settled on a wide branch, where she leaned into the trunk of a sycamore near the milking parlor, hidden by foliage and waiting for dark. And then, after Cabot left in his blue car, and after her brother finished the night milking and walked to her aunt and uncle's farmhouse, and after his light in the upstairs bedroom went out, Aggie crept into the milkhouse, climbed the ladder to the giant tank's lid, and filled her quart bottle with cooling milk.

She drank half of it right there, then dunked the glass again, buffing drips off the stainless tank with her sleeve before she dashed like a rat across the barnyard gravel. At the foot of the haystack, she filled an empty feed sack with baling twine, then returned to the woods and climbed awkwardly, the bag between her teeth, milk sloshing from the bottle tied to her waist.

It took a while to lash herself with twine into a tree's high branches. Afterwards, with her belly full and exhaustion overtaking her, she slept. She later roused to drink more milk and to scoot off the branch to pee, but soon fell into her deepest slumber since the cougar's attack. Only when twittering birds woke her in the warm predawn did she untie herself and finish off the bottle's contents.

At sunrise, the hounds cried again, closer this time, their intermittent bays rolling her way as they moved through the woods. The handlers would have wanted an early start, she figured, when the ground was damp and cool, holding her scent low, clean. Her hands shook as she returned twine to the sack and added her empty bottle.

No old trails, please, please. If the dogs locked in on aging scent, they would go to Mender's and come to the dairy. She wouldn't be safe anywhere.

She quickly moved higher into a tall fir. With the feed sack between herself and the trunk, she shrank behind needled boughs and waited, as hours passed and a pattern repeated: the dogs bayed while they followed her short ground trails, yelped wildly when they thought they had her treed, then whined or went quiet. Men's voices called to the dogs and each other. Terror froze her whenever the sounds grew closer.

But by late morning the barking and baying grew less frequent. By noon, it stopped altogether.

Where were they? Aggie squirmed, tense with uncertainty. Had they set a trap for her? Were they waiting nearby, ready to pounce as soon as she touched the ground? She had watched a coonhound tear a squirrel to ribbons once. Would the men find her like that, torn apart by their dogs?

A shout interrupted the silence. A howl. Baying again, rising in volume and intensity until she *saw* them. Three huge brown dogs yelped and leapt at the tree she'd climbed to reach her current leafy trail, close enough to hit with rocks. She inched around the trunk, squeezing herself and the feed bag behind it, out of sight. Someone crashed through the brush, breathing hard.

"They do it again, Dave?" A man's voice, farther away.

"Uh-huh. Like chasing a ghost. Looka this. Empty. Same as the others." Aggie held her breath, heard the men stomping around the tree, imagined them looking up. Branches crunched underfoot. The dogs bawled relentlessly.

She pushed on her breastbone to quiet her heart. Were they looking her way? She refused to check. Kept her chin against her chest, her eyes squeezed closed.

At last, one man whistled, and the team passed downriver, toward an area where cottonwood fluff would have landed. Before long, the baying and bawling began again. Had they found her dried blood? They howled until midafternoon, so she slept in a tree that night and the next.

During the daytime she traveled through the canopy. She peed from high in the branches of the access tree she'd seen the dogs surround. Wrapped her poop in leaves and stuffed it into crevices. Her feet only touched the ground at night, when she drank her fill of milk, chugged some water from the milkhouse faucet, and topped off her bottle. Dogs would never get her.

Never.

21

—

CELIA

PLAYGROUND

"YOU TWO HAVE UNTIL NINE." Gram said, when Cabot showed up unannounced the day after we drove to the mountain.

I checked my watch: 7:00 pm. He was packing two baseball gloves and a hardball. Gram pointed at the ground in front of her, smiling. "Good yard right here."

"Sure thing, Mrs. B."

He grinned, and I relaxed. He tossed me a glove; we played catch and chased grounders for half an hour before he produced a deck of cards from his glovebox and stumped me with card tricks. Supine on the lawn, he made up ridiculous stories about the clouds, while I lay on my side and watched his hands, his Adam's apple, his eyes. Pondered his lips. Sensed the air pulse with the drum of his voice. He was nonstop entertainment; I didn't have to say a word. At 9:00

sharp, he knocked on the window and saluted Gram, pretended to twist my nose, and drove that throaty car of his away.

What was Gram worried about?

———⚓

He was on my mind when I showed up at the berry field the next day.

"Emily's the row boss." Stout, bearded Herm Leegwater pointed toward one of his employees, a tall, twenty-something blonde in a straw hat. "Check in with her."

Not quite 6:30 a.m. and already hot. Local kids and some fast-picking migrant workers straddled leafy rows, bending low and dropping strawberries into shallow wooden trays. I lifted my empty flat and followed Emily to the far end of my assigned section. "Pick clean," she said. "Unless you want to start over."

It was harder than I expected. I fumbled through the plants, lurched over the foliage. Picked too many green ones. Midmorning, I stood to stretch my back yet again, watching two dark-haired boys no older than thirteen work their rows at twice my pace. I bit into one fruit the size of a tangerine, savoring the spicy sweetness, then refused to eat more. Every berry got me closer to that bus ticket, though I had to say that the prospect of seeing Cabot for the third time in as many days rattled that goal.

I tossed a couple more berries into my half-filled flat and carried it to Emily. "I'm going home."

She checked her watch. "Not even ten thirty yet." She weighed my meager pickings on the white enameled scale and frowned at my punch card. "A sorry way to start a job."

"Other plans."

"We hired you because we *need* you. You coming back?"

My job security was clearly intact. At a going wage of nine cents a pound, Farmer Leegwater wasn't exactly fighting off applicants.

"Sure. Tomorrow." Given the farm's location, they had me. Where else could I jog to work in twenty minutes, give or take?

———⚔

Eighteen minutes later, I was in the shower, sending sweaty grime and berry juice down the drain. By the time Cabot arrived at 11:00, I was on the front porch, squeezing water from my ponytail.

Gram had met Jack Seamus, the "nice young veterinarian" who handled Loomis's weekly herd health, so when I told her Cabot wanted to take me water-skiing with Jack and his girlfriend, she agreed not to turn Cabot's car into a pumpkin before she set dinner on the table at 6:30. After all, we'd be outside. During daylight. In safe company, she must have figured. I'd remember that for next time. And since Daddy had canceled our Lake Chelan trip, perhaps she was trying to make up for it by allowing me to ski at least once before summer was over.

Gram handed Cabot an insulated cooler at the door. "Lunch, kids. On ice. Have fun."

Cabot touched his cap and took the cooler from Gram as if it were a birthday gift. "You the best."

"Remember that." She dropped her chin, knitted her brows.

———⚔

"You ever been on a slalom ski, Celia?" We were heading south to Lake Whatcom, a half hour away. His question confused me. I'd ditched my combo skis for a slalom when I was twelve; I'd told him that on our way up the mountain. I'd spent summers on the water since I was born. I had told him that, too.

"Uh, yeah. A time or two." When he saw me ski, he'd know.

"Nice. We'll get you going behind Jack's boat. Water's cold. Shelly's got a wetsuit for you. Flat as glass out there today, so it shouldn't be too hard for you. You ever ski tandem?"

"Yeah, I—"

"Wait'll you see Jack and me. Shelly's our driver. Solo, we've been pushing speed . . ."

He gave me play-by-plays of his stunts: side slides, jumps, flips, three-sixties, tick-tock landings. As he talked, he occasionally drove the car with his knees, allowing his hands to jump and swerve like racing skis. I couldn't get a word in edgewise, but I didn't mind. His enthusiasm ramped me up. Best-looking guy north of the equator, and he was taking me *skiing*.

We parked next to Jack's truck and his empty boat trailer at a Bellingham city park. Forested foothills rimmed the lake, a "ten-mile, deepwater beauty," as Cabot described it. Jack, a sandy-haired guy about my height, whistled and waved from the dock. A skinny girl with a huge blonde perm was throwing life vests into the boat. *Shelly*. A pharmaceutical rep, Cabot said. Met Jack when she was selling cow drugs to his clinic.

"So, robbing the cradle again, Cabot?" Shelly untied a line from the dock and exchanged a knowing look with Jack.

Cabot laughed. "Celia, meet Shelly, stand-up comic and best driver in the state."

Shelly swatted Cabot with the boat's bumper. "Who's joking?" She tossed me a wetsuit and grinned. "Welcome aboard, Celia."

I slipped out of my shorts and tank top and quickly wrapped my towel over my swimsuit. I sensed Cabot's eyes on me as I pulled on the wetsuit, and I fumbled with the zipper. I wasn't used to anyone watching me like that. I was relieved when Jack pushed the boat away from the dock and Cabot's attention shifted. He coiled the tow rope and sat in the rear-facing seat opposite me, studying the water as the boat planed toward the middle of the lake. Jack faced forward in the seat beside Shelly, reading the surface ahead. These people weren't messing around.

I liked that.

Within minutes, Cabot was in the water, his ski tip pointing at the sky. Jack tossed him the tow line, Cabot signaled, and Shelly cranked the throttle. He rose from the lake and canted, launching a shining wall of lake water. Rainbows caught in it like flags, heralding a series of flawless stunts that *hypnotized* me. I couldn't keep *my* eyes off *him*.

When he pulled himself back into the boat, he shook his head and a thousand drops caught the sunlight in a sparkling arc. Matched the light in his eyes. He was radiant, his muscular good looks almost *feral*. My heart pounded so hard I forced myself to look away.

After Jack skied his own admirable loop, it was my turn. I mentally clicked through his and Cabot's stunts as I dropped into the water. I knew a few of them. Shelly started me out at about twenty miles per hour. I thumbed for more speed, jumped the wake in both directions and caught about four feet of air, finding my rhythm.

What next? I rode straight behind the boat, mentally rehearsing, before I moved up on the wake, crouched, and landed a front flip without falling. *Yes.*

Jack was laughing. Cabot's mouth hung open, and he was pumping his fist. I fell during a hard slide but made up for it with a backward deepwater start. Two laps of the cove later, I climbed back onto the transom. I thought Cabot would give me a medal; he was that excited.

Instead, he pulled me to him, with my back against his chest and his arms around my ribs, swaying with me as the boat turned and rolled in its wake, his chin on my shoulder, his breath hot against my ear. If those wetsuits hadn't been between us, I expect I'd have melted. Even the brush of his legs against mine almost collapsed me.

The day blurred by, mostly. Cabot filled the hours' speed, the day's race. When neither one of us was skiing, we sat in those back seats and spotted for Jack as he rode over the water.

And stole looks at each other.

By 3:00, an afternoon westerly kicked up a chop on the lake's surface. "No point fighting this wind," Jack said. "I'm on call tonight, anyway."

The spell broke. Froth seethed across the lake by the time we trailered the boat.

At the Camaro, Cabot pulled on his sweatshirt and tossed me mine. Jack leaned out the truck window on his elbow as he and Shelly drove up beside us. Cabot called to him. "Vaccinate the dry cows tomorrow?"

"You got it. I'm stopping by the office first. Won't get to the farm until eight."

"While you're there, will you pick up some ketamine? Gotta cut a cat for Loomis."

Jack laughed. "Will do. Anybody but you and I'd tell 'em to shove the cat in a boot like the old-timers do. We're keeping that stuff under lock and key now. Date rape, party drug. Word's out that veterinarians have it. Thefts all over the country."

"That tom's gonna lose his balls, not use them."

Jack laughed again. "Remember what I told you about that scalpel. Bold strokes."

22

CELIA

BLANKET

"WHAT DO YOU MEAN, 'cut a cat'?" We were driving home from the lake through floodplain. Fields of pasture and young corn rolled to the foothills, with the westerly swirling the sunlit grass like cake batter.

"Castrate him. That tom at Eppings'. Good mouser, but Loomis just got rid of the last litter. Doesn't want the place overrun with barn cats."

"You know how? Why can't Jack take care of it?"

"Loomis won't pay him for that. Nothing to it, anyway. Jack showed me on a bull calf at the dairy." And then he was off, describing the process in detail far too vivid for my tastes. I was glad when sleepy little Marmot, population 894, interrupted his monologue, and he pointed to a bakery fronted with peeling, multipaned windows. I caught the aroma of fresh bread pouring through the screens. No reason to go home early. We still had a couple of hours.

He ordered two apple fritters, which the clerk slid into a white bag. I'd asked for a cinnamon twist, but I guess he didn't hear me. Cabot handed them to me and ordered a maple bar.

He bumped the second bag against the fritters in a toast. "For Pam," he said.

"Pam?"

"My mom. You won't mind if we drop it by her house. I'll be quick." The jamb bell jingled, and he held the door. "A few blocks thattaway." He thumbed toward a side street.

"You always call her Pam?"

"I do."

Two minutes later, we pulled up in front of a freshly painted white bungalow with a brown asphalt roof and a deep green, weedless lawn. Not a tree or flower in the yard, but the place was tended, tidy. Someone peeked through closed drapes covering a picture window, then snapped them shut again.

"Wait here," he said. "Three minutes, max." He took the maple bar from my lap and went inside.

Cabot had a mother, and he took her doughnuts.

I could barely claim half of that equation. The pain flared as I waited for him. For three months, the day Mother left had been scorching me. I leaned my head against the side door frame and remembered. Precisely.

———— ⋏ᗺ

Tuesday, March 12, 1985—after track practice. An ice pack wrapped my knee as I hobbled out of the trainer's room with Meredith.

"Uh-oh. Dragon alert." She pointed at a silver Beemer idling at the curb.

Mother. Why now? She hadn't shown for any of my activities all year. I pried Mer's fingers off my arm and lowered myself into the car.

"Hurt it again?" Mother kneaded the ice as if it were putty.

I smiled and shook my head. "Nah. Just a precaution."

Her friendly question unzipped the wariness that usually insulated me against her indifference. Had I moved up on her priority list? I'd never beat out one of her stupid consulting gigs. Still, I felt a ridiculous shred of hope.

"Good. You need your knees." Her voice had a *lilt* in it. She actually hummed as she drove. My heart warmed like a piece of toasting bread, while I sat in surprised silence—until I saw our house ahead.

"Three more driver's ed classes. Come to my test?" When she didn't reply, my voice shrank to that of a shy four-year-old. "You can think about it, I guess." Her humming continued, quieter. "How was work?" We pulled into the garage and I unsnapped my seat belt. "Can you guess my 800-meter strategy for Saturday?"

No answer. I sensed that familiar tide of dread, incoming. "Annie got appendicitis. Her fever—"

"Celia Elizabeth, catch a breath. I came to get you for a reason."

Of course she did. Heat rose in my cheeks. I picked at a fingernail and waited.

"I'm leaving." Mother checked her lipstick in the rearview mirror.

"What do you mean, you're leaving? You just got home."

"Franklin offered me a contract in Chicago and I'm taking it."

"How long this time?"

Judith E. Burke, JD, MBA—a.k.a. my mother—flew away from our family at the first whiff of a business takeover. High-stakes mergers, her specialty.

"This is different. I'm moving out. You and your father will get along fine. Better, probably."

So nonchalant. Like telling me about a hair appointment.

My eyes watered, but I realized I wasn't surprised. "Does Daddy know?"

"I'll tell him tonight."

I closed my eyes as she left the car. Her heels clicked across the garage floor; the door to the house banged shut.

When my father pulled into his stall an hour later, I still sat balled up in Mother's passenger seat, only now my body buzzed and shook. Daddy had no idea what was waiting for him inside. I wanted to intercept him, protect him from her.

Yeah, right. What could I do? I could scarcely breathe, much less help my father. I slid below the windows until he went in the house. Then I stumbled to our side yard and slumped beside a trash can, where my sobs erupted. And wore me out.

When I climbed the stairs to bed, lamplight and my parents' muffled voices leaked under their door. At 1:20 a.m., the garage door rumbled below me and a car drove out. Mother hadn't contacted me since, except for that feeble card on my sixteenth birthday.

Oh, I hated crying over that woman. Hated how she didn't care if I cried or not. Hated what she was doing to my father. And to me. Hated that I'd welcome her back quick as a two-minute egg.

———✿———

Cabot emerged from that little white house scowling. He shoved the key in the ignition, revved hard, and dumped the clutch. Tires squealed.

"She like her doughnut?"

"Too wasted to care."

I opened the glove box. Closed it. "That bites."

"I'm used to it. She spends half her life in bed."

"How often you see her?"

"Actually, every day. I live there. We don't talk much, but I make sure she eats. Try to keep the place up, the outside at least. Inside's another story. She's a pig. Looks like a bomb went off."

"Hm." I turned off the radio. "Rehab?"

"Tried. Digs her heels in. Says she's sterilizing her memory."

"From?"

"My dad, I guess."

"Can't he help her?"

"He's long gone. Started hauling cattle after we lost our dairy."

"You had a farm?"

"Yeah. Out past Deming. Seventy-five cows. Forty acres. Nice little place. Until our herd tested positive for bangs . . . that's brucellosis. Undulant fever . . . when I was eight. Slaughtered every animal. With no milk check, we missed payments. Sold the place cheap. Dad bought a cattle truck and started moving bovines before I turned ten."

"So where is he now?"

"Met a chick at a California farm where he delivered a load of Holsteins. Moved down there. Still comes through occasionally with a shipment, but he doesn't call anymore."

"Man. That hurts." I knew how much.

"I checked out drivers in every cattle truck for years."

I saw the little boy in him as he talked. His yearning for his father. How he wanted to make something of himself, to prove that his dad had made a mistake by tossing him away. No wonder he bragged or monopolized a conversation or didn't listen sometimes. Part of him was still ten years old.

"I made two decisions after he left." Cabot slouched, sullen, his wrist slung over the wheel. "Am sticking by them, too."

"I bet." I touched his shoulder. Let my hand drop.

"Nobody's gonna dump me like that again." His left leg jiggled.

He didn't mention me when he said that, and I was glad. I hadn't known him long enough to dump him, and if I could hold out picking strawberries, I'd be sitting on a bus in a few weeks. Reminding him seemed unwise. He wore a dour look I hadn't seen on him before.

His skunk father had ditched him, just like mine had. And with a mother sailing around in a vodka sloop, of course he'd be pissed.

I could relate. No way I'd talk to my dad when he called. Felt good to hurt him like he had hurt me. He'd written me two letters, but I would *not* tear into those envelopes and let him get to me that way. I'd make my own plans now.

"And?"

"And what?"

"The other decision?"

He downshifted. "Nobody's gonna take what's mine."

"Or?" I shouldn't have asked.

"They'll pay." He punched the accelerator and passed a tractor hauling a silage wagon. Even his car sounded angry.

———⋏⋏———

The rest of Cabot's story unwound along the country roads that led us away from Pam's house—until he braked at an intersection and heaved a sigh. "We've got time yet," he said. "Gotta show you something." We crossed a two-lane bridge over the river and took a hard left down a deserted farm road, where the dirt lane dead-ended at a secluded crescent of sand. "I fish here sometimes," Cabot said. For the first time since we left his mother's, he turned to me and smiled, his expression melancholy, vulnerable.

He pulled a blanket from the car and spread it in the shade at the water's edge. I still carried the weight of his mood, but he brightened some when I sat beside him and bumped my shoulder against his. Dragonflies hovered over the green river's surface. Barn swallows flung themselves after caddisflies in a reckless aerial ballet. The tension I'd felt on the drive eased.

He dropped onto his elbows, then lay on his back and slowly traced circles below my shoulder blades.

"Spell something," I said.

"Huh?"

"With your finger. Draw a word. I'll guess it." I kept my eyes on the water while he wrote SKI on my back. RAVEN. I turned to him and raised my eyebrows. "Too easy. I'm good. Try again."

"That you are."

"Gimme a sentence." I was in uncharted territory, stalling. Wordlessly, he took my shoulders and drew me onto my back beside him. His arm bent under my neck, and he palmed my head.

"My family. Never told anybody all that before, Celia."

"I can relate."

He didn't ask how. Instead, he leaned over me. Brushed my lips with his. Then he lifted his head, searched my eyes, and found my mouth again, seeding me with heat I couldn't arrest.

And didn't want to. I kissed him back this time, pulling him tight against me. His breathing quickened and the muscles in his back tensed. He rolled me up onto his chest, his hands in my hair, his fingers swirling in my scalp as his lips traveled over my cheeks and chin. Down my neck. His hands curved over my shoulders, exploring my sides, kneading my lower back. His kisses grew more urgent.

I took his face in my hands and returned them. I swear my skin purred as he touched me with those inoculating fingers.

His lips grazed my ear. "My beautiful Celia. Made for me." He was whispering. "All mine now."

Though I wasn't thinking too clearly, something seemed off. *All mine now.* All *his*? He'd known me for *days*, and now he was *claiming* me?

I was beginning not to care when he reached under my shirt.

I gripped his wrists. Got to my knees, reeling.

"Time to go, Cabot." I tapped my watch. I had no idea what my tone of voice conveyed. "Mender's waiting." I was the teeniest bit thankful that she was.

He sat up, exhaled through vibrating lips, and ran his hands over his head. Scrubbed his cheeks with his palms. "Yeah." His torso rocked. "Six thirty. Yeah."

FRIEND

ANOTHER RESTLESS NIGHT. The baling twine that held Aggie in the tree rubbed her skin raw, and her muscles ached from sustained contortions in the branches. Again she listened for hounds. Though she hadn't heard them for days, she kept her ears tuned as she dropped to the ground to find food.

Her cheeks swelled with sweet, orange salmonberries when a girl's voice echoed through the trees. "Aaa-gee. Aaa-gee. It's me, Celia. You've seen me before, right? I come every day, looking for you. Well, not yesterday. Yesterday I went to the lake. Want to go to the lake with me? I can be your friend."

Aggie gulped the berries without chewing, and dove into the undergrowth as the singsong voice drew nearer. *Oh. Celia, not Cilia.* The girl she'd seen at Mender's. What made Celia think she was within earshot, anyway?

The dark-haired girl raised her voice. "I know your brother, Aggie. Anything you want me to tell him? He says he misses you."

Aggie shrank under a shrub, listening. *She's lying.* Burnaby didn't say stuff like that.

"You hungry? I brought you a peanut butter sandwich. And this." She tossed a black bundle into the air and caught it. "Are you there, Aggie? Don't know if you like peanut butter, but I thought . . . I can be your friend."

A sandwich?

A hunger filled Aggie far stronger than any her body had known in recent days, and a loneliness so intense she believed it would crush her. Could Celia really be her friend? Could anyone?

She followed until the older girl left the woods, then returned to a thick black sweatshirt draped over a boulder by the pond, its arms spread like an embrace. Big enough for her dad.

Aggie kept a lookout until sunset, when she crept like a coyote to the shirt and sniffed it. Explored beneath it and on the ground for the sandwich, but found only crumbs. She lowered her face to the fabric and licked the remnants. Her belly hurt.

At least she could claim the sweatshirt. At her nearest access tree, she bit the neckline and hauled the shirt between her teeth until she was again above ground, where she scrunched the fabric and buried her face in it. *Laundry fresh.* She rolled the cloth and tied it around her waist to climb higher, then stowed it in the feed bag for bedtime, when she would be thankful that it came past her knees. Food or no food, the sweatshirt and Celia's visit gave her a trace of hope. About what, she wasn't sure.

———✦

But that night, when she skulked back to the dairy and dipped for milk, her fingers slipped, and her bottle sank deep into the creamy liquid. She lunged for it but bumped the tank's lid, which clattered to the concrete below.

She shot a glance at the door, then hooked her feet on a pipe and bent into the tank from her waist—hurrying, stretching as far as she dared, paddling her dirty hands and arms deep in the milk, hoping to snag the bottle's lip. No use. The tank was too big, the bottle too far below her. She emerged drenched to her armpits, then tried again, but nearly fell through the opening.

Distraught, she retrieved the lid and seated it, but in her rush, she knocked the aluminum ladder propped against the tank. It teetered, banged against the sink and fell. Loud. Echoing.

She skidded to the floor, stood the ladder upright, wiped milk drips with paper towels, and ran outside with them stuffed in her shirt.

A light came on in the house as she galloped to the tree.

She would need a friend now.

24

COLOR

"WANT TO SEE THE CUTEST THING EVER?" I asked Cabot, intercepting him when he pulled up in front of Gram's house. I was returning from the berry field, where I'd picked a paltry six flats after leaving a sandwich and freshly laundered sweatshirt in the woods for Aggie. It was my granddaddy's sweatshirt, which I'd found on a hook in the storage room and washed with my dark load.

He pulled Gram's empty lunch cooler from the back seat and smiled. "I'm looking at her."

I laughed and swatted the insulated box. "Aren't *you* smooth as boiled onions. C'mon."

Within minutes, Gram wrestled a raccoon kit into his arms. The twitchy baby patted Cabot's bottle-holding fingers as she suckled, but the man arched away, nowhere near as charmed by the little creature as I was. Before the milk was half gone, he handed baby and bottle off to me, ignoring another kit that rolled and chittered in a cage beside the stove.

"She takes some getting used to," Gram said. She was studying Cabot; I could tell. I'd been too cryptic about our previous day water-skiing, and she was leery. "Nora heard her and her brother whimpering in their crawl space and caught them. I figure they're about five weeks old."

"Have you seen their mother around the farm?" I asked.

"Oh, yeah." Cabot checked his watch. "She got into everything. I didn't know she had babies."

"You know what happened to her? Nora said Loomis was vague."

Cabot rubbed the back of his neck. "No clue."

Gram cleared her throat. Busied herself at the sink.

He winked at me and cracked his knuckles. "Gotta change irrigation. See you tomorrow."

The drowsy kit clung to my arm as Cabot's engine roared to life. I bumped her nose with the bottle. *What did he do to your mother?* She mouthed the nipple, her eyes at half-mast.

"Celia." Gram was on me before Cabot closed the gate.

"Um-hmm?" I rubbed the baby's ear and her slurping resumed. Milky bubbles gathered around her mouth. Gram had moved into emotional strike range. Here came *the talk* I'd been dreading.

"Problems don't go away when you ignore them." Her eyes were on me. I kept mine on the kit. "And refusing to communicate solves nothing. All that bottled up sadness just gives your anger an engine."

"What's that supposed to mean?" There was snot in my words.

She ignored my rudeness. "You and your dad. He loves and misses you."

I purred at the kit, who took in my face with black onyx eyes. "Tough break for him. He should have thought of that."

"You're right. He could have handled his departure better. I understand why you're angry."

"So why are you bugging me to talk to him?"

"Because your anger is coming between the two of you. Maybe affecting your other decisions, too."

"Well, yeah."

"Like how you spend your time? And with whom? Anger steals your curiosity, Celia. Points you at false targets. Its object is rarely the real problem."

So I couldn't aim. If blood could boil, mine was fast approaching 100 degrees. Celsius.

"He lied to me and left me, Gram. Because he was afraid of losing his job. What kind of dad does that?" I kicked at a chair and it crashed against the wall. The raccoon startled; I eased her back into her cage. "I trusted him." At that moment, I felt a mean hatred toward Daddy—and my grandmother. The intensity surprised me. Neither of them cared a whit about my feelings or my needs.

"It might be a good idea if you took a break from that young man. You could think about things for a little while."

I must have looked like a chicken about to peck her, jutting my neck like that. My mouth pursed, beak-like. *No way* she would keep me from seeing Cabot. I bullied the screen door open and stormed outside.

———A———

My allies were at the dairy, so I headed straight up the road. Sprinted, actually. I was out of breath when I got there. I couldn't find Cabot, but Burnaby was in the parlor—in the recessed milker's pit. Cows stood in rows of six on either side of him, their udders even with his chest. He moved down the line of animals, attaching machines to teats.

"Hey, Burn." I leaned against a metal gatepost as I slowed my breathing and examined his profile. His mouth naturally curved upward, with little skin haloes over the corners. Was that an uptick of those lips? A tiny smile when he saw me?

"Celia."

He attached a machine to the teats of a feisty kicker—a Jersey with her hoof aimed right at him. "Easy, Frannie." He calmly pushed his fist into the cow's flank until she lowered her leg. Then he dipped each teat on her bulging udder in iodine and wiped them all with a towel. Vacuum hoses schlupped the milking cups onto her nipples.

"Got a mean one there." I pointed to the agitated Jersey. The cow's eyes rolled wild as she craned her neck to see me. Burnaby flicked a lever and more grain poured into her feed bowl from an overhead pipe.

"She worries. Calved yesterday. Wants her baby, not a machine. I'd kick, too."

Was he empathizing with the cow? I'd misjudged him. So had Gram.

"You ever get mad?" I asked.

"At cows?" He looked bewildered, as if nothing from those lumbering beasts would rile him. Where was Cabot, anyway?

"Sure. Cows. Or at anything else. Mad at anyone."

His eyes darted toward the top of my head, in the vicinity of eye contact. "You mean my gray aspect."

"I do?"

"Annoyance. Outrage. Fury. Varying shades, tints, values. Same family. And yes, regularly."

He sounded like a robot art teacher. I wasn't tracking. "When angry, I see in monochrome. Grays. Apparently negative stress disables reception from my ocular cones . . ." He picked up a hose and sprayed a fresh splat of manure off the elevated ramp before his head snapped toward me. "Shall I keep talking?"

Where was this going? I nodded.

"Cones are cells on the retina that distinguish colors. My brain somehow loses the signal from mine when I'm upset. Therefore, during anxious inflammation, blue skies turn silver. Grass, trees, buildings—all transmute to grays, charcoals. Fortunately, my other feelings evoke different colors. *Synesthesia,* Mama calls it. One of my many conditions."

He talked as if his mother were in the next room. Last I'd heard, her survival was hour to hour. And gray feelings? *Strange.*

Stranger still, I was getting it. His workshop. Those paintings. He was confirming my earlier suspicion: the guy understood his interior state far better than I did mine.

He opened the gates, and the cows moved out, their emptied udders swinging. Six more ambled through the parlor door and into position at their respective stations. Burn released grain from the hopper and the hungry animals nosed it.

Except for one—at the front of the line nearest me. Burnaby assessed her and squeezed each teat. Smooth, bright streams of milk hit the concrete. "Clean. No mastitis." He widened his nostrils and sniffed the giant animal's breath. "Smell that? Like acetone, only sweeter. She's ketotic."

I drew closer and inhaled. I knew that aroma. I used acetone as a polymer solvent in my chemistry lab at school.

"From what?"

He pulled himself up to the cow's level and thumped her belly with his fingers as he bent close, listening. "She's pinging. Displaced abomasum. Twisted gut. Her digestion's shut down." The cow stepped wide, lifted her tail, and released a gush of yellow liquid that splattered against him. His nostrils dilated again. "Ketones in her urine, too."

I stepped backwards. Wearing cow pee would not improve my mood. "What can you do?"

"Loomis will want me to roll her. Flip the displaced stomach back into position. But if it doesn't work, she'll die. I'd prefer to avoid that uncertainty and call the vet. Surgery takes less than an hour. Limits her suffering."

I remembered his painting of the goose. Imagined Jack slicing into the cow's side with bold strokes.

"What color are your feelings about Aggie? And your parents?"

Burnaby rested his hand on the animal's ribs. "Why are you asking?"

"Cause I am gray-hot mad, and I thought you might help me out."

"I understand gray-hot. What's the causality?"

"My parents. My grandmother. I'd be better off without them."

"Duration?"

"Seems pretty permanent."

He ran his hand along the cow's topline. "I suspect that's inaccurate. Imagine other colors in the scene, Celia. Think of those."

"Maybe I like gray."

He frowned. "Think of something that gives you pleasure, that you're thankful for. Find the pleasant feeling's color. Introduce it to the gray. Blend. Change your brain's landscape."

"Where'd you get that crazy idea?"

"Mender. She taught me to mind-paint when I want to ignite things. Sometimes works better than fire or caps." He opened a gate and directed the sick cow into a holding pen.

"Big help you are." I turned to go.

"Starling bones are clean. Come to the barn? Tomorrow?"

"I'll think about it."

Gram had never mentioned mind-painting to *me*.

25

AGGIE

P I

DAYS MERGED. but as Aggie tended her wound, the pain withered and retreated. When she peeled back the flaking edges of the scab, a collar of pink skin rolled toward the shrinking furrow torn by the cougar's claw. She figured her scar would be the size of a new pencil when it finished healing.

She recited the list structuring her hours before the cougar came. *Get water. Pull cattails. Climb. Explore. Spy. Visit nests. Sleep.* Not a bad list. When she followed it every day, she stayed busy. It kept her from thinking about the fire and her parents and jail as much. She had learned her way around and found Burnaby.

But things were different since the cougar. And since the hounds. And since she lost her bottle. During the days she lay healing and couldn't climb, she often imagined her dad hiding in the shrubs during that Homing Pigeon game. "Like the Father," he'd said. "Always with her," he'd said. *Ha.* Where was God when that lion shredded her arm? When her bottle fell in the tank? Now she slept in trees. *Some Father.*

She held a strand of her hair in front of her mouth and blew on it, pulsing her breath while the wind coursed around her, as if keeping time to a song from Dad's fiddle. Things were better when he played. Once, during kitchen church, Mama had even come downstairs and sat on the bottom stair to listen. Dad had kissed her head and played "Swallowtail Jig."

"Lord's Day Nine." Aggie pictured her brother, heard his staccato as he recited catechism while cider steamed on the stove. She pushed on her temples, recalling fragments. ". . . will provide whatever I need . . . will turn adversity to my good . . . in this sad world."

She shook her head. The world was sad, for sure. And some things were too, too sad to use for anything good.

She climbed the dike and found a gray stone, flat and round like a Frisbee, near the waterline. With a walnut-shaped rock, she scratched a white line across the top of the larger stone and wrote *Days* above it. By her calculations, she had been in the woods for five days before her injury and had lost track of three or four days when her infected arm made her delirious. Now she had been healing for at least another six. Total days since the fire? She wasn't sure, but she scraped shorter lines below the heading in sets of five. In each set, four stood upright and a fifth crossed them diagonally. *Fifteen.* She had come here right after her birthday. *Late June already. Or was it July?*

All those days. She drew another horizontal line straight through all the marks. "Done. Over." She made one more slash below them and wrote *Today*, then laid the stone on the calendar rock. "Dad? What now?" Her eyes filled.

She balanced her calendar in a tree and laddered an alder. She would go to the dairy and find her brother. Only this time, she wouldn't simply spy on him. They would talk. She wanted to kick herself for thinking he wouldn't. Despite his quirky brain, he still had to care about her, didn't he? Of their immediate family, only she remained. Since the fire, she hadn't given a thought to how he was faring without her parents and her.

And how was he managing with Uncle Loomis and Aunt Nora? Uncle Loomis made him edgy. Come to think of it, so did Aunt Nora. Would he remember his anchor thoughts? How to calm himself while he lived in their house? He needed her. She thought of Cabot watching Burn ignite the napkin and hoped her brother had left those matches alone.

———⚓———

At the back of the machine shed, she dropped to her hands and knees and squeezed between the wall and a lilac bush. Footsteps crunched the gravel around the corner, coming her way. At least two people. She closed her eyes as they drew nearer.

The crunching stopped. Did they see her?

Keys jingled. A woman hummed. Two car doors opened and shut. An engine turned, then caught, wheels ground into the gravel, and her aunt and uncle drove off down the lane.

She exhaled slowly and smiled. Perfect timing. Now she could talk to Burn without her relatives ruining everything. She stood cautiously and backtracked, circling behind the buildings, and peeked in the parlor's window. No Burnaby. No cows lined up to milk, either. Animals milled in the loafing area, some with their heads through stanchions, their noses buried in hay.

Scanning all directions, she darted between the tires of a tractor closer to the open barnyard. A better vantage point, from which she saw Burn's truck and a blue Camaro parked in front of the milkhouse. A screen door banged, drawing her attention to the house. Maybe her brother had gone inside.

A minute later, a movement in an upstairs window caught her eye. She remembered that room. Stuffy, crowded with furniture and hot, hot, hot all summer. Her aunt and uncle's bedroom. Flung wide open, the window gasped for air, surely a last resort for shuttered Aunt Nora. With the shade raised, Aggie got an unobstructed view of a man crossing the room, and he wasn't her brother.

She watched the window intently, but he didn't reappear, so Aggie edged around the huge tractor tire until the doorway came into view. Seconds later, Cabot exited through it, a Coke in his hand. *Sure, mister. Inside for a little drink, are you?* She shrank as he strode across the barnyard, fingering something in his pocket before he entered the barn, where mingling cows parted as he crossed the concrete slab.

What else did Cabot hide in his pockets? She thought of the caps in the root cellar—exactly like those in Burn's truck. She knew about her brother's stockpile because she had taken some from the glove box herself—with Burnaby's permission, of course. If Cabot had rifled through Burn's truck, he would have found them for sure. Now the thief had been rummaging around upstairs, too. What was he after? What else had he stolen? And why?

A demanding voice interrupted her suspicions. She couldn't make out the words, but realized that Cabot was bellowing at someone or something in the barn. *At Burnaby?* She looped behind the parlor and stopped short of the barn's gaping doorway.

". . . mutt doing in here again?"

". . . with me since she was a pup . . . cattle dog. Bred for this work."

Aggie sidled closer to the opening, her body tight against the jamb.

"Seems to me that her job is to babysit you, Burnpile. So you don't start any more fires."

Not again! She eased her head around the corner. Cabot was clambering up the tall stack of bales toward her brother. Burnaby pitched a forkful of alfalfa to the cows below, then punched the fork's tines into the hay beside him, waiting. As Cabot reached the top, Burnaby dropped to one knee and rested his arm over Pi's back, his chin above the dog's muzzle.

Her brother was feeding cows—with Pi, like always. That was his job. So why was Cabot harassing him?

"What do you mean?" Burnaby sounded confused.

"You got a little carried away at your house, didn't you? When I heard someone set that blaze, I thought of you. Does Loomis know about your little pyromania hobby?"

Burn won't answer him. Her brother never defended himself when anyone teased him. But these were serious accusations. She wanted to shout at that awful man, shout that she did it, that she lit that fire and that he should leave her brother alone. She wished that Burnaby would stand up for himself for once. But as she predicted, he raised his head and focused on something past her, outside.

"For whatever reason, you burned your house down. Then Auntie Nora brings you home like a stray cat." She saw Cabot eye the pitchfork. "Bad enough when you just came here to milk."

"During the school year I only work weekends. Every summer I work full-time."

"And now you *live* here, invading my territory. How convenient."

Burnaby hiccoughed and stood up. Aggie took that as a sign that he heard the man.

Pi leveled her head at Cabot, unblinking. The man eyed the dog warily.

"And Celia is part of my territory."

"Celia?"

"I saw you with her at Mender's barn."

"You did?" Burnaby tilted his head, perplexed.

"Your truck was parked at Mender's yesterday. You were in the barn, right?"

"Yes, I was."

"Celia was leaving there when I drove up. What were you two doing?"

"We worked on birds. Talked."

"She's off limits for you."

With fists balled at his hips, elbows and jaw protruding, Cabot took a step toward Burnaby.

Pi bared her teeth and crouched, ready to vault. Burnaby grabbed her collar, and Cabot seized his chance. He sprang for the pitchfork and jerked it out of the hay. The dog lunged, but Burnaby's grip restrained her. Cabot lowered the fork and aimed.

"Get that mutt outta my barn." He waggled the tines at Pi.

The dog wrenched hard, broke loose from Burnaby's hold and hurled herself at Cabot, who caught her with the sharp tines and thrust them deep into her chest. For a split second Cabot and Burnaby stared at the impaled, squirming animal, then Cabot yanked the fork free. Pi writhed, whining on the bale between them, then slipped off the stack. She twisted in the air and yelped, hit the concrete, and flopped, silent.

Aggie clamped her hands over her mouth, stifling a shriek as Burnaby, wailing eerily, scrambled down the stack and huddled over his limp dog. He ran his fingers fast down her bones, checked her eyes and gums, tamped the bleeding holes. Felt for a pulse.

For a moment Aggie saw Cabot as a terrified little boy, his cheeks flushed, mouth crumpled, eyebrows high. As if it were all an accident. Then his jaw tightened and his eyes narrowed into slits.

"Stay away from my girl."

Burnaby slid his arms under Pi, hoisted her gently and rushed from the barn, his head bent low over the dog. Outside, an engine turned over, rumbled. Wheels spun, bit, and a vehicle sped down the driveway.

Immobilized, a tremor grew in Aggie's gut, then spread into her shoulders and limbs until her body juddered. Her mind raced. She had to run from this horrible place, from this terrible man. *Run.* She tried to palpate her trembling, useless legs. Her fingers refused to engage.

She buried her head in her hands. If Cabot heard her sobs, she didn't care. If he caught her, she would make her limbs work, would fight him with her teeth and fingernails. She'd get away from him and run for help. Tell on him. He wouldn't get away with this.

But Cabot didn't hear her. Stock-still, he watched Burnaby's retreat, then cocked his head at the whine of shifting gears as they faded down the road. Finally, he rammed the fork back into the top of the stack and muttered under his breath. "Leaving early, aren't you, Burnaby? Loomis don't like shirkers." He cracked his knuckles and took his time climbing down. Then he felt in his pocket again and headed Aggie's way, looming as he approached. She cowered against the doorway as he marched right past her, downhill, toward the trail to the river.

CABIN

I WAS THINKING ABOUT MIND-PAINTING the next morning when I jogged to the farm and found Cabot in the dairy's office, next to a chlorine-scrubbed room with a stainless tank the size of a Volkswagen van. He sat at a fly-specked steel desk, writing notes from a list of cows' ear tag numbers onto pages splashed with coffee and who knew what else. He laid his pen down and grinned.

"Couldn't stay away, could you?" As I stepped toward him, he pointed at a chair. "That's far enough, unless you want to wear my cologne."

I did not. Manure splattered his coveralls and neck; cow blood freckled his cheek and ear. I slumped into the bucket chair opposite him. My posture matched my pout.

"Uh-oh. You look like you could start a fight in an empty house. What's up?"

"I'm seeing gray skies. I need to get out of here."

"That can be arranged." He leaned back in his seat and propped his boots on a corner of the grungy desk.

"My dad's harassing me, and Gram keeps pressuring me to talk to him. He and I had *planned* on Lake Chelan, remember? Instead, he dumped me here."

"Sorry you're not liking the company, my lady. What am I then, a way to kill time?"

Actually, he was just that, but in a scrumptious sort of way.

"Of course not. You're the redeeming part of this whole mess. When I'm with you, I don't think about the cabin."

"Cabin?" Cabot dropped his feet to the floor and cocked his head, his radar swiveled toward me.

"Yeah. The one I told you about. Daddy and I were going to paint the outside, build some Adirondack chairs like Gram's. Swim, hike, read. Water-ski. We got a new boat last year."

"Too bad. So who's there now?" He raised an eyebrow. Lifted and lowered his heels.

"Nobody. It's sitting there empty, overlooking that lake, with that clear water lapping the dock like an invitation."

"Maybe we need to accept. Can you get inside?"

I felt a smile climb my face. *The cabin.* No Greyhound necessary. "Oh, yeah. I have the key at Gram's." I tapped my chin, thinking through the week. "You have Wednesdays and Thursdays off, right? We could leave Tuesday after your shift, hang out for a couple of days. Do some skiing. Be back before your shift on Friday."

This plan would give Daddy convulsions. *Yeah.* If I disappeared, that would punish him all right. Gram would have to tell him I was missing. He would wet his pants when he got the call. By the time I got back from the lake, he'd be so deranged he'd come get me and fly me to Houston himself.

Then I thought of Aggie. I had seen heartbreak on the faces of her family and the neighbors searching for her. Disappearing would be downright cruel. I would phone Gram once we arrived and let her know where I was—and that Cabot was with me. That would set Daddy in motion. "Let's do it." I flew from the chair, clapping.

His eyes sparked with . . . uh . . . longing? No, not so affectionate as that. More like the eagerness in Gram's dogs when I waggled steak gristle in front of them, then made them wait until I released them to eat it. *Ravenous.*

I was too jazzed about my ride to Chelan to care.

———✥———

With my escape in the works, I tapped him on the head and danced out of the office, into the sparkling day. Mid-July's morning light webbed me with its rays and towed me away from the road and across the fields, toward the woods below Gram's where I had played as a child. A heron rose from the pasture like an aging pterodactyl and landed in the grass closer to the trees.

In the forest, I crossed over a nurse log to the brimming spring above the pond, where the heron's large, twiggy tracks decorated the mud. Last time I had been to this pool, my granddaddy had braced himself on the mossy log and sipped the sweet water. "Purest in the county," he'd said. Remembering, I bent to copy him, and was drinking straight from the pool when I caught sight of something in my peripheral vision.

A footprint.

Water went down the wrong pipe when I saw it; I got up choking. This was no cryptic tiptoe, but an honest-to-goodness, child's footprint. Barefoot. Fresh.

"Aggie?" I pivoted, calling. "Aggie? You here?" A thrush's song whirled through the trees as I waited, listening. "You don't have to hide from me. I can help you." I circled outward from the pool in a snail shell's curve, a girl-finding Fibonacci spiral that led me to another close-set pair where she had lingered in the squishy earth. She must have drunk here, too. I curled away from the pond looking for more, but the leafy litter hid any other signs of her.

My thoughts raced. Aggie was nearby. Aggie was *alive*.

Search teams from here to the moon had scoured the area for her repeatedly, with nothing to show for it but those vomited berries in the hours after she vanished. I had seen those prints in the garden, *briefly*. No one had found anything since. Now here were these footprints, undeniable.

This was the deal: Aggie was hiding. Not lost, not dead. Hiding.

I tore back to the house to tell Gram and found her and Cabot sitting on the porch with glasses of lemonade. Since I'd left the dairy, he had finished work and scrubbed clean. Plaid shirt, Wrangler jeans, cowboy boots. Dressed for town.

"Footprints! Aggie's!" Gasping for breath, I waved them toward me. "You gotta see."

Gram rose quickly, but Cabot didn't move. "Hold on, Celia. Slow down," he said. "What *exactly* are we talking about here?"

"The little pool above the forest pond. Fresh footprints." I tugged his arm. "C'mon." Gram had already started for the woods. The dogs ran ahead of her, chasing the heron I had spotted earlier until it flew into the trees.

Cabot stalled until Gram crossed the hill. "Where did you go? I've been here for half an hour." His arms snared me. "My girl. I need to know where you are."

"In the *woods*, Cabot. I *found* her!"

"A few prints. Far cry from finding the elusive Agate Hayes."

"You're just jealous, Mr. Search and Rescue." I wrested myself from his hold, poked him in the ribs, and skipped sideways until he followed.

"I don't see anything, honey." Gram bent at the waist over the pool's muddy shore. Across the water, Clover jumped at the heron perched high overhead, splashing each time she landed. Zip spun in place and barked at the disinterested bird.

"Call them off, Gram." I snagged Zip's collar and hauled her from the mud. "It's right—" Dog prints riddled the ground. "It *was* here." Cabot watched from the trail, arms folded.

Gram backtracked to me. "I suppose," she said, stooping low over the pummeled earth.

"Hold on. There are more." I hurried to the pair of prints. But where Aggie had most certainly stood, a rock the diameter of a Frisbee pressed into mud.

"They were *right here*!" I pried up the stone. An impression of its underbelly had replaced any sign of the child.

"Under that rock?" Gram peered at me as if I'd slipped a cog.

"The *rock* wasn't there before."

"*Sure*, Celia." Cabot exaggerated a slow nod. "Neither was that tree."

"But I—"

"I know you want to find her, honey. We all do. But we can't let our imaginations fool us now, can we?" Gram's cheeks sagged. I tried to explain, but she held a finger to my lips, whistled for the dogs, and headed home.

Cabot was studying the ground around the pool. "What were you thinking, Celia? Dirty trick to play on an old lady, even if she is giving you grief."

"I wasn't—" I kicked at the stone. Stubbed my toe. Started back up the trail, away from that miserable pool.

"Hey, hey, hey. Hold on." He grabbed my arm and pulled me toward a downed log, onto his lap. "What time does Mender go to bed?"

I sat stiffly. No use explaining. They didn't believe me? *Fine.* I'd find her on my own.

"About nine. She reads for a while. She'll be asleep by ten."

"That works. I'll pick you up by the road tomorrow night at ten thirty." He settled his chin on my shoulder. Lowered his voice. "If we drive straight through, we should get to the lake before four. Neighbors won't see us arrive at that hour, either."

"There aren't any close neighbors. Nobody will be nosing around. We'll have the place all to ourselves."

I tried to stand, but he held me there, his mouth by my ear. His breath smelled metallic. "We may never want to leave."

A worm of fear crawled up my spine. What had I done?

I tore at his hands.

"Let go of me, Cabot."

He laughed and squeezed me tighter.

Not funny. I bent forward until he relaxed his arms, and I rolled off his knees onto the ground. I couldn't leave for the cabin yet. Aggie was hiding in the woods, possibly within shouting distance. Who else would have planted that rock on her tracks? I would find her before I would go anywhere.

"About tomorrow." I scrambled for an excuse. "I can't just disappear. Gram will call my dad and they'll have the cops hunting for me within hours. You'd be in deep trouble. I'm not eighteen yet, remember?"

"Oh, yeah?" He seemed surprised. Did he pay attention to *anything* I said?

"Um, I'm *sixteen*? A *minor*? If we're taking off, I have to make Gram think I'm staying with some friend from the berry field, so she doesn't come after me. We need to buy ourselves time to make the trip."

This little excursion wouldn't work, anyway. If I called Gram from Chelan to kick Daddy into gear, she'd have Cabot arrested. But if Gram thought I was with a friend, she'd have no *reason* to call Daddy, so what would be the point?

Cabot's eyebrows crouched. "Buy ourselves time. Yeah. Next week." He pulled me to my feet and kissed me, his lips unyielding. Made me think of a cattle brand. When he slid his hands around my waist, he clutched at me, and not in a good way.

I pushed against his chest and forced a smile. "See you tomorrow. I'm going to help Gram feed the kits."

He released his hold. I knew his glare hung on me as I trotted away, but I didn't look back. Despite the warm day, I was shivering by the time I reached the house. I checked windows, expecting him to show up at the door any minute, but after he emerged from the woods, he cut across the lawn and drove off without saying goodbye. Gram watched my hand shake as I lifted the raccoon's bottle out of the steamy water in the sink.

"You all right, Celia?" I nodded, but she wasn't convinced. "Of course you want to find her."

"I saw those footprints, Gram."

"I know, honey. I know." She patted my head as if I were a puppy. "You look a little peaked. Something happen with Cabot?"

There she went, prying again. "I'm fine, Gram. Cabot and I are fine. And I'm sick of you acting like we're not. Like *I'm not*!"

"Oh, dear, you—"

I threw the bottle into the sink; water splashed onto the counter, the cupboards, the floor.

"I care about you, Celia. Want what's best for you."

"Yeah. What you think is best. What about *what I want*?" I tramped to my room and locked the door.

How would she know what was best for me? Times had changed since she was sixteen, in, what, the 1930s? I'd have to figure this out myself. But I knew two things: Aggie was in those woods. And something about Cabot scared me.

27
—
AGGIE

CACHE

AFTER CABOT DESCENDED the haystack, Aggie guessed his
destination. When he bulled his way through a thicket toward the
abandoned farm, she scooted into the brush, rubbed her sweaty palms
on her shirt, and sipped teaspoons of air to calm her erratic breath. If
she circled behind the stone chimney, she would have an unimpeded
view of the root cellar.

At the clearing, the door to the underground room already stood
ajar. She edged past a tangle of blackberry vines, wiped her brimming
eyes, and crouched behind the chimney. A scraping sound came from
inside the cellar, made by something rough. Cabot hadn't appeared
to be carrying anything that would make that noise. What else had
he hidden in there? And why?

She waited until he emerged and strode toward the trail, then
began counting. At fifty-two, she no longer heard him. At one

193

hundred, she crept to the cellar door, propped it open with a stick, and stepped into the small, dim room.

Not much to see. River rock walls. Heavy beams across a low ceiling. Plank shelves. A floor of packed earth, cool on her bare feet. Her eyes adjusted and she noticed a silty layer coating everything horizontal: dust from an overhead ventilation hole, she figured. Years of dirty cobwebs, interrupted only by mouse trails and droppings, stretched across the shelves. The place was humid. Undisturbed.

And too empty. Apart from scuff marks on the dirt floor, she saw no evidence of recent activity and nothing on the shelves, though Cabot had walked inside at least twice, leaving caps and probably something else. She panned the room. Whatever he had hidden here, she would find. She would scour every inch of the place, would uncover *something* that would prove his threat.

She couldn't see onto the top two shelves, much less reach the narrow highest one. If anything was lying flat up there, she would miss it, unless she climbed the planks. If Cabot returned, he would find her hanging like a monkey. She breathed fast at the danger. What if he trapped her?

Again she checked outside, then dropped to her belly and squinted into the space beneath the bottom shelf, where dusty webs waved like flags when she blew on them. A startled wolf spider the size of a quarter scurried past, and she flinched. *Dad said wolf spiders don't spin.* So what species had woven all these webs? Would they bite her?

Not if she was fast. She hesitated, then thrust her hand into the recess and swiped. Nothing there, either. Her eyes lifted to the hundreds of rocks lining the walls. One of them had to be loose. But which one? Where?

Spiders, she quickly realized, helped rather than hindered her search. Where the dusty strands laced over the wall or shelving or formed a filmy barrier between planks, she moved on without lingering. But where the filaments were broken? Clues.

She had inspected halfway up the rear wall when her breath caught. *There.* Webs had been cleared from a foot-long section partially hidden behind a vertical support post. On the shelf, a chalky grit and some soil particles dotted the dusty surface. And something had rested there, marking the layered deposit.

Bingo.

She fingered the first stone in the web-free opening and tried to jiggle it. It didn't budge.

But the stone below it did. Tense, she gripped the curve of the softball-shaped river rock and tugged. Powder sifted to the ledge below as she pulled the stone free, exposing an earth-lined cubby. She set the stone on the shelf and sized up the dark opening. What was he hiding in there that would be worth all this effort?

It was empty—at least straight in and to the left. But then she patted around the corner to the right and released the breath she didn't know she'd been holding. *Yes!* She extracted a syringe—like the one she used to squirt water at their rooster when he came after her, only smaller. This one was about the size of her dad's thumb, with clear liquid in it and something scrawled along its length. She moved to the doorway for light. *Ketamine*, whatever that was. She set it on the shelf and reached again. *Yep.* Just as she thought. The baggie she had seen Cabot carry inside, full of cap rolls.

Anything else? This time her fingers ticked a sealed bag of wooden matches like the ones Burnaby carried and a few paper circles like those he tore when he was nervous. These were her brother's too. What did Cabot want with all this stuff? Why was he nosing around in her brother's things? She wanted to jab him with that pitchfork like he had jabbed Pi.

All that remained in the cubby was a small box. Her dirty fingers smudged the lid as she opened it, and her mouth fell open. *From Aunt Nora's dresser!* Even in the dimness, she could identify that amber agate. She held it to the light. Recognized the seams arching through it like branches. Aunt Nora would miss it for sure. Aggie and Mama had made the necklace a few years back, for her aunt's fortieth birthday.

———⚟———

"See, Aggie? Like sunlight on a winter tree. This will be perfect." Mama had set an agate the size of a robin's egg in the pooling sunlight. Light bounced in the translucent pebble and caught on the ebony threads tracing through its interior. Her mother stroked the surface, rapt. "Most stones want me to lick 'em—or waves to wash them—before they shine. Not my agates. Give 'em a little sun and they glow from the inside." Her mother smiled at her. "Like you."

Aggie held the stone steady while Mama glued a bell cap over its narrow end. The glue dried overnight on the kitchen window ledge before Aggie threaded a skinny rawhide strip through the top of the cap. Mama had knotted the ends together.

Aggie spun the pendant on the dangling hide, aching at the memory—and at the anger she'd aimed at her mother. She held the stone against her cheek, longing to apologize for her sneaky disobedience and her hateful, fire-spreading thoughts. Wishing she could revoke them. Rewind time.

No way Cabot could have this agate. She'd return it to her aunt. For Mama.

Sweat beaded her upper lip as she imagined Cabot opening the empty box, livid that someone had found his cache. Still, she *had* to take the necklace *now*, before he could haul it off and steal it from Aunt Nora forever.

She rolled the agate over in her hand, the inner etchings faint in the murky room. Resolutely, she passed the cord over her head and tucked the necklace inside her shirt, patting the small bulge it made near her sternum. She closed the lid, stowed box and bags and syringe into the cubby precisely as before, and slid the river rock back into the wall. The door latch dropped into place behind her as she crept into the sunshine.

All that powdery dust. Those dirty old webs. Aggie's eyes and nose itched. When rubbing them didn't help, she made her way to the forest pool, where she dunked her face and blinked underwater. *Much better.* She stood and shook her head like a puppy, then climbed an access tree.

None too soon. Celia, heavy-footed, sashayed down the trail, lowered her face to the water and drank. As the black-haired girl raised her head, she coughed and touched something in the soft mud.

Oh no oh no oh no. Aggie shrank against the trunk as Celia, crouching low, crawled around the shore until she came to the spot where Aggie had stood. Celia circled the pool, her eyes on the ground. Aggie curled her muddy toes, cringing as Celia returned to the first footprint, inspected it, and sprinted toward the house.

They found me. Aggie dropped to the ground, frantic. At a dead run, she took off in the opposite direction. Leaping, crashing blindly through the brush, she ran until her lungs cried uncle and she bent over, hands on her knees, sucking air, grasping for a plan.

Only one made sense. She had to go back. Return to the pool and confuse Celia. Get rid of the footprints before the girl showed them to others. But how? If she tried to scrape or dig or pound out the prints, they would know. She massaged her temples, thinking. *Cover them. I can cover them.* She turned and bounded back to the water.

She took too long to find the rock. Too long to carry it and press it over the pair of footprints. Dogs were barking. Coming closer. *Hide! Now!* The remaining footprint shouted at her, untouched. Her failure nearly collapsed her. But she climbed instead.

A heron balanced on a branch high over the pool as Mender's pursuing dogs burst through the undergrowth. Mender appeared behind them, ignoring the bird and the dogs leaping for it as she read the mud. *She knows!* A few more steps and Mender would see the footprint, too.

Then Celia came down the hill with Cabot and caught a dog's collar. They all hovered over the doughy ground, but Aggie's footprint was gone, obliterated by the feet of bird-crazy setters.

LIE

HIDDEN IN BRANCHES near the pond, Aggie watched Mender trudge up the trail behind the dogs. Celia and Cabot stayed behind, talking. Their words sounded mumbly, and Celia worked her hands as if she was scared. Then Cabot kissed her—*ew*—and Celia hurried away from him.

Celia should be afraid. Cabot killed things.

As she ran her thumb over Nora's agate, the murder again consumed her, vivid: the pitchfork's tines punching into Pi, the dog flailing in the air, that single yelp, over and over. She smelled the blood seeping out of the animal's slack body, felt the fur Burn's hands clutched as he held Pi to his chest and ran.

Where had Burnaby taken her?

Pressing tears overpowered her, and she wept for her brother and his little dog. Pi was Burnaby's best friend in all the world. Now she was dead, too. First Mama and Dad, then Pi. *And me—or at least Burn thinks so.*

Oh, she wanted to go to him. Her heart squeezed under her ribs and her core chilled, despite the summer heat. She put her hand under her nostrils and focused on the breath filling her lungs with air, keeping her going.

She pictured Burnaby closing the catechism book during kitchen church, answering for her, reciting from memory there in front of the stove.

———❧

"Lord's Day Nineteen . . . Second, by his power, he defends us and keeps us safe from all enemies."

"Dad. He does not."

"That's my girl, calling life play-by-play." Mirth had crinkled her dad's eyes. "When time makes you more of a historian, you'll see otherwise. His power all around you, inside you. His safety, right here." He tapped her temple, then touched the corner of her eye. "Watch for it."

———❧

For Pi, too? She cried harder as she wove her way back to the homestead, pacing loops of sorrow around the pioneer's chimney, tangles of brush, and old stumps, traipsing on her callused feet through miner's lettuce, jack-in-the-pulpit and wild bleeding hearts. She tore away handfuls of grass and threw them into the air, keening. When she stubbed her foot on a rock half submerged in the cushiony ground, she hurled it into the undergrowth and wailed.

But instead of a thud when the stone landed, a muffled plunk echoed back. A splash from somewhere deep. She hiccoughed and dropped to her knees, alert. *Water?* As she crawled to the rock's landing spot, her arm broke through the ground cover into nothing but air. By reflex, she flung out her other arm and grabbed for a handhold to stop her fall. Her fingers snagged an embedded stone at the hole's edge, arresting her headfirst plunge into an abandoned well.

She lay there shocked at her discovery, stunned by the close call. *Upside down.* That's how she would have landed in this shaft. On her head. She put her hands on either side of the opening.

Not quite three feet wide, she figured, and at least deeper than their flagpole. She shuddered. She would feel so . . . what was the word? . . . *claustrophobic* down there. Even if she screamed her loudest, who would hear her? And headfirst? Her nose and mouth would have been underwater. She wouldn't have screamed at all. She would have drowned.

But she hadn't.

Safe again. She thought of the cougar. And the maggots.

Her rapid breathing calmed. She sat back to inspect the hole, lined with river rocks. Why did the pioneers even want a stupid well, this close to the river? The reason was probably a hundred years old, like the farm. She tossed in another stone. A splash answered. If she kept her head out of the way, a wiggly reflection of sky and leaves shone at her from the water below. A weasel popped over a tree root and chucked a warning at her, twitching his black-tipped tail. Aggie wiped her eyes. *Okay, little guy.* Yes. She would be a weasel now. But not like before. She wasn't play-acting like a kid anymore. That was baby stuff. This was serious business. Now she needed every ounce of a weasel's stealth and cunning—and ferocity—to expose Cabot and put a stop to all his meanness. She squared her shoulders and turned toward the dairy.

For the next hour, she hugged a fat limb on the walnut tree between her aunt and uncle's house and the main barn. The lush leaves hid her well, and she took in a full view of the house's porch, both doors, the barnyard, and the start of the river trail that led past the homestead. She could watch Cabot's comings and goings from here. When her brother returned—*if* he did, after what happened to Pi—she would watch him, too.

She startled at a movement in the kitchen window and sat up. Cabot was in the house again. Her reflex sent some lichen fluttering onto the lawn. Did he see it? No, he was looking down, his curls bobbing under the frilly valance. His head dipped toward the sink as he drank from the faucet. Then the screen door creaked open, and he slid his feet into barn boots on the stair.

Seething, Aggie ran her thumb over her canine teeth and wished they had sharp points. She wanted to jump on him and bury fangs into the back of his neck, like a weasel would do to a rabbit. What did he steal this time?

Cabot was halfway across the barnyard when the Eppings' brown Buick drove into view. At the car's appearance, he bent over as if he were picking something up and, still stooping, pivoted direction. Then he stood and strode back toward the porch, as if he were coming to meet them. *So they won't know you were inside. I'm on to you, dog-killer.*

When the car rolled to a stop, Cabot opened the door for Aunt Nora and wrested a grocery bag from the back seat. At the kitchen door, her aunt patted his cheek, took the bag from him and carried it inside. Uncle Loomis slanted his hip into the car, crossed his arms, and watched.

"You're good to us, Cabot. Above and beyond."

Cabot sauntered back to him, smiling. "No problem." *Fake.* Aggie clenched her jaw.

"I mean it. We're thankful. What with Nora's family and the fire and all, we've been too preoccupied to pay attention around here like we should." He cleared his throat.

Cabot shielded his eyes against the sun and fixed them on her uncle. "Speaking of Nora's family, we had a rough scene here today."

"Oh?" Uncle Loomis's inflection rose.

"That dog of Burnaby's. 'Member how I said she'd growled at me a few times?"

Her uncle nodded and uncrossed his arms. Inclined his head and stepped toward Cabot.

"I was helping Burnaby throw hay to the cows, and the dog attacked me. I lifted the fork to stop her, but she jumped right into it. I feel terrible about it."

Aggie's mouth dropped open. *Liar!*

"She almost knocked both of us off the stack before she went overboard. Hit the concrete hard."

Uncle Loomis worked his jaw as if chewing his tongue; his forehead wrinkled. "Too bad. That dog's been Burnaby's shadow since the kid was little." His voice sounded like gravel. "Will she make it?"

"Doubtful. I tried to fend her off without hurting her, but the tines caught her pretty hard. Burnaby took off with her, hasn't come back. Didn't show for his milking, but I got it done."

Doubtful? Aggie shifted on the branch, furious. Pi was dead when she hit the ground. *You speared her. You wanted her dead!*

Uncle Loomis hung his head. Cleared his throat again and ran his hand under his nose. "Sometimes those old cow dogs get too protective for their own good. Start seeing bogeymen."

"Yeah, I guess."

"These things happen, Cabot. Don't be too tough on yourself. Sounds like the dog couldn't be trusted anymore. At least now she won't bite some unsuspecting visitor." Uncle Loomis squeezed his shoulder. "Thanks for milking for Burnaby. Poor kid."

Aggie measured Cabot's expression but couldn't gauge him. Obviously, her uncle couldn't either.

"And there's more." Cabot drew something from his pocket and opened his hand. "I'm worried about Burnaby for other reasons, too."

"What's this?" Her uncle bent close to some torn red paper in Cabot's outstretched palm.

"Spent caps. I saw Burnaby in the calf shed near the sawdust pile yesterday. He was pounding these on the concrete with his pocketknife. He even lit a strip on fire and threw it in the shavings. Walked away while it was still burning. I stepped on it, so no harm done, but he could have started something big." Cabot handed her uncle a charred ribbon of caps. "Why is he doing that?"

Fresh dread descended on Aggie as she stared at the paper in Cabot's hand. True, Burn fired off cap rolls sometimes, but he would never spark them near a sawdust pile. Or would he, if he really got upset? Or was Cabot making the whole thing up? If not in the calf shed, where else had he seen Burnaby light them?

Worry creased Uncle Loomis's face. "He lit a lot of caps when he was younger. Nora's sister said it calmed him down." He handed the red paper back to Cabot. "His parents spent considerable time teaching him other ways to cope, I never guessed he'd still be setting them off. I'll talk to him."

"Just dangerous, is all." Cabot opened his mouth to say something, then clamped it shut and shoved the evidence in his pocket.

"What?"

"Now I'm not accusing him, Loomis, but I heard that the fire at his house may have been intentionally set. Do you think . . . ?" Cabot's question dangled, unanswered. "I'd hate to see a barn go up in flames or any animals . . ." He shook his head. "Can't take those kinds of chances."

Aggie wanted to jump from the tree and pound on the liar. Tell her uncle what really happened. But Uncle Loomis liked Cabot. He would never believe her.

Loomis muttered something Aggie couldn't hear, then slapped Cabot's back. "Maybe I'll give him a few days off. The boy loved that dog."

Cabot walked to the milkhouse with his head down. Still, Aggie caught the satisfaction in the rise of his brows and cheeks—and in that forced upward curve of his mouth. Wild-eyed, she leapt from the tree and ran to the woods.

29
—
CELIA

SPEED

WHAT WAS I THINKING? If a duck had my brains, it would fly north for the winter. Skipping off to Lake Chelan with Cabot would be even worse than flying north. Much worse, considering how he acted at the pond. Sure, I'd still hang out with him until I earned my money, but on my terms. Our cabin would remain *unoccupied*. How had I been so oblivious? Once again, I'd misjudged a man. First Burnaby. Now, Cabot.

And maybe even my dad? I'd think about that later.

For two days I'd been wondering what Burnaby would say about Cabot. He worked with him, after all. Knew him in a context I didn't. I checked the barn for Burn repeatedly, but he must have gone to Seattle. Mender said his mom had taken a turn for the worse.

How had I so misinterpreted Cabot? He'd been filling every corner of my life that Gram would allow and had seemed just fine, talking about how he'd own a dairy someday, or what car he'd buy next, or how he wanted to reorganize Loomis's milking strings. Regular farm guy stuff, I imagined. And he planned to study business part-time at the community college. That would be good for him. Make his conversation more interesting, maybe.

Frankly, I hadn't cared what he talked about. His kisses made up for whatever he lacked, helped me forget my family wreckage. And since the afternoon I interrupted him on that blanket by the river, he hadn't pushed me for more, either.

Until I invited him to Chelan.

———⋏⋏

The day after we postponed our trip, I hurried home from the berries, but he never showed. I didn't see him the next day, either. I checked the windows for his car so many times that finally I laced on my running shoes and jogged toward the dairy to find him. I figured I'd tell him we couldn't go to the cabin after all, then suggest we go somewhere even more fun. Local. I'd cheer him up. Kiss him. He'd forget Chelan and be his former self in no time.

A familiar tune pestered me all the way to the farm. Only when I turned at the dairy's lane did I recognize it—and how I danced to it. By running to that barn, I was groveling again, chasing Cabot the same way I chased my mother when she was upset with me, even if it wasn't my fault. Afraid of rejection, was that it? Thinking Cabot's or my mother's anger was mine to mend, because they both tried to make me responsible for it? Thinking I needed to placate them to keep them from being mad at me?

Well, no thank you. I would hold my ground about Chelan and if he didn't like it, if he got angry, so be it. His anger was *his*. I was *not*. I made a quick U-turn and hurried home.

———⋏⋏

The following morning, Cabot's day off, he showed up at Gram's at nine, smiling like he hadn't left in a snit three days before. What was the deal? Did he think I would sit there every day waiting for him? What about phoning me and asking if he could come over, instead of assuming?

I should have been out there in the forest looking for Aggie when he arrived. She'd been missing for close to three weeks already, out there eating twigs and berries or whatever. Sleeping with raccoons.

But when he grinned at me, I wavered. The girl was out there *by choice*, and plenty of people were searching. Why did I think she'd let *me* find her? A balmy summer day beckoned. Today would be better with Cabot in it. I wanted to feel his arms around me again and forget that I was practically an orphan. I could at least spend a few hours with him and hunt for Aggie in the afternoon.

"Hey, girl. Have I ever got a day planned for you." He bent over and kissed me full on the mouth, his eyes shining.

"Do you now?" That face. Those lips. Whether or not I wanted him to, the man woke me up inside.

Just go with it. I heard Meredith across the miles.

———⁂———

Mer had attended our school for three months when some senior boys came in the library and sat at a table near my study carrel. When they mentioned her name, I pulled my feet under me, so they wouldn't know I was there. I didn't hear everything, but one guy said something about her strumming his banjo. Another, snickering, said she made him feel so good he wanted to sing. Then their voices muffled, and they all started laughing. That's when Bradley King whammed his books down in the carrel beside me. That boy has the world's worst B.O., so I got up and snuck out the back way.

I told Meredith. "They, uh, said you were . . ."

"I was what? Out with it."

"That you were a fun, *fun* girl. Sounded like you were part of a band."

She laughed. Said our school was one long, hot gig, and she'd play every chance she got. "Better than drugs," she said.

Drugs. Yeah. I guess all those hookups were like drugs to her. She sure never called them *love*, though I thought her eyes welled when Greer McWilliams dumped her.

Mer had her reasons. Her parents were on the ropes. I got that. Where did Daddy's love for Mother get him? Still, was it good for my friend to give herself away like that? Was it worth losing herself for the pleasure—or the comfort? How would she ever gather up all those pieces? How would she find herself again?

How would I, if I took her advice?

———

"Grab your swimsuit," Cabot said. "River level's dropped. We can float the South Fork." An inflated inner tube poked from the Camaro's trunk.

"Um . . . Can't. I tore it the other day." A ridiculous lie, but being mostly naked with the man would not help me figure out our relationship.

He ran his eyes over me, assessing my cutoffs and tank top. "Not a problem. You can wear that. Bring a change of clothes."

"How long you expect to be gone?"

"'Til dinner. Why? You got other plans?" He stood with his feet planted wide, his hands clasped behind him.

"I do." I smiled weakly. "Helping Mender today. You and I have three hours, max." Through the screen door, I saw Gram working at the sink. Her head snapped up when I mentioned her. Eavesdropping.

And I was changing the rules between Cabot and me.

"Ohhh-kay. Plan B, then." He clicked his tongue, thinking, then called to Gram. "Want anything at the C Shop, Mrs. Burke?"

She raised her soapy palms. "Surprise me." Dropping her chin, she pointed at me. "I want you back here by noon. I'll have lunch ready. We'll get started after we eat."

I took the stairs by twos. Gram, frowning and holding a towel, stood on the porch and watched us drive off. From the corner of my eye, I glimpsed Burnaby's pickup, parked by the barn at last. After I got home, I would pick his brain about his coworker.

Birch Bay was half an hour away, Cabot said. He drove with one hand and rested his other first on the gearshift, then above my knee, his fingers wrapping my thigh like a shackle. He chewed a toothpick, pensive.

"How'd work go yesterday?" I asked. Some ice needed chipping here, but I would not get all needy and pry about how he spent our time apart. Better to float a general question, for starters.

"What do you think?" He sounded accusing, as if I had wounded him. Was he still teed off because I'd delayed Chelan? Or because I'd be doing something without him that afternoon? I didn't know. The quiet between us unsettled me, but I let it be. No need to rile the gator.

A few miles out, he suddenly punched the accelerator and veered into the opposing lane to pass a minivan—directly into the path of an oncoming dump truck. It was bearing down on us. Fast.

"Look out!" I screamed at him and grabbed for the wheel as the truck barreled toward us, its horn blaring. He flicked his wrist to the right, and the car swerved nimbly into the narrowing space between the truck and the van. Then he laughed at me.

"Never played chicken, have you, Celia?"

Trapped in that car, I was a bird in the jaws of a dog, waiting for the animal to chew. I crowded the door, my hand near the handle. Why had I agreed to this? Made myself so vulnerable? He *wanted* to scare me. *Why?*

He braked and drove slowly then, and his winning smile returned. At a stop sign at the top of a short hill, he pointed through the windshield toward the water. "Lummi Island's out past the point. We can take a ferry over there one of these days if you want. Walk on the beach and eat at a little café near the landing." I stared at him. This was crazy-making. Jekyll and Hyde.

The car cruised down to a two-lane crescent of pavement squeezed between a clutter of low, multicolored cabins and a bay of wide mud flats, peppered with people digging.

"Clam tide," Cabot said. "We won't be floating for a while yet."

"Butter clams?"

"Littleneck, Manila, Butter, Horse. Almost every variety's out there. Depends on which part of the beach. Most of those diggers are county locals. They know where to find the good ones." Cabot nodded at a small boy toddling in the mud, hugging a plastic shovel and dragging a bucket as his dad trailed him with a clam rake. "They start 'em early. It ain't like digging for razor clams at the ocean, but they can pretend."

Past the exposed shallows, toward the Strait of Georgia, smooth water held more of the San Juan Islands, floating like green dumplings in cool blue soup. Calming. I pulled in a warm, salty breath, held it in until my lungs wanted more, then blew between my pursed lips, forcing myself to relax into the festive beachfront. Teenagers strolling in clusters on the road's shallow shoulder turned and watched the shiny Camaro as it rumbled past.

"Speed limit of twenty-five feels like a cage, don't it, Celia? My car is crying to be let out."

Apparently, while I was taking in the view, he was thinking about racing. His gearshift knob said Hurst on it and had finger grips; the speedometer maxed out at 150 mph. "What's the fastest you've ever driven this thing?" I asked. Screaming past that minivan had seemed way too comfy for him.

"Over 130. On Highway 82, about midnight a year ago. I bought the car from a guy in Pasco—east of the mountains— and gave it a little test run on the way home. I was about to punch it over the top, but my radar detector went off." He tapped a black box sitting on the dash. "My friend."

"Didn't that scare you?"

Cabot shook his head, incredulous. "I felt like God."

"I bet." My hands sweated just thinking about it. Where else did this guy like to go fast?

At the far end of the bay, he parked in front of an old house painted a cheery yellow and with "The C Shop" in huge letters under the gable.

"Ah. The place you mentioned to Gram." I climbed out of the car and stepped under the shady porch awning.

He smacked his lips. "Candy worth the drive, including every flavor of jelly bean known to humankind." I would have followed him inside, but he blocked my path. "Stay here," he said. "I want to surprise Mender *and* you." Through the window, I saw him point as a lady scooped beans into two bags. I snatched at one when he came outside, but he held it overhead and spun away from me, laughing. "Hold your horses, girl. Wait 'til we get there."

Five minutes later, we arrived at the state park at the far end of the beach and lofted inner tubes across a driftwood log. I blinked toward the white ruffle of retreating waves in the distance. "You're an optimist," I said. "The tide's still going out."

"Luxury seating, instead." Cabot laid our tubes against the sun-bleached log and gestured for me to sit in one. I bounced on the edge twice and plopped in the middle as he pulled off his T-shirt and lay back on his tube, a bag of jelly beans in his lap.

My heart started racing. I couldn't take my eyes off him, lying there beside me as a warm, salty breeze blew over us. My mind braked, but the rest of me was drawn to him as if we were magnetized.

"Ready to guess flavors?" His head moved back and forth between a bean he was pinching and a card he pulled from the bag.

I swallowed slowly and shifted my eyes to the paper. "What's that, a cheat sheet?"

"Reference, girl. Jelly Belly has forty official flavors now." He ran the bean down the row of descriptions, searching for a match. "There it is." He rolled onto his side and held the bean poised between us. Then he lowered the candy onto my tongue. Watched me chew.

"That mouth of yours . . ."

"Stop, Cabot." I turned away from him, giggling nervously, but he stroked the side of my face until I felt like a cat, leaning into his touch.

"I have to concentrate." I exaggerated a gulp. "You giving clues?"

"Nope. Let your palate tell you."

Well, my palate and I hadn't talked much, and he could tell. I called cotton candy beans, lemonade; cantaloupe beans, peach. After eight or nine, they all tasted like variations of orange. Blurry orange. The only one I got right was licorice. I didn't care. The only taste I wanted was of him.

"Hm. You need a little help, I see." He leaned over me, his face inches from mine—and popped a white bean into my mouth. "What do you think?"

I chewed. "No clue. Good though."

He brushed my cheek with his nose and kissed me, lingering, before he pulled away and licked his lips. "Gotta be coconut."

I watched his tongue. "Cheater. Gimme that." I lunged for the card, but he swung it out of reach and held out another bean. Pink grapefruit. The entire tasting session grew more and more delicious, no matter which flavor he offered. I had decided to breeze right by my three-hour deadline, until he fed me a bad bean. Figuratively speaking.

"Having fun?"

I stopped chewing and nodded. His chocolate eyes gazed at me from under those thick lashes. "I am now." I walked my eyes over that gorgeous face.

"This is only the beginning, Celia. Wait 'til we get to the lake."

"About the lake—"

"When you changed your mind the other day, I thought you chickened out. After today, I know better. You want to go as much as I do."

"But I don't—"

He pressed his fingers to my lips, shushing me. "And when we have that place all to ourselves?" His hand coasted over the top of my head and down my neck. "Just wait, woman."

My brakes were squealing now. I pushed him off me and sat up. "Cabot, I like you. I really do. But we can't go to Chelan. It was a lousy idea. I was so mad at everyone and I wanted to get out of here. When you offered to take me . . ."

He slid stiffly back onto his tube, his jaw tight. An angry flush crept from his neck to his face.

"I'm sorry." I reached for his hand, but he pulled it away, ignoring me as he watched a woman haul a bucket of clams to her car. A black lab loped along the shore, dragging a piece of kelp.

A minute passed. Two. Gradually, his shoulders relaxed, and his features softened. He turned to me then, his eyes wide, as if someone had switched on a light bulb and he was seeing me for the first time.

"I don't believe you." He spoke so quietly I wasn't sure I'd heard him.

"What did you say?"

He shouted this time. "I said, I don't believe you." Then he laughed. "I get it. You're scared. I know you want to go, but you're afraid. Sure you are. I get that. You've never done anything like this before. There's always a first time, Celia. You just need a little encouragement." He ran the back of a finger down the side of my neck. "Leave it to me. I'll get you over there, and you'll be glad you went."

My skin went cold. I had heard a hundred times that when a girl said no, a guy should comply, no matter what. If he didn't, well, he'd be in deep weeds. I agreed completely. A girl should know she was safe—exactly the opposite of how I felt right then.

Why had I misled him? I had encouraged him by inviting him to sneak off to our empty cabin. And by coming out here and playing games. I had used him like a drug—and hadn't thought about how I would affect him. I was disgusted with myself. Dismayed.

Still. Even if I was an idiot, he had no right to me.

I stood and picked up my tube. "We better go."

The man jabbered all the way back to Gram's in an animated discourse about what we would do tomorrow and next week and when we went to Chelan. *Blah, blah, blah.* His words smeared. I couldn't think straight. I watched trees whir past, felt the engine growl through the floorboards. Smelled that musky Kouros cologne of his in my hair. I said nothing. Did he even notice?

At the gate, he turned off the car. "You don't have to go inside yet."

"Yeah, I do. Gram's waiting. I can walk from here." I gave him a feeble smile and reached for the door, but he grasped my arm.

"Here. For your grandmother." He handed me a small paper bag and pulled me sideways as I took it from him. Kissed me so hard his teeth sliced my lower lip. "I'll see you tomorrow, babe."

It wasn't a question.

If this were quicksand, I was sinking. I had to extricate myself before Cabot's next days off.

I closed the gate between me and his car and licked my bleeding lip.

MOTHER

GRAM MUST HAVE SEEN US sitting in Cabot's car at the end of the drive. By the time I walked in the front door, she was sliding grilled cheese sandwiches off the skillet. I dabbed the strap of my tank top against my lip and examined the cloth. No blood.

"Here you go, Gram. C Shop." I tossed Cabot's bag of jelly beans onto the counter and sat on a barstool. "Make 'em last. No more where those came from."

"Surely the store's not closing?" She unrolled the bag and sniffed the beans. "Mm. That place is a landmark."

"Nope. Going strong. On the other hand, the Celia-Cabot *stor-ee* is shutting down. We won't be going anywhere anytime soon."

"Oh?" She set a sandwich in front of me. I dunked it in the bowl of tomato soup already waiting on the counter. "I wondered why he left you at the gate."

"*I* left *him* down there so he wouldn't follow me. He wants to be with me every second." I shoved a bite in my mouth and talked through the food. "And he's getting pushy as a goat. What Cabot wants, Cabot gets. Or he'll keep trying." Mender set a bowl of sliced apples between us, her brows pinched. "Nobody will hijack me like that ever again. No ma'am. I've got better things to do."

"So did you tell him this?"

"Not in so many words. But I will. Next time he comes over." I wasn't as sure as I sounded. I worried a strand from my ponytail between my fingers and watched Gram's lips move as she ladled soup for herself. Was she praying? Right there at the stove? Couldn't she give it a *rest*? I was about to suggest that when the phone rang.

"I'll get it." Without thinking, I lifted the receiver off the wall phone, untangling the cord as I returned to my stool. "Hello. Burke residence."

"Finally."

I dunked my sandwich again.

"I've heard nothing but an answering machine at the house for days. There's no answer at the cabin. Tight-lipped receptionists at Campos Oil. How are you? Is your dad there?"

"Hello, Mother." Gram faced me, her ladle suspended over the pot. I dropped my sandwich; soup sloshed onto the counter. I was nine years old again. "No, he's working. How are you?"

"I'm fine. Really busy with the Franklin deal. That's why I left so, well, so suddenly, you know? So are you having fun at your grandma's?"

"Well, I—"

"Is Mender there? May I speak to her?"

"She is." I held the phone out to Gram, but she shook her head and returned the ladle to the pot. She flipped her hands, shooing the receiver back to me. "But she's not available." My voice quavered.

"I didn't want to involve you in this, but I have papers for your father to sign. Would you please have him call me?"

I jotted the number on my napkin. "I'll give him the message."

Then her voice again, quieter. "Thank you." Quieter, but not kinder. I knew the difference.

"Anything else?"

"No, just tell him time is of the essence."

"All right."

"And Celia?" *She said my name.* "I'm sure you're having an enjoyable stay. I'll try to see you when you get back. After this contract wraps up."

A dial tone sang through the earpiece and I hung up the phone. My teeth chattered. I leaned over my soup, my head in my hands. "I'm cold, Gram." She pulled a knitted throw off a living room chair and wrapped it around my shoulders. Rubbed my back.

"We'll get through this. You want to call your dad, or shall I?"

"I'm not sure. I need to think." Gram dragged the afghan over her arm as I slid off the stool. "I'm going for a walk by the river." Aggie ran to the woods when her life went haywire. So could I.

"Take your time. I'll be here when you get back."

———Ꮠ———

I could hardly see the ground through my tears. I'd just been stabbed. Stabbed in another Mother ambush. And to think Daddy had endured a zillion more.

I felt ashamed. And selfish. I had frozen Daddy out just like Mother iced me. I had railed at him about how he was like her, but I was blind as a one-eyed mole. The one acting like her? *Moi.*

Sure, my dad had left me here in Washington against my will, but what else could he do? I had backed him into a corner. I'd never have come with him, if I'd known he was leaving. And he'd never have let me stay in Texas if I were within a hundred miles of Meredith. He didn't like this mess any better than I did, but I had snarled at him and my gram as if they had ruined my life.

I had felt so . . . *justified*.

I stumbled past the garden. The first zinnias were showing color. I absently thought about snipping some for Gram's table. *Later*. Reality intruded.

My mother's voice thumped my eardrums. Or was it my own? Hadn't I blistered Daddy? Then when he called to make amends, I still wouldn't talk with him. Wouldn't forgive. And what did I do for an encore? I found the best-looking, scariest guy in Northwest Washington and nearly ran away to the cabin with him. I was as myopic as a wild hog.

Or was I?

My anger protected me, didn't it? Didn't it toughen me up so I could blow off people who hurt me, rather than melting into a puddle when they did? I stopped walking and imagined my face when I yelled at my dad—and at Gram.

I broke down and wept. Who was I kidding? My anger was merely a cover for my sadness. It didn't protect me at all. All that *monochrome*, as Burn put it, was keeping the right people at arm's length and holding the door wide open for Cabot.

Well. I'd just have to change trajectory. I could do that. Sure I could. Maybe Burnaby could give me pointers now and then, when I asked, of course. At the very least, I could quit thinking of myself so much. Stand in other people's shoes for once.

Or in their bare feet. I'd start with that little girl hiding somewhere in those trees—along that sneaky river. I'd show her she wasn't alone.

———— ⚘

At the old horse arena, the dogs jumped at the gate. I held my hands to the mesh; they licked my palms. "Not today, girls. You'll scare off Aggie." They whined until I crossed over the rise, where the Hawley's blue meander popped into view. *Where is she, river?* Where did she sleep? What did she eat?

Did Aggie know how near she was to Burnaby? When her brother wasn't at the hospital, he spent most of his time between Gram's place, the dairy, and those woods. Had she seen him at the farm? Spotted him as he crawled through the brush looking for her? Was *that* why she was hanging around here? If so, I could narrow my search grid.

But what made me think I'd find her by myself? After searchers came up empty downstream, they returned and covered this area repeatedly. I suspected that neither I, nor anyone, would find Aggie without her permission—unless she was trapped. Or dead.

I panned the woods. She was probably watching me that very minute.

So I wouldn't hunt her. I would *draw* her to me with food and whatever else she might need—like that sweatshirt. She would hear my voice, find the provisions, watch me and decide to trust me. *Then* she would come to me. Being found would be her decision, not mine.

Good thing I was breaking up with Cabot. There weren't enough hours for Aggie and him and those miserable strawberries. This could take time, taming a wild, scared girl. But how much time? How long could she last out there?

"Aaaaa-gee, Aaaaa-gee." I sang into the forest and wandered farther downhill, to the first of Burnaby's bone plates. Did she watch her brother visit the anthills? Had she seen us together?

I raised my voice. "I know your brother, Aggie. Anything you want me to tell him? He misses you." I stepped into a sunny patch away from the mosquitoes, listening. "Are you hungry? I can bring you a sandwich."

I passed two hills squirming with ants, then stopped and strained my ears. Birdsong echoed behind me. Yellow jackets, smelling lunch's cheese, I guessed, buzzed near my face. I chatted into the air in a loop along the length of Gram's property, stalling every fifty feet. Did I truly sense her hiding nearby? Or was hope tricking me?

Oh, I wanted to save that little bird.

I returned to the pool where I'd seen her footprints. "Aggie? I know you're listening. I will *not* try to catch you and I *won't* hurt you. I just want to talk. To help you. To be your friend."

A single syllable fell from the trees in response.

"Why?"

I froze.

CONTACT

HER REEDY VOICE DROPPED into the air behind Celia from above the spring. The second she spoke, Aggie regretted it.

"Aggie?" Celia's hands went to her heart.

Aggie blanched, as a tide of doubt rose in her. What had she done? Had Celia really said she'd bring food? *Be my friend?* Could Aggie believe her? A hawk lifted from a nearby branch. She rode him with her eyes, flying away.

Her voice shrank; she forced more words. "Why do you want to help me?"

Celia moved in a slow circle, searching the trees. "I think you must be lonely. Freaked out. You've been hiding for a long time. A friend might, you know, be nice for you."

"Only you. Nobody else."

"Okay." Celia inched toward the pond, perusing the canopy.

"Don't look or I'll go away. Look at the ground."

"Okay." Celia sat cross-legged on the ground and rested her forehead on her hands. Kept her eyes on the thick forest duff between her knees.

"Don't bring the others again. Promise?"

"All right. Not even Burnaby?"

Aggie hiccoughed, stifling a sob.

"No. No!"

"But he misses you, Aggie. He can help, too."

That lie about Burnaby. Was all of this a lie? To trap her?

"You bring him, you bring *anybody* and I'll disappear. I know how. You'll never find me." She did know how.

"Okay. Nobody but me." Celia dropped her hands to her knees. Peeked from the corners of her eyes.

"You try to trick me and I'll know. I'll see."

"I *won't*, Aggie. I promise. Do you—"

"Stay there until I leave. Count to one hundred."

"Got it. Chill out. Just tell me what I can bring you next time. How will I find you?"

"You walk and I'll find you. You tell, you bring anyone, and I won't. I'll know." Her words tripped, tumbled.

"I'll be here tomorrow. You hungry?"

"Yes. So hungry."

"I can go get food right now. Want me to run back and—"

"Count now. You come tomorrow, but I might not."

"Okay. Got it."

Celia kept her face to the ground and counted, loud enough for Aggie to hear. At one hundred, she stood, her eyes moving in all directions before she raised her hands like a megaphone, as if to call. Lowered them.

From her hiding place, Aggie saw Celia's lips move, but couldn't tell what she said.

CASKET

WOBBLY FROM MY ENCOUNTER with Aggie, I wound my way through the grassy north field adjoining Loomis's land and circled back behind Gram's barn. I hugged my body as if I were holding the child. I'd never kept a secret like this. Could I? Should I? Aggie was starving and alone in a forest populated with large predators. Cougars. Even black bears. She needed people to calm and help her. Give her safety. Shelter. Food.

How had people frightened her so badly?

Burnaby's truck was still behind the barn. How could I not tell him? What if she died before I said anything to her family? Or before I brought her home?

But if I told him, obedient, responsible Burnaby would tell others. Searchers who loved her and cried for her return would again converge. Aggie would know I squealed and would go somewhere beyond my or anybody's reach—and smash what was left of their hearts. I would never forgive myself for causing that kind of pain.

Oh, I wanted to tell them Aggie and I had spoken. At least they'd know she was alive. Would they wait for me to bring her in? *Hah. Fat chance.* They'd be hunting for her in a heartbeat.

No, I couldn't say a word. Like it or not, she'd be my secret. I had to trust my plan.

Resolved, I stepped into the workshop, where all my deliberations were promptly flushed by a lamb-sized animal in a wooden box.

Pi?

She didn't jump up when I came in the door. Didn't position herself between me and Burnaby. Horrified, I dropped to the floor and laid my hand on her side, waiting for the rise and fall of her ribs. Burnaby set his hammer on the workbench, his eyes glassy.

"What happened?" I stroked the little dog's muzzle and lifted her flew, exposing white, clammy gums. A fly landed on a black crust on her belly. *Not Pi.* How much more could Burn take? "What happened?" I asked again.

Burnaby propped a wooden lid at the end of the box, then sat beside me and petted his dog's head. His eyes were swollen, his face splotchy. He inhaled sharply and hesitated, as if the words themselves stabbed him. "Pi jumped Cabot. He ran her through with the pitchfork. She fell off the haystack." His voice was flat, mechanical. His eyes, faraway.

My lips tightened, pulling at the workshop's air as if through a tiny straw. "Burnaby, why? Why would Pi attack him?"

The truth crept into my knowing before he responded. I understood what Pi must have sensed, and what I'd been denying. Beneath that charming exterior, the man was dangerous. I thought of the Camaro screaming toward the dump truck. Cabot took what Cabot wanted, and if something got in his way . . . I shivered. Hadn't he said as much? But what could Cabot possibly have against kindhearted, gentle Burnaby? If he would do this—

"He threatened me. Pi was defending me. Cabot murdered her." His account sounded rote, like a stock report. The scene swam in my head.

"Does Loomis know? Does Gram?"

"I don't know. I haven't returned."

"Burnaby, I am so sorry." He tensed when I laid my hand on his knee. "It's okay. I'm as nice as your mama." I rested my head against him and closed my eyes as a stink wafted from the dog's body. "We have to bury her."

He touched Pi's shoulder, wiped his knuckles across his wet cheeks and stood when I did.

I had avoided my grandmother long enough. I stumbled ahead, yelling for her, my voice a croak. She met me at the foot of the porch stairs, her hand at her throat as I wheezed out the awful story. When Burnaby joined us, she pinched his shirt and tugged him to her. Then she climbed a step and touched his face. He stiffened, but she held him there, his cheeks between her hands, her tears spilling. "Dear Burnaby." She stroked his eyebrows with her thumbs and he closed his eyes. I wrapped my arms around them both.

———⋀⋀

When we were breathing again, Gram led us across the lawn. "This is a good spot." She toed the ground under the tree where she liked to pray.

"In your yard? I can bury her in the field."

"This is better. Close to us. Close to you. If you like, you can stay here. Get your things from the farm and move into that bedroom. Your aunt and uncle won't mind." She pointed to a second-story window. Burnaby nodded.

"I'll get Pi."

I sat on a porch step, elbows on knees, my chin in my hands, as we watched him retreat. "The fire, his parents' injuries, his sister's disappearance. And now this."

Gram frowned. "I suspect there's more to come."

BAIT

SECURED BY TWINE IN A TREE-BED. Aggie dreamed of climbing high in a cottonwood, where she hoisted herself through undulating leaves to a hawk's nest. While another nestling slept, a wobbling eyas flapped its baby wings at her, opened its beak, and chirped in Mama's musical voice. "Go-o-o-od morn-ing, Aaaa-gee. Ready for breakfast?"

Warm in the black sweatshirt Celia had left her and clinging to remnants of her broken sleep, Aggie turned her head toward the sound to catch the evaporating dream. Mama, singing through a hawk's mouth. The melody lingered, beautiful.

"I'll put it right here." The voice again. A girl's voice. Louder. Closer. Aggie's eyes flew open, and she stilled her body and breath. A foot crunched tinder beneath her. Whoever was below stopped walking.

Somebody was crinkling up newspaper. No, the sound was more

thumpy, like someone bumping a paper grocery sack. "It's me, Celia. I brought you a bite to eat. I'll set it here, on the stump."

Panic flooded Aggie, eroding all fragments of the beautiful dream. *She knows I'm here!* Her nose itched, but she refused to scratch it. *Celia.* Almost close enough to touch. She waited until the voice faded, then untied herself. A canopy route led her to a decent lookout tree, and she tracked Celia from the branches.

Celia chatted her way along the trail. "Good morning, Aggie. If you can hear me and you want to talk, I won't tell." With every collection of spoken promises, she left a biscuit: one on a stone, another beside the pool, another perched on a head-high branch, like a bird.

Aggie relaxed a little. Obviously, Celia knew she was in the forest, but didn't know *where*. She followed the talking girl, transfixed but suspicious. Why had she decided to trust *Celia,* of all people? Hadn't she seen her kiss Cabot?

If she were Cabot's girlfriend, surely this was a trap. *Those biscuits have something in them to make me sleepy, so she can catch me.* Or worse yet, poison. She bristled. How many birds and animals would find the biscuits and die from them? After Celia left, she would gather them all, every one, and throw them in the well, away from unsuspecting eaters. And she wouldn't talk to that sly girl again.

But when Celia pulled one from the bag and sank her teeth into the puck-shaped delicacy, Aggie doubted herself. Celia waved the half-eaten biscuit like a hello. "Mm. A bacon biscuit. You'll like it." Aggie's shrunken stomach growled. Nobody else tried to talk to her like Celia did. Was she mistaken about her—and the food? Celia seemed to be the only person who didn't want to catch Aggie and throw her in jail.

Aggie shadowed her up the hill until Celia entered Mender's yard, then scurried down the tree and backtracked, collecting biscuits, tucking each one into her pouched shirt. So what if Celia checked and found the treats gone? For all she knew, crows or raccoons filched them, the same way raccoons had filched the hidden eggs she missed on Easter. Had those animals been as excited with their hard-boiled eggs as she was at that moment, with a lap full of biscuits?

She crawled onto the stump near her last sleeping tree and took a slow bite. Buttery flakes and salty bacon bits spread across her tongue. She closed her eyes and chewed. *Heavenly.* She licked crumbs from her grimy fingertips and chowed down three more before her stomach refused the offering. She hadn't eaten food cooked by anyone's hands for such a long, long time.

Celia. Her friend.

She definitely needed one. Her calendar marks told her she'd been hiding for over four weeks. Even with summer in full bloom, she never found enough to eat. Blackberries would help, but after they ripened, the weeds and grasses would age to golden, shrivel and toughen, and there'd be even less food.

And what about later? Cattail stems turned woody, and roots would be harder to get once the water rose with fall rains. She would be cold and would need something besides calluses for shoes. Without a friend, what would she do then—if she lasted that long? Already, she was often dizzy. Climbing took all her strength.

Celia was so nice to her, so kind. Cabot was probably tricking her, too, like he did her aunt and uncle. Wouldn't Celia want to know? She toyed with a plan. Not a lot of details in it yet, but her goal was firm. Aggie would stop Cabot from hurting these people she cared about. She retrieved the feed sack with her sweatshirt and baling twine inside and set out.

———✦———

Which tree? North of the homestead's long-crumbled barn, Aggie tapped one old-growth monster whose beefy limbs overhung the alder-studded barnyard. Easy climbing, even if she was carrying supplies. Those arms would hold an actual bed, twice as high as the boughs she'd been tying herself into, and she'd have a view of the cellar. No cougar would attack her way up there, either.

About eighty feet up, three branches jutted from the trunk like spokes on an olden days wagon wheel, equidistant from the ground, and each as thick as her calf. If Aggie laid more limbs crosswise over them, she could build a hidden, level sleeping platform that would look like an eagle's nest from below. No more binding herself into contortions in skinny, cougar-free trees where anyone could surprise her.

She hoped there were fewer mosquitoes up there, too. Her den had protected her from swarms of biting bugs, but since she'd left the cave, insects had turned her skin into a mass of welts. She climbed the tree to map her best route upward and bounced on the foundation limbs that would hold her bed. *No mosquitoes.* Better yet, along the trail to Uncle Loomis's farm, there was no sign of Cabot.

But the dog-killer was out there, somewhere. She would have to work fast.

First, she gathered branches the diameter of walking sticks, each about five feet long. The sun was high by the time she collected twenty-eight of them from a wide swath of forest floor and laid them side-by-side across the foundation limbs so that messy lateral twigs camouflaged the platform's underside. Lying across the lumpy surface, she took stock of the roof-like greenery above her. This would work.

It was late afternoon when she finished lashing the floor base to the limbs with her sisal baling twine and some cattail reeds. After that, she stripped tender new growth from nearby trees, spread it over the platform and, with a satisfied sigh, admired her handiwork. A modified browse bed, her dad would call it. After more than a dozen trips up the tree, she ate her last biscuit and fell asleep on the cushy bedding.

———✠———

She awoke in waning daylight, disappointed to find mosquitoes already clouding around her and landing on her exposed skin. It was colder this high up, too. The sun had set, but its afterglow would last until she made some changes. She swiped her hands through the veil of insects and hurried down the tree with her sweatshirt.

At the river, she dug her fingers into clay at the water's edge and smeared it over her face and ears, her neck, feet, and the backs of her hands—everywhere her tattered clothing didn't cover. With handfuls of moss from tree trunks and the forest floor, she stuffed her pajama legs. Next, she pulled on the oversized sweatshirt, padded the torso and sleeves with the soft insulation, and tucked the bulky shirt into her bottoms. She smiled as she visualized herself: a puffy, mud-caked tree sloth, a new species for her dad's taxonomy chart.

As twilight advanced, she dragged one more floppy branch of fir needles up the tree. The green blanket covered her body, and she burrowed beneath it—away from the humming mosquitoes. Warmer, and with fewer bugs finding her, she ate cattail stalks gathered that morning when she uprooted the reeds that held her bed together.

Long after dark, she was still awake, her thoughts swirling. When the moon crowned the treetops, a sound below drew her attention to a flashlight beam as it bobbed along the trail from the dairy. Had someone seen her working here? Come to capture her? An owl launched from a nearby tree and flew between Aggie and the moving light. Did the silent bird sense danger, too?

At the clearing, a man stepped into shadowy view. He trained the light on the root cellar latch, disappeared inside with something long and narrow, then hurried back to the trail. Even in the gloom, Aggie harbored little doubt; Cabot had hidden something else. Something bigger this time.

34

CELIA

FUNERAL

GRAM CUT THE GRAVE'S OUTLINE in the lawn with her half-moon edger as Burnaby pushed the wheelbarrow to the side yard and lowered Pi's casket to the ground. He returned to the barn for a shovel and flat-edged spade, ran his thumb along the spade's sharp edge, and carved, loosening sod squares inside the sliced perimeter. I stacked the squares, clearing the level patch of earth. Then Gram and I waited as Burn picked up the shovel and dug fast, his breathing labored, his cheeks wet with tears.

When the depth satisfied him, he eased his arms under Pi and lifted her rigid body from the coffin onto the grass, where she lay curled as if in sleep. I pictured him out there in the barn, bending the little dog before the heat left her, shaping her for the casket that now sat empty beside her. Empty, that is, until he plunged the blade into the dirt pile and shoveled earth *inside,* across the floor of that wooden box.

I opened my mouth to protest, but Gram caught my eye and shook her head. So when he laid Pi back inside and packed dirt along her belly and spine and inside her ears and mouth, when he heaped more soil on top of her and compressed it, I kept my lips sealed.

Good thing I did. As Burn prepared his dog for burial, I realized that after enough time passed, he would extract Pi from her grave, wash her bones, and wire every one of them. It struck me then that all his resurrections weren't merely some quirky hobby. For Burnaby, they were acts of love. He couldn't make those dry bones come alive like in that Ezekiel story of Gram's, but at least they weren't being abandoned to holes in the ground. Burn knew those animals down to their very bones—and *remembered* them in watercolor.

My eyes welled. When Pi stood in front of him in all her bony splendor, how would he paint her? What colors would bring her back to life on his page?

Burn shoveled until the casket brimmed with dirt, then nailed down the slatted lid, slid the box into the cavity, and stood between Gram and me. She rested her hand on his back. He didn't pull away.

"You, Father, who knows when a sparrow falls, heal and welcome this little dog." She said more, but misery plugged my ears. Earth pelted the coffin as we filled the hole, after which Burnaby turned from us and swayed back and forth for the longest time. I patted the mound smooth and sat near it until he put the tools in the wheelbarrow and steered it off toward the barn.

"Time to educate Loomis," Gram said.

"I'm coming." She saluted me and strode straight down the driveway, her arms swinging. I brushed my hands on my cutoffs and skipped to catch up. We turned north toward the dairy.

———⚶———

"Every story has two sides, Mender." Loomis stood by his tractor, a load of silage heaped in the wagon behind it. He pulled off his cap and ran his forearm across his brow, then exhaled wearily. The blue Camaro sat in the barn's shade. "A tragedy for Burnaby and Pi, I know. I hurt for the boy. But Cabot told me she attacked him without provocation. He felt terrible about hurting the dog, but what else could he do? A man's got to defend himself."

"So you take his word for it? You've known Burnaby since he was born. Has he ever lied to you about anything? He doesn't know how. You know this." My tiny grandmother was taking on Ape-Man.

"No, but neither has Cabot. In the eight months he's worked here, I've come to count on him. I trust the man. On the other hand, Burnaby can be, uh, you know. He means well, but he doesn't always interpret situations like you or I would."

"You're making an enormous mistake, Loomis. There's another side to Cabot."

"With all due respect, Mrs. Burke, unless you have proof, I'd prefer that you not malign my herdsman. I'm surprised that you, of all people, would condemn someone without weighing all the angles."

Across the barnyard, Cabot stuck his head out of the office and smiled at me. He raised his index finger in that "hold on a minute" gesture and ducked back inside the room. I pretended not to see him and tugged Gram's shirt. "C'mon. Let's go."

"We've been friends a long time, Loomis. You know I wouldn't say this lightly. For whatever reason, Pi was a casualty of Cabot's vendetta against Burnaby. I don't imagine you want something even worse to happen. I suggest you pay attention to your help's whereabouts." Gram folded her hands at her waist, like a teacher standing before an errant student.

Loomis tipped his cap. "Burnaby can take some time off. He needs it after . . . well . . . everything. His parents. Aggie. Now this. Too much. This is all too much." He wagged his head slowly. "And I agree. Best he stay at your place until his parents can come home. I just hope they both do."

He climbed on his tractor, his movements ponderous. His voice rose above the engine. "Goodbye, Mrs. Burke."

I ran ahead of Gram and was at the road before Cabot reappeared in the office doorway.

"Later," he called.

I lifted my hand in acknowledgement. *I'll be ready for you.* I looped toward my grandmother and ran in place until she caught up. "That was like talking to a rock," I said.

"Yes. An immovable one." She huffed once, then took a giant step into a race walker's pace, her hips, arms, and braid all swinging again. I jogged to keep up. Behind us, Loomis's tractor revved and rolled toward the silo.

———⋀———

When we got home, Gram headed to the study, closed the glass-paned door and sat in the chair beside the bookcase. Sometimes she whispered into the sky or ceiling when she prayed, but today her eyes were clamped shut, her lips tight.

The day's events left me jittery. I shucked off my shoes at the door and made a beeline for the phone. With less than an hour before Cabot arrived, I needed reinforcements. From the minute we left that dairy, I knew I needed my dad.

I hesitated as I held the receiver. What if he was lashed to an oil rig with waves crashing up the sides? Or hunkered down with a team of scientists in one of those endless meetings about viscosity or layered extractions? Or asleep? Or, what if his letter and call the previous week were his last attempts to contact me?

What if I was too late?

With my free hand, I plucked a gingersnap from a plate on the counter and crammed the entire cookie in my mouth. Ginger. Good for the stomach, right? Mine was making funny noises. Understandably so. In the last twenty-four hours I had hunted a phantom child, buried a murdered dog, and talked to a neighbor being duped by a criminal I nearly ran away with. Now I was reaching out to my estranged father. Drama, drama.

I dialed the number Gram had written on the pad under the phone.

"Burke here."

"Daddy?" I whispered to him.

"My girl. I have missed you."

His voice had love in it. All my spitefulness, and what did he do? Hugged me through those phone wires as if I were all sweetness and light. I sniffled into the receiver.

"You okay, Celia?"

"Better, now." I snatched a paper towel and dabbed my nose. "Daddy, I'm sorry."

"Sh. Sh. Sh. I know. You just needed a little time."

"How's it going down there?"

"Like clockwork. A best-case scenario. I should be able to wrap it up by the end of August and be on the plane to pick you up by September third. You'll be late for the start of school, but we can work with that, right? Can you hold out 'til then?"

He was coming back for me. In little more than a month. *My dad.* After all those weeks apart. My leg stopped jiggling. Daddy would come for me. Cabot would fade to a distant memory.

I spilled my guts to him then, catching him up on Mender's birds, strawberries, the kits, Burnaby's artwork. Mother's call. The fire. How I'd found Aggie but nobody believed me and how I'd tell him more about that later, but how I couldn't wait to tell her that her dad would come home.

I started crying again. "Like you will, Daddy."

He waited for my sobs to subside. "Anything else?" It dawned on me that even though I hadn't been talking to him, Gram had. Every week.

"Gram told you about Cabot and me."

"She did."

"Probably not good, huh?"

"She has some concerns. Any you're aware of ?"

Well, yeah. "I did something really stupid."

The line went quiet. "You still there, Daddy?"

"I'm listening, sweetheart."

"I was mad at you and Gram, so I invited him to our cabin. Then I changed my mind. After that, *he* changed. He's been pushing me to . . . well, you know. Acting like he owns me. And he's bad, Daddy. He killed Pi."

"So, what are you going to do?"

"I need to end it, but I'm scared that he won't leave me alone. That I won't be strong enough to stand up to him. What if he . . . what if I'm not?"

The line crackled. "Daddy?"

"Celia. I think you've forgotten the truest thing."

My brain raced. Daddy loved quizzing me. Got a real charge out of how I remembered everything I studied. Took great delight in my accurate answers. So for me to forget something, especially a *truest* something, left me stranded where the buses don't run.

"Dang. So tell me."

"I've told you a million times. Not recently enough, obviously. Think about it."

"I dunno, Dad. What?"

"I love you to the thousandth power. I'm with—"

I started laughing. "You're with me to my farthest stars. You're holding me through every hour. You'll bring me Canada, and Mars." Man oh man, that stupid song. He sang it when I was little.

"Remember it, Celia. Nobody's stronger than a girl who's loved like that."

Warmth washed over me. I felt whole. *Beloved.*

"You can do this, sweetheart. I'm right there with you."

The phone's handset was still warm in its cradle when I heard tapping on the screen door. Cabot stood watching me through the mesh with his piercing eyes, while the afternoon westerly blew around him and into the house. When I turned his way, he stepped over the threshold, through the living room and toward my perch on the barstool.

"Who you talking to?"

"My dad." I smiled, but not at Cabot. I still heard Daddy's voice.

"Yeah? Why'd that jerk call again?" He pulled a stool next to mine and grabbed a cookie.

Did I lead him to believe that about my father? My wonderful daddy?

"I called him." I felt sturdy.

Cabot pushed his stool back from the counter and wheeled it sideways to face me. "You *what*? You turning *unpredictable* on me?" He flicked my ponytail, twirled the end around his finger.

"Mm-hm. Sure am." I pulled my hair away. He didn't notice that I'd been crying, though I must have resembled the bruised peach beside the sink. Or perhaps he didn't care. "Cabot, this . . . we . . . aren't good together. I don't want you coming here again."

He sat still, as if he were waiting for my words to swing from his earlobes, crawl down his auditory canals and coil into his cochleae for a soda before they registered. I kissed this guy? *Oh, barf.*

He laughed derisively. "Yeah, right, Celia. You've been watching for me all day. You even came to the farm. You know I'm the best thing that's ever happened to you."

How did a girl call it quits when a guy wouldn't? For as much talking as Cabot did, he sure didn't listen worth a lick.

"I mean it. We're done." No point explaining. He wouldn't hear me, anyway.

His arm circled my waist, but I squirmed away and scooted to the door. I held the screen open. "Please leave."

He tilted his head and backed over the threshold. His face was open, curious. "That must've been some talk with your dad. I get that. Cool down a bit. I'll come back later."

"No, Cabot. Don't come back *ever*."

He plugged his ears with his thumbs and laced his fingers behind his head. His elbows projected like giant ears. "You don't mean that, Celia. I'll pretend you didn't say it. Get some sleep tonight. I'll see you tomorrow morning at eight. Bring your hiking boots."

"We're not going anywhere!" The hurtled door struck his shoe, slammed inches from his face.

Gram hurried from her study at the commotion, then tracked my glare out the window. Cabot loped across the lawn and waved, a synthetic grin smattered across those cheeks I once found so irresistible. She scowled back at him. *Attagirl, Mender.* Both she and Daddy were backing me up.

Daddy, however, was still thousands of miles away, and Gram was no match for Cabot's manipulation. Her talk with Loomis had proven that.

———Λ

The next morning, I was turning duck eggs in the laundry room incubator when Cabot's car thrummed down the driveway. Gram, poised over the waffle iron, unplugged the appliance and sank her spoon back into the bowl of batter. She slid a stack of cooled waffles into a plastic zip bag and lifted it toward me. "Snacks for you and Burn," she said, and put the bag in the freezer. Then she walked to the front window and peeked between slats in the blinds.

"Go upstairs, Celia. I'll talk to him."

I closed the incubator lid and hurried to the landing at the top of the stairway. I crouched out of sight and pressed my ear between the balusters.

"Hey, Mrs. Burke."

He could charm a pie into cooking itself.

"Celia ready yet?"

"She told you to stay away, remember?"

"Aw, she didn't mean it. She here? Can I talk to her?"

"I insist you—"

"She know you're keeping me from seeing her?" He must have tried to push past her.

"Unh-unh. Not another step."

"Celia? *Celia!*" His voice wound up the stairs. I shrank against the wall.

". . . see you here again, I'll call the sheriff."

"The sheriff ? Ha!" Heels thunked on the porch's floorboards. "Lotta good that'll do you. Tom's a friend of mine."

Aggie's search party. That stodgy sheriff with the dog. Of course Cabot knew him. They worked Search and Rescue together. The man wouldn't believe Cabot over Gram, would he? I chewed a hangnail.

"Friend or no friend, you're trespassing. I'll press charges if you don't leave my property *immediately*." Gram's voice rang like struck iron. She sounded eight feet tall.

"Crazy old woman. I'll see her again. You can't stop me." Gram gasped, and the door whumped closed.

I rushed downstairs, afraid of what I'd find.

35

AGGIE

SURPRISE

AFTER THE FLASHLIGHT MAN left the cellar, Aggie lay awake long enough for the gibbous moon to move and shine onto her platform. Half-light from a half-moon, but still so bright. She thought of her mother turning out her bedside lamp. "You'll sleep better, my Agate."

Mama. Dad. Where were they buried? Did Burnaby visit their graves? Did he miss them as much as she did? She sighed. Mama was right about sleeping in the dark. When that moon bloomed full, it would pummel Aggie, haunt her with memories. Maybe she would slip back to her inky cave for a few nights when its light woke her.

She hadn't realized how her den insulated her from the nocturnal noises and activity, either. Tonight, the forest teemed. An owl floated through the shadowy trees dangling a rodent from its talons. Bats shimmied after mosquitoes around the freestanding chimney. A possum appeared from a burrow and foraged on the ground, while deer browsed near the dilapidated barn. Distant coyotes yipped like fans at a ball game.

She caught the stink of a porcupine somewhere nearby and later awoke with a lurch of fear to a scratching, crackling sound. *Claws!* A cougar? Her breath dammed in her throat, escaping only after a bobcat's dim outline descended an adjacent trunk and blended into the undergrowth.

With the rising sun, the creatures vanished. Aggie rolled to her side on her new bed and shoved knotted hair from her face. Two Steller's jays, their feather crests tall, scolded her as they flitted between branches. "Please, birds. Not yet." Mud flaked off her cheeks as she pressed herself onto her elbows, weary. "You're way, way too loud." More sleep would be impossible with those high-decibel birds harassing her. She rubbed her eyes, stretched, and began pulling moss from her pajamas.

Then she remembered the flashlight man. Her eyes flew to the cellar, its plank door dappled with shade. Before she went inside, she had to *know* that Cabot wouldn't surprise her.

He wouldn't. She found him at the dairy, whistling the next group of cows into the parlor, where they'd keep him occupied for at least an hour. As soon as she saw him, she pivoted and sprang, deer-like, back into the woods and down the hill.

Suspicions doused her with dread as she crept inside the cellar, but as before, the shelves stood empty. Where was it? *Slow down, Aggie.* Her eyes crawled the room until they rested above a top shelf, near the ceiling. She climbed, reached into the narrow slot, and, with her fears realized, extracted a shotgun. She glanced at the door, lowered the gun stock-first to the floor, and shook her head. She didn't want to imagine the worst, but knew he wasn't hunting birds with it.

———✳︎

Before the fire, Aggie's dad had owned a shotgun. When she turned nine, he taught her to shoot, but not with that twelve-gauge. "It'll knock you flat, little girl." Instead, he bought a twenty-gauge over/ under, and showed her how to carry it with its muzzle pointed at the ground or the sky. She learned how to drop open the barrels and slide two shells into the chambers. How to set and release the safety. She could press the gunstock into her shoulder, draw a bead, and squeeze the trigger. Dad threw clays for her; they exploded when she shot.

"You're a natural, Aggie. Excellent form."

She did not, however, enjoy shooting one bit. The kick, even from the smaller gun, left bruises on her shoulder, and the noise jarred her. Even with foam plugs, her ears rang afterwards. And every shotgun killed birds.

———⋏

Aggie hefted the gun and sighted it toward the chimney. This one was the same style as hers, but bigger, heavier. She toggled the safety on, off, on. Was it loaded? That would be dumb—and dangerous, leaving it where anybody could get it. *But he doesn't intend for anybody else to get it.* She cracked the gun open so that the muzzle tipped away at an angle from the stock, exposing the brass ends of two shells. She swallowed hard. The gun was ready to fire.

She considered throwing it in the river. *No, way too obvious.* Cabot still hadn't discovered the empty necklace box, or he wouldn't have brought the gun here. He still thought his hideout was a secret, and she wanted to keep it that way. She fingered the rawhide around her neck. Rubbed the agate pensively.

What if she just removed the shells? There was no extra ammo in the cellar, so unless Cabot brought more, he couldn't reload. If he checked the chambers before he used it, he would know he'd been found out, but she'd take that chance. She'd seen his meanness. If he had rotten plans for this gun, pulling the cartridges might slow him down.

She slid the shells from their chambers, returned the gun to its shelf, and flipped the wooden door latch into place.

DRIVE-BY

"HE'S GONE, HONEY." Gram turned from the door, her chin trembling. Cabot's car roared away.

I hurried to her, quickly looked her over, then wrapped my arms around her, relieved to find her untouched.

"You were somethin', Gram. I expected him to blow right by you." My voice caught, tangling with residual anxiety and awe. Cabot stood six foot two of solid muscle. Mender Burke barely brushed five feet and was so lean she could shade herself with a clothesline, yet she had kept the man outside. Her hand lay open over her chest, forming a V beneath her clavicles. "You okay?" I asked.

She inhaled and grinned. "I had help. I don't know why I was so shocked. It wouldn't have been the first time." I stepped away from the window as she drew all the blinds wide open.

"You don't give yourself enough credit, Gram. I heard the strength in your voice."

"I'm not taking any credit," she said. "The good Lord protected us." She locked the door before she headed for the phone. "I'm calling Deputy Yost. I have a brief report to file."

———✲———

Cabot drove past the gate four times in the next two hours. Fast. Slow. Fast. Then very, very slowly, with a thirty second pause at the gate before he squealed away, his tires smoking. Gram jotted notes on a tablet each time he went by—as calmly as if she were keeping track of eggs poaching. A baby raccoon played with Mason jar rings in my lap as I huddled against a kitchen cabinet and drew strength from my giant of a grandmother.

"He scares me, Gram."

"Me, too." She slid a raspberry cobbler into the oven. Set the timer.

"I'm afraid he's a sugar bird, Celia."

"What do you mean?"

"A term your granddaddy used for someone desperate, scratching and pecking and clawing for a sweet seed that will soothe that ache in his heart." She lowered a mixing bowl into sudsy dishwater. Dried her hands. "Seems like he thinks you're his."

"I'm no *seed*."

"Glad you realize it." Her finger traced my hairline. "I suspect that man will always be hungry."

"Can you imagine if Burnaby'd been here?"

"Good thing he wasn't."

"Where was he off to so early, anyway? I heard his truck leave before I got out of bed."

"Seattle. To see his parents."

"Any news?"

"Harris is on the mend. That shattered leg will take a while, but his doctors hope to release him by this weekend." She untied her apron and hung it on a hook. "Bree's another story. Those third-degree burns on her back . . . She's fighting sepsis. Her organs are stressed."

"That's awful."

Gram's eyes wandered toward the window. "Horrible. Who knows how long they'll keep her in that coma. Nora said Burnaby visits his dad, and then sits by Bree's bed for hours on end, watching a ventilator breathe for her."

Both of us fell silent. I put my fingers on my wrist. My heartbeat matched the ticking kitchen clock. I couldn't keep Aggie a secret much longer. What if Bree died while the girl was hiding in the woods, and Aggie never got to say goodbye? I wished I could read the child's mind. If she learned her mom was near death, would she come with me? Or disappear for good?

"Gram, if someone said they wanted something, and you knew they needed something different, what would you do?"

"Depends. Who are we talking about here?"

"Just somebody I know."

"From the berry fields?"

"Maybe."

"Is the person open to suggestion?"

"Not at all. Won't stick around if I tell anybody, either."

"Is the person in danger?"

"Yes. But it'll get worse if I tell. I promised I wouldn't."

"Can the person's parents help?"

"No. They aren't around."

"What kind of danger?"

"May be deadly."

She crossed the kitchen to where I sat on the floor. Set a hand on my shoulder.

"Can you talk to Mr. Leegwater? Tell someone at the farm?"

I pressed my hands together without answering.

"Celia."

"I guess. Yeah. I'll do that."

I got up and scanned the empty road. No blue car anywhere. "I'm going to check anthills."

"Better not, dear. Stay inside for now."

I *couldn't*. Aggie was hungry. "Maybe I'll lie down."

"Superb idea. Hard morning. Think I'll do the same."

I closed my bedroom door and waited until she padded down the hall. When her door latch clicked, I tiptoed downstairs, filched some waffles from the freezer, and hurried across the yard toward the trees.

NEWS

AGGIE CARRIED THE SHOTGUN SHELLS to the river and threw them far over the water. When a kingfisher plunged near their point of entry, she worried he'd retrieve one. Instead, he rose from the river with a minnow, flew into a cottonwood, and enjoyed his breakfast. Aggie thought of the biscuits, and Celia, her friend. Mama would have been happy for her, knowing she had a human friend. Especially a friend who fed her.

For the next few hours, she poked sticks in anthills. Picked berries. Avoided a skunk, its tail bobbing like a question mark through the dike grass. Retracing the route where she'd found biscuits, she waited, debating with herself how best to convince Celia about Cabot. Drumming up courage.

At last Celia's melodic voice preceded her down the trail. "I have your breakfast, Aggie. Maybe we should call it a brunch today.

Blueberry waffles. Mm-mmm. You'll like these. Here you go. On this branch."

Crouched near a bone plate, Aggie waited until Celia passed her. Did she keep her word and come alone? The waffle dangled feet away. Saliva pooled under Aggie's tongue.

"I have n-e-w-s," Celia sang. "Your dad is coming home from the hospital. Burnaby's visiting him and your mother today. When you're ready, come to me. I can take you to them."

Aggie forgot the waffle. *What did she say?* Her dad was *what? Alive? Mama too?* She leaped upright. The girl wouldn't lie about her *parents.*

Panting, she swiped aside a snowberry bush and sprang toward Celia's trail just as the top of a man's baseball cap bobbed through the undergrowth, coming her way. She dropped like a falling rock and slid back undercover. *She lied! She brought someone!* Footfalls moved, stopped, moved along Celia's path, mimicking her stops and starts. Aggie forced her breath into shallow, noiseless puffs, though her heart battered her insides.

Seconds later, Cabot came into view. Every few steps he stopped and inclined his head, then moved toward Celia's voice. He was chewing a waffle—one of *Aggie's* waffles—and trailing her friend. And when Celia turned, he ducked.

She doesn't know he's there.

Aggie frowned. Celia was broadcasting her message and Cabot was hearing it all. Now he knew she and Celia talked, knew that Celia hung out with Burnaby. Didn't Cabot kill Pi because Celia spent time with her brother? The implications settled on Aggie with horror. Burn was in worse danger than she thought. Perhaps Celia was, too.

Celia's voice faded, and Cabot evaporated into the greenery behind her. Aggie looped wide, like a bird dog circling quail, until she saw the porch door close behind Celia—and watched the stalker slip behind the woodshed and jog toward the barn. With Celia safe,

Aggie hurried after him and crouched behind a rain barrel in time to see Cabot jerk the padlock and tug on the immense barn door's handle. When neither budged, he pounded his fist against the frame, scanned the empty road, and trotted across the field. Then he climbed the fence and sank over the hill near Uncle Loomis's farm.

He was like a coyote. Or a wolf. One who was extending his range.

He dropped out of sight just as Burnaby drove his truck through Mender's gate. *Two minutes. They missed each other by two minutes.* She watched in relief as her brother turned a key in the padlock and slid the barn door open along its overhead runner. The lofty interior swallowed him. Another door inside opened and closed.

Aggie flared her nostrils and inhaled a long draw, trying to catch his scent. She missed everything about him. Now he was alone, not thirty feet away. Hidden by the barrel, she hugged her knees to her chest. Were her parents *alive*? He would know—and he could take her to them. They'd find somewhere to live, all together again. A tremor of hope passed through her.

And doubt. They might be alive, but according to Celia they were still in the hospital. People didn't stay in hospitals that long unless they were so, so, so injured or sick. She hurt them *badly*. Almost *killed* them. They wouldn't want to see her.

All that pain? Her fault.

She rolled onto her knees and bent over them. Pressed her mouth against her leg as cries welled, then heaved from her like vomit. She had to get this out of her. This dirty voice that pressed on her like a stone and crowded out hope.

———Ⓐ———

"Lord's Day Forty-Five." An image of Dad smiling, his fiddle across his lap, seeped like fog around her black thoughts. "Aggie, you ready?" Her turn for catechism. Burnaby stood beside the kitchen table with her.

"Our Father in heaven, hallowed be your name . . ." She knew the words. Spoke them between sobs. "Forgive us our debts—" Would he? If she gave him the fire and what she did to her mama and her dad, would he take them away? She couldn't carry the weight one more day. Her fingers snarled in her matted hair, pulling, pulling. She had to give him those debts. Needed him to lift them off her.

Her words came from a slow faucet at first, but they came. Tears dampened her pajamas as she mumbled into her knees, pouring out her fear and sorrow and guilt. Her regret. Then, from somewhere deeper, her remorse. Talking, crying, talking. Until she made room inside herself. Until she had nothing left to say.

EAGLE

"AAAAA-GEE. AAAAA-GEE." I sang her name to a made-up tune as I carried the waffles to the woods. I would leave a few down by Burnaby's bone plates, along the trail to the anthills. If she hung out near them, she would hear me.

I had to convince her soon. If I didn't find her by Friday, I'd have no choice but to enlist Burnaby's help and hope he wouldn't frighten her off. We didn't have much time. The child was stressed, underfed, and without shelter. The weather was deteriorating. Unseasonably chilly rain and high winds would arrive as soon as the weekend—three days away. Unless Aggie stayed warm and dry, hypothermia could claim her before we got her to her parents.

I called to her. Sang. Told her stories. Told her at least ten times that her parents were alive. Told her I'd be her friend. Twice, I thought

I heard something in the trees behind me, but when I stopped moving, the sound did, too. Creepy. In my Halloween imagination, it sounded like a bear, like something big was in those bushes. Nothing like a small girl.

Cabot's visit still spooked me. I needed to calm down. "I'll be back tomorrow, Aggie." I speared my last waffle on an alder branch and whistled my way home.

———𝒜———

The next morning, the dogs raced ahead when I paused in the field between the barn and the road, breathing in the warm, sweet scent. Pasture grass fell like a swooning crowd behind a sickle mower, pulled by my granddaddy's old Massey Ferguson tractor. A red-tailed hawk landed in the stubble, plucked a dead vole, and flew past its circling mate. Crows scolded and intruded on a mottled young eagle—a female, I figured, given her larger size. She tore at a rabbit, also killed by the passing mower. Scavenging birds popped into the air and relocated as the dogs loped toward the feast.

I held a scrambled egg burrito high in the air. The tractor slowed and the mower bar stopped scissoring. Burnaby climbed to the ground, and I waved the food at the birds. "Might as well join 'em."

Burn ticked his mouth in a fleeting smile and retrieved his breakfast. The tractor engine sputtered idly, and he settled against one of its tires.

"You eat yet?"

"Mine's waiting at the house. I'm fine."

Burnaby held his burrito in front of me. "Some for you, too."

Man oh man, it smelled good. "Twist my arm." I leaned in and took a bite.

Just as I closed my mouth over the tortilla, a blue Camaro charged over the hill and downshifted. The driver slowed to a crawl. Cabot, his elbow jutting from the open window, glared at us. Too close for this girl. He was a mere fifty-yard dash away, with only a fence between us. I chewed twice and swallowed.

The birds in the field erupted with the car's noise. The dogs popped their heads out of the grass, ears forward, alert. The immature eagle flapped over the fence with the rabbit in her talons and landed farther down the road, where she continued shredding the carcass.

Cabot's face contorted. He stuck his head out the window and yelled at us, but I couldn't hear him over the idling tractor and grumbling car.

"What'd he say?"

Burnaby was staring at the treetops across the road, his cheek fluttering. "You should go in the house."

Cabot shouted something else, gunned the engine, and sped forward. Startled, the roadside eagle unfolded her wings to flap upward just as he swerved his car toward the bird. The chrome fender struck her somewhere between wing and body. She careened up the car's hood and, for a split second, seemed to be flying away.

But no. The impact flipped the eagle into the air before she sprawled, her wing torqued sideways, onto the road's shoulder. The car squealed to a halt; the door swung wide and Cabot stood tall on the threshold. He thrust his middle finger in the air before he stabbed it toward the injured bird and yelled, "Next time, Hayes, that's you!"

The Camaro screamed as he punched the pedal and tore down the road. The cloud of his threat settled over us.

I stood immobile, my hands over my mouth, until Burnaby ran ahead and slid onto his knees beside the young eagle, his arms and hands extended, uncertainty on his face.

Three feet tall, the bird held her hooked, razor-sharp beak open wide, menacing. Her concave tongue protruded and pulsed as she panted. She rotated toward Burnaby with her good wing curved, its tip pointed downward. The other wing lay broken and useless at her side.

I approached behind her, assessing, and saw blood on the side of her face—from her mouth! Then she snapped her head toward me. A strand of sinew trailed from her beak down her neck. Her open mouth looked clean.

Just rabbit blood. I exhaled my relief.

But her wing? Now that was ugly. Blood seeped into her feathers near her shoulder, and the pinions twisted at an unnatural angle away from her body. *Broken. Compound fracture.*

My palms were wet, and I breathed through my mouth. How bad was it? A clear membrane blinked over the bird's brown eyes as she took my measure. "We have to get her to the house before she goes into shock, Burn." Apart from that broken wing, she seemed intact, but I couldn't tell for sure. A small hope buoyed me. Without internal injuries, she could survive this.

I should get Mender. I took a step toward the house, then stopped. No. It would take too long. I'd corralled raptors before. I could do this. Burnaby stood and began whistling softly to her. *We* could.

I hesitated. I'd never stabilized a bird this big. We didn't even have gloves. Between her talons and her beak, she could put a serious hurt on a person.

The eagle craned her neck and turned her head toward me, then back to Burnaby. "Quick, Burn. Take off your shirt." He took a step away from that wicked beak, stripped off his T-shirt, and held it in one hand.

"Here's the plan. Move slowly. Count of three, drape your shirt over her head but stay out of range. She'll make ribbons of your skin if you get too close. I'll come from behind and restrain her. Got that?"

Burn nodded. He lifted his shirt at the shoulder seams and gave it a quick shake. It unfurled, ready. We had one good chance at this. I counted.

On three, Burnaby dropped the shirt over the eagle's head and neck. She flipped her head side to side, but he held the cloth fast. I snapped my right hand forward and pulled the bird's good wing into her body as if I were closing a pleated fan, then clamped my arm over it and ran my hand down her leg to her tarsus bone, just above the foot. I gripped it hard, then slid my left arm under the broken wing and clenched her other leg the same way. I pressed her spine into my chest.

Done.

"Easy, girl." I stood upright and held those treacherous feet straight out in front of me, anticipating the bird's resistance. Burnaby waited beside me, holding the provisional hood in place. But she didn't fight. Instead, blinded by the cloth, her head nodded, and she relaxed into the security of my arms and body. Her wing hung useless.

We shuffled to the house, a jumbled assembly of arms and wings, talons and hands. Burnaby opened the door. "Gram?" I called. No answer. In the kitchen, two breakfast burritos sat beside the stove, ready on plates. "Gram? Mender?" The bird jostled against me as I raised my voice.

"Should I go find her?" he asked.

"No. She'll show up." I didn't want Burnaby to leave. Once the eagle collected herself, I could have a fight on my hands, and the broken wing would make it worse. Besides, I couldn't so much as scratch my nose from this position.

"We'll prep her for transport. You can get us to the vet, right?" Burn nodded and jangled the keys in his pocket.

I carried her to the laundry counter, above drawers and cupboards of bird-tending supplies and instruments. Burn took a flannel sheet from a stack beside the sink and spread the cloth over the surface.

"You've done this before."

"A few times. Nothing hands-on. Mender has me pass items to her as she needs them."

Good. He knew where to find things. No way I could dig through cupboards. I repositioned my straightjacket arms and eased the bird down onto the sheet. A jagged white spur jutted from the underside of her wing, its marrow red as jelly. No mistaking Burnaby's fascination. He stared, rapt, at the injury.

"Find the largest hood. Top drawer to the left."

Burn extracted a leather helmet with nut-like bulges to cover the eagle's eyes and keep her quiet.

"That's the one. Lift your shirt, then slide the hood up from below her beak. You want that beak to pass through the hole above the chinstrap. Then slip the hood straight back over her head."

As if he did it every day, Burnaby pinched the braided tassel protruding from the top of the little helmet, clucked his tongue at the bird, and settled the hood into place. He drew the rear thongs snug, then rested his hands on the counter. Focused. Steady. Those fidgety hands of his, calm.

"Good job. Now, those talons." Before I could ask, he set a roll of adhesive tape and an Ace bandage at my elbow and retrieved two wine corks from a bag in the cupboard behind him. "You're on, Burnaby. Give those claws something to grip." He screwed a cork into each clenched talon, and the eagle squeezed them as if she were on a branch. Then he bound her legs and feet together with the Ace wrap and secured it with tape.

"Oh, yeah. Weapons disabled."

I immediately turned to her injury. "Ready for that wing, Burn?" For her ever to fly again, the bone needed to stay viable enough to mend after surgery. We had to keep it moist. "Saline. And gauze. Lots of it."

As best I could, I maneuvered the broken wing into a more natural position, then laid a thick layer of saturated gauze over the break. I shaped the feathered arm against her body, added more wet gauze, and held it there. Then I refolded her intact limb and clasped both wings snug against her.

Burn flew into action. As if he swaddled wrecked eagles every day of his life, he bundled the flannel around the bird until she lay before us like a baby, soothed and comfortable.

"It's a wrap, Burn." I laughed with relief.

"Couldn't have done better myself." Gram stood by the door, smiling. "Go turn off the tractor, Burnaby. I'll get the car."

JUNKYARD

AT A TREE NEAR THE DAIRY, Aggie held one of Celia's waffles
between her teeth and gripped a low alder branch. She flipped backwards until her knees hooked the limb, pulled herself upright, and
devoured the food. Then she tugged her torn, dirty pajamas up to
mid-thigh and ran her hands over her legs, tracing her sinewy muscles
with her fingertips. *So skinny.* Her knees bulged, knobby. Curling her
fist, she raised it over her bent elbow and flexed her biceps like boys
did when they showed off. The muscle looked stringy.

Her body was rapidly growing weaker, and it worried her. She
tripped more now, and her limbs sometimes shook when she climbed.
If she waited much longer, they would fail her altogether. And if they
failed—if she fell and died before she could expose Cabot—what
would happen to Burnaby? And Celia?

Plain and simple, she couldn't hide anymore. Before the day

ended, she would tell on the dog-killer. The gun, the cubby-hole, his threats and lies . . . his murder of Pi. She sighed, resigned. She'd have to tell the *sheriff.* Would he let her see Mama and Dad before he took her away?

Jumpy, she concentrated on bird music from the surrounding trees. Birds had helped her when Mama got sick, cheering and distracting her. And, though she wasn't sure how, they kept her strong. Especially robins, tugging worm ropes from the ground like athletes, chirping their hellos and goodnights from treetops every time the sun rose and set. "Benedictions," her dad said.

And the robins' eggs? Those tiny blue orbs snugged into mud cups like pieces of sky. Aggie savored the hope in them, had captured it in her sketchbook. Wished she could stay in egg season forever.

But it didn't work that way. After eggs hatched and nestlings grew, they flew. Lately, she had spotted fledglings as they dodged predators and learned to find food, copied their parents' flight patterns, and roosted like grownups. Everywhere except their nests.

Her dad had told her she was like one of those birds, growing her own wings. Getting ready to fly. She hummed as she remembered, then stopped short. *Birdsong.* It *sounded* like hope.

A chill wind penetrated her clothes, and she smelled rain. Who could take her to the sheriff ? Who would listen to her? Angling for a view behind the machine shed, she pondered the junkyard of old farm equipment that Loomis kept for parts. One of those truck cabs could shelter her while she decided. While she worked up her nerve.

She crept to a pickup and stuck her head inside. A blackberry vine wove through a broken window and across the floor. Mouse droppings covered the cracked dashboard. The seats stank of mold and mouse urine. *Boo. Not this one.*

Vines also clawed at a silage truck, the last vehicle at the far end of the yard. The cab stood tall above her head and a hawthorn shrub grew along the driver's side. *No one's climbed in here forever.* She slunk past the dirty bumper. Moss grew like a green picture frame on the gasket around the cracked windshield, but it—and the other windows—were still intact. This cab would stay dry when it rained.

At first glance, the far side of the truck seemed neglected, too. But soon Aggie noticed small details that suggested recent activity. A freshly torn, wilted vine threaded the door handle. A thin trail of flattened grass ran the length of the vehicle's bed. A wide smear streaked a dusty side panel. Her curiosity piqued. In the absence of tracks or scent or telltale scat, she could only guess. *Deer? Bear?*

With her back to the cab, she assessed the area. The truck's nose pointed into hilly fields to the north. Dense woods lay fifteen feet east of the passenger door. The rear walls of farm buildings to the south blocked views behind the rear bumper. Large game could easily pass here undetected. Oh well. They wouldn't bother her inside the cab.

But when she gripped the rearview mirror, stepped onto the running board, and looked through the algae-tinged glass, her analysis shifted. *Definitely not deer or bear.* Below window level, tools and boxes of shotgun shells covered the bench seat and floor. A cattle prod like the one her uncle jabbed at cows headed for auction wedged against the driver's door.

She pulled the shiny handle down, blinking in surprise when the door opened quietly at her tug. Too quietly. The hinges showed fresh grease.

A red strip caught her eye. A line of scorched caps lay between a box for an electric sander and a leather tool belt. A few spent matches lay near the charred red strip.

For a fleeting second, she linked her brother to the scene, then rejected the notion. This was all wrong. Burnaby would never stow his stuff here. Burnaby kept his tools in their barn in alphabetical order. But those caps . . . Had he been worrying—and fired them off to calm himself?

Not a chance. Burnaby wasn't stupid. Besides, this was loot, and she didn't believe for a second that Burnaby would steal anything. He followed rules without wavering. Even if he did, he sure wouldn't pop caps right beside his stash. All fingers would point to him as the thief.

Who would do this to frame her brother?

Easy answer.

———⚹———

She left the cab undisturbed, exiting fast. Still perched on the running board, her muscles tightened when an engine fired up in the barnyard. Framed by the dingy cab windows, a green tractor pulled a flatbed trailer around the machine shed, and headed into the junkyard. Toward her. She dropped beneath the window and landed on the ground in a squat, then crawled under the truck and scooted forward between the front tires.

Diesel fumes wafted around her. The tractor motored closer until nothing lay between the noisy engine and Aggie's hiding spot but a stack of aluminum irrigation pipes nested in a fringe of knee-high grass and thistles. The trailer clanked over a rut as the tractor eased it forward, then stopped. Boots passed between her and the pipes, and a deep bass rang over the chug of the idling engine. Uncle Loomis. Singing. His thick hands hoisted one of the thirty-foot tubes as if it were paper and clanged it onto the trailer. Every time he bent for a pipe, she cringed, certain he would see her.

So what? *Go to him, Aggie.*

She tried. Though her voice deserted her, she inched along the truck's underbelly toward her uncle as he loaded the trailer.

But he didn't see her. He climbed back in the tractor. The engine whined, and the machine arced around the silage truck, where it paused, then continued its route north, hauling pipe into the thirsty pasture.

She wasted no time. *Aunt Nora.* She'd tell *her*, not scary Uncle Loomis. Aunt Nora would call the sheriff for her. On hands and knees, she left the underbelly of the truck and sprinted for the house.

Grasshoppers popped like rockets around Aggie as she watched Aunt Nora, purse in hand, pull the kitchen door closed, walk to her car, and drive away. If her aunt had turned, she'd have seen the frightened girl standing in the open, unable to speak—not thirty feet from her porch.

The car bumped down the lane and Aggie, lightheaded, darted back to the junkyard. When she reached an old hay rake, she heard whistling, so she squatted and peeked through its skinny tines.

A hat. Head. Shoulders.

Cabot climbed over the crest of the hill from the direction her uncle had driven the tractor, his mouth a whistling O, his arms swinging. At the front of the silage truck, he jigged in a circle, his head swiveling, checking for onlookers. When he sprang onto the passenger side running board, his upper body showed through the windows. He opened the door, bent over behind the seat, backed out, and closed the door.

An instant later he came around the truck, shoved a box inside the front of his coveralls, and zipped them over it. *Shotgun shells.* Aggie raised her slitted eyes and saw him pass the machine shed toward the woods. Judging by his direction, he was taking the ammo to the cellar. He must have opened the gun. Must have discovered that she pulled those shells. She bit a dirty cuticle and followed.

When she got to the cellar, Cabot's coveralls and the box they hid were nowhere in sight. He stood outside the little door, wearing jeans and a red T-shirt. He lifted a small plastic tube, pushed hard on the cap, and slid it into his back pocket. *The syringe.* Had he reloaded the gun already? Neither his face nor his posture told her.

Instead of returning to the farm, he surprised Aggie when he punched through some twiggy dogwood bushes hiding a faint deer path. What now? She followed him down the game trail as he dropped into a swale, then skirted a car-sized boulder and a windfall of young maples, clearly familiar with the route.

When the green of Mender's fields showed through the trees, he sat behind a smaller boulder and surveyed the house. For at least half an hour, no one showed. Restless, he drummed his knees, tapped his toes. Then the door opened at the landing where Aggie had stolen milk. Now she understood. Cabot spied on Celia from here.

Celia stepped into the wind with a loaf of bread dangling from one hand. Wonder Bread, with those dots on the wrapper. *For me?* A ripple of dizziness fuzzed her vision, and she shook her head to clear it. Celia's breakfast treats had awakened a fierce hunger in her; her body cried constantly for food. She pushed on her stomach to quiet the whine and focused on Celia walking downhill to the woods.

Aggie wanted to shout. Or run to her. She'd point at Cabot's hiding spot so he wouldn't sneak any closer. She nearly did. But Cabot's reaction when he saw Celia scared her. Held her back.

The man extended his neck like a wolf and settled onto the rock, watching Celia walk. He was *hunting* her. His hands lay crosswise on his thighs; his elbows locked at right angles. His jaw worked fast, and the wad of gum in his mouth popped between his front teeth before he pounced.

"Hey, girl." He ambushed Celia after she passed beneath the hill, out of view of the house. Aggie watched in shock as he blocked her retreat.

WOLF

MAKE A RUN FOR IT. CELIA. Get back to the house. Aggie's heart drummed. She wanted to shout, but words tangled in her throat.

Celia startled at Cabot's voice. Aggie was close enough to see fear tighten her shoulders and drain her face. "What are you doing here?"

"Oh, I thought my girl might like some company while she feeds the birds."

"Did you, now?" A bleak smile turned Celia's lips, and she twisted the tie on the bread bag. "What makes you think I'm feeding birds?" She started walking again.

He cocked his head toward the sack, matching her footsteps. "I saw you the other day, hanging waffles from trees like they were Christmas ornaments. Lucky birds, to have such nice fresh treats. I tried one myself."

Celia sped up. She moved laterally, as if to circle back uphill to the house, but Cabot took a giant step in front of her and smiled, his eyes wide and wild. "Don't change your plans on account of me. I'm sure Aggie—uh, I mean your birds—are waiting."

Aggie shrank. She was right. He had heard Celia calling her.

"What do you know about Aggie?" Celia's voice rose. *With fright?* Aggie could no longer see her face to be sure. They had passed her. She scrambled to keep up, shadowing the pair as they approached the anthill trail.

Cabot's words poured like syrup. "Well, I know you're looking for her and that you say you saw her footprints. That you think you can be her new best friend. Just like you and Burnaby."

"Leave Burn out of this."

"He's 'Burn' now, is he?"

Celia neither answered nor opened the bag as Cabot tailed her into the trees. *Stupid move, Celia. I wouldn't lead that creep into the woods for anything.* Celia had missed her chance to escape in the field. How was she going to get away from him now?

Aggie considered jumping onto the trail ahead of them, then thought better of it. What if he trapped them both? *I'm too scrawny. He'd catch me. Use me to get Celia to do what he wants.* But if she ran for help, she'd lose them. And what if nobody was in the house? No, no, no. She wouldn't leave Celia. She'd stay with her friend, find a way to help.

Celia slowed, pulled some bread from the bag. Aggie squinted at her hand. Not just bread, a *sandwich*. Celia flung it like a Frisbee. Aggie wanted to dive for it, but it sank in a thicket.

"Look, Cabot. We hung out for a while. We had a good time. You showed me around and I'm glad about that. And now we're moving on. Why is that so hard for you to get?"

"Your memory's failing you, girl. Last week you were so into me you wanted me to drive you to your empty cabin. You weren't talking about moving on then." He ran his hand over his mouth and back across his chin. "And the way you kiss me? Invitations. Promises."

Celia's head tipped to the side as she listened. She didn't seem so scared of him right then. More perplexed and sad than worried.

Don't let him suck you in! Aggie wanted to scream.

"I think we speak different languages, Cabot. No kiss of mine promised you *anything* more. I was wrong to give you that impression, but you read way too much into it. I read you wrong, too. You seemed like somebody who got how mad I was at my family. Somebody who would understand me, care about what I was going through."

"I get you, all right. Every time I think of my mother sitting in the dark with her cigarette and that bottle, I want to find my dad and . . ." He punched his fist into his hand. "We're alike that way, Celia."

She backed away from him and shook her head so hard her pony-tail slapped her face. "No, we're not. Maybe at first, but not now. I raged at Daddy all the way to my grandmother's, you know that? After months of crying, my anger made me feel alive again. Then what did I do? I flew toward you like a stupid mallard answering a duck call. You were even angrier than I was. I don't want to be like you. We're done, Cabot. You can't have me."

She was scared again. Aggie could tell by the way her voice caught and cracked. *But brave.*

Cabot looked irritated, as if her words bumped him like insects. "This is all Burnaby's fault. He wants my job, and now he's trying to steal you, too. If he had his way, he'd take everything I've got." He moved toward her, lifted a strand of hair off her face. "You're blind, girl. And confused, that's all." He took hold of her arms, kneading them with his thumbs. "C'mere, baby. I don't want to lose you."

She shook him off and trotted backwards down the trail. "I'm sorry about your parents, Cabot. But I can't fix this for you."

"Hey. Nothing to fix. Once Burnaby's out of the way, we'll be fine."

"What does that mean?"

"The guy's got problems, Celia. I think he was stealing tools before Loomis laid him off. He's mental. He starts spazzing when I tell him to do something. He lights fires when the job gets too tough for him. He's not safe to have around the farm. I wouldn't be surprised if he lit his parents' house on fire. Loomis is gonna can him, if I have anything to say about it. I've almost got him convinced."

Aggie wanted to scream at him. She grabbed a rock and cocked her arm, held it poised for a beat, then slowly lowered it.

Celia's face knotted at his accusation. "You're wrong, Cabot. He's not that way at all." She hurried down the trail, flinging more sandwiches. Cabot caught up and bumped her heels, talking close to her ear.

They were outdistancing Aggie. *I can't hear them!* She dipped through the woods, advancing on the pair until the trees thinned, then angled into better cover. By the time she swerved back toward the trail, the low rumble of Cabot's voice had quit. She couldn't hear Celia, either. Panic dropped on her like a noose. Where were they? She launched herself into a tree and climbed, hunting for a glimpse of his bright shirt.

There. A flash of red showed in the clearing near the root cellar. She reached for a cottonwood limb, but instead of her usual quick grip, her hands faltered and she scrambled to hang on. Her legs seesawed as she inched hand over hand, until she planted her feet on a branch. She grunted with the effort, her biceps rubbery. "Please, please, arms, don't let go."

On another limb, she contorted her body for a clearer view through the canopy. A breeze fluttered the leaves, so that they opened and closed over Cabot and Celia below. Cabot's hand gripped the cellar door. Celia twisted the empty Wonder Bread bag like a washcloth, her hands tight.

Aggie laid her head on the branch to see better and scrunched her brow. *Why can't I understand them?* The bark felt cool against her face, and she closed her eyes. If only she could rest here, tune out the blurry voices arguing below her. She stuck out her lower lip and puffed air onto her forehead, as if blowing away fog. Then Cabot shouted, riveting her attention to the scene below.

Purple-faced, he threw his hat to the ground and swore. Then he grabbed Celia's arm and wrenched it, pulling her toward him. She howled with pain and landed on her knees. He dragged her to her feet and shoved her into the root cellar ahead of him. Aggie held her breath until he barged back outside, holding the shotgun. When Celia's knee jutted through the doorway, he kicked it, yanked the door closed, and flipped the heavy latch into place. Inside, Celia screamed.

She's trapped! Aggie lurched, off-balance. Her legs shook like Jell-O, but she managed to stand. Colorful dots sparkled in her field of vision. *I'm on my way, Celia.* She aimed her foot at a lower limb to begin her descent, but missed and fell backwards out of the tree.

41

AGGIE

GAME

AGGIE STIRRED. Was that her brother's scratchy voice? *So far away.* A dream? Her eyes flicked open. She was lying on her back beneath giant trees on a thick mattress of decomposing leaves. But where? And why was she so sore? She raised her arm in front of her and pulled up her sleeve. Skinned. Bloody. Her other arm? Same. Then more voices. Someone screaming, "Let me outta here!" and thumping something. Beating on that door? *Celia?* Another man's voice. Who was he?

She remembered. Cabot kicking Celia, slamming the door, holding the gun. Her own hunger and weakness and the haze clouding her mind like soot. The falling that seemed to last for hours. How long had she been unconscious? And how was Burnaby here, too? Where'd he come from?

She wiggled her fingers and toes. Bent her arms and legs. Everything still worked. She located the branch where she'd been sitting and tracked her route to the ground. Hardly surprising that she ached. If Celia hadn't been screaming and pounding that door, Cabot would have heard Aggie crash through those branches. *He'd have captured me, too.*

Instead, she sprawled flat on the ground between Celia, howling from her prison, and Burnaby, who traversed the anthill trail into the clearing and stood face to face with shotgun-wagging Cabot.

Hold on, Celia. Aggie regarded the door, which vibrated with every thump, then squirmed like a newt toward Burnaby. He needed her more right now.

Her bewildered brother set a basket on the ground. He looked past Cabot as if the man were invisible and stepped toward the cellar.

Cabot glowered. "Can't you leave us alone?"

Burnaby turned back to Cabot. "Who? Leave who alone?"

"Yeah, like you don't know. Dogging me and Celia." Cabot held the shotgun at his hip and leveled it at Burnaby.

"I saw Celia head this way, but she never spoke about meeting you." Burnaby's expression stayed mild, as if Cabot were pointing a feather duster at him.

"She don't tell you everything, moron." Cabot stepped closer to him. "What's that around your neck? A chicken bone? You chew on it between meals?"

Burnaby regarded the curved bone. "An owl ilium. Owl's hipbone. A gift."

You don't have to explain anything, Burnaby. The man's just taunting you.

"Gift huh?" Cabot raised the bone from Burnaby's chest, wrapped his fingers around the chain and yanked. "What's it worth to you?" He shifted the gun and swung the bone on its broken chain like a pendulum.

Burnaby flattened his lips as if he tasted something sour. "It's mine, not yours."

"Maybe. Maybe not. What will you do to get it back?" He balled the chain and bone into his hand and poised to fling it into the underbrush.

Burnaby lunged at his hand, but Cabot stepped out of reach. "Ah, ah, ahh." He ticked his index finger back and forth. "No grabbing." He walked toward the chimney.

"Let's play a little game, Burn. That's what Celia calls you, right? Burn?"

Burnaby's eyes followed Cabot's fist. He didn't answer.

"I see you're watching. Thatta way. Pay attention. Then the game won't be too tough for you." He waggled the white bone inside the old chimney's firebox. "Let's play Finders Keepers. You keep your eye on the chicken bone. I'll drop it. And if you can find it, it's yours. Got it?"

Burnaby locked his eyes on his gift. The broken chain caught the sun and scattered sparks of light.

Cabot brandished the gun. "I didn't hear you."

"I understand."

"Glad to hear that." Cabot hiked backwards up the dike while he kept the gun pointed at Burnaby. He gathered bone and chain into his free hand, wound his arm like a pitcher, and aimed for the river.

Her brother stood motionless, except for that cheek of his.

"Oh, swimming's too hard for you?" Cabot wagged his fist. "Poor baby." He returned to the center of the clearing and pretended to study the fir that held Aggie's treetop bed. "Hm. You like climbing trees better?" He feigned a throw into the branches and looked at stoic Burnaby. "No? Okay. Stand over here so you can see me real clear."

What was he doing? Aggie forgot her pain and hunger. Her muscles wound tight, ready to spring.

Cabot rotated the gun's muzzle. "Move, Burnaby." Her brother walked around the chimney until the barrel stopped revolving. "Yeah. Right there." Cabot swished through the ground cover and stood against a tree, about a horseshoe toss away from Burnaby. "I'll make it easy for you. It'll be somewhere between you and me."

He balanced the gun over his arm as he tied a knot in the broken chain and rocked the bone back and forth like a hypnotist's charm. Then he wadded it into his hand and, as if he were lobbing a softball to third graders, threw the bone a few feet ahead of him. It vanished into the thick greens.

Burnaby's body flinched. His eyes fixed on the spot.

"That's right. Keep your eyes on it. Now all you have to do is walk straight to it and it's yours." Cabot propped the gun against the tree behind him and raised his hands. "No pressure."

What was he doing? Aggie analyzed the ground cover. What had Cabot hidden in there that could hurt her brother? Burnaby walked forward, his eyes still glued to the spot where the bone had fallen through the leaves. Then Aggie remembered. She opened her mouth to scream.

Too late.

Burnaby took four steps toward Cabot. On the fifth, he collapsed into the well.

42

CELIA

CREATURE

"GET AWAY FROM ME, CABOT." He was stepping on my heels. I felt the heat of him on my back, his breath on the side of my face as he talked, inches from my ear. Gram's house shrank behind the hill as he intercepted my retreat and pushed me toward the woods. I wanted to stop walking, slap him and tell him to get lost, but something about the press of him, the way his presence closed around me out there in the open field terrified me. He seemed bigger, more powerful. Menacing. I had to keep moving.

His words blurred—and were so far from what was real. I was walking in a nightmare. He told me I needed him, wanted him. And that he wanted me. That wherever I went, he'd be waiting. He said other stuff, too, about touching me, and my skin crawled as if bugs were swarming on it. Sweat dripped down my chest. My lungs shrank.

In a few minutes, Burnaby would head this way, gathering bones at the anthills. If he encountered Cabot out here . . . I picked up my pace, hoping to put some distance between the two. If I got through the woods, I'd run for it. Find Loomis.

But when we approached that abandoned farm, he said that Burnaby was missing some bricks and was a danger to me and the dairy and that he, Cabot, was here to save me from him.

His words burned little holes in my eardrums. "You are a deluded liar, Cabot, and I think Burnaby has saved me from you."

When I said that, he threw his hat on the ground and swore at me with words so filthy I felt contaminated. Sliced open. I truly expected to see blood. Then he cranked my arm behind me until I cried out and fell over. But bad as the pain was, the fear was worse. He shoved me into that little hobbit cellar and closed us both inside.

I dropped into hell. The terror of it. He held me torqued like that while he pulled a gun from the top shelf.

"Wait for me, sweetheart." His voice flattened to a dead calm. "Be right back. I have something for you . . . You'll forget all this. Gonna make sure nobody interrupts us."

Then he pushed me back against the shelves and opened the door.

Well. He would not lock *me* in that dungeon. I leapt at the opening and shoved my leg between the door and the jamb. Of course he couldn't close the door with my knee right there, so he kicked it. Kicked my knee so hard I toppled back inside. Before I got up, he hurled the door and threw the latch. I do believe that by the time I stood and screamed his name, he had convinced himself that *I* had assaulted *him*. He was that delusional. That crazy.

I screamed until my throat was raw and tightening. Pounded on that door as I leaned against it, supporting my injured knee. I tried to guess his next move, but terrible thoughts intruded, crowding out anything rational. Now, instead of Cabot breathing on me there in the dark, fear pressed into me, drinking oxygen from the dank air around me. I picked a box off a shelf and beat it into the door until the cardboard broke and little tubes scattered all over the floor. Then I heard men's voices.

One of them was *Burnaby's*.

I felt the blood leave my face. Cabot was outside with a gun, alone with Burn. I could tell that Cabot was taunting him, ordering him around. Frantic, I ran my fingers over the door, the hinges, pulling at them. My breath came out ragged. Phantom earwigs crawled across my neck, down my back.

Outside, Cabot laughed. What could be funny? I screamed again and was slamming my fists against the door when the latch rattled, something thudded to the ground, and the door pushed against me. I jumped away as a scrawny, bedraggled creature with matted clumps for hair burst through the door. A girl's soft, high-pitched voice came out of its mouth. She was holding the broken door latch. And she said my name.

"Celia! Get Cabot under this tree—so he's right under me." She pointed at a plum tree and sprang into its limbs. Stunned, I stood there until she blended in with the leaves.

Aggie!

I limped outside. Cabot was pointing his gun into ground cover beyond the chimney.

"What'd you do with him, Cabot?"

He whirled toward me. I ducked as the gun's muzzle moved with him. "How'd you get out?"

He clearly hadn't seen the girl.

"Where's Burnaby?"

"He left. Wanted to give us some time alone. Said to tell you he'd see you around."

"Yeah, *right*. You have another little rabbit burrow to hide him in?"

"My pretty girl sure has grown a mouth on her."

I backed toward the tree as he sauntered my way. The gun rested crosswise in his arms, like a newborn.

I shivered from the ache in my knee, but I stood there like bait. I didn't understand Aggie's plan, but hers was the only one on the table. If she wanted me to lure him under the tree, I would lure like nobody's business.

Cabot stopped about ten feet away. Too far. Aggie said to get him beneath her.

"Why are you backing up, pretty lady? I won't hurt you."

"You already did." I scowled at him as he ran his eyes down my body. More earwigs. "And I'd like to hear why." I tilted my head and hip. Flirty.

I took another step backwards as he approached. *Just one more step, Cabot. One more.* I forced myself to study my fingernails, as if his delay bored me. What would Aggie do once he stepped into that bullseye below her?

I found out.

Her scream preceded her. As she sprang onto Cabot's back, her legs clamped around him like a spider and she clawed his face and gouged at his eyes. Bit his ears. Then she bit his neck as hard as I've ever seen *anyone* bite *anything*. Ever.

Cabot howled and dropped the gun. He flailed at Aggie's arms as her fingernails drew blood from his eyelids and cheeks. She screeched at me. "The gun. Pick it up. Point it at him. At his chest!" My hands and fingers were useless, but I lifted the weapon, held it level, and pointed it in his direction.

Then that little wolverine slipped off him like fog. She ran to me and wrested the gun from my shaky grip. She must have guessed I'd never touched one, must have seen my shock and fear.

Cabot moaned and clamped his hands over his eyes. Blood trickled from his neck and cheeks. He wiped his face with his palms and opened his eyes a slit, then wide—as he took in that dreadlocked, dirty little elf.

Though Aggie barely reached my shoulder and weighed no more than a minute, she held her finger alongside the trigger and was aiming right at his chest.

"Hands on your head." Her voice was thin as thread.

Cabot held his hands at shoulder height and hesitated. His body coiled. He was going to try for the gun.

Aggie saw it too. "On your head!" Her finger went to the trigger.

Cabot sneered at her and laced his fingers over his skull.

"Get over by the well."

He threw me an angry glare and swaggered toward thick ground cover near the chimney.

"On your stomach. Now."

A well? What was she talking about? Aggie walked behind him until he was on the ground, prodding him until he poised for a pushup in a tangle of salad greens. I didn't see a well anywhere.

"Celia. His coveralls should be in the cellar. Get 'em. Quick." She spoke without taking her eyes or the gun off Cabot. "Burnaby can't swim." Her voice shook.

Aggie touched the barrel between Cabot's shoulder blades. "All the way down. Hands on your head." He plopped onto his belly and twined his fingers over his occipital lobe, directly above Aggie's bloody dental impression. His face pressed the ground, and he muttered into the dirt.

I hurried for the coveralls and held them out to her. "Why these?" She didn't answer me, but spoke into the leafy carpet instead.

"Burnaby. Can you hear me?" Her eyes darted to a shaded hole crowded with foliage that opened a few feet from Cabot's head. *The well.* I could have been right on top of it and not noticed. I scrambled to the edge and bent over the rim. Cabot twisted toward me. Aggie jabbed the gun into his ribs.

Burn's voice echoed. "Here. Right here. Aggie? That you?" Water splashed, and I saw his shoulders and yellow head, his face upturned. "Celia?" Aggie spoke before I could answer.

"I'm here, Burn. You hurt?" She stepped around Cabot and leaned over the well so he could see her, but she kept her eyes and the gun tethered to Cabot. Tears streamed down her face.

"Uninjured. Where's Cabot? He said he'd shoot me if I spoke."

"I'm breathing down your neck, you dirty—"

"Shut up, Cabot." Aggie poked him with the muzzle. "He won't be shooting you, Burn. I've got the gun. How far down are you?"

"I'm in water to my waist." Seconds passed. "Distance from my waist to the lip?" He was taking his time to estimate. "Approximately eleven feet. No, twelve."

Aggie evaluated my hoodie, unzipped halfway down my tank top. "Your sweatshirt. Tie it to the coveralls."

The girl was a genius. Talk about being good in a crisis. I knotted our makeshift rope and tossed an end to Burnaby. "We'll get you outta there."

Burn leaped for the hoodie's sleeve. Missed. Jumped again. His fingers found the cuff and gripped. "I've got you at this end," I said. I steadied myself against rocks lining the well's edge and the fabric pulled tight over them. He began to climb.

Cabot was watching me. When he slowly unclasped his hands and lay them on the ground by his head, Aggie didn't react. Then he shot his hand forward and grabbed my ankle. I recoiled, and a few inches of the coveralls slipped through my fingers. I clenched the fabric tighter and held on for all I was worth. Which wasn't much, given my sore knee and Cabot yanking on me.

Aggie jabbed him with the gun. "Let go." Her wispy voice chilled me. I could tell it affected Cabot, too. When he released his hold, I dug my heels into the ground and pulled. Aggie shoved the muzzle into Cabot's kidneys until he returned his hands to his head.

I braced my feet and leveraged my body against the well's rim, straining. My knee ached. For all Burn's skinniness, I could hardly hold him. "You making headway?" I asked.

"Halfway."

Then the rope shifted again under his weight and so did I. The rock supporting me loosened; my foot punched it into the well, and I toppled backwards. Burn's moan and the sound of a splash rose from the hole. The hoodie and coveralls slid into the water.

I dropped to my belly opposite the prostrate Cabot and peered down the well. I nearly cried with relief when I saw Burnaby upright and moving. He was holding his shoulder.

"Oh, Burn. I'm sorry." I rolled to face Aggie. "Let's get Cabot out of here."

Aggie shook her head. "I won't leave Burnaby. Go get Uncle Loomis."

I got to my feet. "You sure? You got Cabot? I don't know, Aggie . . ." Her skinny arms trembled. That gun was heavy.

She nodded. "Hold on a second." Lowering one knee to the ground, she planted her other foot ahead of her and, with her forearm on the upraised thigh, steadied the gun. Aimed it straight at him. I felt better about leaving her then. "He won't be going anywhere." Her steely eyes confirmed her resolve. Her voice was airy, like it came from the sky.

"I'll hurry." I took a dozen slow, painful steps up the trail until the movement loosened my knee enough to speed up. With the wind howling overhead, I limped toward the dairy.

HELP

AS CELIA HOBBLED UP THE TRAIL, Aggie trained the weighty firearm on Cabot and pictured that ammo sinking in the river. If he hadn't reloaded, she was nothing more than a scrubby girl with an empty shotgun, like a terrier with no teeth, barking at a grizzly.

But what if he *had* reloaded? And what if he rushed her and seized the weapon?

Please hurry hurry hurry. She sturdied her arm against the fatigue as a tremor crept into her muscles. How long could she hold this thing? She repositioned again, aiming lower on Cabot's back. Her senses sparked. *He's too still. Planning something.* The gun barrel shook.

His voice came so low she had to strain to hear him. "You've got me all wrong, little girl. If I hadn't stopped Burnaby, he'd have hurt your friend Celia." He looked her way, but kept his hands on his head. "Do you know he lit your house on fire, Aggie? Then he drove off to work, leaving you all to die."

He's trying to distract me. She willed herself to tune him out, but his words attached themselves to her like tentacles, entangling her in doubt. Could Burnaby have lit a second fire? Did that fire, instead of hers, burn their house?

No! Don't listen! He wants you to do something stupid. She tried to block the lies with thoughts of her trees and birds, of her parents smiling and healed. Happy things.

———————

Minutes ticked by. Cabot's words kept coming, fluid and melodious. She thought of Pi, and her brother weeping as he carried the dog to the truck. She exhaled through her teeth. Whispered.

"Help me."

"Who ya talking to, sweetheart?" Cabot lunged for the barrel; Aggie swung it away.

There was no time to answer. Uncle Loomis, breathing hard and sweating, broke into the clearing. When he spotted Aggie, he ran toward her, his mouth open in a wide, delighted grin. "Risen from the dead." His deep voice bounced off the trees. He palmed her head affectionately and took the gun from her, then laid it on the ground before he scooped her into his arms and spun her, laughing. "And risen from the swamp, from the looks of you."

He's being nice to me. He's glad to see me. Her eyes blurred with tears. She wrapped her arms around her uncle's neck and squeezed. He held her like a moorage.

Cabot wasted no time. "Loomis. Good to see a friend. Crazy people down here." He stood and brushed leaves and twigs off his shirt and jeans. Wiped blood from his face.

"I figured as much." Uncle Loomis kissed Aggie on the forehead, then lowered her, retrieved the gun, and took in the scene. Aggie hid behind him and grasped his shirt, the cloth tight between her fingers.

Cabot talked faster now. "Burnaby ripped off your shotgun. I got it back, but then this little monster jumped me."

"M-hm. I see that." Her uncle lifted the gun to study it and Aggie dropped her hands as Celia limped into the clearing with a rope.

"Be right back." Aggie scurried into the root cellar and returned with two shells, which she handed to her uncle. "It's not loaded." Or maybe it was. She was taking a chance. What if Uncle Loomis believed Cabot?

Her uncle cracked the gun open, exposing two empty chambers. Aggie's eyes widened.

"How'd you know it was empty?" He winked at her, his eyes spilling. Over her? Uncle Loomis was crying because of *her*?

Then he did the oddest thing. He turned away from Cabot and Celia so only Aggie could see his hands. He pretended to reload the gun, but instead slipped the shells into his pocket. He snapped the barrel back in place, clicked the safety, and handed the weapon to Cabot. Celia gasped.

"Now that you've caught him, Cabot, let's get him out of here and take him someplace where he won't hurt anybody."

Cabot puffed up like a sage grouse. He sneered at Celia and waggled the gun's butt at Aggie. Her uncle put his hand on Cabot's shoulder. "I'll pull him out. You make sure he doesn't run once I bring him up."

"You bet, Loomis."

Her uncle knelt by the well. "Hey, Burnaby. Ready for daylight? Any injuries I should know about?"

"Yes, I am ready. Surface wounds. A modest amount of blood."

"We'll get you fixed up. Here comes the rope. Remember the snake pops out of the hole, goes around the tree, and dives back in the hole?"

Uncle Loomis should have saved his breath. Burn knew every knot in the book. Aggie danced in place, waiting for her brother.

"Yes. Bowline. Under my arms." Her uncle sat back on his haunches until Burnaby spoke again. "Tied and secure. Ready."

"Elevator going up." Uncle Loomis produced leather gloves from his back pocket and smoothed them over his thick fingers. He docked his sturdy legs, gripped the rope, and pulled like Hercules—or The Incredible Hulk. His muscles bulged from his enormous shoulders down into his forearms. His legs anchored to the ground like ancient stumps, and he hoisted Burnaby out of that hole as if he were a toddler.

When Burn's hands touched the lip of the well, Celia and Aggie converged on him and helped him stand. Celia ran her fingers along a scrape on his face, then stepped away. Sobbing, Aggie clung to her brother, as her threadbare clothes absorbed the well water that dripped from him. "They're alive, Burn? Mama and Dad?"

Burnaby lifted the rope over his head and tossed it aside. He held his hand open above his sister, then gently set it on her head. "They are." She gripped him tighter.

Uncle Loomis kept moving. Aggie pulled her face out of Burnaby's shirt and watched. Whose side was he on? Her uncle coiled the rope and handed it to Celia. He casually retrieved the gun from Cabot, who passed it to him as if he were a fellow soldier. Loomis stood the weapon against a tree.

"Now what do we do with him?" Cabot asked. He stood beside Uncle Loomis, his feet planted wide and his hands clasped behind him. His eyelids were swelling.

"Wanna see?" In a flash, her uncle seized Cabot's arms and locked them behind his back like wings under a roasting chicken. Aggie clapped her hands over her open mouth. Cabot had rotated Celia's arm like that. But her uncle cranked Cabot's arms so hard Aggie thought they might break right off.

Cabot folded at the waist, yowling. He writhed to free himself but was powerless in Uncle Loomis's mighty grip.

"Get moving," her uncle growled and shoved the dog-killer, still bent in half, ahead of him. About fifty feet up the trail, he let go of one arm. "Stand up and walk. Try anything and you'll crawl."

With one arm liberated, Cabot spun down and toward his elbow, uncurling Uncle Loomis's hold on the other arm. He threw a punch, but her uncle dodged it and cocked his own fist. Then, in the split second before Uncle Loomis could strike, Cabot dropped to his knees and hung from Loomis's grasp, surrendered. He held his free hand upright.

Loomis grabbed Cabot's wrist and crossed his arms behind the man's back. "Changed your mind, huh, punk?"

Cabot shook his shoulders angrily, but didn't resist when Uncle Loomis jerked him to his feet.

The girls watched until the pair crossed behind the hill. Aggie pointed after them. "How did Uncle Loomis get him to—*what* just happened?"

"Beats me." Celia said. "Better ask Mender. She claimed she had invisible help with him." Her voice was shaky, but she looked at Aggie and laughed. "Where have you been?"

"All over."

"I bet." She scanned Aggie's skinny body. "You can tell us over a meal. Let's get your brother."

But her brother had evaporated. Aggie shook her head. Her thoughts fuzzed again as she ran back to the clearing. Was she dreaming that they found him? Where was he?

Celia limped after her, calling. "You want to fall in there again, Burn? What are you looking for?"

Burnaby. As soon as she spotted him, Aggie slumped onto the mossy ground and lay on her side, facing his way. Thankful. Exhausted. He crawled through the herbage beyond the well, his hands patting the earth ahead of him like a blind man.

She smiled. Typical Burn, to ignore his brush with death and go on a treasure hunt. She didn't care what he was doing. He was here. A little beat up, but okay, and Cabot wouldn't hurt him anymore.

"Found it." Out of the greens, Burnaby pulled a snarled chain connected to something curved and whitish. *Oh, yeah.* Aggie recognized the necklace Cabot had snatched from her brother. She wanted to ask him about it, but her mouth wouldn't move.

He held it up to Celia. "Your owl ilium. Cabot took it." He twisted the chain's broken ends, and the bone swayed.

"I can fix that." Celia slid the broken chain into her pocket. Then she lifted a leather thong off her chest and over her head. As Burnaby watched, she untied it and removed a shell, gently threaded the cord through the bone, and tied it behind his neck. He blinked hard, held his breath for a second, and bowed his head, the muscles in his neck relaxing. Hardly nervous at all.

Aggie let relief unclench and sedate her. Her body throbbed from the fall, from hunger, from so many adrenaline surges. She just wanted to lie there.

And she wanted her mama.

REUNION

WHEN I TIED THAT OWL'S PELVIS around Burnaby's neck, he ran his fingers along the leather. The corners of his mouth rose in that adorable, crooked uptick. "How'd that thing land in the bushes?" I asked.

Aggie answered for him. "Cabot tore it off Burn and tossed it."

She slowly got to her feet and walked to a spot on the far side of the well. "It landed right there. Burnaby was standing where you are now. He walked in a line from you to me and stepped into the well on his way."

"Cabot must have known I would concentrate on the location. Not recognize the break in the vegetation."

"It's hard to see even if you're staring at it." I parted the plants, exposing the well's crumbling rock rim.

"I'll build a cover for it," Burnaby said. "Deter animals."

"Good thing none have fallen in there so far, Burn. If you'd found any bones down there, we'd never have gotten you out." He gave me that oblique smile again. "Now you've got that hipbone, let's go. Loomis called the sheriff. He'll want our statements."

As soon as I said "sheriff," the girl bit her thumb. Stood on her tiptoes and jigged. "You up for that, Aggie?"

Her eyes flicked toward a tree by the river. I could tell she wanted to make a run for it.

"Are you afraid of the sheriff?" Why was I talking to her as if she were a preschooler, instead of someone who had just rescued me? But she was so tiny.

"He'll take me, too."

"Take you where?"

"Jail." She clamped her arms around Burnaby and buried her face in his shirt, muffling her words. "Mama. Dad. Have you seen them, Burn?"

"I have." He stood like a post.

"So, when? Where are they?" She crouched and fidgeted with some twigs, her shoulders near her ears. "*How* are they?"

He raised his hand against the flood of questions. "Both are at Harborview. Second- and third-degree burns. A surgeon pinned Dad's leg. The doctor released him a week ago. He's staying in Seattle. With Mama." His voice was low and choppier than usual. "He thought you were dead. We all did."

I shouldn't have kept her a secret. I had robbed Burn and his father of hope. Not to mention Loomis and Nora. And Gram.

Aggie's eyes widened. "Mama? How's she?"

"Burns on her back. Arms. Head. Three surgeries. Medications are keeping her comatose for pain control."

"Will she be okay?"

"Prognosis varies day to day."

Pain pinched Aggie's face. "I did that to her."

I stared at her. "Why do you say that?"

"I started that fire. I was only testing a fuzz stick. I was making them for Mama and built a little campfire, and Mama called me for dinner and I kicked dirt on it, I really did, to put it out and instead of water and a shovel I used my foot and Mama would be mad if I didn't come to dinner right away and . . ." And then she was sobbing too much to get the words out.

"Oh, Aggie." I was struggling with the storyline, but I got the gist. "Sounds like an accident to me. You started out doing something nice for your mother, built a small fire, and put it out. Is that right?"

Aggie shoved her fists into her eyes. Her chest heaved. "I don't know. I guess. But—"

"You will not go to jail, Aggie." She backed up when I reached for her.

"I thought I killed them. When I heard you in the woods and you said they were alive, I thought we could all be together again, and that they wouldn't take me away." She pulled at her greasy hair with both hands. "But I lit that fire, Celia. The house is gone and Mama's still in the hospital."

This time she let me draw her into my arms. I could feel her corrugated ribs, her protruding shoulder blades. "An accident, Aggie. An accident. They won't take you anywhere. You've served your time." I thought of that little girl out there in the woods for a month, feeling like a murderer, missing her family. Hungry, dirty.

I rocked her. "It's over, Aggie. Over."

———✈︎———

A sheriff's car was idling in the barnyard when the three of us came over the hill. Cabot sat in the back seat. He pounded the window with his fist and tried to catch my eye, but I hurried past him with my arm around Aggie.

"There." Burnaby pointed into an assembly of old machines where Loomis and an unfamiliar man in a green uniform were sifting through the cab of a big farm truck.

Aggie hung behind me as we approached, then stepped forward like she was reciting her spelling words. Or going to the guillotine. "Burnaby didn't steal those things."

The men bolted upright.

Loomis jumped off the running board and hurried to Aggie. He cupped the top of her head with both hands. "Deputy Yost, meet Aggie. Your missing person." His voice had a hitch in it. "A little worse for wear, but she's back with us." He picked her up and bounced her, as if his arm were a scale. "You're hollow, missy." He poked her belly with a finger. "Time for pie."

The officer walked toward them both, his cheeks stretched in welcome. "Miss Hayes. We have missed you."

Where her tears had washed away mud, I saw her blush. "See the caps in there?" She blinked against a spatter of rain and tightened her arms around her uncle.

The deputy stuck his head in the cab.

"Those are Burnaby's caps, but he didn't put them there. Cabot did. He wanted you to think Burnaby did, but I saw him climb in there and take shotgun shells. They're in the root cellar. He hid other stuff there, too."

He stared at her, his face illegible.

"I believe you, Aggie," Loomis said. "Saw Cabot out here last Saturday. Figured he was scavenging a part for another rig. Today, though, I was out here for pipe. Saw that cab from my tractor. Couldn't believe my eyes.

"Had to be either Cabot or Burnaby, stashing all those goods. Nobody else comes near here. Got me to thinking about what Mender said. So I followed Cabot in from the field. I walked over the rise just as he left the truck with a box.

"I smelled a skunk, so I checked the barns and shop. Sure enough, tools missing everywhere. A full shelf of my ammo was cleared out, too—and one of my shotguns." Loomis tucked a lock of hair behind Aggie's ear before he continued. "I was hunting for Cabot to apply a little justice, when Celia here ran up the trail shouting for me."

Aggie squirmed free and dropped to the ground. "He hid the gun in the root cellar down by the river. And more of Burnaby's caps. And this." She extracted a luminous stone hanging from her neck.

Loomis rolled the agate between his fingers. "That's Nora's," he said. "How'd he get—"

"I was spying from behind the tractor and saw him in your bedroom. He passed by the window." Aggie's head oscillated between the men like an electric fan. "Burnaby didn't steal that stuff. You know that, right?"

Her brother toed a stick in the dirt.

"I do, Aggie," Loomis said. "Cabot has left plenty of evidence. And witnesses." He ticked a finger at Burnaby, Aggie, and me, as if he were tapping us.

Then he frowned. "Hold on a minute. You were in our barnyard? Spying?"

"Lots of times."

Deputy Yost shut the truck door. "Sounds like you have quite a story to tell."

Aggie opened her mouth, closed it, then opened it again. Her words sputtered. "I lit the fire. Burnaby didn't do that, either."

"I'm all ears, young lady. Let's get you out of this wind. I'll get my notebook and you can tell me what's been happening for the last month. You all can."

At that, whatever was holding Aggie together disintegrated. She sank to the ground and broke into sobs. "I am . . ." She struggled for breath. "I am so . . . sorry. You have to arrest me . . . I know."

The deputy dropped to his knees and held her head in his hands until she stopped shaking. "Aggie. You're safe now. Safe."

———✍︎———

Gusts flattened Cabot's hair and clothes as two more officers escorted him, handcuffed and grim, from Deputy Yost's patrol car to the back seat of theirs. I watched the car travel the farm lane and shrink behind the hill.

Burnaby brought me a bag of ice. I held it on my knee as the sky darkened with the changing weather and as Burnaby, Aggie, and I sat at the kitchen table, ate fresh raspberry pie, and told the sheriff everything.

As we were concluding our stories, Nora drove in. When she walked through that door and saw Aggie, I thought the roof would blow right into the next county with all that screaming and fussing. She kissed that girl's grimy little face about a hundred times and cried until she snorted.

My own eyes filled. "I'm sorry I didn't tell you about her," I muttered, but nobody heard. I'd tell them again later. Louder.

Nora dug in her purse and handed several bills to Burnaby. "Can you two make it to town before the stores close?" She pulled out a scrap of paper and sat at the counter, writing. "Oh, never mind. Just get her some clothes. Undies. And a toothbrush." She measured Aggie with her eyes. "Size six? Seven? Your guess is as good as mine."

"C'mon, sweetie." She took Aggie's hand. "Time for a bath."

———✍︎———

I hoisted myself into Burn's truck, my bum leg straight, the other folded under me. Burnaby flipped on the windshield wipers and shifted through the gears. His cheek ticked nonstop; his calf tightened every few seconds. The accelerator responded to his spasms, and the truck pulsed forward. He kept clearing his throat.

"What color've you got in that head of yours?" I yawned and massaged my bad knee. "You look like chewed twine."

"I don't know yet." Burn tapped the turn signal and aimed the truck toward town, heading for Crescent Clothiers. Nora said the store carried Aggie's size, whatever that was.

I imagine I didn't look much better. We needed to get our minds off the day's events if we planned to buy anything remotely suitable for the girl to wear.

"Take your time," I said. I closed my eyes and pressed my head to the glass.

"More rain's forecast for Saturday," he said.

Rain. I officially met Cabot in the rain. I was running. I sat up so fast Burnaby jerked the wheel. His brow bent with concern.

"I've been meaning to ask you this forever," I said. Now he really looked worried. "Ask me what?"

"The rain problem. Mr. Maurer gave it to us at the end of the year to play with over the summer."

Burnaby relaxed. Those parentheses appeared at the corners of his mouth. "'Problem.' As in 'math problem'?"

"Yeah. Sounded trivial at first." I scooted closer to him and aimed my voice at his ear. "It's raining. You're on foot. You want to get home, but also stay as dry as possible. Should you run or walk?"

His hands relaxed on the steering wheel. "We won't need integrals." He thought for a moment. "Velocities, vectors, and variables."

"Okay, Burnaby. Okay. You got something to write with in here?" I rummaged through the glove box and pulled out a pencil and a notepad with mileage numbers on it. Right there beside a bag of caps. "Variables for the amount of rain being dropped in gallons per square feet per second, right? Plus the vertical component and wind speed—each in feet per second."

He shifted in his seat as we pulled up to a stop sign. "And distance traveled, speed of the traveler with respect to a fixed point, and the total surface area of the traveler from the top and, separately, from the front."

I scribbled as a semi crossed in front of us. Burn touched the notepad. "To find the angle of the rain to the direction of the path, we can use arctangent."

Sweetest ride I'd ever taken. By the time we returned with a bag of clothes and a toothbrush, we had pages of answers for different body types and conditions which, summarized, came down to this:

Run, usually; walk sometimes.

Pure bliss.

———

Back in the kitchen, a fair-skinned girl with felted blonde hair sat at the table, an empty dinner plate in front of her. Her skin glowed pink instead of brownish-gray, and she smelled a whole lot better. Her tiny body swam in one of Nora's T-shirts. Scratches and mosquito bites covered her arms and legs. A long, scabby pink scar ran the length of her forearm. The girl had been through the wringer.

Nora snagged a comb in her hair. "No use, sweetie. These mats will never come out. Time for a trim." Aggie lifted scissors and a hand mirror off the table. She frowned at her knotted hair, laid the blades against her head, and sawed. Burnaby and I sat down to watch.

"Here, let me do that. You hold the mirror." Nora seized the scissors and went to work. Half an hour later, Aggie's dreadlocks lay in a heap on the floor like a pile of dead mice. Nora swept them up and carried them outside. The girl sported a pixie cut with bald spots. Trendy.

———

"Think we could see our house?" Aggie asked. The sun dipped below the clouds and the rain had let up. Her fresh clothes hung loose and flapped in the wind, as she, Burnaby, and I sat on the farmhouse porch. I would have taken that girl to the moon if she'd asked.

Burnaby drove, of course. We wound our way through tall firs to a grassy hillside dominated by the Hayes' barn, unpainted and weathered. A brick chimney rose from rubble and charred ground. Somber, Aggie left the truck and crept to the burned site. She shuffled along the perimeter, then paused on a bare patch outside the home's footprint. A few weeds poked through the dirt. "Right here, Burn. Here's where I built the fire."

Burnaby nodded. "The inspector identified this as the point of origin. Without accelerants." His eyes passed over Aggie's. "We'll rebuild. Dad and Mama will come home." She leaned into her brother, holding him tighter than she had by the well.

I found a stick and poked around in the debris, jabbing and scraping the black remains. Not much left. Then I bumped something with my foot. The lid had melted, and the glass was sooty, but intact. "What's this?" Aggie and Burnaby looked up from their crouch over a warped skillet. "Full of rocks." I shook it.

Aggie ran to me. She wrapped both hands around the jar and held it to her chest as if it were sacred. Her face was soft, bright.

"Mama's agates."

———

We pulled into the parking lot of The Regional Burn Center at Harborview at ten the next morning. Burnaby touched Aggie's knee with one finger and pointed. Near the front door, a blond man in a hip-high cast sat outside in a wheelchair, one arm swathed in bandages. Despite the apparent misery he had endured, he smiled and craned his neck, obviously waiting for someone.

That someone was Aggie. Thirty seconds later, the pixie was in his arms.

45
—
AGGIE

SCARS

AGGIE PRESSED HER FINGERS hard against the jar on her lap and watched the tips of her fingernails turn white. Harborview Burn Center filled her passenger window as her dad parked near the same entrance where they'd reunited four weeks earlier, when he'd held her until she finally stopped crying and released her grip on his arm. The same grip she now had on the jar.

"She's awake enough to talk? For sure?"

Her father turned off the engine and smiled at her in the rearview mirror. Healing skin bloomed pink on his neck. Ingrown beard hairs erupted from red bumps along a scar under his chin. "Chatted with her last night. Not for long, but she's back with us."

"With you and Burnaby, maybe."

Her brother unclipped his seatbelt and stepped onto the blacktop. Pushed the car door closed behind him and stood with his back to the wind, yellow hair blowing over his eyes.

"Your mother wants to see you, Aggie."

"She's just saying that." Aggie shrank low in the seat and the agates clinked against the jar. She had replaced the melted lid, buffed soot off the glass.

"C'mon, sweetie. She's still on pain meds, so she'll be a little sleepy, but you'll be glad you came. I promise."

"Dad . . ."

He reached over the seat and rested his hand on her knee. "We've been through this a dozen times. What's the worst that can happen?"

He had a point. Since Mama would hate her forever, she may as well get used to it. The warmth in Dad's eyes whenever he looked at Aggie still surprised her, but she was learning to count on it again, and Burnaby talked to her more. She hoped she could live with two out of three.

"Now I can't pretend, Dad."

He raised his brows, searched her eyes. "About what?"

Her thumbs petted the agate jar. "She used to be happy. Before she got sick, she loved me. With her in that coma, I sat by her bed and pretended those things were still true."

"Oh, Agate." His eyes brimmed. "They are, they are, they are."

Aggie swung her gaze to the heavy clouds overhead. Even the sky was crying.

She set her jaw and trailed him into the hospital, hugging the jar to her chest. He led her to a different room than the one they visited during late July and August, the one where her comatose mama had faced the ground in a sling or lay sideways in that special burn-unit bed.

In this new room, they didn't make Aggie or Dad or Burnaby wear a yellow suit or mask. The air smelled like clean linens, not antiseptic. No ventilator hissed and clicked. Aggie shrank against the wall and fixed her eyes on the single IV line trailing from the hanging plastic bag to her mother's arm. The crowd of hoses and wires she'd seen the previous week were nowhere in sight.

Mama's eyes were closed. Propped on her side at an incline, she faced the door from a plain old hospital bed with rails. Rain battered the window.

"Hey, sweetheart." Dad bent over Mama and kissed her lips lightly. Ran his hand over her close-cropped hair before he rested it against her cheek.

Mama's eyelids fluttered, then closed again.

"We're here. All of us." His voice sounded like feathers.

Her mother's eyes opened and played on the ceiling, unfocused. Then they swerved to Burnaby. Smiling, she ran her hand over the white waffle blanket. Burn stepped closer and touched her knuckles, one by one. "Hello, Mama."

"What time did you leave last night?" she asked, her tongue thick.

"Eight forty-two. Right after you fell asleep."

"Glad you're back, love." She pressed her other hand on top of his. He tensed but left his fingers between hers.

She lifted her head and looked past him to Aggie. "Agate? My Agate?"

Aggie nodded and crept to the bed, raising her eyes to Mama's only after she set the agate jar on the blanket in front of her.

"I ever tell you how I got these?" Mama slowly unscrewed the lid and tipped the jar with the back of her hand. Agates spilled onto the blanket. Her lips barely moved. "Giant waves guarding them."

Aggie leaned closer to hear. Mama reached for her, then dropped her hand to the bed.

"We'll have to go to that beach together sometime."

Together?

Aggie's lips puckered as her mother closed her eyes again. She wanted to believe Mama in the worst way, but she *couldn't*. Hunting agates with her kind mama? The hope was too big. She couldn't hold it inside herself even for a second. She backed up to the wall and slid to the floor, her chin to her chest, her forehead on her knees.

Her dad lowered himself to the linoleum beside her, his injured leg straight out, his side pressing against hers. "Waited a long time for this, haven't we?"

Aggie's face rubbed her jeans as she nodded.

"A little too much?"

She nodded again.

Dad rose and gathered the strewn agates, then set the jar on the bedside table behind a water glass with a bent straw. "We'll be back, Bree. I'm taking Aggie to the cafeteria."

Mama nodded without opening her eyes. Burnaby sat in the chair beside her as Dad pulled Aggie to her feet.

———✣

For the next month, they prepared to bring Mama home.

Deacons from their old church towed in a single wide trailer and connected it to the power pole and the septic field and the well on their property. Dad said they had good insurance so didn't need help from the church's benevolent fund, but that didn't stop the scrubbed-out cattle truck, pickups, and cars. They arrived with clothes and towels and canned goods and pots and pans and dishes and casseroles and beds and dressers and a sofa and recliner and kitchen table with wooden chairs. Friends carried everything inside.

Aggie's father was closing the tailgate on a truck when an old man slipped inside the trailer with a package wrapped in newspaper. Dad found it after dinner and unwrapped the scarred violin and ancient bow with half of the horsehair missing. Lifting the fiddle to his chin, he tuned and plucked the strings.

Insurance bought Mama a wheelchair. She could walk the hospital halls, but not very far before her lungs hurt, so Burnaby built a ramp up to the trailer's door and smoothed a gravel path to her seed barn, so she could get around once she arrived.

Aggie lived on high alert every second after Mama woke up.

Whenever they visited the hospital, she watched her mother for a shift in her mood or tone of voice, something that would confirm what Aggie *knew* would happen: Mama would come to her senses and realize what Aggie did to her. Or her brain would start acting up again. Either way, her mean mama would be back.

So far, Mama hadn't mentioned the fire. She had been . . . well . . . *gentle*. Curious about Aggie's time in the woods. Even a little playful now and then. Aggie didn't trust her for a minute. Pain medications drugged and confused Mama—no more, no less.

Aggie braced herself. The second week of October, Mama would leave the hospital and move back in with Dad and Burnaby and her. By then she'd be *clean*. The doctors had already been weaning her off the painkillers for more than a month. They had stopped her prior psychotropic medications when she was in the coma, Dad said, and she refused to restart them once she regained consciousness. Now Mama's mind was sharper, her eyes clear. What would that mean? Which mother would come home to them? To her?

———ᴀ

"What about her antidepressants, Dad?" Aggie sat across the table from him in the trailer. The aroma of taco filling wafted around them, but Aggie hadn't touched her favorite meal. "And that other pill. The yellow one."

Dad spooned salsa over his beans. "Those side effects . . . As long as she's stable . . . She says she doesn't need them anymore."

"Don't they all say that?"

"Who's they?"

"You know. Mental patients."

"Hard to lump them all together, Aggie. Each one is different. Sometimes people get well."

Another hope she couldn't let inside herself. "What are the chances?"

"I . . . tend to ignore statistics. You know that." He grinned at her. "They kept her in a coma for three solid months. Wouldn't be the first time a brain has healed from all that rest. And everyone we know was praying."

He set the salt shaker in front of her and pointed at it. "Imagine this is a benzodiazepine-induced coma." Then he lifted the pepper shaker to eye level and set it beside the salt. "And this is prayer."

"I don't get it."

"Which one healed her?" He pressed his forearms into the table and leaned toward her. "Does it matter? Nothing short of a miracle, Aggie, straight from the Father."

If it lasts. Aggie rocked in her seat.

———⚓

That night she screamed her cougar scream again. Burnaby, his hair tousled from sleep, stumbled from his room and turned on the lamp. Dad sat her up, wiped her sweaty face with the cool washcloth Burn brought from the bathroom, and crooned to her.

"Another one?" Her father stroked her hair and wrapped his arms around her.

She nodded, whispering. "Worst one yet." *Third time this week.*

Dad held her. This time he didn't ask her what she'd dreamed. She couldn't tell him anyway. As always, the terror slipped away as soon as she roused.

———⚓

She awoke to the sound of Burnaby's truck as he left for school the next morning. *Seven forty-five.* Better than a clock. The nightmare's residue lingered, and she wished she could fall back to sleep. *Mama. Here in two days.* She dressed, gathered her homeschool lessons, and walked the trailer's narrow hallway to the kitchen as her dad hung up the phone, humming.

"We're leaving for Seattle at the crack of dawn on Friday. Have a little airport stop before we go to the hospital."

"*What* are you talking about?"

"Celia has a long weekend. Teachers' workshops. She'll catch a red-eye out tomorrow night and we'll pick her up before we get your mother Friday morning. She can stay until Tuesday."

"Stay *here*?" Aggie's chair toppled as she jumped to her feet.

An elbow sent her books to the floor as she leaped to hug her dad, who held a skillet of eggs and a spatula in his extended arms.

"I take it that's okay with you?"

"Oh, Dad." Things were looking up.

DREAMS

IF CABOT HADN'T RUINED MY KNEE. I'd have been at a cross-country meet during those teacher curriculum days, but given the incompatibility between healing tendons and competitive running, I had the weekend free for my friend Aggie. Daddy booked my flights.

She was having nightmares, Harris told me. Bad ones. And she wouldn't talk about them or about pieces of the trauma that plagued her. He'd taken her to a counselor, but then poor Aggie had really clammed up. And now with Bree coming home? He was at his wits' end. He'd called Gram, who suggested he call me.

Aggie. My little bird. After our August days together, I suspected that the flames inside her had more to do with her guilt and her unpredictable mama than her time in the woods, where even *God* had been kind to her, she said. I didn't get that whole forgiveness and God thing, but my history told me that mothers will do what mothers will do. So will daughters. And sometimes they wish with all their hearts that they could *undo* some of it.

Good luck with that one. No matter what her mother did, unless Aggie learned to show *herself* some mercy, she'd keep right on screaming. I knew *that* for a fact. I'd done a fair bit of screaming myself.

———⚡———

When I walked across the airport's tarmac, Aggie's forehead and nose pancaked against an upstairs window in the terminal. She waved with both arms, then ran down the ramp against traffic to hug me and to commandeer a handle on my duffle. Burnaby retrieved my bag from us both, but not before he made true eye contact and smiled. For half a second, but still.

"Celia."

I felt like Queen of the World, even before Harris wrapped his arms around me, smiling wide as the Mississippi watershed. "You get my letter, Agate Esther?" I poked her midsection. Still skinny. "I picked out that barn swallow stationery just for you."

Aggie blushed, pulled a crinkled letter from her pocket and waved it in front of me.

"Dang, Ags. You're supposed to read it and write back, not haul it around. Here I spend the entire month of August with my new friend Aggie, and as soon as I go back to Texas, she drops me like a hot potato. What've you been doing for the last six weeks?"

"Sorry. I didn't think you'd . . ." She hung her head, sheepish.

I squeezed her close to my side as we walked to the car. "Just teasing you, sweet pea. How're you doing?"

Before we left the airport parking lot, we talked through the surface of her days: homeschool, the trailer, her birds migrating at the equinox. Then, while Harris steered and Burnaby hunched over his homework in the shotgun seat, she and I sat in the back and, for the entire half-hour drive to Harborview, navigated her most immediate worry: her mother's burns and physical healing.

We waited with the car in the hospital loading zone while Harris and Burnaby went inside for Bree. Only then did we begin to rummage around somewhere deeper.

"Think your mama's in those nightmares?"

Aggie shriveled and rubbed her stubby hair. "I can't tell. Sometimes I remember trees, but not much else. Last night was horrible. I woke up feeling sad and dirty and really scared. Something inside me is so afraid, and I don't know why."

I trotted my fingers on her shoulder. "Sounds like that fire's still burning."

"I don't know. Maybe."

I pointed at the hospital entry, where Burnaby and Harris flanked a nurse with Popeye forearms wheeling Aggie's mother across the lobby. Coming our way. At the car, Burnaby folded the wheelchair footrests and opened his mama's door. Bree took Harris's arm and stood, as a grimace crossed her face. Then she placed her hands on the car's roof, lowered her head and passed her eyes over us, her connection remote.

"Hello, kids."

Quiet. Fragile. She seemed exhausted. Harris helped her sit, buckled her seatbelt, and tucked her caftan around her. A knotty scar showed at the edge of a blue scarf wrapping her head like a turban. She didn't say more, and nobody tried to make her.

Harris drove north. Aggie, wedged between me and Burnaby, went silent and held my hand. Burn looked out the window, his legs pleated like an accordion in the cramped back seat. Bree dozed, so I did, too, lulled by Harris's humming, the red-eye catching up with me.

———Ƛ———

Early afternoon, we pulled up in front of a cracker-box trailer near their blackened homesite. At the perimeter's far edge, a bulldozer and excavator stood ready to scrape away the rubble and start over. Harris helped Bree into the recliner in the sparsely furnished living room and Aggie, her cheeks flushed, spread a quilt across her mother's legs. I sat at the kitchen table next to a plate of cookies and reached for one.

Bree shifted in the chair and took in the hand-me-down furniture without comment. Aggie hovered nearby, but her mother was oblivious; the girl could have been invisible. I knew what *that* felt like. Anyone walking into that room would have tripped on the tension.

Then Aggie did exactly that.

"Your favorite, Mama. Chocolate chip oatmeal." She set a napkin and two cookies on a small table beside her mother's chair, returned for some milk, then caught her toe on the carpet and spilled the full glass in her mama's lap.

Aggie gasped, but Bree's features stayed flat as she watched the milk soak through the quilt and into her clothes. Aggie ran for a towel, but Harris got there first.

"Here, love. Let's get you changed."

"I'm tired, Harris. I'd like to lie down."

Aggie returned with the towel and held it out to her, but Bree stepped past her, bumped the table and knocked the napkin and treats to the floor.

For five seconds, the room was as still as the air before a northeaster starts blowing. Except for Bree, all of us—Harris, Burnaby, Aggie, and I—stared at the cookies on the rug. Then I raised my eyes to Aggie.

Her mouth quivered. She clenched her ragged hair and pulled. A wail began low in her throat.

"I . . . didn't . . . MEAN . . . TO!" She screamed the last words. Bree's eyes widened and locked on her daughter, as if Aggie had suddenly materialized out of nowhere.

Aggie dropped to the floor. She clawed at the carpet, at the cookies. Ground them into bits between her fingers. Smashed them with her fists as she howled from deep in her guts. "I. DIDN'T. MEAN. TO!" Each word stood like a soldier between her and her mother. Then she humped over, her face against the rug, sobbing. "Mama, Mama, Mama. I am so *sorry*."

"It's just milk, Aggie." Bree seemed confused. Didn't she know about Aggie's campfire?

How would she know, unless Harris told her? But he *hadn't*. Obviously, he hadn't.

"Not the milk, Mama. The *fire*!" She howled, choking, and threw herself on the sofa, burying her head in the cushions. Burnaby stood near the door, fidgeting with the zipper on his sweatshirt, while I wished I were a mouse. Bree sat on a kitchen chair, her eyebrows tilted with worry. Harris went to Aggie, but she pushed him away and sat up, her eyes squeezed closed.

"I lit it, Mama. I was mad. Mad. I was trying to be better, I really was, but I lit the fire that burned you and Dad. Ohhh, Mama, Mama. I am so *SORRY*."

The word *sorry* erupted from her like a train, its horn blaring. Or like a blowtorch.

And like a broken-winged bird.

Bree braced herself on the table and stood, pausing for breath before she crossed the room to Aggie, whose eyes roved wild over ceiling and walls, her sides heaving with the pent-up stuff of nightmares. So gingerly, Bree sat on a cushion beside her daughter and laid her hand on Aggie's knee.

"My Agate."

It was the kindness, I think. At that moment, Aggie found a tear in that enormous curtain between her and forgiveness—and slipped right through it. She buried her face in the folds of her mother's caftan and sobbed, while Bree traced her ear as if petting a web.

I didn't belong there. Edging past Burnaby, I crept outside, where I walked along the river until evening fog settled in, hours later. A melody wound through the trees as I returned uphill to the trailer.

Someone was playing a fiddle.

———⚡

Personally, I know little about God, whoever he is.

If he is.

I realize, however, that to some, he's downright awesome. From Gram's description, I picture him like a raptor with a sky's wingspan, exhaling love's oxygen on his hatchlings, feeding them comfort and truth and power straight from his beak.

On the other hand, my mother would say that bird sits on people's backs, the god of heavy loads.

I'm still perched on the wire about all that.

But Aggie? I do believe I saw her finally leave one for the other.

MILLIE

A NOVEMBER SNOWSTORM delayed us in Denver, but Daddy and I made it to Gram's by Thanksgiving noon. When I stepped in the door, Aggie jumped on me, her arms and legs like vines. She was taller, I think, and had gained weight. Her dad limped to us and kissed my cheek. Bree, still gaunt, made her way across the room and hugged me. When I let go, she held on, until Gram approached to take our coats.

Burnaby gestured behind them, so I rezipped my jacket and followed him to the barn, where Millie, our eagle, was eating frozen mice and raw beef like a celebrity.

"Four months already, Burn. She using that wing at all?"

He eased into a ten-by-twelve-foot pen of vertical wooden slats. Millie flapped awkwardly to a chest-high perch, the jog in her injured wing obvious. "She's attempting, but the misalignment will prevent her release."

"How'd that surgery get so screwed up?"

"Post-op X-rays looked correct. I suspect she reinjured the wing in transport, but the shift wasn't evident until she began extending it. By then fibrous tissue interfered with calcification."

"So she'll spend her life on a glove, visiting schools."

"Not if I correct it."

"You're making me nervous."

He exited the pen. "I talked to Jack Seamus about her when he was dehorning calves."

"He's a dairy vet. What's he know about eagles?"

"He knows avian anesthesia."

"Burnaby, you can't."

Or maybe he could. Millie lifted her nape feathers and glared at us, then hopped back to her meal. The thought of her never flying again made my stomach hurt. "What if she—"

He looked me square in the face and spoke softly. "I'll keep you informed, Celia."

———⚶———

In December we were back in Washington. Burn joined Daddy and me outside the courtroom as we waited for Cabot's trial to begin. "So how's Millie?" I asked. I hadn't heard a peep from him since Thanksgiving.

"Still researching procedures."

No time to ask him more. As he checked a clipboard on a nearby table, the bailiff opened the doors, and everyone's attention shifted to the judge's bench. Over the next two days, witnesses spilled out facts, attorneys jockeyed, and Cabot stared at his hands.

Until I took the stand.

While I answered the public defender's questions, Cabot's muddy eyes bored into mine until I thought his retinae would combust. His aggression heightened my resolve to stay strong. I said my piece and stared right back at him. He didn't scare me anymore, and my body agreed; I could breathe just fine.

His attorney's defense leaked like a colander. Cabot didn't testify. The man was toast, and three days later everyone knew it. The judge found him guilty of felony assault with a deadly weapon, unlawful imprisonment, grand larceny, and a meaty misdemeanor or two. As the deputy led him from the courtroom, his gaze locked on me, his eyes loaded with emotions I didn't try to read.

And then he was gone. I let relief wash over me, hoping he could start over one day.

The trial ended as Christmas break began, so Daddy and I stayed in Washington through the holidays. Every time I visited Millie huddled in her pen, I fought a wish to break Cabot's arm and see how he liked it. I told Burnaby as much. My call to her original surgeon about further repairs went nowhere. "Too fragile . . . high risk." *Blah, blah.* And impossibly expensive.

I half-wished Burnaby and Jack would try. I told Burn that, too, but he just shrugged and threw her another rat. I couldn't stand it.

———ᐱ———

I spent my last three days of vacation talking and prowling the woods with Aggie. Sleeping in that trundle bed she stored under hers. She didn't scream once.

The day before I left, she woke up *brave*. "Owls are nesting, Mama. Great Horned."

"Aggie, it's snowing."

"She's started laying. I have to see."

Bree walked to a window facing the woods. "How high?"

"Thirty feet."

"Use the harness?"

"I will." Aggie took safety gear from the hook by the door and tossed me my parka. "C'mon, Celia. Show ya."

———⅄⅄———

I hadn't been home a week before a letter arrived from Burnaby, his script tiny, precise.

> *Celia,*
>   *Two-hour surgery on Millie complete. Pulled errant rod. Resectioned. Retained bone length. Placed external metal fixator with seven pins.*
>
>

Sincerely,
Burnaby
>

I ran to the phone and dialed. His dad answered. "Harris! Burnaby there?"

"Hey, Celia. He's at work. You okay?"

"He *operated*? Seriously?"

"That he did." Harris laughed. "The day you left. They didn't tell anyone beforehand. Glad I didn't know."

"How is she?"

"Came home from the clinic yesterday afternoon. Hopping around her pen and wants to bite everyone. Only been a week, but by all appearances, she won't be any worse off than before. Jack said your grandmother nearly took both his and Burnaby's heads off for not asking her to assist."

Seriously. I wanted to clobber that Burnaby. And kiss him.

———⅄⅄———

Six weeks later, his next letter showed up.

Dear Celia,
Cabot is dead.

Burnaby

Gram filled me in by phone. After two months at McNeil Island Corrections Center, Cabot escaped from a work detail outside prison walls. Searchers figured he hid in a marsh until nightfall, then tried to swim to the mainland. He drowned alone in cold, murky water that hid his body for thirty-six hours.

The Hayes' line rang eight times before I hung up. I waited fifteen minutes and dialed again. Where was Burnaby? Oh, I wanted to hear his voice. To hear what he felt when he learned of Cabot's death. What colors did he see? Were the trees indigo? The sky bronze? His hands gray? If I were to see feelings like he did, would all color drain from my world?

I held his letter in my lap and relived summer's iridescent green days, and laughing yellow ones. Would the day Cabot died be yellow? No, not for Burn. He hated death. He wanted to see things resurrected, restored.

I loved that about him.

I smoothed the paper and cried. Such a waste. Cabot fought his pain with the wrong weapons, and they took him down. I shuddered at how I nearly did the same, and thought of Meredith, and that baby she carried for a while. Thought of how we had nothing to say to each other anymore.

Then it dawned on me that we're *all* sugar birds, every single one of us. All scratching far and wide for the sweet seed that will satisfy our deepest hunger. I called Gram back with *that* epiphany. Asked her if she thought I'd ever find mine. If she'd ever found hers.

"Hmm." I could hear the smile in her intonation before she switched metaphors on me. "Pearl of great price," she said. "Remind me to tell you that story when I can look in your eyes."

I would remind her, I decided.

I *would*.

———⋀⋀

Late March, Burnaby wrote me about the flight pen he built for our eagle. I called him immediately.

"Attached to the barn. Twenty by eighty. Sixteen-feet high."

"She's actually flying? Not just gimping around?"

"Early yet, but full, balanced wing extension."

———⋀⋀

Daddy and I pulled into Mender's the day after school let out in June, and there she was. Behind netting in her airy flight corridor, a mottled giant bird eyed us from a sunny perch. I jumped from the car and ran to see her. She sailed farther away and chittered, warning me off.

Millie. Millie the Magnificent, flying again. Inspiration for the rest of us healing birds. Her mouth gaped with threat.

"Good girl for staying wild." I stepped closer and curtsied. "Don't worry, beautiful. After tomorrow, you can ditch this place."

At nine the next morning, we gathered outside the barn for the ceremony. I tossed my sweatshirt on the rain barrel and scanned the happy circle dressed in a colorful array of tank tops and tees in the late spring sun: Nora, Loomis, Gram, Daddy, Aggie, Burnaby, Harris, and even Bree—still free of psychotropics, according to Harris. Her short, patchy curls lifted in the breeze. I had visited once more in May and spent hours with them all at Gram's—and in that trailer next to the new home Harris and Burnaby had begun framing.

These people I love.

Burnaby donned his long leather gloves and retrieved our eagle from the barn. Mender laid one hand on my shoulder and the other on Millie's back. The raptor jostled.

Gram better be quick.

She was.

"Bless this beautiful bird, dear Father. Carry her with your breath."

Burnaby hoisted her upward and let go. The eagle rose overhead, circled the barn, then angled across the road toward the top of a lofty fir. Loomis started singing. Nora jabbed him with her elbow until he hummed.

When Millie landed, a pair of crows mobbed her, diving at her head and back until she launched again and flapped a slow, powerful rhythm across the river and greening valley. We watched her shrink to a black speck before she merged with the forest.

The crows returned to the fir. Aggie looped her arm through her mother's and pointed at their nest. "Three eggs up there, Mama."

Bree planted a kiss in her daughter's hair, tipped back her head and laughed.

Keep an eye out for
a powerful new novel by
award-winning author
Cheryl Grey Bostrom

TURN THE PAGE FOR A SNEAK PEEK

COMING IN 2024 FROM
TYNDALE HOUSE PUBLISHERS

JOIN THE CONVERSATION AT crazy4fiction.com

CP1898

1
CELIA

SCRAPE

NORTHWEST WASHINGTON STATE, 1997

Above the pond, a cloud of gnats shimmered in the July morning, as a Canadian goose rousted her brood through reeds of yellow iris toward a floating gander. On the opposite shore, Celia Burke leaned against a fat alder tree and watched the goose family cross the pond like a giant centipede.

Over them all, its white head a beacon in the green-black needles of a Douglas fir, an enormous bald eagle aimed its beak toward the paddling geese. Celia raised her binoculars slowly, anticipating the apex bird's strike, her eyes peeled for the twin metal leg bands her grandmother had spotted during repeated sightings of this aging raptor.

She didn't wait long. The eagle lifted its wings in feathered angles, flapped, swooped, and snatched a downy chick from the swimming spine of birds. The gosling's parents—their honks frantic, necks extended—launched their heavy bodies after the attacker. But the eagle rose out of range nimbly, the chick in its talons.

Celia dropped her field glasses and sprang from beneath her tree's leafy cover. The raptor passed overhead, swift and low and parallel to the narrow road beside the pond, the gosling a mere ladder's reach away.

She sprinted after it, her ridiculous urge to prevent the baby goose's demise as reflexive for her as breathing. For the next few seconds she chased the eagle, propelled by the illusion that she could mob the raptor like a crow, that she could startle it into dropping the chick. She ran with abandon, watching the bird, not the ground, prepared to catch the baby when those wicked feet let go.

Instead, a rise in the rough country road caught her sneaker edge and sent her sprawling. Midair, she twisted, then hit the road's rough surface in a skid. From her outstretched right arm to her ankle— wherever her tee and jean shorts weren't covering skin—gravel, secure in its tarry substrate, scraped her raw. The spectacular tumble entered her memory in vivid, agonizing slow motion.

A goldfinch sang from a nearby field. Celia lay in the road, listening to it and a distant rumble. Numbed by endorphins from her sprint and the sweet relief of adrenaline, she felt oddly peaceful. Only her hip throbbed. Detached, she envisioned its purpling contusion as she ran her tongue over her teeth. Finding them intact, she inhaled a lungful of fresh rural air. On her exhale, a wave of pain arrived with a motorcycle's roar.

And with a motorcycle. Its tires crunched the shoulder's gravel as the engine's RPMs slowed and stopped. A kickstand scraped, and heavy footfalls hurried toward her. She pushed herself to an upright position with her good hand.

"No paralysis. That's favorable."

She twisted toward the deep, steady voice and craned her neck at the helmeted man in a brown leather jacket and goggles who shaded her like a tree. A smiling tree, with a two-days' growth of blond beard and a wide mouth of straight white teeth.

She rolled her shoulders. "I couldn't jump off a dime right now."

"Think you can stand?"

She nodded, reached, and the man pulled her upright with a leather-gloved hand.

"Oof. Hip pointer." Groaning, she cupped the bony protrusion at the top of her pelvis with her uninjured hand and winced at the condition of her other palm—and the arm attached to it. Blood dripped from her elbow.

"No doubt." He scanned her body-length abrasion. "I do not believe that hip is your immediate concern." Stripping gloves from huge hands, he pulled a thermos of water and a packet of gauze from a saddlebag on his bike, then held the supplies toward her. "May I?"

"Let me get this right. I trip, out here in the boonies, not a soul in sight. Fast as gossip you show up out of nowhere with road rash supplies."

"Ha." He crouched, inspecting her bloody leg. "I'm still awaiting permission."

"Fine. Have at it. I've got a mile hike home and I'm not going to carry half the road with me." She plucked a seed-sized stone from her forearm and flicked it away. "Dang. I'm sandpapered."

"An apt description." He turned from her to the bike, removed his helmet, and placed gloves and goggles inside it. His hands made one smoothing pass over corn-colored hair.

Celia eyed the backs of his ears, tight to his head, their lobes plump and flared. She'd know them anywhere, though nothing else about him matched the seventeen-year-old she hadn't seen for . . . what, almost twelve years? Well, apart from that hair. And his height, though this man seemed even taller.

"Burnaby?"

He answered with a grin, also unfamiliar. Back then, she'd spent a summer coaxing the corners of his mouth to rise.

"Hello, Celia."

Discussion Questions

1. Fathers play meaningful roles in the novel. What are their impacts, both positive and negative, on Aggie, Celia, and Cabot?

2. Reflect on how members of the Hayes family respond to Bree's depression. What helped? What could they have done differently?

3. Aggie's and Celia's mothers hurt them deeply. How do those wounds affect their interactions with others? Their choices?

4. How do Aggie's guilt and shame distort her reality early in the book? At what points do you notice her perception shift?

5. Think back on the ways Celia's grandmother Mender attempts to guide and mentor her. What do you think is positive about her approach? Are there any downsides?

6. What made Aggie's ability to survive more believable for her than it might be for a child that age in your family or neighborhood? What traits seemed typical for her age?

7. How does autism manifest in Burnaby, and how does it both enhance and restrict his keen intelligence? How does it both challenge and benefit his relationships?

8. How does suffering influence Aggie's perception of God throughout the story?

9. The Scripture verse "Consider the birds . . ." appears in the book's front matter. How do birds—and nature in general—illustrate hope in this story? What else does nature reveal to the characters?

10. Look back at Mender's explanation of sugar birds in chapter 36. Do you agree with this description? Why or why not? What do you think of Celia's conclusion that "we're *all* sugar birds, every single one of us"?

Acknowledgments

TREES. A YOUNG GIRL. A FIRE. A few years back these eggs hatched, bare and sightless, into a sketch I wrote for an online fiction-writing class, where fellow writers urged me to develop the story. I don't remember your names, but I'm grateful. Since then, fed encouragement and expertise from a raft of friends, colleagues, and other experts, the story grew feathers. I am thankful for each and every one of you, mentioned here or not.

My cohort at Mt. Hermon—Gayle Roper, Mike Richards, Janet McHenry, Marilyn Siden, and Carolyn Phillips—you shared your wisdom with me in the best of feasts. Mathematician Jerry Maurer, be assured that Celia and Burnaby depended on you. Aubrey Basart, at ten, you helped me know Aggie so much better. And Scott Cameron, because you lived oil exploration in the 1980s, so could Wyatt. Thank you all.

Many of you advised, questioned, believed, prayed, laughed, and cried me through this book, from early drafts to publication. Without you, I'd have stalled. Thank you, Avery Ullman, Laura Buys, Mona Stuart, Bev Den Bleyker, Donna Vander Griend, Ruth Droullard, Darlene Elenbaas, Shelly Kok, Angie Van De Mark, Ashley Sweeney, Mattie Wheeler, Michael Bland, Jacksón Smith, Red House Writers,

Jan Soto, Lisa Largent, Laura Bostrom, Phyllis Kramer, Carol Ouellette, Elle Timmer, Jené Flittie, Dana Vail, Jeff Thomas, Diane Cochrane, Steven Kent, Bryan and Bonnie Korthuis, Mike and Cheryl Grambo, John and Jacquee Larsen, Steve Groen and Lissa Halls Johnson.

Artist Emma VandeVoort Nydam, your map brought the sun out. Thank you.

Thanks, too, you amazing editors. Early on, Sandra Byrd, you helped me build the story's engine, then showed me the rails, and how to keep the narrative within them. Ours was a holy appointment; working with you was pure joy. Alexandra Shelley, thank you for welcoming my manuscript into your editorial gold mine, where learning from you was a life- and craft-changing privilege. Your keen insight made all the difference. Ellen Notbohm, your seasoned eye and smart, creative suggestions helped me dress the story in its party clothes. Burnaby and I thank you. And Sarah Rische, your laser focus makes lines shine.

Agent Cynthia Ruchti, you saw possibilities past my imaginings, and through your skill, diligence, and wisdom they came true. A million thanks for expertly guiding the book to Tyndale House. Jan Stob and Karen Watson, thank YOU for opening Tyndale's doors to *Sugar Birds* and for your team's beautiful, God-honoring delivery of the story into readers' hands.

Blake—my husband, my love, and my best reader—you help me fly and land, no matter the weather. I'll thank you forever.

Most of all, I thank you, Father God. Start to finish, your provision and love mark every page of *Sugar Birds*. Words can't contain my gratitude.

About the Author

FOR MOST OF HER LIFE, Pacific Northwest naturalist, photographer, poet, and award-winning author Cheryl Grey Bostrom, MA, has lived in the rural and wild lands that infuse her writing. Her work has appeared in a variety of publications, including the American Scientific Affiliation's *God and Nature* magazine, for which she's a regular photo essayist. *Sugar Birds* has already garnered recognition that includes a number of key industry awards, with a Carol Award, *Christianity Today*'s Fiction Award of Merit, and Christy Award finalist honors among them. You can connect with her at https://cherylbostrom.com.

CONNECT WITH CHERYL ONLINE AT

cherylbostrom.com

OR FOLLOW HER ON

 facebook.com/cherylgreybostrom

@cherylgreybostrom

@cheryl_bostrom

CP1884

TYNDALE HOUSE PUBLISHERS IS CRAZY4FICTION!

Fiction that entertains and inspires

Get to know us! Become a member of the Crazy4Fiction community. Whether you read our blog, like us on Facebook, follow us on Twitter, or receive our e-newsletter, you're sure to get the latest news on the best in Christian fiction. You might even win something along the way!

JOIN IN THE FUN TODAY.

 crazy4fiction.com

 Crazy4Fiction

 crazy4fiction

 @Crazy4Fiction

FOR MORE GREAT TYNDALE DIGITAL PROMOTIONS, GO TO TYNDALE.COM/EBOOKS

CP0021

By purchasing this book from Tyndale, you have
helped us meet the spiritual and physical needs of
people all around the world.

Tyndale | Trusted. For Life.

CP1704